NEW GIRL

I sat and lowered my head to begin the writing assignment. We all looked up again when we heard a knock on the classroom door. It opened and a girl who looked at least sixteen stepped in.

"Yes, what is it?" Mrs. Morgan asked, not hiding her irritation.

"The principal would like to see Jordan March," she announced.

Mrs. Morgan tightened the corners of her mouth and then looked at me.

"Go ahead," she said, her voice full of annoyance. "You can leave your things right there. Don't dawdle in the hallway when you return either. Get right back to do your work."

I rose and joined the girl at the door. As soon as she closed it behind us, she turned to me and smiled.

"This is your first day here, right?"

"Yes," I said. "Is that why the principal sent for me?"

"No," she said, widening her smile. "Boy, are you in trouble," she said.

V.C. ANDREWS®
SCATTERED LEAVES

This title is also available as an eBook

V. C. Andrews® Books

The Dollanganger Family Series
Flowers in the Attic
Petals on the Wind
If There Be Thorns
Seeds of Yesterday
Garden of Shadows

The Casteel Family Series
Heaven
Dark Angel
Fallen Hearts
Gates of Paradise
Web of Dreams

The Cutler Family Series
Dawn
Secrets of the Morning
Twilight's Child
Midnight Whispers
Darkest Hour

The Landry Family Series
Ruby
Pearl in the Mist
All That Glitters
Hidden Jewel
Tarnished Gold

The Logan Family Series
Melody
Heart Song
Unfinished Symphony
Music in the Night
Olivia

The Orphans Miniseries
Butterfly
Crystal
Brooke
Raven
Runaways (full-length novel)

The Wildflowers Miniseries
Misty
Star
Jade
Cat
Into the Garden (full-length novel)

The Hudson Family Series
Rain
Lightning Strikes
Eye of the Storm
The End of the Rainbow

The Shooting Stars Series
Cinnamon
Ice
Rose
Honey
Falling Stars

The De Beers Family Series
Willow
Wicked Forest
Twisted Roots
Into the Woods
Hidden Leaves

The Broken Wings Series
Broken Wings
Midnight Flight

The Gemini Series
Celeste
Black Cat
Child of Darkness

The Shadows Series
April Shadows
Girl in the Shadows

The Early Spring Series
Broken Flower
Scattered Leaves

My Sweet Audrina
(does not belong to a series)

V.C. ANDREWS®

SCATTERED LEAVES

POCKET STAR BOOKS
New York   London   Toronto   Sydney

Following the death of Virginia Andrews, the Andrews family
worked with a carefully selected writer to organize and complete
Virginia Andrews' stories and to create additional novels, of which
this is one, inspired by her storytelling genius.

This book is a work of fiction. Names, characters, places and
incidents are products of the author's imagination or are used
fictitiously. Any resemblance to actual events or locales or persons,
living or dead, is entirely coincidental.

An *Original* Publication of POCKET BOOKS

A Pocket Star Book published by
POCKET BOOKS, a division of Simon & Schuster, Inc.
1230 Avenue of the Americas, New York, NY 10020

ISBN-13: 978-1-4165-3081-7
ISBN-10:   1-4165-3081-9

This Pocket Star Books paperback edition March 2007

10   9   8   7   6   5   4   3   2

V.C. ANDREWS® and VIRGINIA ANDREWS® are registered
trademarks of the Vanda General Partnership

POCKET STAR BOOKS and colophon are registered
trademarks of Simon & Schuster, Inc.

Cover art by Lisa Falkenstern

Manufactured in the United States of America

For information regarding special discounts for bulk purchases,
please contact Simon & Schuster Special Sales at 1-800-456-6798
or business@simonandschuster.com.

SCATTERED LEAVES

Prologue

With my hands clasped and resting on my lap, I sat at the foot of my bed in my room, waiting for Grandmother Emma March's chauffeur, Felix, to come up for my two suitcases and me. This morning it was so quiet that I imagined I wore invisible earmuffs. I could hear only my memories: the muffled sounds of my mother and father having another argument behind their closed bedroom door across the hallway, the clip-clop footsteps of Nancy, the maid, coming down the hallway to clean either my brother Ian's or my room, Ian imitating the sound of some insect he was studying, Grandmother Emma's voice echoing from the other side of the mansion as she barked out an order to one of the other servants.

As I sat there, it suddenly occurred to me why I wasn't terribly unhappy about leaving my grandmother's magnificent mansion. It had never felt like a home to me. It was more like borrowed space. Mother used to say we were even borrowing the air we breathed here. My brother, Ian, and I had to be so careful about everything we touched, even in our own rooms. So-called unnecessary noise was prohibited. Often, we found ourselves whispering, even when Grandmother Emma wasn't at home. We behaved as if we believed that whenever she went somewhere, she always left her shadow behind to spy on us and make reports. There were tattletales listening in every corner, under every chair, behind closed closet doors.

The rules swirled about us like angry bees ready to swarm down and sting us at the slightest sign of any violation. Just before I fell asleep every night, I could hear the house itself chanting and reminding me, "Beware of smudging furniture or windows. Don't leave anything out of place. Never track in anything from outdoors. Walk on air. Shut off lights. Respect me. Think of me as you would a very famous holy cathedral and treat me with similar reverence."

From the first day after we sold our own home and moved in with Grandmother Emma because of Daddy's economic troubles, my mother dreamed of moving out. The moment she stepped through the tall mahogany double doors, with the gold-painted, hand-carved March crest at the centers, and followed our things in funeral fashion up the stairway to our side of the large mansion, she was draped in dark shadows and weighed down like someone forced to wear layers and layers of heavy overcoats. Each day the brightness seeped more and more out of her eyes, and later I often caught her gazing out the window like someone behind prison bars envisioning an escape. Even in this opulent, rich world, she looked poor, misplaced, homeless and forgotten, or as Ian said, "A prisoner of circumstances beyond her control."

In the end we all were prisoners of these circumstances, even Grandmother Emma.

No one would have suspected that days of happiness and joy were rare for us. After all, we were the rich March family. Those happy days, however, were our private holidays, occurring just often enough to keep us, especially my mother, from drowning in a sea of depression. She would come up from the dark depth of despair, take a breath in the sunshine and then sink again to wait for the next occasion for smiles and laughter.

Too bad we didn't have more good and happy times to deposit in some sort of bank, I thought, and draw from them when we were in need of cheering ourselves. We'd always have something for a rainy day. Whoever could do that, whoever had a vault full of wonderful memories, was rich, even richer than Grandmother Emma, whose husband had been a top executive at Bethlehem Steel during the so-called golden age.

My grandparents had been like royalty then, and in the high society of today's Bethlehem they were still treated like old monarchs. She composed and moved herself as would any queen who merely had to nod or lift her hand to open doors, raise curtains, command the obedience of not only servants but seemingly everything and everyone around her, including birds and clouds. Only Mother was beyond her reach.

Mother and Grandmother Emma never got along. They could pass each other in the hallway without either acknowledging the other's presence. My mother always believed my grandmother thought she was not worthy enough to marry a March. Mother said Grandmother Emma insisted on us moving into her home not because she felt sorry for us and wanted to help us as much as she wanted to control us and be sure we didn't stain the Marches' precious image or put a crack in their solid reputation. There really wasn't much about our lives she didn't know and didn't want to influence or change, and my father put up little resistance.

"You don't just have feet of clay, Christopher," I overheard my mother tell my father once. "Your whole body and soul are made of clay and your mother is molding and sculpting or at least still trying. Anyone would expect her to give up by now, but not Emma March. She never surrenders. Ironically, I'm not the one who will always displease her."

Most of the time, my father ignored my mother's complaints and criticisms or just shrugged and went on doing whatever he was doing. Complaints and criticisms, whether from my mother or from my grandmother, were to him what flies were to an elephant. And even if he paid any attention and really heard them, he would wave them off with a gesture or a laugh. My grandmother said he was a clone of his father in that way. I never knew my grandfather, so I couldn't say. Ian knew him for a while before he died, but he told me he was not old enough to form any opinion except to say he didn't think he would have liked him if he had lived longer anyway. I had no reason to doubt it, because my mother seemed to agree with Grandmother Emma about her description of my father and grandfather.

"March men are selfish. Their eyes are turned inward. They don't see anyone else," she muttered when she voiced a complaint and he ignored her.

I never saw that more clearly than I did when my mother told him his little girl had crossed that mysterious boundary into womanhood. At the age of seven, my body, like some impatient Olympic runner, had charged out of the gate before the sound of the starting pistol. I had lurched forward and at times had felt as if I'd been rushed into my adolescence by a traitorous inner self that, on its own, seemingly overnight, had decided to begin forming my breasts, curving my buttocks, narrowing my waist and then initiating menarche.

The most terrifying thing I had overheard my doctor tell my mother was, "Yes, Carol, it is biologically possible for her to become pregnant," and there I was at the time, finishing the second grade. Living within our protective bubble, attending a private school, and having my friends filtered through Grandmother Emma's eyes, I hadn't been exposed to the worldly side of things very much. I hadn't even known exactly how women became pregnant. It had still been one of those "somedays." Someday I'll tell you this; someday I'll tell you that.

For as long as she could, my mother hid my accelerated development from my grandmother, who made the March family appear so perfect and special that the common cold would turn and flee at the sight of her scowl. We were not permitted to do anything unusual or that could in any way be considered abnormal. In fact, in her eyes members of the March family simply were supposed to be too perfect and too strong to show signs of trouble or illness. If Grandmother Emma had even the slightest symptom of an ailment, she refused to leave her room. The world had to be brought to her until she was a March again.

Knowing this, having lived with it myself and seen firsthand how she could be, I appreciated the deep depression and defeat she was experiencing now back in the hospital, where she remained an invalid, stricken down by a stroke, confined to a bed and at the mercy of doctors, nurses and medicine. She had slipped off March Mountain. Ironically, both of us had been betrayed by our bodies, hers admitting to age and mine refusing to be governed by it.

Ian, who believed that nothing happened by coincidence, that everything had an understandable and explainable explanation, or what he called a cause and effect, once rattled off the downward slide of our family this way:

"Grandmother Emma and her husband, Blake, created Daddy's personality and weaknesses because of the manner in which they brought him up. They spoiled him and made him selfish. That's why he has not been a good father to us and a good husband for our mother, why he failed at business and why he womanized."

"What's womanized?" I asked him.

Ian's vocabulary was years ahead of my age, even years ahead of his own.

"He has sex with other women, Jordan."

"You mean with those tadpoles and eggs?"

He had once explained it all to me and showed me pictures of sperm, which had reminded me of tadpoles. At the time I'd had a great deal of trouble understanding the intricacies of the whole human reproduction process. Ian gave me a book about it on my seventh birthday. My mother was surprised he did that, but she thought it was probably sensible. To her, Ian was always more sensible than even my father, maybe especially my father. My grandmother, on the other hand, thought the book and Ian's giving it to me were disgusting. She, like my father, never understood Ian.

"Just listen," he said, impatient with my questions and interruptions. "I'm talking about our family, our father. His upbringing led him to make these choices and mistakes. Mother reacted to his mistakes and wanted to divorce him. Grandmother Emma, who refused to permit the word *failure* in the March vocabulary, talked Mother into backing down, but as you know, she called them up in the Pocono Mountains at the family cabin where they were meeting to iron out their problems and told them those lies about us, making me look like some pervert just because I was studying your accelerated development and she caught me measuring your budding breasts."

"Perverted isn't nice," I said, shaking my head. I loved demonstrating whatever knowledge I possessed to Ian. I wanted his respect, even more than I wanted his love.

"Of course not. It's disgusting. However, if she hadn't done that, made that phone call, Daddy wouldn't have rushed out in the storm. They wouldn't have had the accident. He wouldn't be a paraplegic, Mother wouldn't be in a coma and Grandmother Emma wouldn't have hired this sadistic woman, Miss Harper, to be our minder."

"And you wouldn't have poisoned her," I could now

add. He had taken rat poison from the groundskeeper's shed and mixed it in the glass of water Miss Harper had kept at her bedside. She'd been very cruel to us, and when Ian had secretly taken me to see our mother at the hospital in Philadelphia, she'd punished him by taking all of his precious scientific things, including his private notebooks, out of his room.

Ian was already gone by the time Grandmother Emma had her stroke. As I sat thinking about the things he had told me, I concluded, as Ian would, that she had her stroke because of all the previous terrible events that now troubled her day and night. Her iron will finally crumbled under the weight of it all, and she collapsed. But even then, even now, in her battered and distorted form, she still managed to hold on to the reins and run our family.

She arranged for me to live with her sister, my great-aunt Frances Wilkens, on a farm my grandfather and grandmother had seized in a foreclosure many years ago. She kept control of the family fortune and forced my father to agree to everything. She wasn't here, but her shadows still lingered on our walls and still reported to her. Every precious piece of antique furniture, every chandelier, every painting and sculpture, the very drapes hung waiting for her commands. The house remained loyal to her. She was still the monarch, the Queen of Bethlehem, Pennsylvania. I could feel it even now as I sat there in my room, stared at the doorway and waited for Felix.

Daddy was below with his old girlfriend Kimberly, the woman who'd started all the recent trouble. He had been seeing her secretly, and Mother had found out. I wondered if he would wheel himself out of his bedroom to say good-bye. With his gaze down, his fingers kneading his palms like Nancy would knead dough for bread, he had told me my grandmother was probably right about my going to live with Great-aunt Frances. He would be unable to be a real father to me and with Ian now in some institution because of what he had done to Miss Harper, I would be terribly alone in this grand old mansion.

It had been on the tip of my tongue to say I had always been alone and he had never been a real father to me, but I'd swallowed it back with my tears and clung instead to my hope that someday soon my mother would get better and come for me. Together then, we would go get Ian and somehow, some way, all of us would be a family again. I wished hard for it as I fingered the locket she had given me for my last birthday. Inside were pictures of her and Daddy just after they had turned their love into a marriage, both wearing smiles trapped in gold. Ian whispered they were photographs of illusions. He made me believe they would simply disappear, so I checked often to see if they were still there.

Maybe he was right about illusions, however. In the hollow silence of this great house, in which even footsteps seemed to sink and be lost, it felt out of place to have any sort of hope. If Ian had been here, he would have analyzed it all carefully and told me why I had all these dark feelings rumbling under my heart.

"You're leaving for a place, a home you've never seen, to live with someone you've never met, someone you've only known through an old picture or some vague reference Grandmother Emma has made. Great-aunt Frances is like some fantasy, a storybook character.

"You're going to be entered into a new school and be alongside students you don't know. You won't have a mother or a father to accompany you and stand up for you. Everything will be unfamiliar, strange, even frightening.

"You won't have anyone to call. I'm in an institution. I haven't even answered your letters to me because Grandmother Emma never mailed them to me. You don't even know where I am exactly. No one will talk about it with you. You can't call me on the telephone. You wrote another letter describing what's happening to you, but you can't depend on Father sending it to me. Mother can't hear you or speak to you even if she could hear you, and as Grandmother Emma would say, our father is lost in his own self-pity.

"You still have your accelerated development to face. When the mothers of other young girls your age see you, they will probably not want their daughters to be around you. Some will think you're older and were left back or something. You saw some of that starting to happen here. They'll be afraid for their daughters. They won't call you a freak to your face, but they'll think of you that way. I'm sorry to have to tell you all this, but we have to think about it all sensibly."

"Then what should I do?" I asked my imaginary Ian.

He was silent. In my mind's eye I could see his eyes narrowing as they did when he gave something great thought. I waited patiently, relying on my imagination and my memory to help me realize what Ian's answer would be.

Suddenly his eyes lit up, his whole face brightening with his successful pursuit of an answer. They always came to him from some magical place. He heard voices no one else could hear.

"Be a March," he replied with his characteristic confidence. "Be like Grandmother Emma."

"Like Grandmother Emma?"

"Yes."

"How?" I asked.

"Even if you are afraid, don't let anyone know it. Not," he added, turning to me and smiling that tight, self-contented, arrogant smile, "even yourself."

1

A New Chapter in a Book
Yet to Be Written

"Time to go, Jordan," Felix said.

He stood there in my bedroom doorway and looked in at me, bracing himself as if he was afraid I might throw a tantrum. I knew that even if I had, it would have been a waste of energy. He had his orders and he wouldn't disobey them, even if it meant risking his life. For as long as I'd known him, Felix had always been very loyal to my grandmother. Mother told me he had been with Grandmother Emma and Grandfather Blake ever since he was in his early twenties.

"What makes some people devote their lives to others like that, I don't know," Mother muttered. "Especially people as arrogant as the Marches."

Felix lived on the property and had never had a family of his own. He had a brother and a sister who were married and had children, but he never talked to us about them. We knew Grandmother Emma always had gifts sent to his family on Christmas and on their birthdays and she gave Felix expensive watches and rings, beautiful leather wallets, and once even a paid vacation to some Caribbean island. He hadn't used it. He'd given it to his nephew. He rarely took a vacation.

"Your grandmother knows how to keep the palace guards loyal," Mother had said. At the time I'd had no idea what she'd meant, but I'd seen that Ian had understood.

I always thought that was unfair. It made me feel like a foreigner in my own home, someone who didn't speak the same language. I could ask Ian to translate and explain later, and most times he did and enjoyed doing it. He liked teaching, but I still felt frustrated.

"What does Mother mean by palace guards? We don't actually live in a palace."

We lived in an enormous mansion, but it didn't look like the palaces I saw in storybooks and on television. There were no moats and high towers.

"Grandmother Emma thinks we do and what she thinks matters," Ian had told me.

"But then who are the palace guards?"

"That just means everyone who works for her. She makes sure they are loyal and in debt to her some way or another, just like we are," Ian had said.

It hadn't exactly explained it all to me, but I'd been able to see that Ian hadn't wanted to talk any more about it. All that seemed so long ago that it felt like I'd dreamed it anyway.

I bit down on my lower lip to keep from showing Felix my emotions. Then I slipped off the bed, and he moved quickly to grasp the handles of my suitcases before I changed my mind. He glanced at me to see if I would cry. I wanted to, but I thought of Grandmother Emma, and just like her I stiffened my shoulders and brought back my pride in full dress parade. I could hear her admonition: "Be a March. Always remember, you are a March and what you say, how you behave, what you do reflect on the whole family, even our dead ancestors, and believe me, they're listening and they're watching."

Not wanting Felix to think I was so sad, I snuck a final look at my room. Without me and my most cherished possessions, it would look abandoned if my mother came home and peered in at it. It would become what Ian called "another museum room in the house." So many rooms were simply there for show, unused and kept spotless. They were there for guests to be paraded past to be impressed. Ian used to say Grandmother Emma wore her house the way other women wear jewelry.

"How can you wear a house?" I asked him.

"In the minds of people who see you, you are inseparable from what you own," he said. "Nobody looks at her and doesn't think of this mansion, the furniture, the limousine, all of it. Understand?"

I nodded, but I didn't. I knew when and how to push on Ian and get him to keep explaining, and when to just pretend I understood what he was saying. Would I ever be as smart as him? I wondered.

"Your brother is a very special person," Mother used to tell me. "When you get older, you'll realize just how special he is."

I had already.

"We have a few hours of riding to do," Felix said,

turning to me in the hallway. I knew that was his way of asking me if I needed to go to the bathroom. In this house, under the cloud of Grandmother Emma, you never said "bathroom." You said "powder room." You went there to "do your private or personal business."

"Toilets are persona non grata," Ian told me.

When I asked him what language he was speaking, he said, "The language of survival."

Maybe my brother is really from another planet, I once thought. Daddy acted as if he believed it.

"I'm okay," I told Felix. I had done my business in preparation.

"Good then," Felix replied and charged forward as if he was afraid I'd change my mind. I trailed behind him so silently that I felt as if I was floating away. Felix didn't look back to see if I was coming or if I was crying. I couldn't say I liked him or disliked him. We'd had so little to do with each other before this.

His short hair was all gray. There were even gray strands in his bushy eyebrows, but he was still broad in the shoulders and stood with a military posture, tall with long arms. My suitcases didn't seem to weigh anything in his large hands. He moved easily ahead of me down the grand stairway. At the bottom he paused, and I knew he was expecting my father to be out in the hallway to say good-bye. We both looked in the direction of Daddy's bedroom, and then he turned to me.

"I'll go let Mr. March know we're leaving," he said. "He must have forgotten."

He lumbered down the hallway, put a suitcase down, and tapped gently on Daddy's bedroom door.

After my parents had the car accident, Daddy went

to therapy to learn how to get around in a wheelchair and take as much care of himself as possible. Grandmother Emma said it was taking longer because he wasn't being cooperative. When it finally came time for him to come home, Grandmother arranged for his bedroom to be downstairs rather than have one of those chair elevators installed. She said she would never mar her beautiful stairway and hand-carved balustrade with some modern mechanical thing.

I heard Felix mumble to the closed door. He waited and then it opened and he spoke again. He picked up the suitcase and started back toward me.

"He'll be right along," Felix said. "I'll go and put your suitcases in the car."

I waited for what seemed like a long time before my father came wheeling out of his room. I was afraid to move, even to sit. The grandfather clock in the living room bonged ten times. To distract myself, I played the same game with the shadows Ian often did. This one looked like a humpback whale, that one looked like a tiger about to pounce, and another resembled a giant hawk.

When my father finally appeared, he was in his bathrobe and barefoot. His hair was as wild as it would have been had he just woken, and his eyes looked swollen and red. He used to attend to his personal hygiene closely and some days even shaved twice. He always smelled good. This morning he looked like he hadn't shaved for a few days. He had a paper bag in his lap.

"Kimberly is in the shower," he told me, as if I cared whether or not his girlfriend said good-bye to me. "You have everything you need?"

I didn't know what that meant. If I'd had everything I needed, I would have had my mother, but I nodded.

"Well, okay. You be a good girl. As I said, we'll come visit you soon. I've finally given into this idea of a specially designed automobile for me to drive, so maybe I'll test it out with a ride out to see you and Aunt Frances."

Of course, I thought he'd be coming not because of a burning desire to see me but instead to test-drive a special car. Again, I just nodded.

"You know," he said suddenly, tipping his head to the side, "until this moment, I've never realized how much you look like your Grandmother Emma. Something about the way you purse your lips, Jordan. You know both she and Frances were pretty good-looking young women in their time. You have good genes and resemble them both."

Ian often talked about our genes. He seemed afraid of what he had inherited from Daddy.

"Are you going to see Ian soon, Daddy?"

"Soon," he said, but without any real enthusiasm.

"Would you please be sure to tell him where I am and please ask him to write back to me when you do see him? I gave you the letter for him. You will give him Great-aunt Frances's address so he can write back to me, okay?"

"He has written to you," he said.

I would swear my heart stopped and started.

"He has?"

"That's what this bag is full of," he explained. "His letters to you. I found them in the office just yesterday, rummaging through the files, looking for some legal tunnel to escape the prison your grandmother and her attorney have put me in."

"Ian's letters?"

"Yeah, your grandmother in her godlike wisdom decided not to give them to you, not that you or anyone normal could make head or tail of what the hell he wrote anyway. I read two and gave up. Kimberly even read a few and was just as lost. Maybe they'll amuse you," he added and handed the bag to me.

I looked in it, surprised and elated over how many I saw bundled with a rubber band.

"Will you ever take me to see him, Daddy?" I asked.

"Sure, sure," he said, waving my request away just as he used to wave away my mother's.

I would ask him to promise, but Daddy's promises were like scattered flowers, beautiful for a short time, and then quickly drying and fading until they crumbled and disappeared in the darkness of the earth, just like people.

"Okay. Give me a kiss and get going," he told me.

I leaned over his lap and kissed his cheek. He grunted something I didn't understand and spun his chair around. I watched him wheel himself down the hallway toward his room and recalled how he used to lumber down the hallways with his boots tapping the tiles, his head high, moving like the prince he was supposed to be, and for the first time all morning, I thought I wouldn't be able to stop myself from crying.

I did, though. I imagined Ian standing at the top of the stairway looking down at me, mouthing, "Remember. Be like Grandmother Emma. Don't cry. Ever."

I clutched the bag of his letters to my breasts, vanquished the throat lump, turned and walked out.

It was a beautiful late August day. Over the horizon, a stream of milky white clouds seemed glued to the sky. Otherwise, the blue extended unstained in every direction. A warm breeze lifted the flower blossoms in Grandmother Emma's beautifully manicured gardens but barely stirred the branches of trees or combed the blades of grass. Felix stood outside the car beside the open rear door, waiting for me the way he often waited for Grandmother Emma. Ian used to say he expected him to snap his boots together and salute when she appeared.

I gazed at the limousine. To me it looked like I was about to enter a dark cave, but I walked ahead and never looked back. I crawled in, sliding way over on the right side and pressing myself against the corner as if there had hardly been any room. Felix closed the door. I glanced back at the front of the mansion as he got in. In my imagination Ian was standing there, watching, waiting to wave good-bye, his gaze firm, his eyes betraying no tears.

"Here we go," Felix said, then he started the engine and drove down the long driveway.

The silence that followed made me shiver. Ian was so correct in my imaginary analysis. I would never feel as alone as I did at this moment. I remembered when my mother and I were once in a crowd after a movie and my hand slipped out of hers. Someone behind me moved me ahead and someone else moved me to the right. I was terrified, but my mother was there quickly, seizing my hand again.

She wasn't here now. Would she ever be again?

The limousine turned and we headed off, my short life at the grand house trailing behind me in memories made of smoke, disappearing like the car's exhaust, unseen and gone so quickly that it made me wonder if any of it ever had happened.

"It's nice where you're going," Felix offered, trying, I suspected, to cheer me up. As when he spoke to my grandmother, he didn't look back.

I used to think it looked like he was talking to himself. It had to be hard never to be able to look at the people to whom you spoke. Ian imagined that he had turned his head when he first started as Grandmother Emma's chauffeur.

"She probably snapped so sharply at him to keep his eyes on the road," he told me, "that he felt the bite on the back of his neck forever."

"I haven't been out there in some time, but I do remember it being a pretty home," Felix added.

"It's a farm, right?"

"Well, it was a farm," Felix said. "They keep a home garden going, but it's not a commercial farm. They don't raise crops to sell. I remember a large pond on the property. Cows used to drink from it back when they had cows."

"Are there any animals there now?"

"Some chickens, I think. You'll have fresh eggs all the time," he added.

I couldn't really see his face in the rearview mirror well, but I felt he was smiling. It occurred to me that Felix was the only one I knew now who wasn't a total stranger. It didn't do any good to be related to someone if you had never met them. My great-aunt Frances would still be a stranger to me. Despite what my grandmother told me in the hospital when I went to see her for the last time, I was afraid Great-aunt Frances wouldn't like me. Maybe she would be very mean to me. Maybe she hated the idea of having to take a young girl into her home to live with her. After all, as far as I knew, she hadn't asked for me to come live with her. Grandmother Emma had just told her it would be so. She could give everyone in the family orders through Mr. Pond, her attorney, even now, even though she couldn't speak well.

But she did assure me that last day in the hospital that her sister would never hate me. She said something even more mysterious to me as well. She said she needed me. How could a woman as old as Great-aunt Frances need a girl my age, especially one who was like me with all my added problems?

Did she need someone to help on the farm even though they didn't sell crops? Would I gather eggs? Would I plant vegetables? Pick wild berries for jams? I had been imagining all those things as this day had drawn closer and closer.

I wondered if Felix really meant it when he made it sound as if he liked Great-aunt Frances's home so much. Maybe he didn't like living in a city.

"Where did you grow up, Felix?"

"Me? Oh, a little town just outside of Philadelphia."

"On a farm?"

"No. My father had a hardware store."

"Did you go to college?"

"No. I was in the army for a few years and through a friend, I met your grandfather and he hired me to be his driver after only an hour or so. He was like that, you know."

"Like what, Felix?"

"He could look at someone and pretty much decide about him or her quickly, and he was unafraid of acting on his impressions. Very decisive man. You know what that means?"

"No."

"He was very self-assured, very confident of himself, never worried about his decisions, no matter how quickly he made them. Sometimes, your brother reminds me of him. Reminded me, I should say."

"Really?"

Ian would be very interested to know that, I thought. I pressed the paper bag of his letters tighter to me. I had to be sure to write it down and put it in my next letter to him. I hoped Great-aunt Frances would make sure the letter was mailed to him.

Then again, perhaps she'd been told not to do that. I had no idea what her instructions about me were. I knew she was younger than Grandmother Emma, but I didn't know exactly how much younger. I wondered if she was as elegant and as aristocratic a woman. Would everything be as formal in her house? Did she bark orders at servants, too? How much did she know about me? The more questions I asked myself, the more anxious I became.

I think Felix was watching me on and off in his rearview mirror. Suddenly he said, "Everything is going to be fine. You'll see."

How could everything be fine? I wanted to ask him, but I didn't want to seem ungrateful either, so I turned instead to look at the scenery and play another one of the games Ian had taught me to play whenever we were trying to ignore a long ride. We'd each choose a color and then claim a point for anything that was that color. Somehow, he always won; he always chose the right colors and got the most points. I didn't mind it. To me it seemed Ian should always win, always be right and correct. It was truly like having a big brother who was solid and strong in very important ways. Maybe he couldn't beat up other boys with his hands, but he certainly could destroy them with his words. He could even do it to adults.

I think I was more frightened about being without him beside me than I was about being without my parents.

Despite the game I tried to play and the beautiful sunny day, the ride began to feel dreary and long. I was going to start reading Ian's letters, but usually when I read in the car, I got carsick faster, and I wanted to save them for when I would be alone.

Twice Felix asked me if I needed to stop or wanted him to stop to buy me something to eat, candy, gum, anything. It surprised me because Grandmother Emma never permitted us to bring gum or candy into her limousine. She insisted on it being kept spotless. It was years old but looked like it had just been built. I wondered if she would ever ride in it again.

Finally, Felix announced we were in the community in which the farm was located. I felt like we were descending into another world, a world stained with shacks and run-down houses, overgrown farm fields, a village with most of the stores boarded up and buildings needing fresh paint. Children along the way gaped in awe at our passing limousine as if they had never seen a car so big on their broken highways. It made me feel as if my grandmother's car had been a space ship and I'd been an extraterrestrial.

Felix pointed out the school, an old-fashioned-looking redbrick building of three floors. I caught a glimpse of the playground and the parking lot. School hadn't started here either yet, so there were only a few cars there and no students around the building.

"It's not too far from your great-aunt's farm," Felix told me.

"I have to ride a school bus," I said. I knew that much. Ian and I had always been driven to our private school and back.

"Well, you'll like that. It's how you can get to know other kids your age, too. I rode a school bus to school until I had my own car."

I couldn't imagine Felix as a young boy. Some people just couldn't be diminished in your mind. They would always be the same size. It was just as impossible, if not more impossible, to imagine Grandmother Emma as a young girl even though I had seen some pictures of her. She looked so different, softer, happier. Were they really pictures of her? Maybe she used someone else's pictures.

It was as if the world was really frozen in time. I was always this age and size, and so were my parents and grandparents, everyone. Everything else, the albums, the stories, all of it, was just make-believe.

We turned down a very long highway where there were fewer and fewer houses, and these, too, weren't very nice. Most were small and old and didn't look well cared for, because their lawns were not neat and there weren't pretty bushes and flowers like there were at Grandmother Emma's home and the homes around it.

Those I saw were far apart from each other. Felix pointed out what he called some working farms and one horse farm, where there were dozens of horses in corrals.

"It's beautiful country here," he said. This time he really did sound as if he was saying that to himself.

Maybe he really does want to live here now, I thought, *even though the houses don't seem as nice as the houses in Bethlehem.* What if Grandmother Emma never came out of the hospital? Would he remain working for my father, or would he retire? Once he dropped me off now, would I ever see him again?

"Daddy told me he's getting a special car that he will be able to drive," I said. I said it to see what Felix would tell me. Would that mean he wouldn't be needed to drive Daddy anywhere anymore?

"Hmm, so I hear," he said. He didn't sound very convinced or at all worried about keeping his job. He sounded confident that my father would always want someone to do things for him. "Okay," he announced a moment later, "get ready. It's right ahead on the left side."

I leaned forward, then slid myself to the left side of the car as we drew closer to the old farm. The property began with a fieldstone wall not much taller than I was. Looking closely at the wall, I saw how weeds and mold had invaded it. Some of the stones appeared ready to topple, and in some places, they had crumbled. Why didn't anyone fix it? I wondered. Grandmother Emma would be very upset.

At the foot of the driveway, there was a tall iron

gate. It was wide open and quite rusted. The gate looked somewhat bent, too, because the hinges had come apart toward the top. The bottom of the right side was stuck in the ground and looked like it hadn't been closed for a hundred years. Was Felix sure this was Great-aunt Frances Wilkens's home? He said he hadn't been here for some time. He could be making a mistake.

"What happened here?" Felix muttered to himself when he slowed down.

"Maybe this isn't it, Felix."

"Oh, this is it. I'm sure."

The driveway itself was nowhere as pretty as Grandmother Emma's. This one was just dirt and crushed stones with ditching on both sides. Weeds grew up out of the ditching, too. Felix had to drive very slowly because there were large potholes to avoid.

"Well, this is gone to the dogs," he said.

I looked to the right and saw the uncut grass full of tall weeds. There was another, much smaller house with a small tractor parked off to the right of that. I could see it had a flat tire and leaned so far to the right that it looked like it might topple. An old-looking, dirty blue car was parked in front, parked on what looked like what little lawn the house had.

The grass on my left wasn't as tall but looked like it hadn't been cut for some time either. There were weeds and untrimmed bushes everywhere. A sick maple tree in front was having an early autumn and dropped its leaves like tears, crying about itself. There was a wheelbarrow turned on its side beneath it, the inside streaked with rust. It looked like it had been left there fifty years ago.

But my attention went quickly to the farmhouse. This was a very different house from the mansion in which we had all lived with Grandmother Emma, and not just because it was much, much smaller. It was still a large house with two stories and an attic. There was a small tower on the right side with arched windows and the front had a wide porch, but it didn't look very nice and certainly not what I'd expect to be the home of Grandmother Emma's sister.

"This was once quite a house," Felix remarked. The way he emphasized "once" told me he didn't think that much of it now either. The wall cladding and roofing were composed of continuous wood shingles that had long ago faded and grayed. As we drew closer, I saw that some windows had just window shades drawn down or a little ways up, but few had curtains. Some spindles in the porch railings were missing and some hung loosely and looked as if they would fall out any moment. I could see that the second step to the porch was broken. Because of the way the porch roof shaded the front of the house now, the windows were dark, more like mirrors.

As we came around, I made out the side of what looked like a small barn behind the house, but the grass was wild and uncut around it as well.

I'm going to live here? I wondered. I suddenly remembered the tale of *The Prince and the Pauper.* I had left the grand castle where I had lived like a princess and now I was going to live like a poor little girl. Why did Grandmother Emma leave her one and only sister in such a place? Didn't she care that people would see how she had left and treated her only sister? How could Grandmother Emma not know how dilapidated and run-down it was? Exactly when had she been here last? Surely it must have been a long time ago, and it must have been beautiful then or she wouldn't have sent me. Maybe she knew but didn't care. And now she was sending me here, too! Wasn't I a March anymore?

Or maybe being sick had made her so unhappy that she wasn't worried whether or not I would be.

When Felix stopped the car, he just sat there staring at the house, shaking his head slowly. He couldn't believe it either. It was all a mistake. He remained seated. For a moment I wondered if he was going to get out at all, or if he was just going to start the engine, turn around, and take me back.

Finally, he opened his door and got out. He stood there for a few moments with his hands on his hips, gazing at the property. He shook his head more vigorously this time, then finally reached for my door and opened it for me.

"I'll get your things," he said. "Just wait here."

I got out slowly while he went to the trunk to fetch my suitcases. There was still no sign of anyone either at the farmhouse or the smaller house to my right. *Perhaps everyone left,* I thought. *That could be it. Everyone left a long time ago.* No one lived here anymore and Grandmother Emma just didn't know yet. I couldn't help wishing that was so.

Felix came around and started for the front porch.

"Come along," he said, "but watch the step," he warned. I could hear the underfloor of anger growling in his throat. He stepped over the broken step, glaring back at it.

Closer now, I could see that even some porch floor-

boards were cracked, a few broken enough to have
fallen in, leaving gaping holes. The front windows
were stained with dust and dirt. There were pieces
of bushes and tree branches scattered over the porch
floor. No one had swept it for some time. There was a
flannel shirt crumpled in the corner.

Felix lowered my suitcases carefully to the porch
floor, as if he thought the weight of them might cave
it in. He searched for a door buzzer and found a hole
with a wire. He plucked it and glanced at it, and then at
me, with disgust before turning to the door and knocking hard on it—so hard that the panel windows rattled.
I thought they'd fall out and shatter. Again, he looked
at me, his face dark and gray with displeasure.

I was overcome and depressed by the same disappointment. When I first had heard I was going to live
with Great-aunt Frances on a farm, I immediately
envisioned the farms I had seen in my storybooks and
on television, farms with whitewashed picket fences,
pretty, well-kept corrals and lots of fun farm animals.
Surely, I kept hoping, Grandmother Emma and the
March family couldn't own anything as dreary as this.

I remembered hearing how my grandfather had
gotten the property in a foreclosure, but I also remembered either my grandmother or my father saying he
wanted it to be their rural retreat, a vacation home. I
knew they had fixed it up. It was all so confusing. If
they had fixed it up, how could it look like this? Why
or how Great-aunt Frances had ended up living here,
I did not know, and I certainly didn't know or understand how she could be living here now.

No one came to the door, so Felix rapped on it
again, this time taking care to hit only the solid sec-

tion, really pounding on the jamb itself. Finally, we heard footsteps and a high-pitched, "Coming, coming. Don't bust a gut."

The door did not open easily. It caught on the jamb as if it hadn't been opened for centuries and looked like it would be torn in half with any effort to open it. Finally, it did, and my great-aunt Frances stepped out to greet us. Felix, who assuredly had seen her before, actually recoiled at the sight of her. I stood there, gaping in disbelief.

I could hear my grandmother Emma's chiding. "Don't stare at someone like that. It's impolite."

But how could I not? Great-aunt Frances's dark gray hair was in clumsily spun pigtails, strands curling off like broken guitar strings. It looked like a poor attempt to make her aged face youthful.

She was about Grandmother Emma's height, but she was heavier, both in her bosom and hips. She wore a dull blue one-piece dress that had a tear in the skirt hem. The sleeves had a frilly white trim and the bodice had a collar that fit snugly around her neck, just opened at the base. She wore a light red lipstick and had some faint rouge on her cheeks, but her eyebrows were untrimmed. I saw she had a gold teardrop earring on her right ear but none on her left. A charm bracelet dangled off her right wrist. However, it looked like a child's toy bracelet made of plastic.

"Sorry, Miss Wilkens," Felix said, "but do you know your door buzzer is broken?"

"Is it? I haven't had anyone come calling for so long, I didn't know," she said, looking at the wires Felix showed her. "Oh, how terrible. Someone could get a nasty shock."

"No. It's dead," Felix said dryly. Then he turned to me. "This is Jordan."

"Jordan?"

"Jordan March, Miss Wilkens, your grandniece. I know you were informed we'd be here today."

"Oh, dear me, is today the day? How did I forget?" She looked at me and smiled. "Oh, good," she said, clapping her hands. "You're not a baby. I didn't know how I could look after a baby."

Felix turned to me. I think we were both thinking the same thing: *Look after a baby? You don't look like you can look after yourself.*

"Anyway, hello, Miss Wilkens," Felix said. "How are you?"

"How am I? Oh, I'm doing just fine, thank you. Thank you for asking." She looked at him, obviously just realizing who he was. "Oh, yes, you're Felix, Emma's chauffeur." Her eyes narrowed and then widened. "Never mind how I am. How's my sister?" she followed quickly.

"She's about the same, Miss Wilkens."

"Oh?"

She brought her hands to the base of her neck. She looked from him to me and then back to him.

"Does that mean she's not getting better?"

"Not yet, Miss Wilkens."

"Oh, dear. Emma will be very vexed about that. She will give her doctors a piece of her mind if she's not better soon," she added, nodding.

"Yes," Felix said, finally smiling. "She's already done that."

"Well," Great-aunt Frances said after taking a deep breath, "is that all you have, dear, those two suitcases?"

"That's all she has right now," Felix replied for me. "I'll bring other things as time goes by and we see what she needs."

I could almost hear him add, "If she stays here, that is."

"No matter. There are so many, many things you can wear. I never threw anything out. Emma was always complaining to our parents about that. 'She hoards everything like a squirrel,' she cried. I even saved my first lost tooth. It's in a little box my mother gave me when it fell out of my mouth. Did you save your first tooth?"

"No," I said.

"Don't you believe in the tooth fairy?"

I smirked, thinking of how Ian would have reacted to such a question. How could she think a girl my age would still believe in the tooth fairy, especially a girl who looked as old as I did?

"No."

"That's sad. There are so few nice things to believe in. We have to hold on to them. Here's another thing I won't ever throw away," she said, holding up her wrist to dangle the charm bracelet. "It's the first birthday gift I remember my father giving me."

I smiled, but I didn't know what to say. Grandmother Emma would certainly never wear anything a child would wear, even if it held some precious memory for her.

"Oh," she said, realizing where we were all standing to continue the discussion. "I'm sorry. I've been living alone for so long, I've forgotten my manners. Emma would have me locked in a closet, but manners are important only when you're with other people. You don't have to be polite to yourself. Well, it's time you came in, dear. It's time you came into your new home. How exciting it must be for you. Welcome," she added and stepped back.

Felix looked at me. I could see it in his face, the question: Would I just turn and bolt for the car, or would I step into the house? I imagined he wouldn't blame me if I ran, even if it made Grandmother Emma angry.

I closed my eyes and held my breath for a moment.

"Show no fear," I imagined Ian telling me. "You're a March. You can be as strong as Grandmother Emma. Show them all right from the start."

Clutching the bag of his letters to me as if I thought they would somehow protect me from anything unpleasant, I stepped into the house.

It was like starting a new chapter in a book that had yet to be written, a book that I feared had a sad ending and certainly not an ending written by me.

2

At Great-aunt Frances's

The only light inside the house came from the sunlight that poured either through the windows without shades or the windows with curtains that weren't drawn closed. The entryway was wide but short, with a dull brass chandelier that was missing bulbs. A wooden coat hanger stood almost in our way on our right. What looked like a man's black wool overcoat hung on it, with a black woolen hat hanging beside it. Below were a pair of old-fashioned galoshes and what looked like the left foot of a pair of men's black leather slippers. On the other side of the entryway was a mirror in a gilded frame that practically cried out for cleaning and polishing. I saw gobs of dust in the corners as well. A thin gray rug sat unevenly on the hardwood floor. It was so dirty and worn I could see the wood through the torn threads.

I was immediately taken with the odor of burned

toast and bacon, but the scents smelled old, like the
aromas of foods cooked days ago and trapped inside.
The house did seem stuffy and dank. I wondered why
all the windows weren't thrown open on such a nice
day. Nancy, who wouldn't hesitate to open the windows in my and Ian's rooms, even on cloudy days,
would say, "A room has to breathe fresh air once in a
while, too." She made it sound as if the walls and furniture could suffocate.

Directly ahead of us and to the left was a stairway
not half the width and height of the one in Grandmother
Emma's mansion. It, too, had a worn gray carpet over
its steps. The railing was much thinner than the beautiful balustrade Grandmother Emma took pride in. It
wasn't as elaborately designed. I saw that the knob at
the bottom was missing. Only a stem stuck up.

Along the corridor to the stairway and beyond were
framed photographs of people I thought might be family. I was sure one was of Grandmother Emma when
she graduated from college. Some were awkwardly
tilted, and the one nearest to me tilted forward and
looked like it was ready to fall. How could anyone
walk by it and not fix it? I wondered.

My gaze went to the walls themselves. They were
covered in a faded Wedgwood blue wallpaper with
edges curled out and actual tears in some places that
made it look like someone had been scratching at it.
Maybe the house is going to be renovated, I thought.
That was a sensible explanation for all this. Before we
had to move to Grandmother Emma's mansion, my
mother once took Ian and me to a house she was considering renovating. It didn't look in any better condi-

tion, but she said that was all we could afford without depending on Grandmother Emma.

Suddenly, a large gray cat with spotted gold eyes stepped out of the room on our right. It arched its back at the sight of us and then relaxed and sauntered down the hallway, bored and disinterested. Ian would say it had the March arrogance.

"That's Miss Puss," Great-aunt Frances told me. "She's twelve years old so she thinks she owns the house and will go anywhere she wants. Don't be surprised to see her under your bed or on the kitchen table. I should be more stern with her, but thanks to her, we don't have mice."

Grandmother Emma never permitted us to have a pet. She was of the belief that all animals were wild by nature and domesticating them was a futile endeavor, which Ian explained meant a waste of time. She said they brought in dirt and odor and were not kind to furniture. Once, Ian asked to have a dog, but only because he wanted to study the animal and repeat some experiments someone named Pavlov had done establishing some important scientific facts. Grandmother Emma wouldn't hear of it.

"You're not allergic to cats, are you?" Great-aunt Frances suddenly thought to ask.

"No, I don't think so," I said. "We never had a cat or a dog."

"Lester Marshall has a hound dog named Bones, but he doesn't come into the house. I think he's afraid of Miss Puss, even though a dog would never admit being afraid of a cat," she told me almost in a whisper. She was so serious-looking when she said it that anyone listening might think she really believed dogs could talk.

She just assumed I knew who Lester Marshall was, I guess.

I glanced at Felix, who was studying everything in the house and shaking his head. He looked at Great-aunt Frances and then at me, and I thought there was some real hesitation in his face. He was gripping my suitcases tightly now. I could see it in the way his hands hardened; the veins in them were embossed and his knuckles had turned white. He knew that Grandmother Emma wouldn't set foot in here, I thought. She would turn around and order an army of house cleaners to report immediately.

Great-aunt Frances moved the coat hanger back. She saw the way I was looking at the coat.

"This was my father's coat and hat and those were his boots. I put them there to keep him close," she said, smiling. "If you throw away or hide everything that belonged to the people you loved, you make their spirits feel unwanted. Oh, I know, Emma would say that's silly," she added, gazing at Felix. He forced a smile.

I wasn't sure if I would or not. It sounded sensible, and Grandmother Emma did tell us our ancestors were always watching and listening.

"I'm sure you're getting hungry for lunch and your little stomach is growling angrily. I'll make some lunch for you, too, Felix."

"No, Miss Wilkens, I'm not staying for lunch. I have to start back as soon as I see to Jordan's being settled. I have things to do back in Bethlehem for Mrs. March."

"Oh." She shook her head and scrunched her nose,

making ripples in her forehead. "My sister always worked her help too much," she told me and turned to Felix. "Let's show Jordan to her room right away then," she declared, clapping her hands together as if she had just thought of the idea. "Follow me up the stairway."

She kept her palms pressed together and waddled toward the stairs. A hailstorm of questions peppered my mind. When had she stopped being the beautiful, trim-figured woman in the March family albums? How long had she been living here? Was she always by herself? Why hadn't she ever married? Why didn't she have children of her own?

Felix waited for me to follow her first. I gazed through the doorway of what was surely the living room and saw it was a very messy room. There were magazines strewn about the furniture and on the floor. A blanket was crumpled at the foot of the large dark-brown pillow sofa. Glasses and dishes were on the long, narrow, wooden coffee table, and a towel had been tossed to or dropped on the other side of that. I couldn't see much more because we were walking too quickly for me to pause, but I did catch a glimpse of stockings hanging on the fireplace, Christmas stockings. What were they doing there now? It was only August.

The stairs creaked and moaned as we ascended, and the railing shook. I looked back and saw that Felix was eyeing it with some concern and caution.

"Don't lean on it," he warned.

When we reached the second landing, Great-aunt Frances paused and gazed about, as if she was trying to remember where my room was herself. Then she smiled and started down to our right. Because there were no windows in the hallway and the chandeliers in the ceiling were unlit and also missing bulbs, it was so dark that I felt we were walking through a tunnel of shadows. I could barely make out the few pictures hung along the way. They were depictions of country scenes, men and women riding horses with dogs trailing along. There was a picture of a lake with a young woman looking out over it as if she was waiting desperately for someone.

I wasn't watching where I was going, so I nearly screamed when Miss Puss charged past me, grazing my lower leg and shooting ahead into the first open doorway.

Great-aunt Frances paused there and turned to me.

"This is it," she said. I wondered if she had seen the cat go in.

I stepped up beside her and looked into what was to be my room. My heart bobbed like a yo-yo in my chest. There was a very large bed with a heavy-looking, dark oak headboard and footboard, but the bed obviously had been made hastily. The bedsheet hung too far on one side, and the pillows were stuffed too tightly into their cases, making them look bumpy and too rounded. There was a dull, cream-colored comforter with thread hanging from its edges. It appeared to have been tossed over the bed at the last moment. Grandmother Emma would have fired Nancy if she had made a bed like this, I thought. And our minder, Miss Harper? She would have had a heart attack and Ian wouldn't have had to poison her.

Curtains dangled limply around the two large windows, one to the right and the other to the left of the headboard. There were no shades to stop the morning sunlight, and the grime around the corners of the casings, the moldings and around the shelves on the wall to the left announced that the room was in desperate need of housekeeping. There were cobwebs, too, in every corner of the ceiling. Whereas Ian would call Grandmother Emma's house a museum of antiques, he would surely call this house a museum of dust. No one had been sent to greet us at the door, but didn't Greataunt Frances at least have a housekeeper?

Again, I looked at Felix. Now he looked like he would break into tears leaving me here. He was paused just behind me, shaking his head gently. I looked around the room again, at least pleased to see the small desk and chair even though they were both quite scratched. The desk was a little like the one I had back at the mansion. I'd sit there and do my homework. To the right of it was a large dresser that didn't match the bed. It was a much lighter shade of wood and a different style. It, too, had scratches.

"Here's the closet," Great-aunt Frances cried and opened the closet door to reveal clothes on hangers tightly stuffed against each other, squeezed in to fit. "Oh, dear," she said, realizing there was no space for my clothes. "I forgot to take my things out. This was once my room," she said, smiling. "But maybe some of those things would fit you. I tell you what. You take everything out and try anything on and choose anything you want, okay? And what you don't want we'll have Lester take to the Salvation Army, unless it fits his granddaughter."

After she said that a tiny buzzer went off, and she raised her wrist so quickly that I thought something living in the closet might have bitten her, but she was looking at her large-face watch.

"Oh, dear me, dear me. It's time for *Hearts and Flowers*. I never miss it. Never, never. I'll leave you to get organized," she added and hurried past us, out the door and down the corridor.

Miss Puss crawled out from under the bed and looked up at us. Then she shot past and after Great-aunt Frances.

Felix finally lowered my bags to the floor. He sighed deeply and shook his head again as he looked around the room.

"Yep. Mrs. March would sure be surprised," he muttered. He approached the dresser. There were old photographs in frames, a dark wooden jewelry box and two ceramic angels on it. After he ran his hand over the dresser, we could see the top was crusted in dust.

"That daughter of Lester Marshall is supposed to be caring for this house. That was the agreement she made with your grandmother when Lester asked if his daughter and her daughter could move onto the property. Looks like she's got some back rent due," he added. "I'm going to go have a word with her. Why don't you look around and see what you need before I leave for Bethlehem," he added. "I'm just afraid I'd set your grandmother's recovery back a decade if I described all this to her." He tightened his face and straightened his shoulders. "I'll handle it myself.

"Damn," I heard him mutter as he turned and walked out.

I stood alone, feeling as if I had been deposited in someone else's nightmare. Felix wanted me to see what else I needed? I needed my family back. I needed to go home. For a moment I debated whether or not I should just run out after him and cry for him to take me home, but what would that do to Grandmother Emma? And to Daddy? I'd be the cause of so much more trouble. And then, of course, Ian would be disappointed in me.

"Open your suitcases, unpack and settle down," I could hear him whisper.

I put the bag of his letters on the small desk, then I went to the dresser, but when I opened the drawers to put in my things, I found they were full of socks, underwear, and blouses. Actually, nothing had been removed to make room for me. When had Great-aunt Frances learned I was coming? Hadn't she had any time to prepare? What was I supposed to do? I took out a blouse and held it up. It was small enough to fit someone like me, I thought. I probably could fit into some of her old clothes. This had definitely been her room when she was a little girl, and from the looks of it, no one had been in it since. I wondered where she slept now.

I condensed her things to make room for my own things in the drawers. How fortunate it was that I hadn't brought all my clothing. There would simply be no room. When I finished unpacking, I realized Great-aunt Frances had not shown me where the bathroom I was to use was located. There was none in the room, as there was in my room back at the mansion. I had to put away my bathroom things. *Where do I go? It can't be far,* I thought and went out searching.

The first door on my right opened on another bedroom. There was a similar-size bed, but this one wasn't even poorly made. The blanket was tossed back and dangled off the side, and the four pillows were all over the bed. It looked like the bed a person having a terrible nightmare had just slept in or had tried to sleep in.

I gazed around. This room had an oval area rug under and around the bed. It was a light shade of ruby, but splotched and stained, with a few rips along the edges. I saw that a dish had been put there for Miss Puss to lick out the remains of something.

Clothing was strewn about everywhere, as if someone had gone mad and torn everything out of the closets and drawers and flung them in the air. Just as in the living room, I saw dishes and glasses with caked, old food. They were on the vanity table, the vanity table chair and the bedside tables. The windows in this room had shades, but one was inoperative and hung on a slant. On the dresser to my left, I saw a picture I recognized. It was similar to a picture I had seen in one of Grandmother Emma's old albums, a picture of her and Great-aunt Frances when they were both young women. Great-aunt Frances was by far the prettier one back then, I thought.

I turned to a door across the hall and found the bathroom. When I looked at it, I hoped there was another. It was barely bigger than the powder room on the first floor of Grandmother Emma's mansion. The right sink faucet had a slow but continuous drip that had long ago discolored the basin with streaks of rust. Over the counter beside it were an open tube of toothpaste with toothpaste dripped around it, a toothbrush, a hairbrush full of hair, pieces of soap and an open bottle of antacid. There were articles of clothing, panties, slips and socks scattered on the floor and over the sides of the tub. A blouse hung from the shower curtain and looked like it had been soaked in water and soap and then just left there dripping. Whoever had done it hadn't noticed it would drip on the floor and not into the tub.

The cabinet over the sink was open. Inside, the shelves were crowded with all sorts of over-the-counter medicines, loose Band-Aids and another tube of toothpaste without a cap. A bottle of cough medicine had spilled as well, the liquid sticking to one of the shelves and dripping down to another. It was hard and discolored. It had obviously spilled quite a while ago. Why hadn't it been cleaned up?

When I looked at the tub and the shower, I saw they weren't in much better condition than the sink. The tub also had rust stains and a ring around it, from when it had last been used, perhaps. There was a damp washcloth crumpled in it and a bar of soap. Along the far side were jars of bath powders lined up, two without caps.

Was this to be my bathroom, too?

I hoped not and quickly walked out and to the other side of the stairway, where there were two other rooms. The first door was closed, but it wasn't locked. I opened it and looked in on a very nice bedroom. It had a canopy bed with a lighter shade of wood for the headboard, posts and footboard. The dressers matched and the oval area rug was a pretty shade of light blue and in very good shape. Everything was neat in the room. There were no articles of clothing cast about, and nothing looked out of place. All the articles on the dresser were carefully placed. I saw there was another doorway, so I walked in to discover a bathroom in which the fixtures, although not modern, looked newer and clean.

The windows in the room were the ones I had seen with curtains and shades when we'd driven up. Nothing looked worn or torn. Why couldn't this be my bedroom? I wondered. Was it Great-aunt Frances's bedroom? On closer inspection, I could see that although it was well put together, it still had thin layers of dust over the furnishings. It was simply an unused room, but the nicest room in the house I had seen so far. I couldn't imagine why Great-aunt Frances wasn't using it.

Confused, I left it and tried the last door, but it was locked. I thought about it for a moment and then returned to the stairway. I could hear the television, so I descended and walked into the living room, where I found Great-aunt Frances sprawled on the sofa looking dreamily at the set and following the drama. Miss Puss was sprawled on the floor and looked up at me, then lowered her head to her paws. Great-aunt Frances didn't even notice I had entered. It was almost as if she had forgotten my arrival, just the way a child might. She was totally absorbed in her show and looked like she would cry if I interrupted. I decided to wait for the commercial.

Before it came, I heard the front door forcefully opened. Felix stepped in and then stepped to the side to permit a tall, thin, African American woman, with short hair cropped more like a man's hair, to enter as well. Her facial features were childlike, diminutive, with a pair of blazing ebony eyes and firm, taught lips. She wore a dark blue blouse, opened nearly to her belly button. She didn't seem to care that her breasts were almost entirely visible. Her jeans were so tight that I wondered how she could put them on and take them off. I saw she wore no socks with her battered old running shoes. Her ankles looked bruised and swollen.

"It makes no sense for me coming here to clean. Believe me, ten minutes after I'm gone, she gonna turn it back to a pigsty," she whined.

Felix closed the door by pounding it with his sledgehammer fist. He glared at her.

"And believe me it makes no sense your living here rent free without doing the work," he responded.

"I do the work!" she moaned. "She ruins it, so I just give up. I ain't a slave, you know."

"You don't decide when to give up," he said firmly. "Or if you do, you move off the property."

She looked away angrily, her gaze falling on me with stinging fury. I immediately thought she believed I was the reason she was being chastised. If I hadn't come, no one would have discovered how poorly she was keeping the house.

Felix lifted his right hand and pointed to the chandelier.

"No one can change a lightbulb? What's that got to do with how Miss Wilkens conducts herself? And this doorjamb. Why hasn't it been sanded and adjusted? Look at those shades dangling in rooms. What about the ones missing from the upstairs bedroom? I'm afraid to inspect the rest of the house. Minor repairs have been neglected everywhere you look here: the porch steps, porch floor, railings, that stairway and banister. The place is a disaster and it was once a prime property."

"None of that's my fault. I just agreed to clean up. That other stuff's my father's job," she said. "He was hired to be the property manager, not me."

I was shocked to hear a daughter shift blame toward her own father.

Felix grunted.

"Don't worry. I'll be talking with him shortly. Let's first get this place liveable. There's a young girl going to be living here now."

"Well, don't blame me if it turns back to a pigsty before you even drive away," she muttered and charged past me down the hallway to a closet. She jerked it open and pulled out a pail and a mop, glared back at us and continued into another room, probably the kitchen. I had yet to explore the downstairs.

Felix watched her and then walked slowly to the living room doorway, where I stood waiting. Great-aunt Frances either hadn't heard the commotion or had ignored it. She was still transfixed on her soap opera.

"Miss Wilkens," Felix said.

She just waved at him. He looked at me quizzically. I smiled and shrugged. Finally, the commercial came on and she turned to us.

"Oh, are you all unpacked, dear?" she asked.

"Not yet. I had to find the bathroom first. Is that the one I'll be using, the one across the hall?"

"Yes, it is. We'll arrange it together. Now that you're here, I'll have to get myself more organized," she said. "I'll have to be more like Emma."

More organized? I don't see any organization, I thought.

"You mentioned you were going to make her some lunch," Felix said.

"Lunch? Oh, right, lunch. In a few minutes. Debbie has just learned that her sister's child is her husband's, too, and her husband is in a panic and just wandering aimlessly in the city. Marcia says he's like an amnesiac. They don't know if he's pretending."

"Miss Wilkens, I have Mae Betty here cleaning up the house."

"Oh, wasn't she just here? I can't remember."

"If she was, she forgot some things," Felix said and glanced at me. "I'm sure you want it to be in better shape than it is. It was once a prime property. Mrs. March would have a second stroke if she set eyes on it the way it is now."

"What? Yes." Great-aunt Frances considered what he said, and then her eyes widened. "Emma's not coming soon, is she?" she asked, obviously terrified of the possibility and forgetting what Felix had already told her about Grandmother Emma.

"No, Miss Wilkens. She won't be coming in the near future, but eventually, she might."

"Well, let me know first. I'd like to get her room fixed up the way she likes it. She so likes fresh flowers in vases on the night tables. No one dares use that room but Emma, even though she hasn't used it since . . . since I can't remember." She laughed.

"Yes, well, as I said, things have to be taken care of better than they are, Miss Wilkens, whether Mrs. March comes or not," Felix said. "I'm—"

"Oh, it's starting!"

She waved her hand at us to tell us to shut up and leave her alone.

"I have to go talk to Lester now," Felix said, his voice filled with frustration. "Just wait a little longer. I'll return to see that you're getting your lunch."

"I'm not that hungry anyway," I said.

He went out again. I thought a moment and decided

to walk down the hallway rather than go in and watch
a soap opera with Great-aunt Frances. The kitchen was
down the hall on the right. Just past it was the dining
room, and across from it was an office and another
door. All the furniture I saw looked old and worn.
Nothing was polished and sparkling like the furniture
in Grandmother Emma's house.

I opened the closed door and saw a stairway going
down into the basement. Then I heard Lester Marshall's daughter Mae Betty filling the pail with water
somewhere behind me, so I closed the door and went
to the kitchen. Looking through it into the laundry
room, I saw her fuming over the sink and mumbling
to herself.

I was glad Felix hadn't come this far into the house
and seen the kitchen. If he thought the other parts of
the house were bad, he would think this was a disaster.
It looked like it hadn't been cleaned up not only after
breakfast but after last night's dinner and maybe even
yesterday's lunch, too. The table was covered with
dishes and glasses and some open food containers. I
wondered how long the bottle of milk had been out
and if it had turned sour.

The sink was filled with dishes. Why hadn't they
been put in the dishwasher? I wondered, but then again,
I didn't see anything that resembled a dishwasher. The
small refrigerator and the gas stove looked old to me.
However, although it was not nearly as big as Grandmother Emma's kitchen, it was a nice-size kitchen
with plenty of counter space. When it was cleaned up,
it would probably look very nice, I thought.

"What's your name?" Mae Betty demanded as she
turned to me from the laundry room doorway.

"Jordan March," I said.

"I knew you was a March," she said, twisting her lips. "Why you come living here?"

"My parents were in a bad car accident and my grandmother had a stroke."

"They all dead?"

"No," I said emphatically.

"So? Why you here?"

"My grandmother is in the hospital. My father is in a wheelchair."

"What about your mother?"

"She's in a coma in a hospital, but she'll get better," I added.

"Right. And I'll be the queen of England someday," she muttered, picked up the pail and started out. "You'll see," she said after she passed me and stopped in the hallway. "I'll get this place looking decent and she'll turn it back to a pigsty."

"Why are the dishes piled up in the sink? Isn't there a dishwasher?" I asked.

"Dishwasher? You're looking at the dishwasher," she said, "but she don't make it easy. She'll use a new dish and a new glass every five minutes. I tried to get her to use paper plates and plastic forks once and she threw it all in the garbage, telling me her sister would be furious. What sister? I asked. I ain't seen a sister here since I come, but you'd think she visits her every day the way she carries on about her."

She walked down the hallway to the front entrance, pushed the coat hanger back, rolled up the old rug, and began to wash the wood floor. As she worked, she continued to mumble under her breath. I thought I heard a slew of curse words, so I pretended not to hear and instead started to clean up the kitchen. Once in a while, back at Grandmother Emma's house, her maid, Nancy, let me help.

I found the dish soap and began to do the dishes in the sink. As I worked, I suddenly thought that maybe this was what Grandmother Emma had meant when she'd told me my great-aunt Frances needed me. She didn't need me to work on her farm, but she needed me to help with taking care of her home, with taking care of her.

"Oh, my, my," Great-aunt Frances said, coming to the kitchen doorway when her soap opera had ended. "Look at you. Not here ten minutes and you're helping out like a little trouper already. That's the way I was when I was your age, too. I always helped out. My sister never helped out. She always said, 'We have servants for that, Frances. If you do their work, what will they do? You'll put them out of work. Or you'll make them lazy.'

"Now, guess what I have here for you," she said, coming into the kitchen and going to a drawer under the counter. She opened the drawer and took out a large manila envelope. "You know what this is?"

I shook my head.

"It's all the arrangements for your school." She handed the envelope to me.

I wiped my hands on a dish towel and opened the packet. There were directions about the bus I was to take, and there was information about my class with my teacher's name, Mrs. Morgan. There was a diagram showing where my classroom was, and then there was a page about how we were to dress and behave. Grandmother Emma had somehow taken care of all the arrangements through her attorney. School was starting the day after tomorrow.

"You should put all that in your room, dear. As my sister, Emma, always says, 'As soon as you're capable of brushing your own teeth, you're responsible for yourself, which means you're responsible for your own things.'

"Now what do we have for lunch today?" she asked me. "Of course, you don't know. You just arrived. Let's look in the refrigerator."

She opened it and stood back, nodding.

"Wouldn't you just love peaches and cream? I have the cream, and the peaches are in jars down in the basement. I must have eaten all the peaches I had Mae Betty bring up, or else," she added, leaning toward me with her eyes on the doorway, "Mae Betty ate them."

"I never had peaches and cream for lunch," I said.

"Well now you will. Just go down the stairs and to your right you will see the shelves and shelves of canned peaches, tomatoes and onions. Lester Marshall does that every year for me. I'll set out our dishes and give you a glass of milk with a chocolate cream cookie, too."

She looked at the table. I hadn't cleared it yet.

"I'll make some room for us. It will be our first meal together," she said, smiling. "I'll tell you all about *Hearts and Flowers,* too. The peaches," she reminded me when I didn't move. She smiled and nodded at the doorway.

Peaches and cream sounded like a dessert, not a meal, I thought, but I didn't want to be impolite, so I went to the basement door. She poked her head out of the kitchen.

"Oh, Jordan, the light switch is on your right," she said. "Be careful. My cousin Arnold fell down those stairs and broke his ankle when he was ten. He was always a careless person, and eventually he got hit by a car and died. It was so long ago, I can't remember the exact day, but I still have a letter Emma sent me. She wrote, 'Arnold was hit by a car and died.' That's all she wrote and the date, of course. Emma always puts the date on her letters so we can look at it when we want and know exactly when they were sent."

She pulled back into the kitchen, and I searched for the light switch. A single dangling weak bulb seemed to struggle to throw enough of a glow down the stairway. There were so many cobwebs along the walls and rafters that it looked like spiders had woven the wallpaper. I certainly wasn't happy about going down the stairs. The steps felt like they were on the verge of cracking as I descended. I was practically on tiptoe to keep from placing all my weight down on them.

The switch at the top of the stairway controlled another dangling lightbulb below. Although weak, it did clearly show me the shelves. They were filled with jars of peaches, tomatoes and onions, as she had said. Just as I plucked one off the shelf, I heard the sound of a girl laughing. Then I heard some muffled conversation and looked toward the left, where there was another door.

Who was down here?

Clutching the jar of peaches tightly, I went to the door and listened. There were definitely two people talking very low. The girl laughed again. I tried the doorknob, and it clicked open. Very slowly, I pulled the door back and gazed into this part of the basement.

Two windows in the foundation provided enough light for me to make out what looked like a living room thrown together with old furniture: a sofa, a chair, a table. There were cartons and pieces of other furniture all around, including armoires, dressers, and chairs, some piled on each other.

At first I saw no one. Then a head lifted over the wide-armed sofa and I saw a girl. She pulled back even farther until she was sitting up.

She was naked to her waist, and her jeans looked unfastened. Her bosom was small, but perky. She had a silver cross on a silver chain that sat between her breasts.

A boy, who had been beneath her, appeared quickly, turning on the sofa.

He was wearing only his underwear. The sight stole my breath.

They were both African Americans. The girl noticed the light pouring in from behind me and turned my way.

"What is it? Why you stop?" the boy asked her.

"Who the hell are you?" she demanded, looking at me and not bothering to cover up. She put her hands on her hips.

I closed the door quickly, my heart thumping so hard that I thought I wouldn't be able to catch my breath. Without hesitation, I charged up the stairway, not worrying about the weak steps. I switched off the light and stepped into the hallway, closing the door quickly behind me.

I stood there gasping like someone who had been underwater a little too long.

"Good," I heard Great-aunt Frances say. She was peering out the kitchen doorway again. She didn't notice anything unusual about me. "Now let's have our first meal together and get to be great friends."

She clapped her hands.

I looked back at the basement door and then at the peaches in my hand. *I don't care what I imagined you told me, Ian,* I thought. *Even you would think about running out of the house and begging Felix to take you home.*

3

Alanis and Chad

Before I reached the kitchen, the front door opened and Felix entered, followed by an African American man a few inches taller, who, I imagined, was Lester Marshall. He had milk-white hair and a very closely cut white beard and mustache that looked more like rock salt sprinkled over his face. He was stout and wore a long-sleeved blue shirt outside his jeans and a pair of very dirty black shoe boots. His shoulders were thicker and wider than Felix's, but he had a little stoop. Grandmother Emma would make him parade about with a book on his head while she cried, "Posture, posture, posture!"

Felix pointed to the chandelier and said, "Well?"

"I asked her about it," Mr. Marshall said. "She told me she didn't want so much light in the house. She said she'd rather hide herself in shadows and not be reminded about how she looked. That's why I ain't done nothing with the ones upstairs either. I swear," he added, raising his right hand.

"Everything's changed now," Felix said. "There's a little girl here. Mrs. March wants this house brought up to speed quickly. You follow?"

"Yes, sir, I do. Nothing is seriously broken. I'll fix this door promptly and mend the porch in a day. She forgets, but I wanted to fix the doorbell and she told me not to bother. No one comes to visit. Plumbing is fine. Oil burner is fine. Ain't a single short in any of the electric either. Winter comes, this house be as warm as fresh toast."

"All that doesn't explain why the grounds look like no one's lived here for years."

"Oh, I had some back problems and some equipment broke down so it just got away from me, but I'll get it looking shipshape real soon."

"If Mrs. March drove up here with me today, you'd be on a ship all right, a ship sailing for the South Pole," Felix replied.

Mae Betty stepped out of the living room. She clutched bags of garbage in each hand as if she'd been holding two errant boys by their hair. She looked as worn and frazzled as a maid who had been working for hours and hours.

"This is just a tenth of it!" she said.

"I warned you that you had to stay on it or it would get far past you, girl," Lester told his daughter.

"Don't put no act on now, Daddy. You agreed it was a waste of time cleaning up this place."

"There's a little girl come here to live now," Lester told her.

"Well, how's I supposed to know about it? You never said nothing."

"I told her, but she forgot," Lester explained to Felix. "She works nights at the Canary Bar and—"

"I don't care. Just get it all up to speed quickly. I'll be back with Mrs. March soon, or they'll send me back with young Mr. March, and you don't want to disappoint the Marches, especially now with all their personal troubles. You'll be out of here in a heartbeat," he warned.

"No problem," Lester said. He glared at his daughter, who pulled her shoulders back and headed toward me. Her eyes looked like they could shoot flames in my direction. I fled into the kitchen. My heart was still pounding from what I had seen in the basement, and Mae Betty's glaring at me didn't slow it down.

Great-aunt Frances was seated at the kitchen table. She had cleared away some space for two bowls and two spoons on napkins beside them. She had poured a glass of milk for me and laid two cookies beside it. I saw that the cream for the peaches was already in the bowls.

Mae Betty came in behind me, nudging me out of her way without saying "Excuse me," as she started across the kitchen toward the laundry room. Miss Puss practically leaped under the table to avoid being stepped on.

"Oh," Great-aunt Frances said. "I forgot it's hard to open those jars. You can't do it, and my hands are as soft as cotton candy."

"Don't ask me. I got more than enough to do with the mess you made," Mae Betty tossed back at us and continued walking toward the laundry room.

Felix and Lester Marshall were walking by, and Great-aunt Frances called out to Lester.

"Yes, ma'am?" he said, stopping.

"Would you be so kind as to open that jar of peaches for us, Lester?"

"Glad to," he said, taking it from me. He clutched it in his big hand and almost effortlessly turned the cover. We heard it snap, and Great-aunt Frances clapped.

"Lester is about the strongest man I ever met," she told me.

"Not anymore, Miss Wilkens. I'm not what I was. Bones are creaking so loud, they keep me up nights. I'm about to reach Social Security."

When he smiled, I saw he was missing teeth on both sides of his mouth. He glanced at me with kind eyes. He had the sort of face that gave birth to a smile around his eyes that rippled down to the corners of his lips.

"Welcome, Missy," he said.

"Her name is Jordan, Jordan March," Great-aunt Frances told him.

"A truly holy and wonderful name. You know it was in the river Jordan that Jesus was baptized?"

I nodded.

"Welcome, Jordan."

"Thank you," I said.

He handed the jar of peaches back to me and hurried out to join Felix, who was taking him through a survey of the house. We heard them talking in the hallway. It was mostly Felix rattling off this and that for repair and Lester saying, "Yes sir, got it. Yes sir, I'll be on that right away."

"Scoop the peaches into the cream," Great-aunt Frances told me.

As I did so, Mae Betty returned from the laundry room. There was a door that opened to the outside, through which she had gone to dump garbage. She glared at us and shook her head as she walked by toward the hallway. She paused in the doorway.

"I ain't tending to that cat's litter box. That's not part of my job," she declared, and as she walked away, she added, "it's overflowing."

"I always forget," Great-aunt Frances said. "Miss Puss never makes a mess anyway. You take enough?"

"Yes," I said and handed the jar to her so she could scoop out peaches for herself.

I wondered if I should now tell her what I had seen in her basement. *Surely, she should know there is a half-naked girl down there and a boy down to his underpants,* I thought, but I was afraid of starting trouble so soon after I had come, especially with all this commotion going on. So I didn't say anything.

"You must tell me all about yourself, about living with my sister, about her grand house, about your mother and your father. You must tell me all the things you like to eat, too. I'll have Mae Betty and Lester buy them for us, but don't expect me to be as good a cook as Emma's cook."

"I can make some things, too," I said. "Like scrambled eggs and toast, oatmeal, and—"

"Oatmeal? Ugh. You like it?"

"Nancy makes it with honey and raisins. It's good."

"Who's Nancy?"

"Grandmother Emma's maid and cook."

"Oh. Good. I'm glad you learned how to make things. We'll help each other. I just love having you here. When Emma's lawyer, Mr. Pond, called to tell me about Emma and how she was sending you to live with me, I thought, finally, finally my family remembers me. I thought I had been put on a raft and shoved out to sea. I can't remember when I last got a telephone call from anyone in my family.

"So," she said, folding her hands together. "Where do you want to start?"

"Start?"

"With yourself, talking about yourself? You can start as far back as you remember. I don't care. I love stories. Oh, I have all the soap opera magazines, so you can catch up and watch them with me. I also love to watch *Yesterday's Hungry Heart.* It's about romance during the time when there were lords and ladies, knights and princesses. You'll be home from school before it goes on, too. I checked the time. The moment the bus drops you off, just come into the living room and we'll watch it together, okay?"

I didn't know what to say. I never watched television right after school at Grandmother Emma's house and certainly never watched a soap opera. I couldn't imagine doing it instead of schoolwork, and I could never imagine Grandmother Emma watching such a thing.

"You look so serious. Oh, I know. You're worried about doing your homework, but you don't want to start right in on schoolwork after you've just come home from school, do you? I never did. Emma did," she revealed. "She always addressed her responsibilities before anything else. She loved to say, 'If you do what's expected of you, you'll do what you expect of yourself.' Well, I never expected anything of myself." She laughed. "Whenever I told her that, she would get so angry that her ears would turn red." She leaned toward me to whisper. "You know what Emma's fond of telling people about us?"

I shook my head.

"She's fond of saying we're so different we're like night and day. It must have been another postman. Do you know what that means?"

I shook my head even harder.

"Good. Don't ask," she said, pulling back. She began to eat her peaches and cream, obviously savoring every bite.

I tasted mine and thought it was delicious even though it was probably not the proper thing for lunch.

"Do you like it?"

"Yes."

"Good. We only do things we like here. No one tells us what to do, what to eat, when to go to sleep and get up and what to wear."

She paused, as if she was afraid someone was listening, and then she added in another loud whisper, "No one except Emma, of course. Emma always told everyone what to do, even our mother. But let's not think about it," she followed quickly. "Let's not think about anything unpleasant. Happiness and joy," she said, holding up her child's charm bracelet. "That's what each of these means. This is a smiling face. See?"

I nodded.

"You saw my Christmas stockings hanging on the fireplace, didn't you?"

"Yes, why are they there now?"

"Every day is Christmas in my house," she said and leaned toward me. "And here, we can still believe in Santa Claus if we want to."

She laughed and continued to eat.

She was right, I thought. She and Grandmother Emma were like night and day. Whatever "it must have been another postman" meant, it was probably right.

"Where's your other earring?" I asked her, now that she was showing me her jewelry.

She put her hand to her ear.

"Did it fall off again? We'll have to go on a treasure hunt. Later, we'll try to find it, and whoever finds it gets a prize. What will the prize be?"

"A clean towel," Mae Betty said, returning with two more bags of garbage, which she had picked up from the living room. "In this house, that's a prize."

Great-aunt Frances laughed.

"Oh, don't exaggerate, Mae Betty," she said, waving at her.

"You can wash up your own lunch dishes at least," Mae Betty muttered at us as she went by.

"Of course we can. But will we?" Great-aunt Frances added and laughed.

"I can," I said.

Great-aunt Frances didn't look up to reply. She ate much faster than I did and when she finished, she rose and took her bowl and spoon to the sink. I watched to see if she was going to wash anything. She looked at the dishes left to wash and the things in the kitchen that had to be cleaned and thrown out, and then she shook her head and spoke to the dishes.

"We haven't time for you right now," she said.

"You'll have to be patient. I have to go upstairs with Jordan and organize our bathroom and help her with her clothes. Mae Betty will just have to put up with it." She turned to me. "Are you finished yet, dear?"

"Yes," I said. I brought my bowl and spoon to the sink, and she took it immediately from me and put it on top of hers.

Felix and Lester Marshall were coming up the hallway toward us. I saw that Lester had two window shades under his arm.

"I'll be installing these in the young lady's room," he told Great-aunt Frances.

"How thoughtful," she said. "We're going upstairs now, too."

Felix looked at his watch. He was obviously staying longer than he had intended, but he urged Lester on and followed. We all ascended the stairway, Great-aunt Frances enjoying the fact that she was leading the little parade.

"Let's fix up the bathroom while they work on your bedroom," she told me when we reached the top.

I followed her in, and she immediately began to pick up things.

"Emma would burst a blood vessel if she saw this bathroom, I'm sure, but I'm so used to living alone that even after I knew you were coming, I just simply went on in my usual way. You get forgetful when you reach my age, Jordan. I'll be depending on you to remind me about things all the time. Little girls don't forget anywhere as much."

She knelt by the tub and began to wash it. I gathered as much as I could off the sink and began to straighten up the cabinet. I thought I would keep one shelf for my own things. I had enough tampons for a while, but I wondered now what Great-aunt Frances had been told about me. How would she react to the news? Did she know all about Ian and Miss Harper?

"Do you know where Ian is?" I asked, hoping she had been told.

She paused and turned, sitting on the floor.

"Ian?"

"My brother."

"Oh, Ian. Yes. I do remember there's an Ian. That's right. He's not all that much older than you. He needs to be with someone, too. Where is he?"

"He's in some institution. I have letters from him to read and then I'm going to write letters to him. Will you mail them for me?"

"Of course I will. I mean, I'll tell Lester to mail them. I haven't mailed anything to anyone for years. We have rural free delivery here. The postman drives up, puts mail in our mailbox and takes away the mail Lester sends. I don't even pay bills. Emma's always taken care of the bills—or someone who works for her. Oh. I had better be sure to have Lester buy us stamps." She laughed. "I don't even know how much a stamp costs these days. But," she said, waving at me, "I'm sure you know all about it. Children know so much these days. When I was your age, I was lucky to know the way home."

She turned again to the tub, then paused and turned back. "Where did you say Ian was?"

"It's an institution where children go when they do a bad thing."

"A bad thing?"

"I don't know how long he'll be there or much

more about it," I said. "Maybe he tells in his letters. I wasn't given the letters until this morning. Grandmother Emma had them in her office but never gave them to me."

"Emma decides everything for everyone," she said. "I told you. Ian did a bad thing?"

"Maybe you should call Grandmother Emma's attorney and ask him all about it. You can't call Grandmother Emma herself. She can't talk on the phone yet because of her stroke."

"She can't talk at all?"

"She tries, but it's hard to understand what she says. They're giving her speech therapy."

I shook my head. Why hadn't they told Great-aunt Frances everything? I wondered.

"Emma must be so furious. I wouldn't want to be in the same room with her." She thought again. "I'm afraid Emma has told me so little about our family." She smiled. "That's why I am so happy, so very happy you're here. We'll spend hours and hours talking, and you'll tell me everything about everyone. That is, anything you remember and are permitted to tell me, of course. You don't have to talk about the bad thing, whatever it was. In fact, try not to tell me anything unpleasant, and remember, we don't gossip. Gossip, Emma used to say, is words full of air. Real conversation is full of facts. You know what facts are, right?"

"Yes," I said. "My brother was full of facts."

"Good. So we won't gossip."

She turned back to the tub. How could she not want to know why Ian was in the institution? Wouldn't she be curious, at least? Should I just blurt it all? What if I told her what I had seen in the basement? Would she be upset? What would she do if she was? Cry hysterically? Throw a tantrum? Would I be blamed for whatever she did?

She looked up at me again.

"Do you have something else to say? Something pleasant?"

I shook my head. *No matter what happens,* I decided, *I really should come right out and tell her everything about Ian. She has a right to know. He's her grandnephew, after all,* I thought, but she put her right forefinger to her lips.

"Swallow bad news," she said, seeing that the words were nearly dripping from my lips. "That's what I do. Swallow it quickly and never bring it up again."

She turned away from me. *Maybe it's just not the right time,* I thought. *Grandmother Emma always said there's a right time for everything. First, determine that.*

"There's enough room in the cabinet now. I'll go get my things," I told Great-aunt Frances.

She nodded without looking back at me. Just as I started to leave, she did turn.

"Wait," she said. *She wants to know after all,* I thought, but that wasn't it. "I know just what we'll have for dinner," she said, her voice suddenly full of childish excitement. "We'll send Lester for Southern fried chicken and a quart of chocolate marshmallow ice cream. Okay?"

I nodded, even though chicken and ice cream didn't sound like a dinner.

Felix stepped into the bathroom and looked around, then he looked at me.

"Lester," he called without turning away.

"Yes, sir, I'm here."

Lester joined him quickly.

"Any reason why you haven't fixed that faucet?" Felix asked, nodding at the dripping.

"Didn't know it was leaking. She never said. I don't come up here much. Don't like to invade her privacy."

"Yeah, well, invade it and fix the faucet. Looks like you have a leak around that toilet, too."

"I'll be on it."

Felix turned back to me.

"I'll be returning to Bethlehem now, Jordan, but I'll be returning here very soon," he said, raising his voice. "Keep a list of anything you find that needs attention, understand?"

"Yes," I said, glancing at Lester Marshall. I didn't like being a tattletale, and that's what it sounded like I would become.

"Don't worry. Your grandmother would expect you to do so," Felix told me.

"Okay," I said. If it was what Grandmother Emma would want, I'd have to do it.

"I'm going now," he said. "But I'll be back very soon," he repeated, this time looking pointedly at Lester. He put his hand on my shoulder for a moment, and then he walked toward the stairway.

I looked back at Great-aunt Frances, who was still on her knees washing the tub, and Lester Marshall, who was examining the sink faucet. Once again, I felt a great urge to run after Felix to beg him to take me home, but I didn't. I watched him disappear down the stairs, then I went to my room to get my bathroom things. I did go to the window, where I looked out for one last look at Felix. I saw him pause, gaze back at the house, shake his head, then get into Grandmother Emma's limousine. A few moments later he was driving off. He was the last person connecting me to my past world. All I had now were Ian's letters waiting to be read.

As the limousine made its way down the gravel drive, the girl and the boy I had seen in the basement crossed in front of the house and walked toward the small house. The girl wore an apricot-colored round crown hat. They were laughing, but suddenly the girl pushed the boy away. He looked like he protested, but she ran and he ran after her. I watched them until they disappeared from my view. Then I returned to the bathroom with my toilet articles.

Lester was gone, but Great-aunt Frances was sitting on the side of the tub looking exhausted. She had her hand over her breast.

"It takes so little to tire me out these days. That's why I can't do very much. Mae Betty will just have to work harder now that you're here, too. I'm not used to house cleaning," she whined. "And I'm too old now to start. You can't teach an old dog new tricks. The tub is as clean as I can get it." She paused and then smiled. "But don't worry, dear. We'll be all right. Everything will be all right. We don't have to be so uppity about ourselves, do we? If Emma doesn't like it, she'll just have to hire more help for me."

While she spoke, I put my things in the medicine cabinet.

She saw me put the tampons in the bottom cabinet, but she looked away quickly.

"You know I had my first period already, right?" I asked her.

She shook her head, keeping her gaze on the floor.

"I don't talk about that. I hate to talk about anything that isn't pleasant. That goes for doctors and hospitals especially. I don't like to think about them. I hate going to the dentist, too. Dr. Evans comes to see me once in a while, and he's going to come see you soon, too. Emma's lawyer told me it's all arranged, so I don't have to be concerned about any of that," she said, looking at me again and smiling. "We don't want to even think about unpleasant things, now do we, Jordan? Okay? Okay?" she pursued, now with more urgency.

I nodded. What else couldn't I tell her about? What was I supposed to do about my problems? How could I swallow back everything?

"The only unhappiness we will permit in the house will come over the television set in my programs. That's all right, isn't it? If someone says anything unpleasant to us, we'll just pretend he or she is not there. It's like changing the channel on the television set. It's that easy. You just close your eyes for a second and go, 'Click!' in your mind and poof, whoever it is and whatever unpleasant thing they said or did will be gone."

She stood up quickly.

"I must remember to go tell Lester what we want him to get us for our dinner. Because it's Southern, I'm going to put on a *Gone With the Wind* dress. I have all sorts of old clothes stored in the basement. I'll find something you can wear, too. I'll go look right now.

What a fun, wonderful way to have our first dinner together."

She hurried out of the bathroom and down the hall before I could ask any questions. What was a *Gone With the Wind* dress? I also wondered if she would realize those kids had been down there.

More important, I wondered why Grandmother Emma thought I would be better off living here than back at the mansion with my father, even with his girlfriend there.

I closed the medicine cabinet and left the bathroom as Lester returned with tools to fix the faucet.

"It's a beautiful day," he said. "You shouldn't shut yourself up in here. Why don't you go over to the house and see what Alanis is doing."

"Who's Alanis?"

"That's my granddaughter."

The girl in the basement, I thought.

"Is there a boy there, too?"

"Oh, that's her latest, Chad Washington. By the time you walk over there, he might be gone and some other boy will be knocking on the door."

He laughed and went into the bathroom.

As Ian might say, the door to my curiosity was thrown open. I started for the stairway. I could hear Mae Betty cleaning up the kitchen. The clanging of pots and pans, the sound of silverware being tossed and the jerking and pushing of the chairs and table told me she was still in a rage. I avoided her and quickly went to the front door and outside.

It was still a warm day, only more clouds had come slipping in under the blue so that the sun was hidden enough to cast a layer of light gray over the property.

I could hear music coming from Lester Marshall's house. Some of the windows were open, and whatever was playing the music—radio or CD player—was turned up to be very loud.

I walked down the steps carefully and started slowly toward the house. I could hear the chickens Felix had told me about. They were in a pen next to the barn in the rear of the main house. When I drew closer to the Marshall house, I heard another window being thrown open. The curtain parted and the girl I had seen in the basement leaned out. The music was turned down, too.

"Hey!" she called. I walked a little faster toward her. "Who are you? What are you doing snooping around here?"

The boy she was with appeared over her shoulder and looked out at me.

"I'm not snooping," I said. "Mr. Marshall told me to come over here. Are you Alanis?"

"Mr. Marshall told you?" She laughed, looked at the boy and then at me again. "So who are you?"

"I'm Jordan March," I said.

"March? You related to Miss Piggy?"

I glared back at her a moment. That was a nasty thing to say. *Maybe I should just return to the house,* I thought.

"You mean my great-aunt Frances?"

"Oh, she's your great-aunt? What's so great about her?" she asked and laughed again. The boy laughed, too.

"That means she's my grandmother's sister," I said.

"I know what it means. I'm just teasing you, girl." She continued to look at me a moment. "Okay, come on in. Chad and I are bored anyway, or at least I am."

She backed away from the window and the curtain fell together again. I hesitated, looked back at the house, then walked slowly toward the front of the Marshall house. I saw a dark-brown hound dog lying on the front porch. It lifted its head off its paws to look my way, then lowered it again. Before I got there, Alanis opened the door and stood there with her arms folded.

Like her mother, she was tall and slim, but her facial features were bigger, so I thought she must look more like her father. Where was her father? I wondered. No one had even mentioned him. Her hat was tilted back and I saw that her hair was slightly lighter than her mother's and longer. However, her jeans were just as tight-fitting. She wore nothing more than what looked like a man's undershirt, and I could see that just like me, she wore no bra.

"Did you get an eyeful in Miss Piggy's basement before?" she asked. Her boyfriend stepped up beside her and laughed.

"How much is an eyeful?" I asked.

"Depends how long you were watching us."

"I wasn't watching you. I heard you laughing and just looked in."

"Too bad. You'd get an education," her boyfriend said, and she laughed.

"Don't tease her, Chad. She doesn't look much more than fourteen. How old are you?"

She thought I was fourteen?

"I'm seven," I said.

"Get out. Seven?"

"Can't wait until she's eight," Chad said.

"What you say your name was again?"

"Jordan."

"Okay, Jordan. You can come in. Just step over Bones," she said. The dog did not move when I approached it, so I stepped over it as she had said. She pushed Chad in the stomach. "Get out of the way, stupid."

He stepped back and I entered the house. There was a very short entryway, and the living room was very small. The hallway was narrow and not very long. I saw three doors and imagined one was the kitchen and the other two were bedrooms, but then I realized one of the three had to be the bathroom.

"Go on in," Alanis said.

When I stepped into the living room, I saw that the sofa was used as a bed. There was a bed pillow on it and a blanket folded on one side.

"I bet your house is ten times this cardboard box, huh?" she asked me.

"My grandmother's house is. It's probably twenty times, maybe thirty," I said.

"Thirty! You kidding?" Chad said.

I shook my head. "No, it's a famous mansion in Bethlehem. My grandfather was an executive at Bethlehem Steel during the golden age."

"Yeah, I heard something about that," Alanis said. "She ain't lying. They're a rich family, owning all sorts of buildings and such."

"Man," Chad said, "what you doing here then?"

"I came to live with my great-aunt Frances," I said. "My father and mother were in a bad car accident. My father's in a wheelchair now and my mother is still in a coma. My grandmother had a stroke."

"You full of good news," Chad said and laughed.

"Go on. Sit down. Don't mind him. He's practicing to be an idiot and he's almost perfect," Alanis said.

"Hey."

"Ain't it time for you to get back to your cage?" she asked him.

"Oh, you're so smart," he said. He looked at me and then he shrugged. "What's the difference? I don't care. I don't want to be in any kindergarten class," he added, looking at me. "I'll see you tomorrow."

"Maybe," Alanis said. "I'll have to check my schedule and see if I can fit you in."

"Yeah, right," he said and left.

"Time's up on him," Alanis said after he was gone.

"Time's up?"

"Yeah. I put love into boys like people put coins in a parking meter. He's expired," she said. "Go on, sit down. You don't look as young as you say you are. Your parents tall?"

"Yes."

I sat on the big, soft chair. The pillow was so worn that I sank until I felt something hard beneath me. She flopped back on the sofa.

"Look, girl," she said with great forcefulness, "I'm no fool, hear? I know you're no seven-year-old," she said, her eyes narrow. "Are you lying for some reason? Trying to keep being left back a secret or something? I know girls did that."

"No. I'm seven. That's the truth."

"Look at you. You're bigger than me upstairs. I didn't have any sign of boobs until I was almost fourteen," she said. "And certainly not as far along as you are at seven," she added, nodding.

"How old are you?" I asked.

"I'm sixteen going on thirty. That's what my grandfather says. Mr. Marshall." She laughed. "So you're going to school here then?"

"Uh-huh. I got my packet."

"Packet?"

"Papers in an envelope telling about the bus, where my class is, my teacher's name."

"Who's your teacher?"

"Mrs. Morgan."

"Well, you'll be in the third grade. You're telling the truth about that. I had her. She's all right when her husband's home. When he's not, she's cranky."

"Why isn't her husband home?"

"He's some kind of salesman. Sells dental stuff. You know why she's happy when he's home, right?"

I nodded. Why wouldn't she be happy to have her husband home?

"I don't think you do," Alanis said. "Never mind for now. You here by yourself?"

"Yes."

"I guess you don't have no brother or sister, huh?"

"I have a brother named Ian."

"Where's he?"

"In an institution," I said.

"Institution? What institution?"

"I don't know the name of it."

"Well, why's he there? Is it a military school or something?"

"No. He had to go because of what he did to Miss Harper."

"Who's Miss Harper? A teacher?"

"She was our minder."

"What's a minder?"

"After my parents got into their accident, she came to live with us and take care of us. She was in charge, but she was very mean to Ian and he put rat poison in her glass of water. She kept a glass by her bed."

"Rat poison! Holy crap."

She sat up as if she had a spring in her spine. Her eyes grew narrow, suspicious.

"You ain't just having fun with me, are you?"

I shook my head.

"Are you telling me the truth, because if you're lying to me . . ."

"I don't lie. My grandmother Emma says people who lie are afraid and weak."

She stared at me and then relaxed again.

"Okay. Your brother put rat poison in Miss Harper's glass of water. So what happened to her?"

"She died."

"You're sitting there and telling me your brother murdered her? I never heard such a story about any March. Didn't your great-aunt know?"

"No. She doesn't remember Ian, and she doesn't know where he is now or what he did. I haven't told her yet. She doesn't like to hear about bad things, unhappy things."

Alanis sat back and stared at me a moment. Then she shook her head.

"I know what you're saying. If something like that really happened, I can believe they wouldn't care about telling your great-aunt. She's on another planet."

She stared at me, then nodded, leaning forward.

"But I'll tell you something, girl. You look older than you say you are. Your parents were in a bad accident. You say your brother poisoned some witchy woman and he's now in an institution, and you're here to live with Miss Piggy?"

"You shouldn't call her that. It's not nice."

"Well, you seen how she lives."

"I'm going to help with the housework," I said. "It's not nice to call her names," I insisted. "She's an adult."

"If she's an adult, I'm a senior citizen."

"She is!"

"Whatever you say."

She thought again for a moment, then smiled.

"Life 'round here has been pretty boring, but something tells me we're going to have a good time," she said. "Right?"

I shrugged. "I don't know."

"Take my word for it. So tell me all about this brother of yours and this mansion your grandmother owns. Don't hold back on nothing neither. You can trust me. I ride the same bus and go to the same school, so we're going to be friends, okay?"

I nodded. "Will you tell me things, too?" I asked her.

"Sure, I will," she said, laughing. "You can just ask away anytime you want."

That's good, I thought. Ian always said questions were the steps on the ladder we climbed to becoming adults.

"Go ahead, in fact," she said, sitting back with her arms folded, as if she was ready for anything. "You can have the first question. We'll take turns."

I can? That's really very nice of her, I thought. I knew exactly what my first question would be.

"Go ahead," she challenged more firmly. "What's your first question?"

I leaned toward her, and her eyes widened with expectation.

"Well?"

"What were you doing with that boy in the basement?"

4

Closets Full of People

"**W**hat do you think we were doing in the basement?" Alanis fired back. She wore a crooked smile over her lips.

I tried to think of the best way to answer, the way Ian would answer.

"Well?"

"It looked like that boy was putting tadpoles in you," I said.

I never had anyone laugh so hard at something I had said, but I wasn't happy about it. No one laughed at Ian's answers.

"Tadpoles, huh? I know what you mean. We had a health class last year and the teacher, the school nurse, put on a slide show about human reproduction. The things boys have in them did look like tadpoles. Hey, I think that's what I'll call Chad next time I see him, Tadpole."

"Was that what he was doing? Aren't you worried about getting pregnant?" I asked quickly. Ian had made it sound as if that always happened.

"Worried about getting pregnant, huh? You're absolutely sure you're telling me the truth about your age?" she asked, tilting her head and squinting at me.

"Yes, I am."

She stared at me a moment longer and relaxed.

"I guess you might be. I know some other girls younger than me who look older, too. I even know a girl in fourth grade who looks like she could be in ninth."

"Maybe she has precocious puberty. My brother Ian told me all about it."

"What's that?"

"It's when your body grows faster than it's supposed to."

She nodded slowly.

"I bet that's what's wrong with Janet Ward's sister."

"My doctor told my mother it's happening a lot more than ever."

She sat forward, her eyes widening.

"That so? I want you to tell me all about it," she said.

"I don't remember that much. Ian did his research and . . ."

We heard Mae Betty calling for Alanis.

"Oh, damn," Alanis said. "Just when we were getting to a good part." She went to the window to shout back. "What, Mama?"

"You get your booty over here, Alanis, and help me with this cleaning up right now."

"Oh, Ma."

"You get over here, girl. I ain't fooling."

"Damn," she said, turning back to me. "That chauffeur sure raised hell around here. C'mon," she said. "We can talk while I work on Miss . . . on your great-aunt's house. Here," she said, handing me a stick of bubble gum.

I looked at it and shook my head.

"Ian says not to eat stuff like this. It will make holes in your teeth."

"Ian says? Ian ain't telling you what to do here, is he?"

"Yes, he is," I said.

"What?" She stopped in the doorway. "I thought you just said he was in an institution for killing that woman with rat poison."

"He is."

"Then how can he be here telling you what to do?"

"He's in here," I said, pointing to my head. "I always hear things he said long after he said them. Ian's very smart, so I try to listen to him."

I wasn't going to tell her about his letters. I was sure he had all sorts of advice for me. Or at least I hoped he had, and it would be personal.

She stared at me with her mouth open, and then she smiled.

"C'mon," she said, took back her stick of gum and hurried out and down the steps.

Bones rose and followed us, but when it was obvious we were heading for the house, he turned around and returned to the porch. I guess he really was afraid of Miss Puss, I thought.

"You didn't answer my question and you said I could have the first question," I reminded her as we continued quickly to Great-aunt Frances's house.

"I didn't, did I? No, no tadpoles today. He tried, but I wasn't doing it with him."

"Why were you with him with nothing on top and he only in his underwear then?"

"Damn, girl, don't go saying that so loud," she warned, pausing and looking at the house. She thought a moment, then asked, "You ever go fishing?"

"Not really. I was in a boat on the lake but I didn't go fishing. Ian did."

"Good for Ian. My granddaddy will probably talk you into fishing with him in the lake back there. Anyway," she said as she continued toward the house, "it's like fishing."

"What is?"

"Being with a boy like Chad. You put bait on a hook and get him to nibble. If you want, you pull him all the way. If you don't, you tease him to death or until he begs and promises so much, you throw up, give in or leave him dangling. Sometimes it's more fun to leave them dangling. Boys need to be taught a lesson, otherwise they treat you like you're their property and I ain't being any boy's property."

"Property? I don't know what you mean," I said.

"Yeah, you will. You got the body started. You might as well start on the rest of it, learning about it and boys especially. And you're lucky, girl, 'cause you got me to be your new . . . what you call it, minder? Just don't put rat poison in my water," she added, laughing, and ran the rest of the way to the house. I hurried after her. As soon as we entered, Mae Betty gave her work to do.

Despite what Great-aunt Frances said Grandmother Emma had told her concerning the work servants were supposed to do and how we were to treat them, I didn't like standing around and watching other people clean up for me while I did nothing. Ian hated Nancy coming into his room and once locked her out, but that was for other reasons. He liked his privacy and hated snoops. I really liked helping. Besides, I thought, Grandmother Emma wouldn't have told me Great-aunt Frances needed me if she hadn't expected I would help with some things.

Mae Betty had Alanis finish washing and vacuuming the floors downstairs and finish straightening up the rooms while she went upstairs to straighten up the bedrooms and collect the dirty dishes and glasses. With her father working on the plumbing and window curtains, bulbs and other things Felix had assigned him, the house was undergoing what Great-aunt Frances called "a face-lift."

"I know it's what Emma wants, and we'd better do what Emma wants," she sang.

She fluttered about from room to room doing little things herself, but spending most of her time planning what she had called our *Gone With the Wind* dinner. I had heard about *Gone With the Wind,* but I had never seen it. She went down to the basement and came up with an armful of dresses that smelled strange. She told me they had been kept in mothballs, but not to worry because we would wear enough perfume to drown out the odor.

While she went upstairs to sort it all, I helped Alanis clean up the kitchen and then the dining room. I found dirty cups and glasses everywhere and imagined that some had been left for weeks, if not months. Whatever had been in them had caked over and was hard and crusted.

"There are rats here," Alanis insisted. "So don't depend on that lazy cat to keep them away. I seen them traveling over the pipes in the basement, and now you know why. She as much as invites them in, my mother says. Lucky you come here to live, otherwise this place would get so bad, it would be condemned by the health department. How come your grandmother let it be like this if she's such a wealthy, high-and-mighty woman, huh?"

"I don't think she knew about it," I said.

"Well, why not? Don't she have all sorts of people working for her, checking up on things? How come she waited until now to send that chauffeur around, huh?"

"I don't know," I said, but what she asked made me wonder again. Grandmother Emma had too much pride to have anyone see this, I thought. What was stronger than her pride, strong enough to keep her from caring?

"You know what I think? I think your great-aunt is an embarrassment for her so she ignored her and couldn't care less what happened out here. My grand-daddy was never worried too much about it. I can tell you that. Matter of fact, this is the first time I can remember anyone came here to look things over."

"How long have you been living here?"

"Two years, and some. We came after my daddy took off with Marlene Lilly, a strip dancer who worked in the club he supposedly owned with two other men. Turned out they didn't own nothing and we had nothing, so we moved in with my granddaddy. My mother's bartender over at a club called the Canary. She says no man's worth trusting. She says it's like putting your money in quicksand. She says she'll never get married again."

"I'm sorry your father left you," I said.

"Yeah, me too, but I'm through crying about it," she told me. However, when I looked at her, she looked like tears had come into her eyes.

She knelt down and started pulling things out from under the sofa in the living room. A box of crackers had been kicked underneath and there were pieces of bread and a quarter of a rotten apple.

"Damn, she got ants," she said. "I'd better get the vacuum cleaner," she told me. "The gobs of dust under there would choke a horse. Like I said, lucky you came. Maybe your grandmother knew what she was doing. Maybe this was her way to save her sister."

Maybe, I thought, although I still had no firm idea why she would have waited this long.

Something told me it wouldn't be too long before I found out.

I stood off to the side and watched Alanis do the vacuuming. No matter what she did, she didn't take off her hat.

"I hate doing this in our place," she muttered. She saw me just standing there and asked me if I wanted to do it. "You said you wanted to help your great-aunt."

"I guess so," I said, so she handed the vacuum cleaner to me and I started. Nancy never let me do it back at the mansion. Although Alanis hated it, I thought it was fun. Soon after I had started, however, I heard her mother screaming from the doorway. Alanis had sprawled on the sofa and was reading Great-aunt Frances's soap opera magazines while I continued vacuuming. I shut it off quickly.

"What'cha making that little girl do that? You want them all after us?"

"Look at her. She's not such a little girl and she wanted to do it," Alanis whined.

"She don't know what she's doing. Get this room finished. I need to get ready to go to work at the Canary. Go on before I put your grandfather on you," she threatened.

Alanis took back the vacuum cleaner.

"You better go see your great-aunt or something. I don't need my mother on my back," she said. "I'll come look for you after dinner and we'll go down into the basement and talk and you can tell me all about that puberty thing and your brother and all. Your great-aunt will probably fall asleep watching television. Most nights she don't even go up to bed."

"How do you know?"

"I know." She smiled. "Chad's not the first boy I brought to the basement. It's like having my own apartment. Boys are impressed with stuff like that."

She turned on the vacuum cleaner. I watched her a moment, then walked out and up the stairs. When I looked in on Great-aunt Frances, I saw she had put on one of the old dresses. It was too tight around her bosom. She couldn't button it all the way up in the back, but she twirled about in front of her full-length mirror, smiling as if she saw a completely different woman wearing a dress that fit perfectly.

"Why, Miss Melody Ann," she cried when she saw me in the mirror. She spun around. "Shouldn't you be preparing for the gala dinner? You need to start on your clothes and your hair."

Who's Miss Melody Ann? I wondered. I actually turned to look behind me.

She laughed and twirled and then she flopped on the bed, the wide, long skirt falling around her. For a moment she just stared at me. Then she shook her head and dropped her arms to her sides as if her arms had turned into lead pipes. The smile flew off her face like a bird frightened off a branch.

"You look too much like my sister when you scowl like that, Jordan. Don't you want to have fun, be happy?"

I nodded.

"So, smile, don't scowl," she said. She looked like she was about to start crying. "Emma would never pretend when we were children. She never appreciated her toys like I did. None of her dolls meant anything to her. You know what I told her once? I told her one day you were ten and the next day you were twenty. I bet she's sorry now. I bet she wishes she could be ten again and wait until she was twenty." She pulled her shoulders up, folded her arms under her breasts and narrowed her eyelids. "Okay, who do you want to be more like, Emma or me?" she asked.

The question terrified me. She sat there, waiting, not moving her gaze off my face.

If I said Grandmother Emma, which was what I imagined Ian would want me to say, Great-aunt Frances would be sad, upset, maybe even angry at me. On the other hand, I didn't want to be like she was.

"I don't want to be anybody else," I said, and she clapped her hands and smiled.

"What a bright reply. Oh, I'm so happy you didn't say Emma. That means you can be either one of us anytime you want to be. Tonight, you can be like me," she said, rising.

She went to the pile of clothes on the floor and pulled apart dresses and skirts and blouses until she settled on a dress she wanted me to wear. It was blue and white with pink swirls through the white. It had frilly sleeves and a frilly collar. When she held it up, I thought it looked more like a costume than a dress.

"Go try this on. It will be too big and too long, but I'll fix it for you. Come back as soon as you get into it," she said, handing me the dress.

She returned to her mirror and began to undo her pigtails.

"I have to do my hair in the meantime. Go on," she said, waving at the door.

I looked down at the dress. I couldn't imagine wearing it, but I went to my room and took off what I was wearing to put it on. I was swimming in it. The bodice fell forward, the sleeves were too long and the skirt dragged on the floor. It was like wearing a sheet. I lifted the skirt so I could walk and returned to her bedroom.

She turned away from the mirror and immediately smiled.

"Oh, it's nearly perfect!" she cried. "Come on in and let me make some small adjustments for you."

Nearly perfect? Small adjustments?

I stepped in farther, and she went to her vanity table, opened a drawer, and came up with handfuls of safety pins.

"C'mon, c'mon. Don't be shy. I mean, don't be too shy. A young lady of quality should be shy. Bold women get reputations very quickly, you know."

I realized she was speaking in a Southern accent. It didn't sound phony either. She was good at it, and it made me smile. I saw she liked that. She started to pull gobs of the material together around my body and use the safety pins to keep them folded. I watched her face as she worked. She seemed to glow with pleasure, little girl pleasure, the smile deepening around her lips and eyes. She used dozens and dozens of pins until she had the dress tightened and formed so I could move about with it on.

"There," she said finally. "Perfect. Go look at yourself, Melody Ann Pinewood."

"Melody Ann Pinewood?"

"That's your name tonight. And I'll be Louise Parker Farthingham. Both of us have beaus, too. You know what a beau is?"

"Like in your hair?"

"No, you silly heart," she said, gently squeezing my upper arm. "A beau is a boyfriend. We're not quite engaged yet, but we're close. We're worried about them, you see. They've gone on to fight the Yankees and we decided to wait. I didn't want to wait, did you?"

I shrugged. Wait for what?

"No, you didn't either, but our beaus wouldn't hear of it. They both told us they might die on the battlefield and make us widows before we were wives." She leaned toward me to whisper. "I heard that line in a movie." She pulled back, then took me to stand in front of the mirror. "Well?" she asked. "Do you like your dress?"

I squinted. The odor made my eyes burn. I scrunched up my nose.

"Don't worry about the smell. I told you I would spray you with lots of perfume."

I couldn't imagine looking more silly. The clumps of material bubbled out around my waist and chest, and the skirt had been pulled up unevenly so that more of my right leg showed than my left.

"Well?" she asked again. "Isn't it a beautiful dress?" She looked like she was holding her breath, waiting for my answer. I was afraid to disappoint her.

"Yes."

She clapped and seized my shoulders to turn me back to the mirror.

"Now let me do something with your hair and then we'll do some makeup and we'll be ready to have a mint julep before dinner in our parlor."

"What's a mint julep?"

"Oh, it's a civilized, polite drink. You'll love it, darlin' Melody. I had my first mint julep with my daddy on a summer night when the sky was streaking with shooting stars. He said, 'Make a wish, my little princess, for tonight it will come true,' and you know what I wished for?"

I shook my head.

"I wished for a friend like you, a wonderful, precious friend like you and here you are, Melody Ann, my own precious little friend. You came from a shooting star. Now sit right here and I'll do your hair right and proper and then"—she paused to bring her lips to my ear—"and then we'll sneak on some rouge before anyone sees."

She took a brush to my hair and began.

"What the hell . . ." we heard and both turned to see Mae Betty in the doorway, holding a pail and a mop.

"What do you think you and that child are doing, Miss Wilkens?"

"Miss Wilkens? I do believe you have made a mistake. There's no Miss Wilkens here. My name is Louise Parker Farthingham and this is Melody Ann Pinewood. You can tell them we'll be down for our gala dinner shortly."

"Damn," she said, shaking her head. "Rich people," she added and walked off.

"Don't mind that, Melody Ann. There are all sorts of confused people about these days. Pity their poor souls. They might just make a wrong turn and end up in some swamp. Now where was I?" she asked and returned to my hair. "You have such beautiful hair," she said, running her hand over my head. Her eyes grew sad, and she stopped talking like a Southerner.

"I had hair like that once," she said with a note of sadness. "It was exactly the same color as yours, too. I would sit in front of my mirror and brush it for hours while I listened to music or just dreamed. Emma would come behind me and complain about all the time I was wasting, but what would I have done with the time anyway? She always worried about time, as if there was a giant hourglass in our house and the sand was running down. Once, I turned all my clocks on their faces in my room and she hurried off to tell our father. He came to my room and looked, and then he laughed and said he wished he could do the same. Emma was fit to be tied.

"You know what I think?" she continued. "I think we should have clocks with no hands on them." She smiled. "That's what I have now, you know, clocks with no hands. It's one o'clock when I say it's one o'clock and not when some watch says it is.

"Of course, I have to be careful I don't miss my programs so I can't be completely oblivious. That's why I have this watch with an alarm. Lester got it for me and showed me how to use it. Now I won't be oblivious.

"Isn't that a nice big word? Oblivious. Emma used it all the time. Frances is oblivious. I finally looked it up. It means 'lacking conscious awareness' or 'unmindful.' What a silly word, I thought. I would tell people I was oblivious, but I didn't sound ashamed or embarrassed, and that would make Emma even angrier.

"I'll tell you a little secret," she said, actually glancing at the doorway first. "I liked making Emma angry. You mustn't tell her. It would make her even angrier," she said, "and she might do something to spoil our fun. She might even send you away to live with strangers."

She brushed and brushed my hair and began to hum to herself. As I studied her face in the mirror, I thought she looked lonely, lost. She went in and out of her imagination to keep from being sad. I felt sorry for her, living here all alone with people nearby who really didn't take care of her as they should have. Why hadn't Grandmother Emma been closer to her, taken better care of her? It was mean.

"There now," she said after she pinned my hair in the back. "Don't you look absolutely beautiful? You'll break hearts downstairs. Remember, we're devoted to our beaus. We can flirt a little, but nothing more. That's all right. Don't look at me like that, Melody.

Young women like us are expected to be flirtatious. Now then," she said, "a little rouge on your cheeks."

She brushed some on me, then stood back and looked at me in the mirror.

"A little more, I think," she said. I thought she had put on too much and I looked silly, but I didn't say so. She put too much on herself as well. "Now let me spray you with perfume," she said and put on so much that I reeked enough to be smelled back in Bethlehem. "Ready?" she asked. "We'll go down and have our mint juleps on the veranda and wait for dinner."

She took my hand and led me out and down the stairs. When I looked at her, I saw she wore a smile of expectation so real that it made me wonder if we would indeed find people and music and food below. Maybe she could wave a wand and perform something magical. I used to dream of doing that to make the mansion a happier place for all of us. How could she be so happy in such a run-down house as this if she didn't have a way to do something magical?

Lester had completed the work he'd had to do in the bathroom, and he'd put bulbs in the hallway chandeliers. The light they dropped around us revealed more scuffs on the walls, and I saw just how dull and dirty the floor still was. Maybe it was too late to make the house look clean again. Maybe it was too far gone and that was why Grandmother Emma didn't really care or worry about it.

I thought Alanis must have finished the work her mother had given her, because I didn't hear the vacuum cleaner or anyone talking below. As we descended the stairs, I saw Lester on a ladder in the entryway putting bulbs in that chandelier. He turned and looked at us. He didn't look as surprised as I imagined he would be.

"Oh, Southern fried chicken tonight," he said.

"And please don't forget the chocolate marshmallow ice cream, Lester."

"No, ma'am. I'll be off to the store as soon as I can."

He put in the last bulb and stepped down. We watched him fold up the ladder. He nodded at us and went out the front door.

"We should take a short walk before dinner," Great-aunt Frances said. "This way."

She led me down the hallway, through the kitchen and out the door in the laundry room. The late afternoon sun was just behind the tops of the trees to the west. I saw the chickens in the pen with the rooster marching about them proudly, and then I looked at the barn. The doors had swung open and I could see there was nothing in it, no cows, no horses, just empty stalls and old hay on the floor. Beyond it was a large pond that went around the trees on our left. A rowboat bobbed gently by a short dock. Suddenly, we heard the honking of geese and looked up to see them in a perfect A-formation.

"There it is," Great-aunt Frances said, "the first good-bye to summer. They're going south. My father used to start his winter preparations on the first sign of them heading for warmer weather."

That memory brought a fresh smile to her face. She looked about, and the joy came into her eyes as if she saw a brand-new farm with beautiful landscaping, clean and neat.

"Now that you're here, we should get Lester to clear

all the land. There will still be warm enough days for us to enjoy the grounds, going rowing and drift with the breeze, and maybe roast marshmallows around a fire at night. Doesn't that all sound wonderful?"

I nodded. It did.

She held on to my arm and walked us toward the lake.

"I never really minded living here. Isn't it still very pretty?"

"Yes," I said. I tried hard to see it the way I imagined she was seeing it.

"When I first came here," she said, "I spent a great deal of my time sitting by the lake. There were so many different birds, and it was pleasant to watch how the breeze made the water ripple. We'll do that on nice afternoons."

"Where did you live before you lived here?" I asked.

"I lived in my father and mother's home until Emma had it sold."

"Why did she sell it if you were living in it?"

She didn't answer. I thought she might not have heard me because she was thinking so hard about happier times.

"Why did you come here to live?" I pursued.

Finally, she looked at me. Her smile didn't fade, but it seemed to lose its energy and freeze. There was a tightening around her eyes. I thought she was going to tell me, but instead, she turned her head to look back at the house. Her Southern accent returned when she spoke.

"Oh, listen. The music has started. People must be arriving. We'll have to go back to help greet the guests. Mama would be upset if we didn't," she said.

Music? Mama?

She turned and started us toward the rear entrance. Before we reached it, the door opened and Alanis stepped out on the short landing. She put her hands on her hips and looked at us, a wide grin washing through her face.

"Mama just told me about you. What are you two doing?" she asked and laughed.

"Get back to the kitchen, Tessie, before I tell Mr. Farthingham," Great-aunt Frances replied.

"Huh? Tessie? Who you calling Tessie? And who's Mr. Farthingham? Get back into the kitchen? You don't know how foolish you look, girl," Alanis said to me. She shook her head, then went back inside.

"Daddy says the servants are gettin' uppity and restless ever since the Yankees won at Gettysburg. I'm afraid we're looking at the twilight of the world as we knew it, Melody Ann. We might as well enjoy what we can. There's a storm on the horizon."

I looked at her and saw how she had turned very sad. Being in this oversize dress, having too much rouge on my cheeks, and my hair brushed down and pinned, I did feel as if we were both in a school play and we were both supposed to look a little sad at this point.

We went into the living room to wait for Lester to bring the Southern fried chicken and ice cream. I sat on the sofa, and with Miss Puss curled up below me, I listened to Great-aunt Frances continue to talk about life in the South back at the time of the Civil War. She appeared to have memorized all sorts of speeches and stories she had seen and heard on television or in movies, and even though I did feel silly after a while, I still listened and enjoyed the way she paraded about the room, gesturing toward invisible guests who arrived, telling me all about this one or that. Everyone had a story attached to his or her name. I imagined that years and years of watching soap operas and reading her stories had given her a rich well of information from which she could draw pails and pails of love, of comedy and of tragedy.

"We feast on gossip, dear Melody Ann," she said. "It's like eating chocolate cake and never getting full or fat because gossip is light and airy but delicious, don't you think?

"Now," she said before I could think of an answer. "I've talked enough. It's your turn. You must tell me all about life in the big city. Go on, start with describing the mansion," she said and dropped herself into the big easy chair, exhausted from her long speeches and dramatics. She stared with anticipation. "Tell me about Bethlehem," she added when I said nothing.

"Bethlehem?" So we were no longer in a play?

"Bethlehem, Bethlehem. Emma's kingdom. I've never been invited, you know."

Never invited? Was this just part of her pretending?

"Didn't you ever see Grandmother Emma's mansion?"

"You know I haven't, Melody Ann. I've been waiting for a proper invitation. Go on, tell me about it all, and don't leave out a single detail."

I began, but I felt strange telling my great-aunt Frances about her own sister's house. She had so many questions about everything I described that I was convinced she really had never seen it or been there to visit. Why hadn't she ever been invited? I wondered.

"It sounds as wonderful as I imagined it to be," she said. "I do want to hear all about your parents, too, but I see it's time for us to go to dinner."

Lester had returned with his arms full of bags, and he'd gone into the kitchen. He peered in at us on his way out.

"Don't leave the ice cream out too long, Miss Wilkens."

Great-aunt Frances didn't reply. She looked at me and smiled as if Lester had been the one lost in some imaginary world and not us. After he left, she rose, and we went into the kitchen. She put the ice cream in the freezer, then took out the boxes of Southern fried chicken dinners. She gazed at them for a moment, then smiled at me.

"We should heat it up, but I bet you're like me, too hungry to wait for that and for us to set the table in the dining room. Let's just eat cold chicken in here and pretend we're eating in there," she said and sat at the kitchen table. "Oh, do get us knives and forks, dear."

I knew where they were and did so. I got us some napkins as well, and she began to eat as if she hadn't for days. I watched her a moment, then sat and began to eat myself. It was good and we did enjoy it. As strange as it had all been, I couldn't say I wasn't having fun. I really didn't mind pretending. After all, like her, I hadn't had many close friends to have over and play imaginary games. Grandmother Emma had been very strict about whom we could bring to the house.

Ian certainly hadn't pretended and played anything with me unless it had had an educational reason. Ian hadn't minded our being alone. He'd been happy being by himself, but there had been many times when I'd wished I'd had someone sleep over.

Great-aunt Frances took out the ice cream and two bowls before I was finished eating. She brought it to the table with two spoons and began to scoop it out. At Grandmother Emma's house, we never ate dessert before everyone was finished with his or her meal and those dinner plates were removed. Of course, we didn't have a maid to serve us dinner here, but still, I would think Great-aunt Frances knew that. Hadn't she been taught the same manners taught to Grandmother Emma?

I quickly rose and took her plate and mine to the sink, where I scraped off the dishes the way Nancy always did before she placed them in the dishwasher.

"Just leave that now," Great-aunt Frances said. "We don't have to do anything until we want to do it."

I returned to the table, and she pushed my bowl of ice cream to me and smiled.

She ate hers as quickly as she had eaten her dinner. I wasn't even half finished with mine before she was done.

"Isn't this fun?" she asked. Before I could answer she said, "I wonder who we'll be tomorrow. If you have anyone you want to be, don't hesitate to tell me and I'll arrange it for us, okay?"

I shrugged. "I don't know," I said.

"Don't you worry one bit. I have closets and closets full of people," she told me. "We can pluck a princess off a hanger any time we want."

She laughed. I had to smile. What a funny, wonderful idea: pluck a princess off a hanger. I started to clean up for us, but she insisted we leave everything in the sink. She said she was too tired to wash and dry dishes, even though we didn't have very many, and besides, there was a program on television she didn't want to miss. She made me go with her to the living room, but not ten minutes into watching her show, she fell asleep in her chair and began to snore. I returned to the kitchen and washed and dried the dishes and silverware. I put it all away, cleaned the table, then went back to the living room.

Great-aunt Frances was still asleep and still snoring. I was thinking that now I would go up and start to read Ian's letters.

"Hey!" I heard coming from the hallway. I looked out and saw Alanis standing in the open basement doorway. She was wearing her hat, a black camisole and jeans. "C'mon. She's not going to wake up until much later."

I looked back at Great-aunt Frances. Her head was tilted to the side and she was breathing through her slightly open mouth now.

"C'mon," Alanis called again in a loud whisper.

"What are we going to do?" I asked when I joined her.

She turned to show me a bottle of whiskey and a pack of cigarettes stuck inside her waist.

"Let's have a private party," she said. "I promise. It will be better than the one you were just at. This one will be real!"

She laughed and disappeared down the stairway.

I looked back toward the living room.

Great-aunt Frances was right. There was no one here to tell me what to do or when to do it. No rules hung above our heads. There were no tattletales in the corners, and even if there had been, who would they have reported to now? Certainly no one would have gone to Grandmother Emma or my father.

I was excited about this new freedom, but it was confusing, too, because I felt as if all the strings that had tied me to everyone I knew were now untied and I was floating with no idea where I would go.

Would I drift into the world in which Great-aunt Frances lived?

Would I have to pretend for the rest of my life to be happy?

My mother's voice would continue to fade.

Even Ian's words were drifting away.

I had gone much further from who I had been than I ever dreamed I would.

Who would I become?

5

Turning the Tables

I followed Alanis to the basement living room, where she sat down on the old sofa, put the whiskey bottle and cigarettes on the table, then turned on a small portable radio. She found the station she wanted and smiled at me.

"Don't worry. She won't hear anything with that television going upstairs. She never does. C'mon. Sit down already." She laughed, pulling her legs up and folding them under her. "You sure look silly in that dress. Why did you put it on?"

I went to the chair. It was as dusty down here as it had been upstairs, I thought, but Alanis didn't seem to mind or care.

"My great-aunt asked me to. She wanted us to pretend."

"Why would a grown woman ask you to do that? I

told you she's bonkers. Aren't you afraid of living here with her?"

I shook my head. What was there to fear? So far, it looked only like fun.

"Couldn't your father keep you?"

"He said my grandmother was right. He wouldn't be able to look after me properly because he was in the wheelchair."

"Like your great-aunt can?"

"I don't know," I said. I could feel myself crumbling inside. She was right. There was so much I didn't understand. Tears were gathering to charge out of my eyes.

Alanis saw she was pushing me over an emotional cliff.

"Well, you'll have more fun here, so don't worry about it," she said, then she leaped off the sofa and started to dance to the music. "You dance?"

I shook my head.

"Don't worry. I'll teach you some great steps." She stopped and reached for the pack of cigarettes on the table. "Neat, huh?" she said, looking around as she pounded a cigarette out of the pack. "It's just like having your own apartment. I discovered it by accident one day when I was bored. You ever smoke?"

"No. Ian says it's really bad for you."

"Ian says this; Ian says that. Sounds to me like Ian's a drag. Except," she said, pausing in lighting her cigarette, "if what you told me he did to that minder is true, he sure is weird enough to make me want to know more about him."

She lit her cigarette and squinted as the smoke

reached her eyes. She waved the air in front of her face, then coughed.

"Your body's telling you not to do it," I said, recalling a time Ian pointed out exactly that. We'd been watching some kids smoking in the mall, and when some of them had coughed, he'd said, "See?"

"That so? What's your body tell you not to do?" she snapped back at me. I could see she didn't like being told anything. "Your body tell you to put on that silly dress and pretend you're living on some beautiful Southern plantation instead of this dumpy house?"

"No. I told you I did it because Great-aunt Frances wanted us to have fun."

"Yeah, right, have fun. You know lots of times, I seen her walking about talking aloud as if she was walking with someone. This ain't the first time I seen her wearing funny clothes either. Why, once . . ." She puffed on her cigarette and blew the smoke behind her. "Once, she laid out a blanket and had herself a good old picnic, blabbering away as if there were a dozen people with her. And there were nights when she lit candles all over the house acting like electricity hadn't been invented yet or something. She made my granddaddy buy her some oil that burns in them old-time lamps she has, too. I see her through the window, playing her old music and dancing as if some man was holding her in his arms.

"My mother says she should be in a mental institution. She says one of these days she'll burn down the house or something. Just wait and see. That's why I think it's weird your grandmother sent you here to live with her. You better keep your eyes and nose open all the time," she said, waving her lit cigarette at me. "One night you'll wake up and find yourself dead."

She paused to puff again.

"How can you wake up and be dead at the same time?" I asked her.

"It's just something my granddaddy says. You know what I mean. It'll be too late. Ain't you got any other relatives to live with?"

"I have an uncle, but he lives far away and he has his own children. I haven't seen him for a long time. I forgot what he looks like," I added. "Besides, I don't want to go very far away. My mother will be getting better and come home soon to get me and take me home."

She shrugged. "Maybe." She opened the bottle of whiskey, took a sip and offered it to me. I shook my head.

"Ian says this is bad too, huh?"

"I tasted wine once. I didn't like it."

"Yeah, well this tastes better and makes you feel good and happy." To illustrate, she took another drink and wiped her lips with the back of her hand. Then she took another puff of her cigarette. She started to dance again. "You like this music?"

"It's all right," I said. I didn't really like it.

"I need a new CD player. The one I have is Chad's and he's going to want it back when I give him his walking papers." She puffed her cigarette and continued to dance.

"Won't Great-aunt Frances smell the smoke?" I asked. I imagined she would think the house had caught on fire and when she found us down here, she would be very angry.

Grandmother Emma not only forbade anyone to smoke in her house; she didn't let them smoke on her grounds. She said once the smoke gets into the furniture and walls, you might as well move out. It was why she hated to go to the cabin at the lake. My grandfather and his friends used to smoke cigars there.

"You kidding? With all the stink upstairs, she wouldn't know the difference if she did smell it. Anyway, I seen her smoke once."

"Really?"

Grandmother Emma would never, ever smoke. How could they be so different?

"She had one of these long cigarette holders and she was wearing a silly hat with a feather and walking and talking down by the pond."

Alanis thought a moment, then put out the cigarette by squashing it on a plate. Then she sat and leaned back with her arms spread over the top of the sofa. "Okay, so tell me what your brother said about that puberty thing?"

"Precocious puberty."

"What's precocious?"

"Ian told me precocious means developing sooner than you're supposed to. He said he was precocious, but in a different way."

"How's that?"

"He was smarter and more mature than boys his age were supposed to be."

"Doesn't sound like something bad."

"He didn't say it was for him. Anyway, the doctor said I'd be all right," I added with emphasis.

"But my mother was still worried what my grand-mother might think, but that was something different."

"What?"

I shrugged. "She was worried I was too young to be able to have a baby and I could get into trouble. That's what Ian said."

"Ian, Ian," Alanis muttered and drank some more whiskey. She stared at me a moment. "Is he funny-looking? Big ears or something?"

"No. Ian's very handsome. Lots of girls wanted him to be their boyfriend, but he wasn't interested."

"Why not? He gay, likes boys more than girls?"

"No. He said the girls were stupid. He used bigger words, words I can't remember, too. He always says he has no time to waste on stupidity."

"Yeah, well it sounds like he's wasting plenty of time where he's at. He can't be that smart if he got caught."

She sat thinking for a few moments, then she took another sip of her whiskey and sat back again, this time turning the radio volume down.

"So you had a period then?"

I nodded.

"Damn," she said. "Granddaddy would say you're armed for bear."

"I don't know what that means."

"Your doctor say you could get pregnant, right?"

I nodded and began to explain it the way Ian had explained it to me.

"You have a period when you're making eggs and—"

"I know all that stuff," she said, waving her hand.

Then she laughed. "Can you imagine being a mother? You probably still play with dolls yourself."

"No, I don't. I'm not a baby."

"You were acting like it with your great-aunt, pretending like two children."

"I told you. We were just having fun. Maybe she wanted me not to be sad."

"Right." Alanis stared at me again. "Boys I know ain't gonna believe you're just seven, girl. They'll think you were left back for sure."

"I wasn't."

"How old does your great-aunt think you are?"

"I'm sure she knows I'm seven," I said even though I wasn't sure.

"Sometimes, I don't think she knows the time of day," she said and drank again from her bottle.

"She said she doesn't care about time, except when it comes to her television shows."

"Lucky her. You're not gonna tell her about me and you being down here and you didn't tell her about me down here with Chad, right?"

I shook my head.

"Good. Let's keep it all a secret, okay? You good at keeping secrets?"

I nodded. "There were lots of things Ian told me not to tell anyone, and I never did."

"I bet he told you lots of things. Whatever he told you, you can tell me."

I shook my head.

"No. Ian wouldn't like it."

"You'll tell me stuff and I'll tell you stuff," she said confidently. "We'll be best friends, and best friends don't keep secrets from each other, otherwise they wouldn't be best friends, right?"

"I suppose," I said, although I didn't like the idea of betraying Ian.

"You have a best friend back home, someone you had over and had you over?"

"No. Grandmother Emma wouldn't let me have anyone stay over."

"She sounds like a real winner, too. Sure you don't want to just taste this?" She held up the bottle. "You don't taste it, you won't ever know if you like it." She kept it up, holding it toward me. "You don't have to be afraid doing anything with me. I wouldn't tell. It would just get me into bigger trouble. Go on," she urged, jerking the bottle toward me. "You can't know how good something is if you don't try it, right?"

I saw she wasn't going to be satisfied until I did try it, so I slipped out of the chair and took it and stood there looking at it.

"Just take a sip, girl. It won't turn you into stone or something."

I did. It burned my throat and I spit. She laughed and took back the bottle.

"Don't worry about it. That's just what it does the first time. You'll get used to it."

"Why?"

"Why what?"

"Why would I want to?"

"You won't know why for sure until you drink more of it," she said. She smiled. "Then you'll thank me."

She took another sip from the bottle to show me how much she enjoyed it. I looked toward the stairway. It was getting late, and I wondered if Great-aunt Frances had woken up and realized I wasn't there by now. I really wanted to start reading Ian's letters, too. Alanis saw how fidgety I was.

"Relax. We don't have no curfew. My mother's at work and my granddaddy's already asleep himself, just like your great-aunt. We're on our own," she said, smiling. "It's early and we're just starting to have some fun, right?"

It was interesting talking to her, but nothing was really any fun to me yet. However, I nodded and sat again. I was getting tired, but I was afraid to say so. It had been a long day for me, so long it seemed more like a week. My body felt as if I had ridden a roller coaster because I'd had so many ups and downs emotionally and I'd had to fight continuously to keep my tears under lock and key.

"We can have a lot of fun together, more fun than you would ever have back at that mansion." Alanis leaned forward. "Are you rich, too? I mean, do you have your own money?"

"No. I don't have any money."

She grimaced. "Don't give me that."

"I don't."

"Don't you get an allowance or something?"

I shook my head.

"They didn't give you money when they sent you here?"

"No."

"What if you want to buy something?"

"Everything is bought for me. It was always that way."

"Damn. Well, maybe there's a way you can get

some money when we need it. My mother thinks your great-aunt must have a fortune buried or hidden somewhere in this house. Your grandmother has an account set up so my granddaddy can buy or charge things that are needed, but he can't get money out of it. Wait," she said after taking another sip from her bottle of whiskey. "I got an idea. You'll need money for things in school, you know?"

"What things?"

"Lunch, for starters, unless she prepares some for you, which I doubt. Tell her you need ten dollars a day. She won't know the difference."

"What will I do with it?"

"What will you do with it? You kidding? We'll buy stuff, like the booze and music and cigarettes and magazines. This is our clubhouse. We don't want to invite boys over unless we have stuff, right?"

I shrugged. "What boys?"

"Boys, boys. Damn. Don't you want a boyfriend now?"

"No, but I would like a girlfriend who could stay over," I said.

"A girl to stay over? I don't know what girl's going to want to stay over here. Maybe we'll invite some girls to our clubhouse, but we have to be very careful who we invite. We don't want no blabbermouth here telling people about what we have and what we do. I'll introduce you to my best friends."

"What will we do here?"

"Lots of stuff. Look," she said, getting frustrated with me, as Ian often did. "Don't worry about it for now. I'll educate you as we go along. Believe me, you're going to have more fun than you ever had, than you ever dreamed you would have. You're in good hands when you're with Alanis King."

"Your name is Alanis King?"

"Yeah, although since Daddy run off, Mama's been talking about calling ourselves Marshall. I'm kinda used to Alanis King. Changing our names is like burying him."

"Who?"

"My daddy, that's who. Don't you listen?"

She stared at me, then she drank some more of her whiskey.

"Try it again," she said, offering me the bottle. "You have to get used to it first. Go on. You don't want to be a child. Not with your body and stuff. Besides, this is like training. First time I drank something, I got sick as hell because I didn't have any training." She pumped the bottle at me, and I slipped off the chair and took it. "Just do it slower, a little at a time. Go ahead."

I sipped and swallowed. It was still hot in my throat and chest, but I didn't cough. She nodded, happy, and encouraged me to take another drink and another.

"That's it. You got it. See. Go ahead, take one long swallow now."

I did. She was happy and took the bottle back.

"This is some of Granddaddy's finest. He don't know how much he has. Sometimes, I pour a little water in a bottle and he can't tell what I took and what I didn't."

I sat again. I could feel it bubbling in my stomach.

"You like sitting there in that stupid dress?"

"I don't know."

"You don't know? How can you not know? You

look stupid. Just take it off. She's asleep and won't care anymore anyway. Here," she said, rising. "I'll help you by undoing these dumb safety pins. I swear, this is the silliest . . ."

She started to undo them, and the dress began to float around me again. She helped me take it off completely and tossed it on the floor. Then she stared at me. I was wearing an undershirt and panties. I could smell the whiskey on her breath and wondered if it was that strong a smell on mine.

"What's this?" she asked, lifting my locket in her palm.

"Pictures of my parents," I said.

She dropped it as if it had been hot.

"Lotta good that does," she muttered, then looked at me hard again and smiled. "You're going to have a dynamite figure in no time. Boys be drooling around you. When I was your age, all I did was dream about growing."

"My mother was sad that I was going to miss too much."

"Too much of what?" She smirked. "The fun starts now, Jordan. You just don't know it yet."

She drank some more of her whiskey and shook her head. "You want to try some more?" she asked, offering me the bottle again.

"No, thanks."

My head felt strange and my eyelids became heavier and heavier. The churning in my stomach increased, reminding me about the chicken and ice cream I had eaten for dinner. Alanis got up, paced about and kept talking as if she couldn't stop. She didn't even pause for a breath, and she waved her arms and hands as she spoke. Half of what she said I didn't hear. She noticed I wasn't paying attention and stopped in front of me.

"Listen to me so I don't waste my breath. Boys your age are babies, you know. You got to have a boyfriend who's older. I'll help you find the right one. We'll sit together on the school bus, but I won't see you much in school. You're down on the first floor and I'm up on the second and third, but we have lunch the same time, so don't you worry about it. I'll see you whenever I can, and if you have any problems, you come find me. I'll give you my room schedule." She started to pace again. "You just look through the window in the doorway and I'll see you and come out."

"Maybe my teacher won't let me out of the classroom."

She stopped walking and turned to me. "Just say you gotta go to the bathroom. She gotta let you out then. Or you can say you got your period. They hate hearing that, and when you tell them, especially the man teachers, they let you do whatever you want. Just to get you away from them. It always works for me. 'Course, you have Mrs. Morgan, but she hates hearing about it as much as men do."

"Oh."

"Yeah, oh. I can see there's lots of stuff you gotta learn," she said. "You've been living too long in some castle."

My eyes widened. That was what Ian thought Grandmother believed the mansion was, a castle. How did Alanis know?

"I've been living too long in a grass hut," she muttered to herself. She suddenly looked very angry. I was beginning to feel chilled. Even though it was warm upstairs and outside, the basement was dank and cool. I embraced myself and moaned.

"I need to put on something else," I said. She stopped pacing and talking and looked at me. "I'd better go upstairs now."

"Yeah, right. It's getting late anyway."

I started to get up, and she put her hand on my shoulder.

"Before you go up, let me see your boobs, how they're cooking."

"My boobs?"

"Breasts." She put her fingers at my undershirt and started to lift it. "It's just us, two girls. Don't worry," she said, and I lifted my arms.

She stared at me almost the way I remembered Ian staring, and then she nodded.

"Yep, you're well on your way, girl. Look at those stretch marks." She squinted. "No one tell you to wear a bra?"

I shook my head.

"You don't have to. I hate wearing a bra. Your brother ever see you naked?"

"Uh-huh. I was his Sister Project."

"Sister Project? What's that mean?"

"He was studying me and keeping records. That's why he was so angry at Miss Harper. She took his records and showed them to Grandmother Emma."

"I'll bet that made him angry. Tell me about it," she said, getting more excited. "How'd he study you?"

"He measured me and kept records."

"Kept records?" She laughed. "Is that what he called it?"

"Why shouldn't he call it that?"

"Yeah, I want to meet your brother one of these days."

"He can't come here."

"Well," she said, swaying a little, "maybe we'll find out where he is exactly and go see him."

"We will?"

"Why not? We get the money, we can do anything we want, right?"

"I don't know."

"Well, I do, damn it, so stop saying 'I don't know.' You just work on getting us the money."

She let go of my shirt and I rose quickly.

"Trust me. I'm the best friend you gonna ever have," she said. She hugged me and stepped away. "I'm going out this way," she said, nodding at the basement door and turning off the radio. "I'll see you tomorrow. Remember, don't tell your great-aunt about this clubhouse. Don't tell anyone and don't mention it around my mother or my granddaddy, okay?"

"Okay," I said.

"Take that dumb dress up with you in case she asks about it," she called to me.

I returned from the stairway and scooped it into my arms.

"I'll see if I can get Granddaddy to drive us into town tomorrow. We can hang out at the mall or something. Don't you have any money at all?"

"No," I said.

"Well, ask her for some in the morning. Tell her you need stuff for school like notebooks and pens and things. You do anyway, and if I tell Granddaddy that, he'll be more apt to drive us there, okay?"

"Okay," I said.

"I still want to hear more about that weird brother of yours," she called from the basement door.

"He's not weird. He's smart," I said.

"Same thing to me," she said and left laughing.

As I started up the stairs, my chicken and ice cream dinner, mixed with the whiskey I had drunk, announced itself again in my throat and I gagged before I opened the door and entered the hallway. I felt very dizzy, too. For a moment I just stood there, confused. Then I went to the living room and looked in at Great-aunt Frances.

She had slid down on the sofa so that her head was on the arm and her feet were dangling. I didn't see how she could stay asleep in such an uncomfortable position. The television was still on with the volume as loud as it had been, but she was fast asleep. I wanted to wake her and tell her I wasn't feeling well, but I was too frightened to do it. She would want to know where I'd been, and she might smell the whiskey on my breath, I thought, so I turned and started up the stairway to my room.

Before I got to the top, the food came up again and I had to cover my mouth and hurry down the hallway to the bathroom. I made it to the toilet just in time and started to heave up everything. I was so loud, crying and vomiting, that I thought Great-aunt Frances would hear me for sure, but when I stopped and sat on the floor, I didn't hear anything but my own moaning.

I was surprised to discover I was still clinging to the big dress. I was hugging it to me, in fact. Finally, I was able to stand and walk. I went to my bedroom and looked for my pajamas. My head was pounding and tears were streaming down my cheeks, but I managed to change and crawl into bed. I was too tired to read Ian's letters, and that made me angry at myself.

I realized I had left the light on in the bathroom and the bedroom door open, but I was too sick to get up and go out to turn it off. I just wanted to close my eyes. I embraced the bag of Ian's letters and turned on my side.

Images of the long and troubling day flashed on the insides of my eyelids. I moaned. I called out for Mommy and for Ian and I crunched my legs up against my stomach to make it feel better. Finally, I fell asleep, but I woke up with a start in the middle of the night, confused and lost. It took me a while to realize where I was. It was dark now. I imagined that Great-aunt Frances had finally come up to bed and put out the lights in the bathroom and hallway.

The shades had been drawn down on my windows so that even the moonlight was locked out. My eyes slowly got used to it, and suddenly, I saw someone sitting across from me. My heart stopped and started, and then I shifted and heard, "How are you feeling, dear?" I realized it was Great-aunt Frances.

"My tummy hurts," I said.

"Yes, I saw what went on in the bathroom. Don't worry. I've taken care of it. It was just too much excitement too fast, coming to a new home, meeting me for the first time, getting used to your new bed. That's what my mother would tell me, and she would be right, of course. Mothers are usually always right. I've been sitting here worrying about you."

She rose and came to the bed to stroke my hair.

"You'll be fine in the morning. You just need to

sleep and sleep and sleep. Don't worry about getting up early. Whenever you get up, that's when morning begins in this house. Sometimes, I sleep until noon. No one rings any bells here. Of course, it'll be different when you start school. You'll have to get up and have breakfast and get on the bus. The bus won't wait for you, but on weekends, you can sleep as long as your little heart wants, okay?"

"Okay," I said in a little voice that made me sound even younger than I was.

"We're going to have so much fun together, but you're going to do well in school, too. I'll help you as much as I can, although I wasn't half as good a student as Emma was. I promise I'll do more and more around the house. We'll think about fixing it up and making it prettier. Maybe new curtains and new carpets and even new furniture, if Emma agrees, of course. But don't worry. We'll make sure you have everything you need. We're going to be our own little family, and we're going to be so happy that Emma will be surprised.

"You know why she'll be surprised?" she asked me.

I couldn't make out her expression that well, but I thought she was smiling.

"No," I said. "Why?"

"Because she sent you here to punish me," she said. She laughed as she adjusted my blanket around me and stroked my hair again. "But we're going to turn the tables on her. You know what that means?"

"No."

"It means she'll have punished herself," she told me, kissed my forehead and walked to the doorway. "Sweet dreams, Melody Ann Pinewood," she said and closed the door softly, laughing to herself in the darkness.

Why would my coming here be a way of punishing her? Why would Grandmother Emma want to do that anyway?

I was too tired to think about it. I curled against the blanket and closed my eyes. When I did, I saw my mother's smiling face and heard her singing that soft lullaby she sang to me when I was very little. Like an incoming tide, the visions of her in her coma came rushing in to chase away my happy memories. I felt an ache in my chest and the tears pushing at my eyelids.

"Mama," I whispered, as if I'd only been two or three.

I was grateful for my descent into the darkness of my own deep sleep, but late at night I woke up with a start, forgetting where I was. I sat up, my heart beating hard and fast. After a moment I remembered and started to lower my head to the pillow when all of a sudden, I heard what I was positive sounded like someone sobbing. It was muffled and seemed as if it was coming from far away. I listened hard and thought the crying was above me. After a few more moments of it, it stopped. I remained awake, listening, and now thought there was the sound of someone shuffling along. Then, even that stopped and the house was quiet again, dark and quiet. I closed my eyes, and soon what I had heard felt more like a dream.

Because the shades didn't quite fit the windows, the morning light slipped in all around me and teased my eyelids until they reluctantly opened and I saw a rag doll sitting up on the chair brought close to the bed. It looked brand new. I reached out for it, and a note fell off. I sat up, then picked up the note.

To Jordan, it read.

> *Every little girl needs a doll to hold and talk to, especially at night when it's dark and she's all alone.*
> *This belonged to Emma but she never held it once.*
> *Now it's yours.*
>
> > *Great-aunt Frances.*

6

Lost and Forgotten

The moment the sunlight woke me, I thought there were two small drums being pounded behind my eyes. I closed them quickly and waited, but it didn't help. The thumping was so loud that I imagined Great-aunt Frances could hear it through the walls. When I sat up, a deep, bass moan came out of my mouth like a hiccup. Then I really did start to hiccup. I hurried to the bathroom to wash my face in cold water and drink some. My hiccups were so loud I was sure I would wake Great-aunt Frances if she wasn't already up. I listened for her and heard nothing, not a sound. I didn't even hear a breeze outside the windows or any creaks in the floors, walls and pipes, as I expected I would in such an old house. I did hear the rooster, but he sounded far away.

Back in Grandmother Emma's mansion, where we'd been forbidden to make unnecessary noise, there had been the sounds of work being done most of the time, either by Nancy somewhere in the house or the grounds people, but from what I had learned about Mae Betty's night job, I didn't expect to see her or hear her over here early. I wondered if I would see her here at all, since Felix had left and wasn't around to threaten her. I thought if he returned today, he would be very upset. She really hadn't done as much as she should have with the upstairs. There were still cobwebs and gobs of dust in the hallway, and except for the repair of the window shades in my room, nothing looked any better or any different. Lester had fixed the leaks in the bathroom, however.

I returned to my bedroom and got dressed to have breakfast. I wanted to just lie there and begin reading Ian's letters, but my gurgling stomach was telling me I needed good food. I made my bed as quickly as I could, satisfied that I had done a far better job than Great-aunt Frances had. I told myself that maybe I should make it my job to make hers as well every day. I could keep a list of chores the way our minder, Miss Harper, had wanted me to keep. Great-aunt Frances would surely appreciate that, and when Grandmother Emma found out, she would be very proud of me.

I hesitated in the hallway, listening for Great-aunt Frances. Why wasn't she up and about? I still didn't hear anything, so I went to look in on her. Her bedroom door was open. She was wrapped up in her blanket so tightly that it looked like a giant spider had spun it around her. She slept across the bed as if the bed had turned under her during the night. Her *Gone With the Wind* costume was in a pile on the floor, and her shoes lay where she had kicked them off. I saw that her hair was down and over her cheeks, the strands so close to her mouth that she could have been chewing on them.

Miss Puss was in the bed with her. The cat opened her eyes to look at me but didn't move. She closed her eyes again, as if she wasn't permitted to wake up before Great-aunt Frances. I shifted my feet and cleared my throat, but she didn't stir, so I left her and went down to the kitchen. I thought I would surprise her by making breakfast for both of us.

I explored every cabinet and drawer to learn where everything was, and then I started to make scrambled eggs. There was nearly a dozen in the refrigerator, and they did look recently gathered. There were still smudges of dirt on the shells, but I didn't find any orange or grapefruit juice. There was no fresh fruit. As long as I could remember, I'd had juice or fresh fruit with my breakfast. I had forgotten my vitamins. If Ian had been here, he would have lectured Great-aunt Frances about the basic foods.

The bread I found in the bread box was covered with mold. I wondered why Mae Betty hadn't thrown it out. There was part of another loaf in the refrigerator, however, and I found the toaster in a cabinet. It was full of old crumbs. I shook them out over the sink, then thought about making Great-aunt Frances coffee, too. Nancy had shown me how. I found the coffeemaker, but I couldn't find any coffee. I found some tea and a can of hot chocolate. I didn't know which to make but decided to do the hot chocolate.

Suddenly, I heard the sound of an engine. I peered out the window and saw Lester Marshall on the tractor. The wheel had been repaired and he was cutting the grass and weeds at the side of the house, working his way toward the barn with his dog, Bones, trailing lazily behind. Neither Alanis nor her mother was anywhere in sight, and the shades on the windows of their house were drawn down.

After I finished making the scrambled eggs and toast, I found some jam and a silver tray. Surely, I thought, Great-aunt Frances would have to be awake by now. I started up the stairs, carrying it all carefully. I had once made breakfast with Nancy and brought it to my mother and father. However, when Grandmother Emma had found out, she'd warned Nancy to be sure every crumb had been cleaned up in my parents' bedroom. She hadn't been happy about food in either my or Ian's room either, but she'd had no problem with being served in her room whenever she'd been under the weather.

When I returned to Great-aunt Frances's bedroom, I was surprised to see that she still hadn't moved. Miss Puss raised her head, however, and this time stood and stretched. I waited in her room with the tray, not sure what I should do. Finally, my great-aunt's eyelids fluttered and she saw me. From the puzzled look on her face, I thought she had forgotten who I was. Then she sat up, ground the sleep out of her eyes and clapped her hands together.

Miss Puss leaped off the bed and walked cautiously in my direction.

"You made breakfast?"

I nodded and brought the tray to her, stepping around the discarded costume and away from Miss Puss, who was looking up at me with some expectation.

"Oh," she said, looking at the cup. "How did you know I drink hot chocolate in the morning?"

"I couldn't find any coffee, so I took a guess," I said.

"Good guessing, only I always have it with a doughnut. Weren't there any doughnuts?"

"Yes, but I didn't think that was a proper breakfast," I said.

She looked at the eggs and the toast, and then at me, and smiled.

"That is exactly what Emma would tell me," she said. "But don't worry," she added quickly, as if she thought comparing me to my grandmother would upset me. "This will do today. Did you have breakfast?"

"Not yet."

"Well, wasn't that nice of you to think of me first. I must think of something nice to do for you today," she said and tasted the eggs. "Very good. Very, very, very good," she declared, holding out the spoon like a sword. "You are hereby given the title of chief cook and bottle washer." She laughed. "My father once gave me that title. You know what he called Emma, what title he gave her?"

I shook my head.

"He called her Mrs. President and told her she would be president of something someday because she knows how to assign work but not do any. Whenever I called her Mrs. President after that, she wanted to slap me. Sometimes she did."

She laughed and continued to eat. Then she broke off a piece of toast and threw it to Miss Puss, who smelled it, looked at me, then took it and crawled under the bed.

"Go make yourself breakfast, dear. I'll be down in a while and we'll think of things to do."

"Okay," I said and started out. I stopped when I remembered what Alanis had said. "Oh, I might go to the mall today with Alanis and get things I need for school. She said her father would take us."

"What a smart idea. It's good to have someone older like Alanis to look after you. She'll know what you have to have for school."

"Only, I don't have any money."

"Money," she said, nodding. "Yes, I think I might have some money. I'll look for it."

She thought she might have some money? She would have to look for it?

"Don't you ever go shopping?"

"No, Lester and Mae Betty get everything I need."

"Don't you have any friends to go places with or who visit you?"

"Not for a long time," she said. She looked like she might start to cry, so I didn't ask her why. I continued out and heard her shout after me, "But now I have you. Remember, the shooting star?"

How could I be that sort of friend? I was just a little girl.

I returned to the kitchen. After I had made my own scrambled eggs and toast and sat at the table, I heard the front door open and close. I wondered if Great-aunt Frances ever thought to lock it. Footsteps drew closer, and then Alanis appeared in the doorway. She had on her hat, a light green oversize blouse and her tight jeans. Her running shoes had words scribbled in black over them. I read a few quickly and realized they were all boys' names.

"You need clothes," she said, grimacing. "You dress like you just landed this year."

I was wearing the button-down blue blouse and long skirt Grandmother Emma had bought for me before she had suffered her stroke.

"And those shoes . . . ugh. You didn't borrow them from your grandmother, did you?"

"No," I said. "She has a smaller foot."

"Otherwise you would? Is that it? Forget it. Did you get any money from your great-aunt?"

"Not yet. I told her about your father taking us to the mall so I can buy some school supplies and she said she thought she might have some money somewhere."

"Yeah, right. She might have some somewhere. She's got plenty stashed in a can or something," she said. "You can bet on that."

"Whose names are on your shoes?"

She laughed. "Those are the boys I shot down one way or another."

"Why are their names on your shoes?"

"It's like, you know, like gunslingers used to notch the handles of their guns?"

I nodded, but I really didn't understand. She walked around the kitchen, looking in cabinets, finding a cookie and sitting at the table.

"Who made that? Your great-aunt?"

"No, I did, and I brought her breakfast in bed."

"So you're a little cook, too?" she said, plucking some of my scrambled egg off the plate with her fingers and tasting it.

"Just a little," I said.

"I hate cooking. Lots of times, I have to fix dinner for my grandfather even though my mother isn't at work because she's too occupied with other things."

"Other things?"

"Yeah, other things, like one of her customers from the Canary."

"Doing what?"

"What do you think?"

"I don't know."

"Right. I forgot you just look like you should know. Okay," she said, getting up. "Go find out about the money. My grandfather will take us soon. I've got my friends joining us. They want to meet you."

"Me?"

"No, the other person sitting here. Of course you. I told them all about you. We've got a lot to do. Now get after her," she said. She paused in the doorway. "We have one more day and night to party before we have to return to school, not that it will make a difference anyway," she said and laughed. "C'mon, c'mon," she urged, gesturing at me. "Get yourself moving. We're wasting time."

I stood up and then she left. Great-aunt Frances hadn't come down yet, so I put my dishes in the sink and went up to get hers and see about the money. I found her foraging about, looking through drawers. When she saw me, she held up a fistful of dollars. Miss Puss was back on the bed, lying suspiciously close to the tray. The plate looked licked clean.

"I hope this is enough," she said, handing it to me. "How much is it?"

I counted twenty singles, a ten and a five.

"It's thirty-five dollars."

"Thirty-five? I know I have more around here somewhere. I've never treated money with the proper respect. Emma always said that. She would be infuriated whenever I found a fifty-dollar bill in a jacket pocket. My father was always giving me money, but I never knew what to do with it. I'd usually give it to Emma whenever we went anywhere together."

She squatted in front of the dresser and sifted some clothing around in a bottom drawer.

"I remember I had a credit card, too, but I think Lester told me it expired."

"I think this will be enough," I said.

She stood up. She was still in her nightgown. It was faded and yellow, like the pages of an old book. I saw how dry her skin was around her elbows. She realized I was looking more closely at her.

"I didn't used to look this way," she said, touching her face. "I've just not been taking good care of myself. But I will now," she added quickly. "Now that you're here, we'll both take care of each other, okay?"

I nodded.

"Oh," she said, going to her closet. "Look at what I found in my closet."

She held up an embroidered schoolbag with a strap that went over your shoulder.

"My mother gave this to me when I went into the sixth grade, and now I'm giving it to you," she said.

I took it and saw the inside had a lining and the top had a zipper.

"Thank you."

"You're welcome, dear. Now, I'm going to take a bath and brush my hair and maybe even do my toenails," she said. "I haven't done my toenails in a long time, and I haven't put on nail polish since . . . since I can't remember."

I put the schoolbag over my shoulder and picked up the tray.

"Miss Puss is as good as a dishwasher," Great-aunt Frances said.

Surely, she didn't think that was the proper way to clean the dishes. The way she had said it made me worry, however. I put it on the tray.

"Do you want me to buy you anything when I'm at the mall?" I asked.

"Oh, you don't have enough money for me, too. You might not have enough for yourself. I'll keep looking for more," she said. "And next time he calls, I'm going to tell Emma's lawyer to send us some. We need petty cash now that I have a young girl living with me!" she declared. She grew serious. "I'm surprised Emma didn't think of it. She really must be sick. No one could think of everything necessary better than my sister. She could have been the first female American president."

I stood there for a moment with the tray. She'd said the last sentence with respect and admiration.

"You do like my grandmother?"

"Of course, I don't like her. I love her. She's my sister. However," she said, lowering her voice and looking at the doorway, as if she was afraid someone might be listening, "she doesn't love me right now. But," she added, raising her voice and smiling. "now that you're here and she sees how wonderful things will be, she'll love me again."

"She's your sister, too. She should love you even if I wasn't here."

"I suppose."

"What made her stop loving you?"

She stared a moment and then she shook her head.

"What did I say?" she asked, waving her right fore-finger at me. "What did we agree about? Never talk about anything unpleasant, remember? No sadness or unhappiness can come into this house. Only over the television set. Otherwise, what do we do? We go click our eyes closed and when we open them, whatever was unpleasant is gone, remember?"

I nodded. I wondered if she was saying this because she didn't want me to be sad or if she never wanted anything sad around her. She couldn't bury her head in the sand, but she could pretend to be some imaginary person and flee from tears as easily as opening and closing a door.

"Good," she said, smiling brightly again. "I'll be down after I get dressed. Don't worry if you have to leave before I come down, because I'm going to take much more time brushing my hair. I'm going to start to do all the things I used to do when I cared about myself."

"Okay," I said and left her humming and rushing about behind me. Before I went down with the tray, I left the schoolbag on my little desk, next to the bag of Ian's letters. I thought I would come up to read them after washing and putting away all the dishes and silverware, but Alanis returned before I could.

"Well, how much did you get out of her?" she asked immediately. I held up the money. She took it from me and counted it. "That's it?"

"That's all she could find right away," I said. "Isn't it enough?"

"It's never enough. We'll have to buy some school

supplies so she won't wonder about it, but that won't leave much for our party needs."

She thought a moment, then smiled with crooked lips.

"After she goes asleep one night, we'll start our own search through this house. We'll find it."

"No, I wouldn't do that. It would be like stealing," I said. Ian would surely agree.

"You're not stealing if you're taking it from your own family. She would have given it to you anyway eventually. I swear, you do have a lot to learn, and fast, too. This ain't Wonderland and you ain't Alice. C'mon. Let's get my granddad to take us now."

I followed her out of the house. Lester Marshall was cutting the weeds that had grown in the driveway.

"Granddad!" Alanis screamed. "Damn, he's deaf," she muttered when he didn't look our way. She took a few steps toward him, cupped her mouth and shouted again. He turned. "We gotta go now."

He nodded, took a few more swipes with his tool, then dropped it to walk toward the car.

"C'mon, and don't say anything about anything," she warned me.

What did that mean?

I followed her to her granddad's car. She told me to get into the backseat. The seat was ripped, and some of the stuffing was leaking out. There was a tear on the back of the driver's seat, too. *How old is this car?* I wondered.

Alanis got into the front seat and leaned over before her granddad got in.

"Put on the seat belt. He's a nutcase for seat belts ever since my uncle Roland died in a car crash."

"Your uncle died in a car crash?"

"When he was only nine. He was in the backseat and . . ."

She raised her eyebrows when her granddad opened the door to get in.

"Well, how do, Miss Jordan," he said, smiling at me. "How was your first night at the farm?"

"Okay," I said.

"I don't know why you still call it a farm, Granddad," Alanis said. "There's only a few scrabbly hens and that old rooster, and half the time we don't get any eggs."

"A farm's always a farm," he said, closing the door. The car's engine groaned with reluctance. He pumped his pedal and turned the key again.

"Time for the junk heap," Alanis said.

"People's always so eager to give up on things and each other, too," he said as soon as the engine started. He turned back to me. "Good, you wearing your belt. Well, then, let's get started. It's not the limousine that brought you, but it will get us where we got to go," he said, shifted and started down the driveway. "And how's Miss Wilkens doing today?"

"She's fine," I said. "I made her breakfast and brought it to her room."

"Did you now? Hear that, Alanis?"

"I'm not deaf, Granddad."

"I bet she just loves having you, having company," he told me.

"She makes up her own company," Alanis said. "She doesn't need her for that."

"Watch what you say," her granddad warned. He smiled back at me. "I'm sure you were brought up right and proper, Miss Jordan. You know it's not nice to say bad things about your elders, now, don't you?"

"Yes, sir."

"I'm sure," he said. "Maybe some of that will rub off on my granddaughter here."

Alanis groaned and wrapped her arms around herself. She turned away and stared out the window, and she was silent almost all the way to the mall, only complaining about how slowly her grandfather drove.

"People behind us would like to strangle you," she told him.

"They all in a rush to get nowhere," he replied and didn't speed up.

The moment we pulled up to the entrance, Alanis leaped out of the car, slamming the door behind her and crying, "Finally. I nearly had another birthday."

"Don't be sassy, Alanis. You be careful, and don't you get Miss Jordan into any trouble," Lester Marshall called to her. He nodded at me. "Alanis knows how to reach me when it's time for you to come home."

"Thank you," I said and got out.

"C'mon," Alanis said, grabbing my left wrist and tugging me hard. "Hurry before he decides to park and stay here, too. He can haunt you worse than any ghost."

I looked back at her grandfather. He was still parked, watching us, a look of worry on his face. Before we entered the mall, he pulled away.

Alanis led me into the mall to the food court, where two of her girlfriends were waiting. They waved as soon as they saw us.

"This is Nikki, and that's Raspberry," Alanis told me when we stepped up to them.

Nikki wasn't much taller than I was, if she was any taller. Her light brown hair was cut stylishly over her ears and midway down her neck. She had large turquoise eyes and shapely thin lips, but her nose was just a little too big for her face. As to her figure, she looked more like a girl in sixth grade than I did. Ian would say she was doomed to be a late bloomer.

Raspberry, on the other hand, had a heavy bosom, wide hips and was taller than all three of us. Her reddish blond hair looked like it had dripped freckles down her bloated cheeks. She wore a thick, brassy-looking bracelet and a ring of some kind or another on almost all her fingers. When she turned to look at me closer, I saw she had a tattoo on the right side of her neck. It looked like a butterfly.

"This is Jordan," Alanis said and put on a smile that made it seem like I was some sort of an accomplishment. The two girls ran their eyes up and down my body and smiled back at her.

"Third grade?" Nikki asked.

"Going into," Alanis underlined.

"How old are you really?" Raspberry asked me. When she spoke, her whole face became animated. Her eyebrows lifted and her cheeks seemed to rumble, as if they hadn't been attached to her bones.

"I'm seven."

"She's lying," Nikki told Alanis. "She just moved here, so you don't know for sure anyway. She can tell you anything she wants."

"I'm not lying," I said.

"We know your great-aunt," Raspberry said. "Why would your family send you to live with her unless you were in trouble? What you do? Did you get pregnant or something?"

"No! I didn't do anything."

All three were staring at me now. I realized Alanis really hadn't believed everything I had told her and wanted her friends to consider me.

"I was left back," Nikki admitted. "They said I wasn't ready for social intercourse, so I didn't go to first grade until I was seven instead of six. Okay," she said, putting her hands on her hips. "Now it's your turn to tell the truth."

"I did," I whined, tears coming to my eyes.

"You're making her cry, Nikki," Raspberry said. "Maybe she ain't lying."

"I believe her," Alanis finally declared. "It's okay," she told me. "My granddad says she ain't lying about what happened to her parents, and if you're nice to her, she'll tell you all about her brother, Ian, and why he's in a mental institution. Right, Jordan?"

I nodded.

"That's a story I want to hear," Raspberry said.

"Is that really your name?" I asked.

She laughed.

"No, it's Wilhelmina Jean. I hate my name, so don't call me that."

"C'mon. Let's go get a piece of pizza and talk," Nikki said. "You got any money?"

"She got thirty-five dollars from her great-aunt, but we can't spend it all. I need to get her some notebooks, pens and stuff," Alanis said.

"That's no problem," Raspberry said. "We'll steal most of it."

She and Nikki laughed. Alanis looked at me and shook her head.

"They're just kidding," she said. I saw her give them a side look of reprimand.

They just smiled, and we walked on to the fast-food pizza. I wasn't really hungry yet. It hadn't been that long since breakfast.

"Shouldn't we wait for lunch?" I asked.

"Lunch? This is going to be our breakfast," Raspberry said and they all laughed again.

Maybe hanging out with older girls wasn't going to be as much fun as I had imagined, I thought, but I wasn't going to start complaining. It was better if I didn't say anything. I just listened to them talk about their summer and some of the things they had done. Almost everything involved one boy or another I didn't know, of course.

"Wait," Alanis said suddenly, putting up her hand like a traffic policeman. "I got to tell you how Jordan here nicknamed Chad Tadpole."

I looked up sharply.

"No, I didn't," I said.

"Sure, you did. Here's what happened," Alanis began, and she told her girlfriends how I had discovered her and Chad in the basement and what I had asked her about it later. I wondered why she wasn't too embarrassed to tell, but soon, they were all laughing so hard that other kids were looking enviously at us.

"I can see you're going to be lots of fun to be with, Jordan," Nikki said.

I know I should have been happy they wanted to be my friends, but if anything, their laughter and smiles made me feel smaller and even more of an outsider. I knew they were taking advantage of me. None of them had any money. They spent nearly twenty of my thirty-five dollars before they were finished. I watched Alanis pay the bill. She glanced at me, and then she gave Nikki and Raspberry the remaining fifteen dollars.

"You two go get Jordan some notebooks, pens and pencils. I'll show her around the mall and we'll meet back here in twenty minutes," she said.

Nikki took the money.

"Sure, we don't mind, and we know just what you'll need for third grade."

"C'mon," Alanis said, guiding me out and off to the left. "Let's go window shopping for when we get some real money. We both need new clothes. You like my friends?"

I nodded even though I didn't.

"We'll invite them to our party tonight," she said. "It'll just be us girls. Next time, we'll invite some boys, too. We'll have to put our heads together and think of someone for you."

"Someone for me? You mean, a boyfriend?"

"He doesn't have to become your boyfriend, Jordan. But boys are like shoes."

"Shoes? How are they like shoes?"

"If you don't try them on, you don't know if they fit, right?"

She laughed and we walked on. I did enjoy listening to her talk about the boyfriends whose names she had written on her shoes. She was proud of how badly she had treated each eventually. She also talked about the girls she liked and disliked at school.

"Just because we have a small school doesn't mean

we don't have our share of snobs," she said. "Someone bothers you, you come tell me, hear?"

"Why would they bother me?"

"They just will," she insisted. She paused and added, "Especially when they hear or see where you live and who you're living with. Whenever I ride the school bus, they jeer and howl when it stops at the gate. A few times, they saw your great-aunt out walking, wearing one of her silly hats or walking with an umbrella when it wasn't raining."

"She didn't want the sun on her. I know people, my grandmother's friends, who do that."

"All I'm saying is they make fun of her and they will of you, so be ready for it. They don't dare make fun of me," she added, already looking furious enough to get into a fight.

What she was telling me made me even more nervous about attending a new school.

By the time we went from one end of the mall to the other, Nikki and Raspberry rejoined us. Raspberry handed me a bag with notebooks, pens and pencils and a ruler in it. I saw what looked like a little calculator, too, and plucked it out.

"What's this?"

"We thought you might need it," Nikki said.

"It was free today if you bought ten dollars' worth," Raspberry added.

"Thank you," I said.

"Jordan and I decided to have a party tonight in Miss Pig—I mean, her great-aunt's basement."

"Great, who we inviting?" Raspberry asked.

"Just us. It's a planning party. We'll plan who we

are going to be friends with and who we ain't and what boys are worth our time and what ain't."

"Good idea," Nikki said.

"What do we have to drink? Any alcopops?" Raspberry asked.

"No. You guys bring them. You got money, I suppose," Alanis said. "Right?"

"Right," Nikki said, smiling.

"What's an alcopop?" I asked.

"You never heard of it?" Raspberry asked me.

I shook my head.

"Don't forget she lived in a castle," Alanis told them.

"It wasn't really a castle. It's just a big house."

"And she's only seven."

"So? I drank vodka and orange juice when I was seven," Nikki bragged. They all laughed.

"Alcopops is just fruit-flavored rum and stuff," Alanis said quickly. "Don't worry about it. We got something more important to think about," she told the other two.

"What's that?" Nikki asked.

"I'd like us to think of someone for Jordan for later."

"She's only in the third grade!" Raspberry said.

"That's why we have to think of him, stupid," Alanis responded.

"Yeah, well, you tell me a boy who's gonna wanna be with a girl in the third grade," Raspberry countered.

I looked from one to the other, not sure what I should say but sure I should be saying something. After all, they were talking about me.

"Look at her. She's pretty cute," Alanis said, but not with as much confidence.

The three of them turned their gazes on me, making me feel very uncomfortable.

Then Nikki poked Raspberry with her elbow and nodded at someone down the mall corridor.

"You see who I see?"

They all turned to look.

"Stuart Gavin?" Alanis said, then nodded. "Yeah, good idea, Stuart Gavin."

A tall, lanky boy with hair the color of faded hay thatched over his head lumbered down the mall. He carried a box under his right arm.

"He's only in the eighth grade," Raspberry said.

"Stuart works for his father. He drives a truck and delivers propane gas after school and on weekends," Nikki explained.

"He's only in the eighth grade and he drives and has a job?" I asked.

"He's like us. He was left behind a year," Nikki said.

"I wasn't left behind," I said. "I wasn't!" Wouldn't she ever believe me?

She shrugged.

"When you meet him, tell him you were anyway. He'll be happier."

"I don't tell lies," I said.

Raspberry and Nikki laughed.

"I don't!"

"Take it easy," Alanis said. "They're just teasing you. I'm sure Stuart will like you when he meets you."

"When will he meet me?"

"Tonight," Alanis declared. She turned to her friends. "No sense wasting time. We'll have to guide them into a romance—you know, be Jordan's romance advisers or romance minders."

The other two laughed.

Alanis leaned in to whisper to me.

"We'll make you our Love Project just the way your brother made you his Sister Project."

"Sister Project? What's that?" Nikki asked.

I felt blood come into my face. Alanis saw and said, "Forget about it for now."

I was happy she didn't tell. I didn't want to say anything about it. They were nowhere near as smart as Ian.

"Well, what's it about?"

"We'll tell you later," Alanis said, then nodded at Nikki. "Go invite him. Tell him to be there at eight and tell him to wash behind his neck."

Nikki's eyes brightened with excitement. She looked at me, then charged off after Stuart Gavin. We all watched her catch up with him and seize his arm. He almost dropped his carton. After she spoke, he looked back at us and shrugged.

Then he walked on.

My heart was pounding with expectation.

"What he say?" Alanis demanded as soon as Nikki returned.

"He said he had to bring a tank of gas to her great-aunt tomorrow anyway so he'll just bring it tonight and hook it up before we party or right after."

"See. That's a responsible boy. He don't want to waste his time or his daddy's gas," Raspberry said, and they all laughed.

"What gas would he hook up?" I asked.

"For your great-aunt's stove," Alanis said. "Didn't they bring gas for your grandmother's stove, or was everything electric?"

"I don't know what was or wasn't brought. The deliveries were always made in the rear of the mansion."

"Rear of the mansion?" Nikki asked. "What's she talking about?"

"Oh, forget about it. We'll see you girls later. C'mon, Jordan, we'll start for home. There's this candy store on the way that sells cigarettes to minors. The old lady running it can hardly see or hear and I'll tell her I'm eighteen. We'll call Granddad from the pay phone there and get him to pick us up."

"See you later," Nikki said.

"Don't forget. I want to hear about Jordan's brother, Ian," Raspberry said. "And the Sister Project!"

We watched them walk off, then started for the exit.

"See? They're very interested in you. I knew they would like you and want to be your friend, too. You can see why those two are my best friends," Alanis said. "And best of all, you don't have to worry about anything you tell them."

If I had anything to worry about, I thought, looking at Nikki and Raspberry, it was whatever I would tell them. In my heart I knew they weren't trustworthy. Ian would say they had mouths with broken zippers.

I kept it to myself and walked on, thinking about what Alanis said about boys. It applied to friends, too, I thought. You had to try them on for size. Right now, I didn't think Alanis and her friends fit, but I was too frightened to say so. I didn't want Alanis to get angry at me and think I was a snob.

What should I do? I wondered. *What should I tell them and what shouldn't I tell them?* Whom could I ask about it?

I certainly couldn't ask my mother, who was in a coma, or my father, who had gladly sent me off, or my grandmother, who was in a hospital and would never want to be bothered with such questions. Certainly I couldn't ask my great-aunt Frances, who made me feel as if I'd been the adult. For one reason or another, none of them could help me understand and make the right decisions now.

I'm not just lost, I thought.

I'm lost and forgotten.

Maybe, just maybe, Ian can help me. I'll find his address on the envelopes in the paper bag and then I'll write to him and ask him questions. Great-aunt Frances had already said she would mail my letters to him, and now that I was at her house, I would get the letters he would send to me. She wouldn't hide them from me as Grandmother Emma had done.

Ian and I would be brother and sister again.

And maybe I wouldn't feel so alone.

7

My New Minder

Alanis wasn't kidding about the woman in the candy store. She wore glasses so thick that they looked like a pair of goggles, and she didn't really look at us when she handed Alanis the cigarettes. After Alanis bought them, she went to a pay phone to call her granddad to come for us. I waited outside while she talked.

"I told him we were walking along because it's such a nice day, so don't mention the candy store and the cigarettes," she warned when she stepped out. We started walking. "You've got to think about everything you tell adults before you speak. Sometimes, they listen very closely and pick up on things. Always do what I do, count at least to five before you answer any questions. That will give you a little time to be sure you don't make mistakes and dig a hole for yourself."

She paused to look at me and I stopped walking, too.

"You come from a rich family, but you ain't rich right now and you're more alone than I am, girl. You better be listening to all the advice I give you, hear?"

I nodded. I didn't mean for her to think I wasn't listening, but I was thinking about so many other things while she talked. I wondered how I was ever going to visit my mother. Would my father take me in his special car? When would I ever speak to or see Grandmother Emma again? What if I hated it here, hated the school? Would my grandmother Emma let my father take me back? Would he want to?

"Now then," she continued as we walked on, "just because your family's scattered and broken, it don't mean you can't be happy and have fun. No one is exactly jealous of my life, but do I look like someone who mopes about all day? No," she said, answering for me before I could even think of it. "That's because I know how to look after number one. You know who number one is, right?"

"No," I said.

"Number one is you, girl. You have to be number one to yourself. Forget about everyone else, that brother in that place, your mother, who you can't help now, and your father, too, who ain't doing much to help you anyway. Your great-aunt lives on another planet. You and me ain't really that different. We both got to look out for ourselves."

She stopped again and I stopped. Her eyelids narrowed.

"I don't trust no one," she said, "but I'll take a big chance with you. You want to be more than a best friend? You want to be like my sister? Well?" she snapped.

"Yes," I said, and she smiled.

"Okay, then. We'll be like sisters. Between us there will be no secrets, no lies. That's our motto. Whenever I look at you and you look at me, no matter where we are, we think, no secrets, no lies. Deal?" she asked, holding out her hand. I looked at it and then slowly put my hand into hers. She held on to it and whispered, "No secrets, no lies. Say it."

"No secrets, no lies," I repeated.

"Sisters protect each other first and worry about everything else second. No matter what, you never tell on me and I never tell on you. We die first. Say it. We die first."

"We die first."

"Good."

We walked on in silence, she with a big grin on her face and me worrying about all that I had sworn to do and not to do. Suddenly, we heard her granddad's car horn and saw him pull to the side of the road. He didn't look happy.

"Why did you take that girl on the highway, Alanis? I told you I'd come for you at the mall!" he shouted as we crossed the street to the car.

I thought she had said she'd told him we were walking. Why was he so surprised?

"Stop treating her like a baby, Granddad. And me, too. I think I know how to walk along the side of a highway. Besides, she wanted to see what it's like here. She got to know her way around. I won't always be hanging around with her. She's only in the third grade."

"One thing you'll never run low on is smart answers. Get in," he ordered.

Alanis flashed a smile at me and opened the rear door. We both got into the rear seat this time.

"Home, please, Mr. Marshall," Alanis told him.

He glared at us. "Put on them seat belts!"

We did, and he pulled away from the curb, drove to a place where he could turn around, and did so.

"Mama still home?" Alanis asked him.

"Yeah, she's home. Matter of fact, she just got herself up. I told her to get herself over to the farmhouse and finish cleaning before she thinks of doing anything else today. I told her you'd be on our house as soon as I brought you back. The kitchen needs tending to," he added.

"That chauffeur come back?" she asked him. I perked up. Had Felix returned? Had Grandmother Emma sent him back to take me home after all? Maybe he had told her how run-down everything was and she didn't want me living here.

"No, but he'll be back. That's for sure," Lester Marshall said.

"Well, I know you're doing the best you can, Granddad. They can't blame you."

He looked back at her and shook his head.

"Don't sweet-talk me, Alanis. You do your chores and you don't get yourself in no trouble at school this year. I don't want to hear about no cigarettes or you bad-mouthing your teachers or nothing."

"Yes, Granddad."

He grunted. I was sure he would be very angry if he knew what she had just bought. How could she lie to him so easily and quickly? I think she saw the shock in my face. She reached across the seat to squeeze my hand so I would look at her.

"We die first," she whispered.

I bit down on my lower lip, looked at her granddad and nodded.

She smiled and looked out the window. When we arrived at the farm, her granddad reminded her about cleaning up the kitchen. She told me she would see me later.

"You know where and when," she added and hurried to her house. Mr. Marshall went to the porch, where he was repairing floorboards, and I went in to look for Great-aunt Frances. I had no trouble finding her. It was her soap opera hour, and she was sprawled on the sofa just as she had been yesterday, her eyes and ears fixed so hard on the television set that she didn't hear me enter or realize I was standing in the doorway. I heard the vacuum cleaner going upstairs and went up to put my school supplies in the bag Great-aunt Frances had given me.

When I entered my bedroom, the first thing I noticed was that all the letters had been taken out of the paper bag and two of them had been taken out of their envelopes. I put the school supplies down and looked at the letters. Would Great-aunt Frances have come into my bedroom and started reading these even before I had? Looking around the room, I noticed that it was cleaner, the furniture dusted and the cobwebs gone. *It was Mae Betty,* I thought. *She snooped.*

I heard a door close down the hallway and looked toward the room reserved for Grandmother Emma. Mae Betty emerged, carrying a fistful of dust rags and a can of some polish. She looked back toward me.

"Make sure you don't leave things lying about your room, and don't leave no wet towels on the bathroom floor," she warned. "I'm not coming up here more than once a week."

"Did you look at my brother's letters?" I asked her.

"I don't know nothing about no brother's letters," she replied and went to the stairway. She glanced back at me and then descended.

Was she telling the truth?

I felt guilty about anyone else reading the letters before I had. Ian would be very disappointed. I returned to my desk and took them out one by one. The return address on every envelope had been torn off. Had Grandmother Emma done that? How was I going to write back to him? I took the bag and lay back on my bed. I decided I would do nothing else before starting to read his letters. There was no address on the letters themselves, either, but at least they were dated, so I knew which one came first.

Dear Jordan,

I am sorry I never had the chance to say good-bye to you. I did ask to see you first, but they rushed me out of the house and took me to see a child psychiatrist, Dr. Walker. It didn't take me long to understand what was going on. They didn't realize what I could see, what I could hear, and what I could smell. I knew almost immediately that Dr. Walker was a praying mantis.

As I sat there and he listened to me, I saw his real body under the disguise. Remember when I showed you a praying mantis and we saw how still it could be for so long? Remember when I explained that it tries to fool other insects by staying so still it's hard to spot? Well, Dr. Walker was that still. He was looking for a way to trap me, but I was very careful and he finally had to move.

He was even more surprised when I told him I knew Miss Harper was a parasite.

"What do you mean?" Dr. Walker asked.

"Specifically," I told him, "she's a sucking louse, one of some 3300 species of wingless creatures of the order of Phthiraptera."

"How do you know this?" he asked.

"She lived off others and had hoped to suck everything possible out of me, out of my sister and even out of Grandmother Emma," I replied.

You should have seen the look on his face. I could see he was very impressed. I told him about the other insects I had seen, especially the hornets who were disguised as policemen. I told him I knew the institution was really an ant farm. He wrote everything down, and then he smiled and told me he and I would talk often.

Of course I knew we would. He was hoping I would tell him everything so he could warn the others.

Instead, I'm warning you. One of these days, someone will come around to see you and ask you questions about me.

Don't answer any questions until they let you speak to me.

Most important, Jordan. Don't let anyone read the letters I write to you. By now, they have surely sent someone to spy. You won't know who

it is and you won't be able to tell what he or
she is.
    Just be cautious and alert.

Your brother Ian

I folded the letter and put it back into the envelope.
As I did so, I saw that my fingers were trembling.
What Ian wrote frightened me. I knew he wasn't jok-
ing. Ian rarely told jokes. If he said anything that made
other people laugh, it was usually because they didn't
understand him. He didn't mean it to be funny; he
meant it to be critical.

Things that made other people laugh didn't make
him laugh. He barely smiled at something that was
supposed to be funny on television, something that
would make our father laugh hysterically or even
our mother. I would hold back my laugh sometimes
and look first at him to see if he thought it was even
slightly humorous. It took a lot to get him to go from
a smirk to a smile, and I suppose I could count on the
fingers of one hand how many times I actually heard
the sound of laughter come from his lips.

Despite all that, he never seemed to be particularly sad to me. Things that should have made him
unhappy hadn't appeared to bother him at all. No one
could ignore people better than Ian could. Up until
the moment Miss Harper had taken his private things,
he'd acted as if she hadn't been there whenever he'd
wanted. I knew that had bothered her more than any
complaint I could have made.

If he wasn't being funny in his first letter, then what
was he being?

I took out the second letter and unfolded it carefully. Taped to the bottom of a page was what looked like a piece of thread, but next to it he had written: *the antennae of a black ant.*

Dear Jordan,

Let me describe the place I am in. It is not exactly a prison even though there are bars on the windows. They won't let me go outside on my own or when I want to go outside. I can go outside only during exercise hours. They have a limited library here. I've asked for some books, but I don't think they'll get them for me. I can't ask you to try to get them because they won't let them through the mail.

I eat in a very small cafeteria. There are five other boys here, but I haven't spoken to any of them yet. I'm not sure what they are, but I'm studying them carefully.

My room is very small, only about an eighth of the size of the room I had at Grandmother Emma's, if that. There are two windows in the room, neither with curtains. They have black shades. My bed is about a third of the size of the bed I had and the mattress is very hard, as hard as board. There is a weak single ceiling fixture. I've asked for a desk lamp, but no one has brought one. When you ask for things here, they nod, but no one says yes or no.

I try to get information about Mother. The best I've gotten is she is unchanged. There are no other details. I haven't asked about Father, and from what I gather, he hasn't asked much about me. They tell me nothing about Grandmother Emma, not even "unchanged." I know, however, that she thinks about me. She has hired an attorney and he has come to see me twice already. It's not Mr. Pond. Mr. Pond is a business lawyer. I need a criminal attorney. His name is Jack Cassidy. He asked me to call him Jack instead of Mr. Cassidy. He wants me to think he's my pal. He is bald with gray eyebrows and a pinkish nose and lips. I was immediately concerned.

Yesterday, after he left my room, I was able to see him talking to one of the hall monitors, and when the light went on, I saw he had a tail and I realized he was a hairless rat. I should have known by the way his lips twitch and the way he clenches his teeth before he writes something in his long, yellow pad.

"I want you to be honest with me," he told me. "I can't help you unless you're absolutely honest with me."

"Will you be honest with me?" I replied, and he smiled and said, "Of course."

Of course, he won't be. I don't mind being honest with him, however. I would rather everyone know that I know what's going on here.

I am keeping my own notebook and I am making copies of all the letters I send you. Some day, all this will be very valuable and I want you to have it all.

I am not confident about ever getting out of here.

But make no mistake about it, I'm not upset or unhappy. I have a wonderful opportunity.

I can expose them all.
Remember, be extra careful and tell no one
any of this.

                              Your brother Ian

I folded this letter up and stuck it back in its envelope. Before I could read another, I heard Great-aunt
Frances calling to me from the bottom of the stairway.
I quickly looked for a place to hide Ian's letters and
decided to put them in the corner of the closet floor
behind the shoe boxes. Then I hurried out, down the
hall and to the stairway.

"I thought you were home," Great-aunt Frances
said. "Did you get what you needed for school?"

"Yes."

"Good. Come on downstairs and we'll think about
dinner. I have to tell you what happened on my soap
opera today, too."

Mae Betty was back in the kitchen washing the
floor and mumbling loudly about all the food that had
been dropped and things that had been spilled and not
wiped up before they'd become sticky and hard. She
stuck her head out of the door as I came down the
stairs to say, "You would think a blind person lived
here!"

Great-aunt Frances only smiled.

"Don't mind her," she whispered. "I heard Lester
complain about how lazy his daughter is many times.
He swears she was so lazy it took her ten months to
give birth to his granddaughter."

Could that be true? I wondered. And then I thought,
How could Great-aunt Frances call anyone else lazy?
Look at how little she will do, even for herself. It

helped me understand a little as to why Grandmother Emma was dissatisfied with her, but that surely wasn't enough to ignore her for so many years and let her live like this.

Before I could say or do anything else, Great-aunt Frances went into a long speech about her characters on her soap opera. She talked about them as if they'd been real people and not actors pretending. As she described the story, she actually had tears in her eyes.

"I don't know how people can be so mean to each other, Jordan, do you?"

Before I could even think to reply, she went on and on about a different soap opera and the things people had done to each other in that one. Finally, exhausted, she dropped herself to the sofa and took a deep breath. Her face hardened in a way I hadn't seen it harden before: her eyes colder, her lips firmer. She looked more like Grandmother Emma, and the childlike softness I had seen in her face evaporated.

"Didn't Emma talk about me at all?" she asked. "Didn't she say anything to you before she sent you here to live?"

I nodded.

"What did she say? Tell me," she demanded.

"She told me you wouldn't hate me and you needed me," I revealed.

She just stared.

"She told me that when I saw her in the hospital just before I came here," I added.

"Nothing else?"

I shook my head. She never really told Ian or me much about Great-aunt Frances, and Mother knew so little about her.

"My name burns her lips, is that it?" she asked with the first sign of anger in her face and voice.

I didn't know how to answer.

"You don't have to answer," she decided. "I know the answer."

She looked away, her face still hard, tight.

"Maybe you should go visit her in the hospital now," I suggested.

She turned to me slowly, her eyes widening as she nodded.

"I should do that, shouldn't I? I should just surprise her."

"I'll go with you," I offered. "And maybe we can go visit my mother, too."

"Yes, that would be nice. I'll think about it. I'll think about what we should wear, too. It will have to be something very special, and we'll have to do something different with my hair. I used to go on car trips all the time. I would go whenever my father would take me, no matter where.

"Emma wouldn't go unless it made sense. 'Why ride to a gas station or to a hardware store?' she would ask me. 'What are you going to look at when you get to the garage or the hardware store? How can you just tag along like a puppy dog?' "

"Maybe you just wanted to go for a ride," I said.

"Of course. No maybe's about it, and my father liked me to be with him. But that wasn't enough for Emma. Nothing I did was right according to Emma. I used to stand in the middle of the room and think, 'If I turn left, she will complain, and if I turn right, she will complain.' Once, she saw me just standing there and asked me what I was doing. I said, 'I don't know which way to turn, Emma.' "

"What did she say?"

"She said, 'Turn around and go back to your room and close the door.' Isn't that funny? Emma could be very funny, only she didn't like to be thought of as funny. If I told her she said something funny, she told me I missed the point."

Ian's more like Grandmother Emma than he thinks he is, I thought.

"When would we go visit her and my mother?" I pursued.

"Oh, I don't know. Soon, soon," she said. She didn't sound as positive about it as she first had. "Now then," Great-aunt Frances continued, her face returning to the face I was accustomed to seeing, "let's think about tonight's dinner. I can make spaghetti and meatballs. That's not hard. We still have lots of ice cream for dessert. Is that all right? Is it enough?"

"We always have a salad with our dinner," I said.

"Salad? Oh, yes. I'm sorry I didn't think of it last night."

"I can make a salad for us."

"Oh, could you? Good. You make the salad. I'll cook the spaghetti and meatballs and I'll find Italian music and we'll pretend we're in Italy being serenaded under the window by some handsome young men. We'll look out the window and imagine them below us in the piazza. We'll smile at them, but we won't say anything or do too much of anything to give them hope. We're supposed to tease them. They expect it."

Why did we have to pretend something every time we had dinner? I wondered, but I didn't ask.

Mae Betty came out of the kitchen and stopped in the doorway.

"I've done the best I can with that kitchen and the downstairs bathroom. You got to wipe up when you spill something."

"Oh, we surely will," Great-aunt Frances said.

"Make sure she does," Mae Betty told me.

"We're going to make a salad," Great-aunt Frances said instead of listening to her. "Do we have tomatoes, lettuce and . . . what else, Jordan?"

"I like celery, onions, green olives, too."

"Oh, do we have that?"

"I don't know what you have, woman," Mae Betty said. She threw her arms down in frustration and returned to the kitchen. I looked at Great-aunt Frances, who shrugged, and then I followed Mae Betty. She looked in the refrigerator and in the bin by the sink.

"There's onions in there. They look older than me. You got tomatoes and lettuce from the garden. My father must've put it in here recently. I never saw her make a salad. She eats tomatoes like apples and lets it drip down her clothes and all over the chairs, table, floor. I can't imagine what her salad will look like."

"I'll make the salad," I said.

"You will?"

I nodded. She almost smiled before she started out. She stopped in the doorway and turned back to me. "I heard you went shopping today with that daughter of mine. She steal anything?"

"No," I said, shaking my head, shocked at the question.

"Because if she does and you're with her, they'll blame you, too, you know. Well?"

"She didn't steal anything."

"Um," she said, her eyes dark and narrow with disbelief. "She smoke at the mall?"

I shook my head again. Alanis hadn't smoked at the mall, but I was sure I wasn't very convincing.

"She teach you how to lie already?" she asked me. "You don't need to answer, but I'm warning you. You get in trouble 'cause of her, it's still your own fault. I can't be looking after you, and I about gave up looking after her."

I felt my forehead scrunch up. How can a mother not like her own daughter so much? Maybe she saw the question in my face. She shook her head.

"I do all this work just to keep clothes on her back and food in her stomach because I don't have a man to take care of us anymore, and you think she would say thank you, just once? You think she would help on her own without being reminded and chased? You just watch out. That girl will lead you to the Devil himself," she said, waving her finger at me. Then she turned and walked out of the house.

How could a mother speak like that about her own daughter? I stood there looking after her. Maybe she was one of Ian's insects, I thought, and worried more about her being the one who had read his letters.

I started to prepare a salad, slicing the tomatoes, onions and the lettuce the way I remembered Nancy would. I didn't find anything to use as a salad dressing, so I just squeezed a lemon over it. I'd once seen her do that. I waited for Great-aunt Frances to come in to start making the spaghetti and meatballs, but she didn't. I heard the television set again and went to see what she was doing.

"I'll be right there," she said, glancing at me in the doorway. "I just love this movie."

I watched her watching the movie and thought if she could crawl into the television set, she would. She didn't look out the window as much as she looked at that set. I returned to the kitchen, where I waited and waited and began to nibble on the salad. Finally, I went to the pantry to find the box of spaghetti and read the directions to make it myself.

After that I wondered about the meatballs. When I looked in the freezer, I didn't see any meat. And what would be our spaghetti sauce?

Finally, she came to the kitchen, but she was crying, tears streaming down her face. She wiped her cheeks. I froze, waiting to hear the terrible news. Had someone come to tell her my mother had died or Grandmother Emma?

"I always cry when I see that movie," she said. "Why did he have to die? Why?"

I just stared at her. Never in my wildest imaginings could I envision Grandmother Emma crying over a movie. In fact, I never saw her cry over anything, even the terrible car accident that had crippled my father and put my mother in a coma.

"Oh," she said, flicking a tear off her face as if it had been a fly. "You're making the spaghetti?"

"Yes, but there is no meat for meatballs, and what should we use as sauce?"

"No meat? I thought there was. Maybe that was last week. I usually use tomato soup for a sauce."

"Tomato soup?"

She smiled. "Isn't that all right?"

I shrugged. Was it? I went to the pantry and found a can of tomato soup. She took it, opened it and poured it into a pan.

"I have grape juice, don't I?" she asked me.

I checked. There was.

"Good," she said when I told her. "We'll pretend it's wine. You set the table, dear."

I did, and I put out our salad. Before she served the spaghetti, she went to the window.

"Listen," she said, beckoning to me. I joined her at the window. "Do you hear that?" she asked, but I heard nothing. "Don't they sing beautifully? You can wave, but don't say anything. Go on, just a wave," she said. She waved, and then, even though I felt very silly, I waved, too. "Poor dears. They are so in love with us. Shall we eat our dinner?"

She complimented me on my salad. The spaghetti with the tomato soup didn't taste terrible. Afterward, she leaped up to get the ice cream. When we were finished, I cleared off the table and started to wash the dishes. I thought she would just return to the living room and her television shows, but she took out a dish towel and began to wipe and put away the plates, bowls and silverware.

"Look at what a wonderful team we are," she said. "I'm sure Emma would be proud of you."

Afterward, she surprised me by taking a carton of photo albums out of a closet and showing them to me in the living room. There were pictures of her parents, of her and Grandmother Emma when they were little girls and older, and pictures of Grandfather Blake. Some had been taken on holidays and some had been taken at the homes of other relatives I had never been told about. Great-aunt Frances explained them all, the cousins, her father and mother's brothers and sisters and even her grandparents and their brothers and sisters. We spent nearly two hours looking at it all.

Although Grandmother Emma had allowed me to see some of her photographic albums, she'd never spent time explaining everyone to me and to Ian. It was almost as if we'd been looking at illustrations in a history book. This was more interesting because it was about our family, and for the first time, really, I felt I had an extended family, a history that was mine and not just Grandmother Emma's.

Afterward, I put away the carton, and Great-aunt Frances began to watch something on television. As before, she grew groggy, sleepy and eventually closed her eyes. I looked at the clock and saw it was nearly eight. Alanis would be going into the basement with her girlfriends soon.

I tiptoed out and went to the basement door. Part of me felt terribly guilty about doing all this right under Great-aunt Frances's nose. It was sneaky, and if and when she did find out, I was sure she would be very disappointed in me, but I was also intrigued with what the older girls would do and say, and there was that boy they invited. Would he be there? After all, I had never gone to a party with so many older girls. For that matter, I had hardly gone to any parties after we had moved in with Grandmother Emma. It seemed harder to turn the basement doorknob, because half my hand was trying to stop me from doing so.

It opened, and I flipped on the light switch and

started down. Before I even reached the bottom of the rickety stairway, I heard the sound of their laughter. And then I heard the music, too. I opened the second door slowly and peered in at what Alanis was now calling her private club. The girls were dancing.

"There she is!" she cried as soon as she saw me. "The guest of honor."

Nikki and Raspberry stopped dancing, then Stuart Gavin stepped out of the shadows and looked at me. He was wearing a short-sleeve blue shirt and a pair of jeans. I hadn't really looked at him in the mall, but now I saw he was taller than the girls and wide-shouldered. In fact, he looked more like a man than a boy. His dark brown hair was cut short.

"Well?" Alanis asked him, tilting her hat back. "What do you think of her?"

He stepped toward me into the light. I didn't think he was ugly, but he wasn't terribly good-looking either, because he had a long, pointed nose and the corners of his mouth turned downward sharply. He had a cleft chin, and his jaw was more square than round.

"I wouldn't have been fooled," he said. "You didn't have to tell me nothing."

"I'm sorry, Jordan, but we told Stuart the truth about you," Alanis said.

"The truth?"

"How you started kindergarten late because you were sickly as a baby, and then how you were left back and then lost another year moving."

She winked at me. I looked at Nikki and Raspberry. They were both smiling.

"It's all right," Stuart said. "I was left back once."

"But . . ."

Alanis moved quickly to stand between me and Stuart.

"We have the rum alcopop," she told me. "The one you liked the most, remember?"

"What?"

Nikki and Raspberry gave Stuart one and started to talk to him. Alanis moved closer.

"Keep your mouth zipped and go along with it," she told me in a raspy whisper. "Otherwise, he'll head for the hills."

She threaded her arm through mine.

"Don't worry," she continued, "I'll be right beside you. I'm your new minder, remember, sister dear?"

"But I told you," I protested. "I don't like to lie."

"Take it easy. Not telling boys the truth isn't lying, Jordan. It's self-defense," she said and handed me the bottle of rum alcopop. "Take a sip," she said. "You're about to grow up overnight."

8

Another First Day at School

I didn't mind the taste of this as much as I had the burning whiskey she had given me the night before. Stuart, showing off, drank his bottle in one long gulp, his Adam's apple bobbing like a frog. Nikki and Raspberry clapped and squealed as he reached the end and pulled the bottle out of his mouth.

"Hell, that was nothing," he said. "I can do it with a quart of beer."

"Wow," Nikki said. "A whole quart at once."

"I could probably do more if the bottle was bigger," Stuart bragged.

I saw the girls stifle giggles behind his back when he turned to me.

"You're going to live here now?" he asked.

I nodded.

"I deliver gas to your . . . what is she, your aunt?"

"Great-aunt."

"What's a great-aunt?"

"She's my grandmother's sister, so she's called a great-aunt," I explained, speaking as carefully as Ian would. "If she were my mother's sister, then she would be just an aunt."

"Oh, yeah? I don't know if I have any great-aunts."

"Are any of your grandparents alive?" Alanis asked him, still stifling a laugh to keep it from bursting out of her lips.

"Yeah, my dad's father."

"Well, does he have any brothers or sisters alive?" Nikki asked him.

He stared, and then he shrugged.

"I don't know."

"So ask him and let us know," Raspberry said. "We'll hold our breath until you tell us."

"You do that and you'll suffocate," he replied.

That did it. They all let loose with laughter.

"What's so funny?" Stuart asked and looked to me, since I wasn't laughing.

"Everything makes them laugh," I said and thought if Ian had been here, he would have tagged them with one of his fancy synonyms for "stupid."

Stuart nodded and sipped on another alcopop.

"Your great-aunt is nice," he said. "She always gives me something when I deliver a tank."

"Money?" Alanis asked, breaking her laugh quickly and throwing a glance my way.

"Naw. Just stuff. Once she gave me a leather wallet. Here," he said, reaching into his back pocket. "This is it." He offered it to me to examine.

It had tiny letters in gold on the outside: BM.

"There are letters," I said.

"Let me see," Nikki demanded and pulled it out of my hands. "BM. What's that, bowel movement?"

They were hysterical again. I took the wallet back quickly.

"No. It probably belonged to my grandfather. His name was Blake March," I said.

Stuart smiled and sipped his drink.

Why had my great-aunt given him this wallet? I wondered. How come she had it?

"What else has she given you?" I asked him, handing the wallet back.

He looked at the girls, and then, after a moment, he extended his left arm and I looked at his watch.

"She gave you that?" Raspberry said, moving quickly to look at it. "That's a good watch, ain't it, Alanis?"

Alanis seized Stuart's arm and studied the watch.

"Maybe. Looks like it might be. Who knows what else is in this house?" she muttered at me. "It's crazy giving away stuff like that just for delivery of a gas tank."

"Maybe you should start working for my father," Stuart countered so quickly that it took all three of them and me by surprise. For a moment no one spoke. The girls held their half smiles.

"Oh, that's funny, Stuart," Alanis finally said. Her face turned mean and ugly. "You must have done something extra for her to get those things, and anyway you shouldn't take things from her. She's not all there. She's bonkers. You should give it all back. Give it all to Jordan," she insisted.

He turned to me.

"If my great-aunt gave it to him, she wanted to give it to him," I said. "She'd be upset if I took it back."

Stuart smiled, and, surprisingly, so did Alanis.

"Well, you can see Jordan clearly likes you, Stuart," she told him. "A girl like this needs someone big and strong like you to look after her, especially when she just starts in a new school. Ain't I right, girls?"

"Oh, yeah," Nikki said. "The creeps will be bothering her right off."

"She hasn't got anyone to protect her from the riff-raff," Raspberry told him. "A girl looking that good is going to be annoyed all the time."

He looked at me and shrugged.

"Sure, I'll be glad to help," he said.

"See?" Alanis said. "I told you Stuart was a nice boy. C'mon. You two sit here," she directed, taking me by the arm and moving me to the sofa. "Stuart, sit next to her." She sat him beside me. "You two get to know each other."

The three of them looked at us, all with silly smirks on their faces, then Alanis started to dance again and the other two joined her.

"I hear your teacher's Mrs. Morgan," Stuart said. "She can be damn mean sometimes, especially if she catches you doing something while she's talking. And if you scratch your head too much, she'll send you to the nurse right away to have her check for lice. She says it so loud that everyone thinks you have lice even if the nurse says you don't. I don't," he emphasized.

"There was a girl in my class last year who had ringworm on her head and had to have her hair shaved," I told him.

"Ugh," he said and drank some more. "Don't you

like yours?" he asked, nodding at the bottle in my hands. I looked at it and then took a sip. "Hey, sometimes, if I have my truck at school, I could maybe take you home and you won't have to ride the bus. You'll get home faster," he added when I didn't respond.

"I'll have to tell my great-aunt," I said.

"How long you been here already?"

"Just a few days."

"You like it?"

I shrugged. "It's all right," I said. "I have to get used to it."

"You got a nice little lake in the back. I once went fishing in it, but from the other side so no one knew. Didn't catch anything anyway," he added and sipped his drink.

"Stuart," Alanis said. "She looks cold. Why don't you at least put your arm around her?"

He stared at Alanis for a moment and then he looked at me. I started to say I wasn't cold, but he put his arm around my shoulders.

"Now that's nice," Nikki said. "See, you're protecting her already."

They didn't laugh, but I saw they were smiling and stuffing their giggles in their bloated cheeks.

"Take another sip of your alcopop," Alanis advised me and winked. "She's been to plenty parties, Stuart," she added. His eyes widened.

"I don't go to many parties," he told me. "I work a lot. I'm saving my money to get my own car. I could buy a used one right now, but I'm better off waiting until I can get a better one. The truck's okay for now."

I was afraid to turn and look at him, but I didn't know what to do because we were sitting so close that our legs were touching and his arm was so big and firm that I couldn't budge.

"If you want, I'll come get you tomorrow and take you to school. My dad's letting me have the truck tomorrow," he continued. "He wants me to start deliveries as soon as school ends. Want me to come get you?"

I shook my head.

"I can. It's not a big deal. I pass this place on the way."

I didn't respond. I didn't even shake my head.

"What are you whispering about?" Alanis asked and stopped dancing.

"I just told her I could come by in the morning and take her to school," Stuart replied and finished what remained in his bottle of alcopop.

"Well, that's nice, isn't it, Jordan? Tell you what," she said. "I'll go along, unless you don't want me." She turned to Nikki and Raspberry. "Unless you want to be alone."

"I don't care. You can come," Stuart said quickly.

"Good. We'll be out front by the gate. Be sure you get here ahead of the bus or we'll hafta get on the bus."

"I'll be here."

"C'mon, you two," Nikki said, reaching for my hand. "Start dancing."

Raspberry pulled on Stuart.

"Hey," he complained but looked at me and then got up.

"I'll show you some new steps," Alanis told me. She made me stand across from Stuart. He was trying to get the right rhythm, but he looked awkward. I followed Alanis's lead and she nodded. "You got it, girl.

Go!" she said, pushing me closer to Stuart. He tried to imitate my dancing, but I didn't think he looked good. The three of them danced around us. Nikki turned up the music. They all drank their alcopops as they danced. Every once in a while, either Nikki or Raspberry pulled on Stuart and made him dance with her.

Nikki gave him another alcopop. Everyone was so loud now that I was sure we'd wake Great-aunt Frances. I guess I looked worried. Alanis paused, put her hands on her hips and turned to me.

"Stop worrying," she told me. "Just have a good time, girl. Ian ain't here," she added and laughed.

We danced and danced. Finally, Nikki and Raspberry were tired enough to stop. Alanis danced some more, but I sat and Stuart sat beside me. He finished his bottle with two large gulps. A wide smile settled on his face.

"You get cuter and cuter as the party goes on," Nikki told him and nudged him.

"Leave him be," Raspberry said. "He's spoken for, girl."

They laughed. Nikki leaned into him and I heard her say, "You should give her a kiss at least."

His eyes widened. He glanced at me.

"She thinks you don't like her enough," Nikki added.

"I like her."

He turned and put his right hand behind my head, pulling my face toward his to spread his lips over mine. I didn't think it was a kiss. I didn't hear the sound of a kiss. It was more like someone wiping his mouth over someone else's. The only kisses I had ever had were kisses on the cheeks. I'd seen kissing in movies and on television, but I had no idea what to expect. I just knew what he had done wasn't anything like it was supposed to be. Stuart pulled back quickly. The girls cheered and he smiled.

"What do you think, Jordan?" Raspberry asked. "Was that a good kiss?"

I shrugged. I didn't want to hurt his feelings.

"You put your tongue in her mouth?" Nikki asked him.

Tongue in my mouth? My jaw fell, pulling my lips apart. I looked at Alanis, who was drinking another alcopop and moving to the music as if she'd been dancing with someone. She looked like she was in another world.

"You don't do that on your first kiss," Stuart told her.

"So do it on a second," Raspberry told him.

"She thinks you don't like her," Nikki said.

"I like her. I said she's cute."

"Prove it," Raspberry told him.

He turned back to me. I started to lean away, but he moved quickly, holding my head even firmer, and kissed me again, this time jetting his tongue into my mouth so hard that I nearly gagged. I started to push him away. He held on to me and then let me go, and Nikki and Raspberry cheered.

"Very good, Stuart," Nikki told him and pulled him up to his feet. She started dancing with him again. I gasped for breath.

"Hey," Raspberry told me as I wiped my mouth with the back of my right hand. "Don't look so worried. You're one of the girls now. We look out for each other. He gets too nasty with you, we'll smash in his face."

She got up and danced with Stuart, too. Alanis paused, looked at me, saw the terrified expression on my face, then turned off the music. They all groaned. Stuart, his eyes closed, kept moving anyway.

"It's getting late," Alanis said. "We'd better end before my granddad comes looking around." Stuart continued to dance, as though he was in his own world. "Stuart!" she screamed, and he stopped and opened his eyes. "Party's over. Tomorrow's school, remember?"

"Yeah," he said. "It was a great party."

"If you behave yourself, you can come to the next one."

"Good. When is it?"

"We'll tell you. Stand by," she said, and Nikki laughed.

"Stuart, can you drop Nikki and me at the gas station?" Raspberry asked him.

"Sure," he said. Then he batted his eyelashes and asked, "What gas station?"

"The one on the corner of Main and Lake," Nikki said.

"That's out of my way, but okay," he said.

"C'mon," Alanis urged them, and they started toward the door. I rose and followed, feeling dazed and confused. The music seemed to still be echoing in my head.

We stepped outside, and Nikki and Raspberry turned to say good night to me.

"Welcome. We're going to have some great times together," Nikki told me and hugged me.

"Yeah," Raspberry said. "Glad you're here, girl. Hey," she told Stuart, who seemed to wobble, "say good night properly to your date, boy."

He turned back to me, smiled, then stepped over to kiss me again. I recoiled when his lips touched mine.

"Whew," Nikki cried, "you're too much for her too soon."

They laughed. Stuart smiled and blew out his chest.

"I'll see you in the morning," he told me.

"We'll be waiting," Alanis told him. "Remember, come before the bus, hear?"

"Yes, ma'am," he said, saluting her.

"Go on home, you idiot," she said and pushed him toward the truck.

Nikki and Raspberry got in, and he climbed in behind the steering wheel.

"Thanks," he called back to us. He started the engine, and then he shut it off.

"What's wrong?" Alanis asked first.

"I forgot to take the gas tank out and hook it up."

"Well, you can't do it now, Stuart. It's too late and you'll make too much noise," she said. "Come even earlier tomorrow morning and do it. Stuart, are you listening?"

"Okay, okay," he said and restarted the engine.

"Make sure he goes straight home, girls. No hanky-panky," Alanis called to them.

Nikki muttered something I didn't hear. She and Raspberry laughed, then Stuart turned the truck around and went bouncing down the driveway a little too fast. We could hear Nikki and Raspberry screaming. They paused at the bottom and turned left to disappear into the night.

"Well, that was fun, wasn't it?" Alanis asked.

I nodded. I wasn't feeling well and it really hadn't been all that much fun for me, but I could see it was important to her that I thought it was.

"Don't worry about Stuart. If you don't like him, we'll find someone else. You better go in and get to bed. You know what time to get up and all, right?"

"Yes."

"Don't depend on your aunt to wake you, girl. You got an alarm clock or something?"

I shook my head. I'd never thought of it. All my life my mother or Ian would wake me for anything.

"Well, I do. It's my granddad. He could wake the dead. Don't worry. I'll come around as soon as I get on my clothes and make sure you're up and ready. Remember our motto," she warned. "We die first."

She started toward her house, then turned.

"Go on inside, Jordan, and get yourself to bed."

"Okay," I said and ran around to the front of the house.

The television was still on. Great-aunt Frances was asleep. I hurried up the stairs and to the bathroom to get my teeth brushed, my face washed, and then into my pajamas. When I crawled into bed and pulled the blanket toward my chin, I moaned regret. I hadn't read another of Ian's letters, and I'd so wanted to read them all already. I vowed to do it as soon as I returned from school.

My brain was in such turmoil that I didn't see how I would fall asleep. The music, the alcopops, Stuart's tongue kiss, all of it whirled around. I felt as if I'd been spinning in the bed. I finally fell asleep, but again I woke up in the middle of the night. Vaguely, I remembered the sobbing I had heard the night before, but this time I could hear Great-aunt Frances washing her face in the bathroom and humming something. I knew she had looked in on me, but I didn't think I should show her I was awake. Minutes later, I was asleep again, and this time, I didn't wake up until I felt myself being shaken.

Alanis was standing at the side of my bed.

"Damn, girl, you gonna need an alarm clock. She's dead asleep, too. Lucky for Granddad. Get up and dressed quickly. Stuart should be here by now if he's going to hook up that gas tank before he takes us to school. Hurry," she urged.

I was so confused. To me it was as if I'd still been in a dream. I didn't wake up fully until after I had washed and dressed and gone down to at least have a piece of orange. Great-aunt Frances finally rose herself and hurried down the stairs in her nightgown.

"Oh, good, you're up," she cried. "I'm sorry I overslept. We'll make sure the clocks are on alarm for tomorrow. Did you have some breakfast?"

I nodded. I really wasn't very hungry, but I remembered what Alanis had told me.

"I need lunch money," I said.

"Oh, dear, lunch money. Yes, I found some money yesterday. I had forgotten about it." Her eyes widened with excitement, and she went to the cabinet under the sink. She pulled out a can of soap powder and opened the top. It was full of tens and twenties. "I don't know why I forgot this," she said. "It's been under here so long."

Lucky Mae Betty doesn't do her job that well, I

thought. She would have found it for sure, and I had no doubt she would have taken it.

"Take all that to your room, Great-aunt Frances," I told her. "Otherwise, it will disappear."

"Yes, I will. Yes. Here," she said, handing me a twenty. "That should be enough."

"Thanks," I said and reminded her to take the money to her room. "Put it somewhere safe," I said.

"I will. Oh, look at you. That's a lovely dress, a wonderful dress for the first day of school."

"Thank you. Grandmother Emma bought it for me."

"Emma can be generous when she wants to be. Oh, dear, where's your schoolbag?"

"I forgot it," I said. "Thanks for reminding me."

I ran back upstairs to get it, then hurried back down. She stood at the doorway, waiting.

"Good luck to you, dear. I remember my first day of school like it was yesterday."

"It's not my first day of school," I reminded her. "It's my first day here."

"Oh, yes. Funny," she said, thinking for a moment, "but it's as if you were always here. I must be still dreaming."

She leaned over to give me a kiss, then I opened the door and stepped out. Alanis was in the driveway, waiting, the brim of her hat down nearly over her eyes. She kicked a stone and looked up at me. "That idiot didn't show to hook up the tank. They'll be no time for it now. C'mon," she said, walking ahead down the driveway. She looked at her watch when I caught up. "He'd better be here in five minutes or we'll have to take the bus."

She leaned to look down the road. A car came by and then a bigger truck than Stuart's, but he didn't appear. Alanis looked very annoyed.

"See?" she said. "Boys can't be trusted with anything. Their promises aren't worth a damn," she added when the school bus appeared. It slowed and then stopped in front us. I looked at Alanis, who made no move to board the bus. "C'mon," she said finally and tugged me to walk around and go up the stairway. The bus driver, a round-faced, stout man with just a ribbon of hair above his temples and down over his ears, smiled at us.

"Welcome, girls. Now take your seats and stay in them until the bus comes to a stop at the school. No wandering about in motion," he warned.

Alanis ignored him. She paused and looked down the aisle at the other riders. Everyone looked primped and prepared, especially the other girls. Two older boys sat opposite each other, both taking up the entire seat by putting their legs across them.

I could see that some of the children had their faces pressed to the window, looking up the driveway to catch a glimpse, perhaps, of Great-aunt Frances. Alanis nudged me and nodded at them.

"What are you looking at so hard?" she snapped at them, and they turned away quickly.

The rear seat was empty. Alanis headed for it and dropped herself onto it, folding her arms and glaring out the window. I joined her and the bus started again. She looked back once and then at me. Her face brightened with a thought.

"Hey, did you get your lunch money?"

"Yes."

"How much?"

I showed her and she beamed.

"I told you she had money buried. Did you see where she got it?"

I hesitated just long enough for the smile to fade from her face.

"Remember, Sister, no secrets, no lies. Well?"

It seemed to me that there was a time to lie. If I told her what Great-aunt Frances had, she would want to go look for it and might steal it.

"She just gave it to me," I said.

"You didn't see where she took it?"

I shook my head.

"You lying, girl," she said. "You're not good at it. You'll have to study me. That's okay. You'll tell me." She smiled with confidence. "Yes, you will. And soon, too. You'll see that I'm the best friend you ever had and ever will have."

She sat back, looked out the window, thought a moment, then leaned forward to take the twenty from me.

"I better hold this for you. Too many thieves in that school."

She stuffed the twenty into her jeans and leaned back again.

The bus rolled along, stopping to pick up students along the way. By the time we arrived at the school, I felt nauseous, but I swallowed it back and followed everyone out. This was, after all, the first time I had ever ridden a bus to school. All my school life, my mother had brought me to school on the first day. She'd been there holding my hand and assuring me I was fine and I was going to enjoy the experience. My teachers had been nice and full of smiles. They'd all known who we were.

Because other buses from other directions were unloading at about the same time, a sea of students poured into the entrance. Most were talking loudly, calling to each other and laughing. Everyone seemed to know everyone else. Was I the only new student in the whole school this year? If anyone looked at me, it was just a glance. Everyone was more interested in hearing from students he or she knew. For a while, I felt invisible, even though I was being bumped and pushed along. I reached into my bag to get my diagram of the school, but Alanis seized my elbow before I could get the paper out.

"Forget that. I'll show you where you go, Jordan. Just move or we'll get trampled."

She held on to me firmly and took me around a corner and down another corridor.

"You're in here," she said, stopping at my classroom. "The cafeteria is down this hall. You turn right and it's right there. I gotta go upstairs. Uh-oh," she said, "here comes Chad."

He approached us quickly.

"Ah, you and the little rich girl," he said. "How cozy."

"Do I know you?" she asked him.

"Funny. Why didn't you call me?"

"I've lost your phone number," she said. "For good."

"Yeah, right. You'll be back," he said, but not with great confidence.

"If I'm desperate," she told him. He smirked,

looked at me and walked away. "See?" she said to me. "Keep them in their place. I'll see you at lunch."

You better, I thought. *You have my lunch money.*

"When I see that Stuart, I'm going to tear off an ear," she added and walked on.

I watched her for a moment. Some girls and a boy jostled me back as they hurried into the classroom. I followed slowly. When I entered, I noted that everyone was rushing to choose his or her seat. Our teacher wasn't in the room yet. Those who had sat turned to look my way. Their faces were full of curiosity.

I really am the only new student, I thought. *They're not looking at anyone else the same way.*

"This is Mrs. Morgan's third grade," a tall, thin, dark-haired girl with thin, almost nonexistent lips told me. The right corner of her mouth dipped at the end of her sentence.

"I know," I said.

"You're in third grade?" she asked and left her mouth open.

I didn't answer. I looked to the seat on the far side in the rear and headed toward it, but just before I reached it, another student, a chubby boy with hair the color of wet hay, charged past me and slid into the chair as if he'd been sliding into first base in a baseball game. The students around us laughed.

"That's not very polite," I said. He smiled and looked at the students seated around us. I thought of what Alanis had just said and folded my arms, stepping closer to him. "Get out of my seat or I'll rip off your ear," I told him.

His face seemed to sink in, the thin smile falling to

shatter at his feet. He glanced at the others, at me, and then got up and slid into the desk two desks ahead. Everyone else stared at me as I took the seat.

Moments later, Mrs. Morgan entered. She was tall, with graying dark-brown hair cut sharply at her ears, every strand perfect. She wore no earrings, but she had a necklace of small pearls that lay just under the open collar of her one-piece dark-blue dress, which fell in a baggy fashion to about two inches above her ankles. The dress seemed to erase any figure she might have. There was no way to distinguish her waist, and she looked to be as flat chested as some of her sixth-grade girls, but certainly not me.

Her gaunt cheeks were tightened at the corners of her thin pale lips, which pursed as she put her bag on the desk and took out her class register. She put on a pair of dark-rimmed glasses that magnified her dull brown eyes. The other students apparently knew her well enough to quiet down and sit still while she flipped silently through pages, cleared her throat and looked up. She panned the room slowly, nodding, until she reached me. She stared at me so long that I felt like I was under a microscope.

"I know all of you, of course, from move-up day last year, except our new student, Jordan March. Jordan, please stand," she said.

I did, and she looked at me even harder. I didn't know what to do or say because she wasn't saying anything. She looked again at something in her register and then at me.

"Jordan," she said, "has just moved here from Bethlehem. Let's welcome her."

She nodded, and the class clapped.

"I begin every class year with my students writing their biographies. We pass them around so everyone gets to know everyone else well," she said. "Take out a sheet of paper and your pens, please."

Instantly, the chubby boy who had slid into the seat I wanted raised his hand.

"Yes, Gary?"

"I didn't bring a pen and paper yet."

"Why not? What did you think we would do today?"

He shrugged.

She looked around.

"Anyone else ill prepared?"

No one raised his or her hand.

"Apparently, you are the only negligent student, Gary. You'll start the sixth-grade year with a negative point." She opened her top desk drawer, took out a pen, ripped a sheet of paper off a pad, and brought it to him.

"Okay," she said when she returned to her desk. "Who can tell me what you all should include in your biography?"

Many hands went up.

"Mona," she said.

A small girl with pretty light-brown hair stood up.

"We should tell about our family, where we were born and where we live and lived, what we like to do, what we want to be, places we have gone and favorite things like favorite foods and shows and stuff," she recited.

"Don't say 'stuff.' Otherwise, you are correct. All right, begin please and write clearly, neatly and carefully," she said.

Everyone started. What should I tell about my family? I wondered. Should I tell anything about Ian?

"Miss March," Mrs. Morgan said. "Please come up front."

All the students stopped writing and looked at me. I rose and walked to her desk.

"I understand you are living with your great-aunt," she said.

"Yes."

"When you go home after school today, I want you to go directly to her and tell her that you cannot return to school if you do not wear a brassiere. You know what that is, of course?"

I nodded.

"I will not permit you to return to my class unless you do. Do you understand?"

"Yes, ma'am," I said.

"Get back to your seat, please," she said.

I felt the blood rise to my face as I turned and saw all the students looking at me. Some of the boys were smiling, especially chubby Gary. I sat and lowered my head to begin writing. We all looked up again when we heard a knock on the door. It opened, and a girl who looked at least sixteen stepped in.

"Yes, what is it?" Mrs. Morgan asked, not hiding her annoyance.

"The principal would like to see Jordan March," she announced.

Mrs. Morgan tightened the corners of her mouth, then looked at me.

"Go ahead," she said, her voice full of annoyance. "You can leave your things right there. Don't dawdle in the hallway when you return either. Get right back to do your work."

I rose and joined the girl at the door. As soon as she closed it behind us, she turned to me and smiled.

"This is your first day here, right?"

"Yes," I said. "Is that why the principal sent for me?"

"No," she said, widening her smile. "Boy, are you in trouble," she said.

9

Parfait

In the principal's outer office, where, behind the long counter, two secretaries scurried between two desks and large file cabinets, Alanis, Nikki and Raspberry sat on the black sofa, waiting. They looked up at me as soon as I entered, my appearance obviously taking them all by surprise.

"Her, too?" Nikki muttered.

"Jordan March is here," the student helper announced. One of the secretaries paused, her face twisting like a rubber mask with displeasure at being interrupted.

"Take a seat with the others," she told me. "And no talking. Mrs. Browne will tell us when to send you in to see her."

Alanis sat between Nikki and Raspberry on the settee. I sat quickly in the only chair. Of course, I wondered why we were all here. I had never been called out of class to go to the principal's office at my school in Bethlehem.

"What is this?" Nikki moaned. "Why did she call all of us to the office? Maybe it's got something to do with last night. Why else would she be here?"

"Shut up," Alanis said. She watched the secretaries and the student helper, and then she leaned toward me.

"Remember. Whatever it is, we die first," she whispered and then sat back.

The door to the principal's office opened, and a policeman stepped out, his hat in his hands. He gazed at us a moment, shook his head and walked out of the office.

"Police! We're in trouble," Nikki muttered, her voice cracking. "Oh, we're in some kind of big trouble."

"I told you to shut up," Alanis said. "Whatever it is, I'll do all the talking."

We heard a buzzer. One of the secretaries picked up a phone and said, "Right away, Mrs. Browne." She hung up and turned to us. "All of you go in now," she said.

We rose. I was too frightened to take a breath. I looked at Alanis, but she didn't seem in the least afraid. She actually smiled at me.

Mrs. Browne's office had a nicer leather sofa and two leather chairs. One wall was covered with shelves of books, and another had plaques and pictures. The walnut brown rug looked brand new. She had a large, dark cherrywood desk with everything on it neatly organized. With her hands clasped behind her back, she was standing by her window and looking out when we entered. It was a large, two-paneled window that faced the ballfield. It had blinds that were pulled up evenly and dark-brown dress curtains with gold tassels.

"Close the door," she said. I imagined she could see it reflected in the window glass. Raspberry hurried to do so. Then Mrs. Browne turned slowly.

I thought she had wide shoulders for a woman. She had a heavy bosom and wide hips, too, but her face frightened me because it looked like someone had taken an ice pick and poked tiny holes in her cheeks and even in the sides of her chin. She wore a dark red lipstick, which picked up the reddish brown hair she had cut stylishly at the base of her neck. Her eyes were a bright shade of blue. *If it weren't for her pockmarks, she would be pretty,* I thought.

"Sit," she commanded, as if she'd been speaking to four dogs. "And you, Alanis, take off that hat. You don't wear your hat in school."

Sullenly, Alanis took it off.

I went for the chair. Alanis sat in the other chair, and Nikki and Raspberry sat on the sofa.

We waited, no one moving, me holding my breath, as Mrs. Browne paused and looked up. It was as if she was reading something off the ceiling or saying some prayer. Then she lowered her head and fixed her eyes on each of us the way someone might fix her target in her gun sights. I had never seen anyone who could turn her eyes into cold, piercing orbs like this. It was as if she'd had tiny flashlights behind them. I felt myself actually shudder with a stab of ice at the base of my neck.

"Let me begin by telling the four of you that I've been principal here for nearly twenty-eight years and this is the first time I've had a serious problem brought to me on the first day, actually even before the day has had a chance to begin. With all the work we have getting organized, I have little or no time for behavioral problems, but this one is so serious . . ." She paused, put her hand over her heart and took a breath. "Perhaps the most serious one I've had in my twenty-eight years, and I have no choice but to deal with it immediately.

"All of your parents are in the process of being contacted," she continued. "You," she said, turning to me, "are living with your great-aunt?"

I nodded. I was afraid that if I spoke, my voice would fail me and nothing would come from my lips.

"I have papers from your grandmother's attorney assigning guardian rights to your great-aunt, Frances Wilkens," she added, tapping some papers on her desk. "So, unfortunately for her, she will have this. She will have to face something terribly unpleasant immediately."

"What will she face? Why did you contact our parents? Why are we here?" Alanis demanded firmly.

Slowly, Mrs. Browne turned to her.

"Oh, don't worry, Alanis. I'm getting to it, to all of it." She took a deep breath, sat and leaned back. "Last night, a student at our school named Stuart Gavin drove his father's gas delivery truck off the road and hit a tree. He wasn't wearing a seat belt, and he was thrown from the vehicle and broke his left arm in two places. He was fortunate that nothing more serious happened to him.

"A passing motorist noticed the accident and called

the police. It seems young Mr. Gavin was intoxicated. The police discovered that the level of alcohol in his blood was way above what is acceptable when driving. Do you know what that means?"

"He was drunk," Alanis said as casually as someone might say *"He had a cold."* It didn't sound bad at all when it came from her lips. "So?"

"So? So?" Mrs. Browne sat forward. "I imagine that you might see so many people in that condition that it means little to you anymore. However, driving under the influence of alcohol is a serious, very serious, crime. He will probably lose his license for a considerable period of time, and his father depends on him to help with their company's gas deliveries."

"I still don't get why you called our parents about it, and why did you call us to your office? We didn't do anything," Alanis pursued, undaunted.

I didn't know whether to admire her courage or criticize her stupidity.

"Oh, you don't?" She panned all of us slowly and returned her gaze to Alanis. "Young Mr. Gavin has told the police that he drank all this alcohol at a party you girls had at Jordan March's great-aunt's home," Mrs. Browne responded and turned toward me. I pressed my lips together quickly. "He has named each and every one of you."

"He's a liar," Alanis said without hesitation. "He came to Jordan's great-aunt's house, but he was already drunk and we told him to go home. He nearly threw up in the driveway. He had those sweet alcopops that can make you sick to your stomach," she added. "He wanted us to drink them, but we wouldn't." She turned to Nikki and Raspberry. "Right?"

They both nodded, but Nikki looked surprised.

Mrs. Browne sat back again, then slowly turned her gaze on me.

"As I understand it, you haven't been living with your great-aunt very long, have you, Jordan?"

"No," I said. My throat threatened to close and smother any other words.

"In this case adults can be held responsible. She could be in very big trouble. You're all underage. I'm sure you don't want to get her in any trouble, too, do you?"

"Oh, no," I said. The tears were building under my eyelids so fast that I was positive now that I wouldn't be able to keep them from spilling out and down my cheeks.

The softness she pretended evaporated as she leaned toward me sharply.

"Then you had better tell the truth, young lady. Did you have a party at your great-aunt's house and give young Mr. Gavin alcohol to drink?" she questioned. With her gaze firmly on me, I felt like I was in a spotlight.

I glanced at Alanis. *What would Ian do?* I wondered. He would answer correctly, but also exactly to how the question was asked. I hadn't given Stuart any alcopops and I hadn't had the party. Nikki, Raspberry and Alanis had had the party.

"Well?"

"No," I said.

She stared at me. I wasn't lying, but I wasn't sure I didn't look like a liar.

She smiled coldly. "Why would he tell this to the police?" she calmly asked all of us.

"Simple," Alanis said, shrugging and sitting back in her seat. "To get himself out of trouble." Then she sat forward quickly. "We ain't getting into trouble because of him," she added more forcefully. "He got no right telling that story and causing you to call our parents. He's stupid. There's going to be hell to pay. Maybe we should sue him or something," she told Nikki and Raspberry, who both sat wide-eyed.

"Sue him? You haven't exactly been an angel here, Alanis King," Mrs. Browne countered. "I wouldn't press my luck."

"It's not luck. It's the truth. You can't put the blame on us just because we done something bad once."

"Once?"

"It ain't right to blame us for his stupidity," Alanis insisted. "My mother ain't going to like this. You just taking his side right away. None of our mothers will," she added, nodding at Nikki and Raspberry, who still looked frozen. "I bet Jordan's family really won't like it, and they could afford big lawyers. We all probably have the right to a lawyer or something, don't we? I know my mother's going to call a lawyer and I bet yours does, too, Nikki. Her sister works for a lawyer, don't she?"

Nikki nodded, and Alanis smiled and turned back to Mrs. Browne. "Maybe she'll get him to do it for nothing or part of the money we'll win against the school and the Gavins."

Mrs. Browne thought a moment. Her firm demeanor seemed to crack a little. I could see it in the way her eyes shifted. She nodded softly.

"Yes, you all might very well need to have lawyers." She cleared her throat with a low growl. "This matter will continue under investigation. If it results in proof that you're lying, you will be in even more serious trouble. I will turn the matter over to the police to handle and it won't be a school issue. You'll all go to court. Is that understood?"

Alanis shrugged again. "What's to understand? He's lying. We didn't do it. I ain't afraid of going to court."

How could she be so strong and unafraid? I wondered.

"We'll see," Mrs. Browne said, but her voice didn't have the same confidence and authority it had when we first entered. I could see she wasn't sure who was telling the truth now and she had gone as far as she could.

My respect for Alanis grew instantly. She looked at me with a smile around her eyes.

"In any case, young lady, I would hope you improve your grammar this year. 'Ain't' is not proper."

"Yes, ma'am, I will certainly try my best," Alanis replied.

Her tone was so obviously false that it made Nikki and Raspberry smile. Mrs. Browne snapped herself back in her seat. She glared at her, and then she looked hard at me.

"I know it's difficult to start at a new school, but I would be very careful about whom you choose to be your friends. Now all of you return to your classes. We'll see where this ends."

Alanis stood quickly, and so did Nikki and Raspberry. I slipped off my seat and followed them out the door. Alanis didn't turn to me until we were in the hallway. Then she put on her hat again and embraced me.

"You did real good in there, Jordan. You are my sister now," she said and squeezed me to her.

"Damn, I was sweating in there," Nikki said.

"You're always sweating," Alanis told her. "You almost gave it all away, trembling so much and looking so gaga-eyed. Don't say anything to anybody, hear? Let's keep all this to ourselves until lunch. See you soon," she told me, and they headed for the stairway.

I returned to my classroom, where everyone was busy writing his or her biography. They all looked up curiously when I entered. Mrs. Morgan didn't say anything. I wondered if she could see how I was still shaking. She nodded at my desk, and I sat and began again. My hand trembled as I picked up my pen to begin writing. I wrote about all the terrible things that had happened to our family when my parents had their accident, but I didn't write about Ian and Miss Harper. All I said about him was that he was very, very smart and wanted to be a medical research scientist someday. Of course, I explained why I had come to live with my great-aunt Frances.

Afterward, Mrs. Morgan collected our biographies. Then she passed our textbooks and workbooks to us. We began reading aloud so she could evaluate how we all read. I thought I did as well as anyone else. By lunchtime, we had been introduced to our English, math and science books. We would start our history book after lunch, and then she said she would give us our homework assignments. Tomorrow morning, after she had read our biographies to be sure there was nothing offensive in them, she would circulate them so we could all get to know each other better, but I thought they all knew each other well enough. They were all going to learn about me mostly.

She then went into a lecture about class behavior. She told us that everything we did that was wrong carried what she called negative points. She explained that at the end of the quarter she would subtract those points from our class averages and we could actually fail even though we'd passed all the tests. Everyone looked frightened about it, especially Gary, the chubby boy who had come unprepared. I thought she was looking hard at me the whole time.

When the bell rang for lunch, Mrs. Morgan called me to her desk as the class began leaving the room. She waited until everyone was gone.

"I have been told by the school nurse that she has been informed you have had menarche, is that correct? I assume you know what it means."

"Yes, Mrs. Morgan."

"If you should have any problems while you are in my classroom, I don't want you blurting it out, understand? You simply raise your hand and ask to go to the nurse. If you need to go to the nurse, go there. If you can handle yourself on your own, go to the girls' room. I can tell you that I've never in all my years had a girl in my class with this problem," she added.

I don't know why she told me that. It made me feel even more terrible.

"Now go to lunch and be sure you obey all our school rules. I'm sure," she added as I started to turn away, "that I'll learn the reason for your being called to the principal's office only minutes after you began here. This is a very busy school year for everyone in this class. I have absolutely no time or tolerance for interruptions."

I said nothing. *I guess her husband's not home,* I thought, recalling what Alanis had told me about her. I lowered my head and hurried out of the room. The hallway was already cleared, because the students were in the cafeteria. When I arrived there, I found the line was long at the counters, but Alanis appeared quickly and seized my right arm. She was still wearing her hat. Apparently, only Mrs. Browne took the time to tell her not to wear it in school.

"Where were you? We're all waiting. We gotta talk and make sure we're all on the same page."

"Mrs. Morgan kept me back to tell me things," I said.

"What things?"

"About what to do if I should have a period while I'm in her room. She said I was the first girl she had in class with the problem."

"I bet she's lying."

"Why would she lie?"

"I don't know. Teachers lie, too. Don't be surprised. C'mon," she said and took me by the hand to cut us in front of some younger students who were too afraid of her to complain. "Pick anything you want. You have more than enough money," she said. "We'll keep the change in our own private bank."

"We're not going to have another party, are we?"

"Sure we are. Don't let Mrs. Dart-face scare you."

"Dart-face?"

"Mrs. Browne. Doesn't her face look like someone used it for a dartboard?"

"Oh. Yes," I said. "It does."

We ordered our food, then took our trays to the table where Nikki and Raspberry were sitting. I saw the way some of the students from my class were looking at us. They were probably wondering how I'd come to be sitting with older girls. I was sure that now they would all firmly believe I had been left back and these girls I was with were not all that much older than me.

Chad was two tables down right, glaring angrily our way and mumbling something to his friends. Alanis pretended she didn't see him.

"Okay, listen up. We just stick to our story," Alanis advised us all at the table. "It will be Stuart's word against ours. Remember. He came drunk and we got rid of him. Anyone see you two in his truck afterward?" she asked Nikki and Raspberry.

"No, there was no one around when he dropped us off," Raspberry said.

"Good."

"What about the bottles in the basement?" Nikki asked. "There's all those empty ones and some more full ones."

"Yeah. Right after school, I'll take care of it," Alanis said.

"Crashed into a tree and broke his arm in two places," Raspberry said, shaking her head. "And arrested for drunken driving. That sounds very serious."

"Didn't you two see how drunk he was when he let you off at the corner?" Alanis asked her.

"Sure we did, but what could we do about it?" Raspberry asked. "I feel sorry for him. His father probably will break his other arm."

"Forget about him. He was a creep for trying to get

us in trouble," Alanis told her. "You don't tell on your friends," she added, glancing at me. "Never."

"Maybe he just doesn't know how to lie," I said. "I'm not too good at it," I added, and they all stopped eating and looked at me as if I had said the weirdest thing.

"Everyone knows how to lie, Jordan. He just didn't care about us. He tried to push off his own blame on us," Alanis said.

"Raspberry's right. He's probably afraid of his father," Nikki said. "I've seen him. He's a really big man."

"Doesn't matter. I'm not afraid of his father," Alanis told her and then turned to me. "Look, Jordan. Here's how you do it. First, you tell yourself you're not lying. You force yourself to believe what you're saying and then when you say it, everyone else will believe you if you do it that way, understand?"

"I suppose," I said.

"We're just lucky she didn't say too much in Dart-face's office," Nikki said.

"What'dya mean? She did better than you did," Alanis told her. "You were nearly in tears and getting ready to throw yourself on the floor and beg for mercy until I came up with the story."

"Shut up. I was not."

"Just make sure you're the one who shuts up," Alanis said. "For your information, Jordan could get into the most trouble. It was her great-aunt's house. They might send her away to some institution like they sent her brother."

"What about her brother? You never told us what he did exactly," Raspberry said.

We heard the warning bell.

"She'll tell you some other time. Everyone just watch out. Dart-face could call us in one at a time and try to get one of us to say something different. Remember. Stick to the story or else," Alanis warned, standing. "C'mon, Jordan. Get your booty back to class and stay out of Mrs. Morgan's way. In her case her bite is worse than her bark."

"What's that mean?"

"It means watch out what you say to her, stupid," Nikki said.

"I'm not stupid," I said.

"Yeah. Don't call her stupid. She may look older than you, but she's not," Alanis told her. "Although sometimes I wonder," she added in a mutter.

Nikki's eyes flared. She pressed her lips together, then started away.

"What'cha go take her side for over Nikki's?" Raspberry asked Alanis.

"I'm not taking sides."

"Right," Raspberry said and hurried to join Nikki before she left the cafeteria.

"Sometimes they act like they're the ones in the third grade, not you," Alanis said. "Don't worry about it. I'll take care of them."

We started out of the cafeteria.

"Everything's going to be all right, Jordan," she told me before we parted in the hallway. "Just hang tough."

I tried, but all the while I was in Mrs. Morgan's classroom, I expected the door to open and Mrs. Browne to send for me to do just what Alanis had predicted: speak with us one at a time, especially me, to get one of us to contradict Alanis's story. I even imagined the police would come and take me away. How would I hang tough then? I wondered, but thankfully no one came.

We went through the first chapter in our history book, then Mrs. Morgan gave us our homework. It seemed like a lot. There was something to do for every subject. I would surely have to get started as soon as I was home and not join Great-aunt Frances to watch some afternoon soap opera. I didn't want to make her feel bad, but I had never been given so much homework.

When the bell rang to end the school day, I gathered my books and workbooks, stuffed them into my schoolbag and started out. No one in my class spoke to me, but I felt many looking at me. Alanis was waiting for me in the hallway.

"Nobody came back for you, right?"

"No."

"Good. We'll be fine. Let's go home. I better get down to the basement and get rid of that stuff quickly," she said. We headed out to the buses, but when we stepped outside, Alanis moaned, "Oh, no."

There, standing and waiting by his old car, was Mr. Marshall, Alanis's granddad, and it wasn't hard to see that he was fuming.

"Get over here," he called to her.

She paused.

"You go on the bus," she said. "I better deal with him myself."

I watched her walk to him and his car. He turned as she walked past him to get into the car, and he slapped her sharply on the back of her head. I could swear I felt it, too. She spun around on him, but he grabbed her shoulder and forced her into the car, slamming the door shut. He glared my way but got into his car quickly.

I hurried into my bus, my legs trembling so much that I thought I would trip on the steps.

One of the girls in my class was seated up front, and she put her hand out to stop me from going down the aisle.

"How come you're in the third grade?" she asked.

"Because that's where I'm supposed to be," I replied. She looked at her friend sitting beside her and they smiled. "It is!" I said. They both started to giggle. I walked all the way to the back quickly and sat by myself. Looking out the window, I saw Lester Marshall drive away. Alanis had her hand over her eyes and her head against the window.

It took much longer for me to get home because of all the stops along the way. By that time, almost three-quarters of the bus had gotten off. I hurried down the aisle without looking at anyone and got off. Then I charged up the driveway. I saw Lester Marshall's car, but I didn't see him or Alanis.

"Oh, Jordan," Great-aunt Frances cried as soon as I entered the house. She stepped out of the living room. I thought she was going to ask me to come in to watch the soap opera. "I had a phone call from the school principal today. She wanted to know if you had a party here last night. How silly, I told her. There was no party. You went to sleep to get ready for school. She asked me if I had seen Stuart Gavin here, the boy who delivers propane gas. I said no but I better see him soon, I think. Then she told me he was in an accident with his truck and he had been drinking alcohol. I told her I thought he was a nice boy and I was sorry to hear it. She said I should be sure to question you, but about what?"

I thought about trying to lie to her and decided instead to just be quiet.

"Did you like your first day of school?" she asked instead of asking anything about Stuart.

"No," I said. "My teacher isn't very nice and I have lots and lots of homework to do."

"Oh, dear. Not nice, you say?" She thought a moment, then smiled. "Well, maybe that's because it's the first day and she wants all the students to be sure they behave. You must not judge too quickly. My father used to tell me that. Take a deep breath, Frances, he told me, and listen again or look again. So take a deep breath and let's see how you feel tomorrow, okay?"

I nodded.

"I have to get started on my homework," I said. "It's a lot, more than I ever had," I emphasized.

"Oh? Well, that might be because it's the first day, too. You do what you think you should. We're going to have something called a quiche for dinner tonight. I took it out of the freezer and defrosted it. It's French, so we'll have French music, and I have two very pretty skirts for us to wear and French hats. My parents went to France a long time ago and brought them back for Emma and me, but Emma hated hers. I know how to say some things in French. I'll teach them to you later, okay? I also had this chocolate fudge cake in the freezer I had forgotten. Won't that be a wonderful dessert. We'll have a good time," she promised.

I nodded quickly and ran up the stairs. I was very worried about the bottles of alcopops in the basement. If Alanis's granddad punished her and made her stay in the house, she couldn't get over here to get rid of them, and then, if the police came to look, they would see we were all lying.

I decided to sneak down into the basement and take care of it myself. Great-aunt Frances was watching her show, so it wasn't hard. I was glad I had done it because the bottles were everywhere and there were seven full ones left in a bag at the side of the sofa. I gathered it all as quickly and quietly as I could and then took it all upstairs. Before I stepped out, I listened for Great-aunt Frances. I just heard the television, so I went quickly through the kitchen and out the door to the big garbage cans. I put it all in one and then hurried back inside and up to my room to start my homework. I wanted to get it done as quickly as I could so I could get back to Ian's letters and finish reading them. Maybe there was something about Mother in one of the letters he'd written later. Surely, they wouldn't all be about insects, I hoped.

The homework wasn't difficult, but there were so many math problems to do that I thought I would be working on it until I went to sleep. I lost track of time, so when I heard footsteps in the hallway, I was sure it was Great-aunt Frances coming to tell me to get ready for our French dinner. I wasn't excited about getting dressed up as a French lady, but considering the phone call she received and the trouble we could still be in, I thought I should do whatever she wanted.

When I looked up, however, I saw it was Alanis.

"You took away the bottles, I hope?" she asked. "I

went down there but they were gone. It wasn't your great-aunt, was it?"

"No, I did it. I put them all in the garbage can."

"What? We can't do that. My granddad takes the garbage down to the front of the driveway for the garbagemen. He's liable to see it. He thinks I might be telling the truth right now, otherwise, he'd whip me good."

"He whips you?"

"Not with a whip, but it might as well be. He's got this thick leather belt leaves welts the size of quarters. Your parents never whipped you?"

I shook my head.

"Not your grandmother either?"

"No." I didn't say it, but her whipping us with her words stung enough.

"I'll take care of the bottles. I'll hide it all behind the barn in a hole where I've thrown other stuff. What did your great-aunt say when you got home?"

"She said Mrs. Browne called and asked about a party."

"What did she say?"

"She told her I was asleep and she hadn't seen Stuart."

"Good. That's perfect. We'll be fine. You did real good today, Jordan."

I knew it wasn't something to be proud about, but her smile and compliment made me feel better.

"The bottles," she said and hurried away. Not ten minutes later, I heard Great-aunt Frances coming with the skirt, hat and blouse she wanted me to wear.

After I dressed, I looked at myself in the mirror. Suddenly, I was surprised myself at how comfortable and relieved I felt escaping from reality and pretending to be in one of Great-aunt Frances's make-believe worlds. In those worlds, we had no Mrs. Brownes and no policemen, no lying and trembling with fear.

When I stepped into the kitchen, I found her in her skirt and blouse and French hat. The French music was playing. She turned from the oven.

"Bonsoir, ma peu assez un. Comment allez-vous?"

I didn't know what to say.

"That means 'Good evening, my little pretty one. How are you?' Go on and say 'How are you?' in French."

She repeated it for me, and I said it.

"Parfait. That's 'perfect' in French. Now I'll tell you to sit at the table. *Reposez-vous à la table, s'il vous plaît.* The last part means 'please.' Always say 'please' when you ask someone to do something. Go on, say 'please' in French." She repeated it, and I did it, and she clapped. *"Parfait.* What's that mean?"

"Perfect."

"See? You're speaking French."

"How did you learn it?" I asked, impressed.

She served the quiche and poured us each a glass of grape juice. Then she lit a candle she had placed on the table.

"We had a French maid and she spent a lot of time teaching me. It annoyed Emma because she thought I wasn't learning it properly. I should learn it in school only. It bothered her that I could speak French and she couldn't. I remember," she said smiling, "when this boyfriend of hers came to the house and I started to speak French to him. Suddenly, he was more interested in me, and Emma was fit to be tied. He even called me for a date once, but I said no. I didn't want Emma to hate me more than she did."

"She hated you?"

"She couldn't help it," Great-aunt Frances said.

"But why?"

"Let's not talk about it. I'll teach you French, too, and someday, you'll impress everyone. You hear that song?" she asked. "That's a famous French singer, Edith Piaf. My father loved her and he loved when I could sing, too. Emma couldn't carry a tune in a suit-case." She laughed. "That's what my father told me once and right in front of her."

How cruel, I thought, and like a fog starting to thin out and disappear, I began to see through the clouded past and understand why my grandmother might have resented her sister, who'd been prettier, softer, more like the little girl her father had wanted. In fact, I suddenly thought Grandmother Emma was like the little girl outside the storefront window looking in at the rich little girl inside surrounded by the things she would never have.

But why, then, had she sent me here? Had she known I would be more trouble?

Was I really what Great-aunt Frances suspected, Grandmother Emma's revenge lobbed like a ball of fire and pain from her bed of misery where she lay condemned by her own bitter heart?

Or was I somehow her plea for forgiveness?

I believed the answer waited impatiently to be heard somewhere within the shadows in this old house.

10

My First Brassiere

After dinner, as usual, Great-aunt Frances went to watch television. She wanted to leave the dishes for the morning, but as soon as she left the kitchen, I cleaned up. Then I hurried back to my room to complete my homework so I could dig into Ian's letters again. Finally, I was able to pull out the bag of them from the closet and begin.

> Dear Jordan,
>   Today, when they brought me to see Dr. Walker, he wasn't in his office yet, so I had the chance to look at some of the paperwork on his desk, and I made a terribly sad discovery. Our own father is spineless. He gave them terrible lies about me and then he signed the bottom of the paper. I studied his signature carefully and made another discovery. Our father is a cockroach. I should

*have known. He always ran or hid from any
threat, any criticism. He looks for a safe hole
and crawls in it.*

*I confirmed this after Dr. Walker came in, sat
behind his desk and started to question me. I told
him I was very saddened to realize that my father
was a cowardice insect. I explained it all carefully so he would see there was no sense in trying
to get me to change my mind.*

"It's my grandmother's fault," I told him.

"Why?" he wanted to know.

*"My grandmother is a spider," I said. "She
wove a web and trapped us all in it. She caught
our father in the web shortly after he was born
and she kept him under her control. Now that he
is injured and can't even crawl away, he can do
nothing but what she tells him to do."*

*Dr. Walker looked very impressed. He nodded
and took his notes and then he asked me what I
thought that made me.*

"You are, after all, his son, are you not?"

*"I'm not sure," I said. "I'm not finished with
my research about that."*

"What about your sister?"

*"The same," I told him. "Let's just say the
jury is still out. We are still weighing all the evidence before we decide."*

He smiled.

*We then got into a long conversation about
good and evil and I told him neither existed.
Things are simply what they are. Is it bad that we
eat cows, lamb and chicken? It's not too good for
them, I said and he laughed.*

"Everything that lives," I said, "lives off something else that lives, especially you."

"Me?" He lost his smile. "Why especially me?"

"You live off of me and the others here," I said. "If we didn't exist, neither could you."

"Well, do I have a right to exist?" he asked me.

I told him in this world even a black widow has a right to exist. Existence is in and of itself a reason to exist. It wouldn't have been created if nature didn't want it created. Once something is born, no matter what it is, it fights to stay alive, so it must have as much of a right to exist as anything.

He looked confused for a moment and then he smiled and said that I had given him something interesting to ponder.

"See?" I told him then. "Thinking is what gives you meaning. Without me, you wouldn't have a reason to be."

He laughed. Despite his orders concerning me, I think he's getting to like me. I don't care, of course, but I might find a way to use that someday. He'll trust me.

Which brings me to why I'm writing this letter to you, Jordan. Do not trust our father, especially if Grandmother Emma dies. I'm not sure yet, but I think when that happens, he will turn into a spider and you might get caught in his web.

I'll let you know what else I learn.

Ian

This letter frightened me so much that I threw it down quickly and took deep breaths. Then I folded it and stuffed it into the envelope. I put all the letters back in the bag and hid them again in the closet, closing the door as if I thought they could come crawling out like the insects Ian had described. Oh, why did I start reading his letters now? I asked myself. Because I had, I was afraid to go to sleep, afraid I would surely have nightmares. My gaze went around the bedroom, searching for any spiders, flies, anything. I did see a small spider in the corner and quickly squashed it with the back of my history book. Then I wiped it off and went around the room searching for any other insects. I saw none, but I had to look under the bed, too.

"What are you looking for, dear?" I heard Great-aunt Frances ask. I stood up. I hadn't heard her come up the stairs and down the hallway. Maybe that was because she was barefoot.

"Bugs," I said.

"Oh, you mustn't worry over bugs. No matter what we do, they'll come around. Ignore them and they'll leave," she said. "I've decided to go to sleep earlier tonight and be sure to set the alarm clock so I don't oversleep and let you go off without a proper breakfast again. We'll have scrambled eggs and toast and hot chocolates together, okay? And before I forget," she said, coming into the room, "here's more money for lunches and whatever else they ask you to pay for at school. I remember they sometimes ask you to put deposits down on things or make you buy the school physical education uniforms."

She handed me a fifty-dollar bill.

"I swear that bill has been in my pocket for twenty years," she said. "Don't tell Emma," she whispered, as if Grandmother Emma had been just down the hallway in that nice bedroom.

Suddenly, a panic came over me. She saw it in my face and she looked like I had stolen her breath. She brought her hand to her breast.

"What is it, Jordan?"

I started to cry.

"Oh, dear, what is it?"

"I forgot. My teacher told me I have to wear a brassiere or she won't let me in her room."

"A brassiere? Yes," she said, nodding, "you should wear a brassiere. Well, don't cry. Let's go look for one that will fit you."

She went to the dresser where many of her things remained and started to sift through the drawer.

"I wasn't all that much older than you are when I started to wear one. My mother insisted. Rather, Emma made her insist," she told me. "She said I was an embarrassment because I was younger than she was and I needed it and she didn't. She didn't want to be seen with me. Now where did I put . . . here we go," she said, pulling a brassiere out from under some panties. "I'm sure this will do fine."

I took it from her. It looked faded, more yellow than white, but the clips that fastened it were fine.

"See? Nothing to cry over." She stood up and smiled. "Did you brush your teeth? Don't forget," she sang and headed out.

I put the fifty-dollar bill in my schoolbag with my books, then went to the bathroom to wash and brush my teeth. I took the brassiere with me to try it on. It felt too tight, and I thought it might stop me from breathing when I managed to fasten the clips. It cut into my skin as well, but what could I do? It was a relief to get it off when I went to bed.

My first day at school, with all the added excitement and tension, had drained me more than I imagined. I don't think I'd ever fallen asleep as fast. I tossed and turned, however, and thought I heard sobbing again, but this time I was too tired to listen hard. *It's just a dream,* I told myself and fell into a deeper sleep. If Great-aunt Frances hadn't turned on her alarm clock and come to wake me, I would have overslept again for sure. Even so, I was in a daze getting myself washed and dressed. It took forever this time to get the brassiere clips hooked, and again, I felt I would suffocate. By the time I descended the stairway and entered the kitchen, Great-aunt Frances had prepared the breakfast she had promised.

"I hope you like everything. I'm afraid I burned the toast a little."

It was more than a little burned, but I didn't complain. The eggs weren't cooked enough either and had too much salt on them. The only thing that tasted good was the hot chocolate. I ate what I could, and when she wasn't looking, I dumped out the rest. Alanis came to the door just as I finished.

"Good. You got up yourself this time," she said.

"No. My great-aunt woke me," I said.

"I had to wake myself first with my alarm clock," she told Alanis. "It's been a long time since I had to get up for school."

"No kidding?" Alanis looked at me and shook her head. "Better get moving. We can't miss the bus. No one is taking us to school," she said dryly. She started to turn, then stopped and smiled. "You wearing a bra?"

"Mrs. Morgan told me to wear it or else she won't let me into her classroom."

"Oh, yeah? Well, we don't want to upset Mrs. Morgan."

"It's very nice of you to look after her, Alanis," Great-aunt Frances said. "You're like a big sister. My sister never had the patience. She once left me alone after school and I waited and waited until a teacher saw me crying in a corner. My father was very upset with her. I was only seven!"

"How sad," Alanis said, but didn't sound really sad about it. "C'mon."

I picked up my schoolbag and followed her out to the door.

"I gave her money for school uniforms and things," Great-aunt Frances called after us. I wished she hadn't told.

"She did?" Alanis asked the moment we stepped outside. "How much this time?"

"Fifty dollars," I said.

"That's good. Good work, Jordan."

"I didn't do anything. She just gave it to me."

"I told you she has lots of money hidden in there. We've got to look for it. You better let me hold on to the fifty. You don't want to lose it."

I didn't want to give it to her, but I didn't know what to say that wouldn't make her angry, so I dug it out of the schoolbag.

"Don't worry. I'll make sure we buy anything you need at school."

We walked down the driveway. I saw where her granddad had filled in holes and trimmed the grass. Suddenly, he appeared at the gate. He was repairing the hinges. He stopped working and looked at us as we approached.

"I don't want to hear nothing from that principal today—or any day, for that matter," he warned. He pointed his finger at me. "You watch yourself now, Miss Jordan. Your family has enough trouble. You don't want to make new problems."

"Stop picking on her, Granddad. I told you we didn't do nothing wrong. That boy lied."

"Only thing I believe, Alanis, is you know what a lie is so you'd recognize it."

She turned away to sulk. He looked at me, then went back to repairing the hinges. We heard the bus coming and stepped out to board it when it stopped.

"No trouble now!" he warned.

"Don't listen to him. He babbles," Alanis said. "I can't wait 'til I can live somewhere on my own. That's why I love your great-aunt's basement. It's like having my own place."

We got onto the bus, and to both our surprise, we saw Stuart Gavin sitting in the seat on the right side, right before the last seat. His arm was in a cast, and his forehead had a scrape on the right side.

"Well, look what the wind blew in, Jordan," Alanis said as we approached. "The rat himself."

Stuart looked down and we took our seat. The bus started away.

"We didn't think you'd have the nerve to show your face, Stuart," Alanis continued, poking him in the shoulder of the arm in the cast. "We're going to make sure everyone in school knows what a fink you are."

He turned to face us.

"It's not my fault," he whined. "I didn't know what

I was saying. I was in pain and the cops were asking me questions quickly. I was drunk and they scared me. I'm sorry. If I wasn't drunk, I wouldn't have told them anything."

"Yeah, right."

"It's true. I'm sorry," he said. He looked at me, and I thought he really was sorry. "I didn't mean to get you into trouble, Jordan. It just came out."

"Yeah, you threw up your guts just like all cowards," Alanis said.

He looked like he was going to cry. Some of the students close by listened carefully and looked at him with disapproval.

"I told my father I was lying," he said. "I'm going to see Mrs. Browne first thing and tell her the same thing. I'm taking all the blame."

Alanis looked at him with some new interest.

"You better not be lying again, Stuart Gavin, 'cause if you are this time, I swear—"

"No. You watch me. You can follow me to the office, if you want. I'm going right there and ask to speak with her as soon as I walk in the building."

"What are you going to tell her?"

"What you told her. She told my father your story. I came with the alcopops and you and your friends told me to leave. Then I crashed. I won't even mention giving Nikki and Raspberry a ride home."

Alanis nodded.

"Good," she said. "After you do that, I'm going to let Mrs. Browne have it between the eyes for accusing us and calling my granddad. He told my mother, but she was too drunk to understand," she whispered.

"I'm sorry, Jordan," Stuart said. I glanced at Alanis

first, and then I nodded and smiled at him. I could see that made him very happy.

"He really likes you," Alanis whispered. "That's why he's doing it. He couldn't care a speck about me and Nikki and Raspberry. See?" she added. "You already begun fishing and you already hooked him."

I looked at her and then at Stuart. I didn't know what I had done, but whatever it was, it made me feel good. I even suspected Ian would approve.

When we arrived at school, Alanis decided we should follow Stuart to see if he was telling the truth about what he was going to do. He didn't look back. He walked directly to the principal's office and went in.

"This will be interesting," Alanis said. "You'd better get to class. You don't want to be late for Mrs. Morgan. We'll group at lunch again and see what we can find out from Stuart."

I hurried to my classroom, getting there just before the first bell rang. Mrs. Morgan was at the door, ready to check my clothing, I thought. She looked me over carefully, then nodded. I went to my desk and took out my books. Before she went to her desk, she crossed the room and paused at mine.

"I understand, Miss March, that you're not here a day and you're already in serious trouble."

"No, I'm not," I said firmly. She pulled her head back.

"Oh?"

"You'll see," I said, my heart thumping, for I thought I might not be able to sound and look as brave as I wanted.

"Yes, I will see," she said, smiling. Everyone in the class was looking and listening.

When Mrs. Morgan passed the autobiographies around, mine was the most popular. I saw some of the students rushing others to finish reading it. As soon as one did, he or she looked at me again. Most looked very sad for me, but some just shook their heads.

Afterward, I did as well as anyone else in the room when it came to our homework and the questions Mrs. Morgan asked. She collected our papers, and we went on to do reading in our history textbooks. She then announced that we would have to buy physical education outfits, and she told how much it would cost. When the bell rang for lunch, I hurried out with the others, anxious to find out what Stuart had actually done.

"I bought you the same lunch you had yesterday with the fifty-dollar bill," Alanis told me as soon as I entered.

"I need thirty dollars for a physical education uniform."

"Yeah, I know. I'll have it for you. Don't worry. Just go to the table. I'm waiting for our hero."

I joined Nikki and Raspberry, who were already eating. *How did they get here so fast?* I wondered.

"I hope Stuart did what he said he would do," Nikki told me. "There he is."

I turned and saw Alanis talking to him. He nodded, and then she came to the table.

"He'll be here after he buys his sandwich. He said he did it."

We all waited anxiously. He came and sat.

"Lucky for me I'm right-handed," he said.

"Does that hurt?" Raspberry asked him, nodding at his cast.

"A little. I gotta wear it for a long time, and of course, I can't work. I could drive with one hand, but delivering the tanks is impossible. My dad got the truck running. It's smashed up, but it runs. Needs a headlight," he added and bit into his sandwich.

"Mrs. Browne said you would lose your license."

"I might. I gotta go to court, but until I do, I still have it," he told us.

"That's all great news, Stuart, but we want to hear what you told Mrs. Browne and what she said," Alanis said. He nodded, hurriedly chewed and swallowed.

"Just what I said I would tell her. I told her I came with the alcopops and you guys told me to leave. She sat there looking angry and told me it was just as much a crime to lie about a crime as it was to commit it. She tried to scare me," he added, "but I told her I wasn't lying. I was wrong to try to blame you guys. I think she believed me finally."

"Good," Nikki said.

"We won't have you assassinated now," Raspberry told him. He laughed and turned to me.

"Sorry I got you in trouble, Jordan."

"Let's forget about it already," Alanis said. "Next time, we'll all be more careful."

Stuart nodded and ate and smiled at me. I could see the smiles on the three girls.

"You want us all to sign your cast?" Nikki asked him.

"Sure," he said and again looked at me.

"Who would you like to do it first?" Raspberry asked him.

"Jordan's closest," he said, digging into his pocket

to get a pen. He handed it to me. "You can write anything you want," he said.

I wrote, *Get better, Jordan.*

"Nice," he told me. I gave him his pen.

"Do you even want anyone else to write on it, Stuart?" Nikki asked, teasing.

"If you want," he said.

"Naw. Raspberry?"

"I'm too tired to write anything."

"I don't put anything in writing," Alanis said, and the three of them laughed.

"So, tell us everything, Stuart. Are you confined to quarters like a bad sailor boy?" Nikki asked him.

"Hell, yeah. I gotta go right home after school every day forever. But," he added with a wide smile of his own, "I can sneak out when I want. I still got my old motor scooter, and it's not hard to drive it with one hand. My dad's going to his small-business company convention this weekend, in fact. Maybe I'll come over to see you," he told me.

"We'll let you know if we're having any guests this weekend," Alanis answered for me. "I can't wait to see Mrs. Browne in the hall. I'm going to ask her if she thinks we still need lawyers."

Everyone laughed, even Stuart.

"You better take off your hat before you ask her that," I said.

"Don't worry about it. Okay, Stuart," Alanis said. "You can eat lunch with us every day, if you want."

"I could? Thanks," he said.

"How do you get here so quickly?" I asked Nikki. "You're upstairs and I'm just down the hall."

"We ask to go to the bathroom sometimes and just come to the lunchroom."

"Won't you get into trouble?"

"Naw," Raspberry said. "Our teachers are happy to see us go."

They laughed again.

Afterward, I looked for Mrs. Browne in the hallway to see if Alanis would do what she said she would, but I didn't see her. Stuart walked with me back to my classroom.

"Maybe I'll call you," he said. "I know your aunt's number."

"Great-aunt," I reminded him.

"Oh, yeah, right. See you," he said and hurried away.

Mrs. Morgan gave us as much homework, if not more, as she had the first day, so Great-aunt Frances's theory about first-day assignments didn't work. Just thinking about it all made my schoolbooks feel heavier in my bag.

"Stuart is smitten with love," Alanis told me when we boarded the bus.

"Smitten?"

"He's got a big crush on you. Don't worry. I'll tell you exactly what to do. It'll be fun," she said. "I can't wait to lay it into Granddad now that Stuart did that. Not that he'll apologize. It's just good to make him feel bad."

"Why? He's your grandfather."

"Trust me. Whenever you can make an adult feel sorry about what he or she said to you, you're better off."

There was so much to learn, I thought, so much that was new and different in this world.

When the school bus let us off at the end of the day,

I saw Grandmother Emma's limousine parked in front of the house. My first thought was that she had gotten better and she'd had Felix drive her here—or else, I thought, he really had told her everything and she had sent him back to get me. Alanis thought otherwise.

"That chauffeur came back here fast to check on my granddad. He's going to be in a bad mood now no matter what," she said. "I think I'll hang out with you a while longer."

We hurried up the driveway. When we entered, we heard Great-aunt Frances talking to Felix in the living room. They both turned when we appeared in the doorway.

"How are you doing, Jordan?" Felix asked. "Getting along at your new school?"

"It's harder," I said. "My teacher gives us too much homework."

"Alanis is being a big sister," Great-aunt Frances told him. "I'm sure she can help her."

Felix looked at Alanis, but suspiciously. I wondered if Great-aunt Frances had told him anything about Mrs. Browne calling.

"Her teacher ain't so nice," Alanis said, "but I'll do what I can."

"Thank you, dear," Great-aunt Frances said.

"How come you came back so soon, Felix?" I asked him, still hoping he had been sent to bring me home.

"Your grandmother sent me back to check on things for her. I see the house is in a little better order and the grounds are better. Anything on your list that needs attending?"

I'd forgotten to start one, but I didn't say so. I just shook my head.

"How is Grandmother Emma?"

"Well, she's made some progress. She's in active therapy now and her doctors are pleased."

"What about my mother?" I asked quickly.

"I haven't heard anything new, Jordan. Sorry about that."

"Does my father know anything?"

"Maybe. If so, he hasn't told me."

"Did he get that special car?"

"Not yet."

"Didn't he want to come see me, come with you?"

"He took a little vacation," Felix said. "He and Kimberly went to Florida for a week."

"Oh. Do you know anything about Ian?"

He just shook his head.

"Will you take us to see Grandmother Emma?" I asked. I was sorry about firing one question after another at him, but he wasn't telling me anything about my family.

"She doesn't want any visitors at the moment," Felix said.

"What about taking us to see my mother. Can you?"

"I'll ask your grandmother," he said. He didn't sound hopeful.

"I want to write to Ian, but I don't know where to send the letter, Felix."

"I'll see if I can find that out for you," he said, but again, it didn't sound hopeful. It sounded empty, words without letters, words made of air.

"It does sound as if Emma will be here someday," Great-aunt Frances said. She looked very troubled.

Felix rose.

"Yes, I would expect so, Miss Wilkens. When she has her mind made up to do something, Mrs. March will do it one way or another."

"I know. You don't have to tell me about my sister," she said.

He looked at Alanis and then at me.

"You just do the best you can for now, Jordan," he said. "I have a few matters more to discuss with Mr. Marshall, and then I'll be heading back. I brought some things for you and left them in a carton in your room," he added.

"Things for me?"

"Just stuff from your room back at the March house. Nancy packed them for me. She's given her notice," he said. "She's leaving in two weeks." He turned to Great-aunt Frances. "Nancy was your sister's housekeeper and cook."

"Yes. Jordan told me."

"I've got to find a new one now," Felix said.

He started out. I hated to see him go. Just talking to him about my family made me feel closer to them. He turned, and I think he saw the sadness in my face.

"I'll return again in a short time," he told me. "If something comes up, you know how to reach me."

I knew I would call my grandmother's house and press two when the telephone answering service rattled off the extensions. Two went directly to Felix. I nodded.

"Take care, Miss Wilkens," he told Great-aunt Frances.

As soon as he left, I turned to Alanis and said, "Let's go see what's in the carton."

She followed me up. It was a big carton on the floor

at the foot of my bed. I hurried to it and opened it quickly. In it I found my framed pictures of my parents and Ian, which I showed to Alanis.

"Your mother's pretty and your father's pretty good-looking too. So this is Ian," she said, studying his picture. "He's not bad-looking either."

"Oh, here's my Sleeping Beauty clock," I said, showing it to her. "Now I can set my alarm myself."

I continued to take things out of the carton. There was more of my clothing, blouses, skirts, socks and a pair of sandals, too, but the most surprising thing of all was the book Ian had bought me, *I Was a Girl and Now I Am a Woman*. How had it gotten back to the mansion? I had left it in the cabin in the Poconos when Grandmother Emma had taken Ian and me home so my parents could meet there alone and discuss their problems. I was sure Grandmother Emma would be very angry if she found out that Nancy had sent my book along with the other things.

"Let me see that," Alanis said and plucked it out of my hands. "This the book you said your brother gave you?"

"Yes."

She started to flip through it and then stopped and smiled.

"This could be fun to read. Look at this chapter," she said, turning it to me. " 'Female Pleasure Zones, Knowing Your Own Body.' I like the idea of that. You read this chapter?"

"Not yet."

"Well, we'll read it together," she said, sitting with her back to the bed. However, she began by reading to herself. While she did, I began to put away my clothing and set my pictures up on the dresser and on the desk.

"Damn," she said, looking up at me. "I never knew reading could be this much fun. There's lots of stuff here I never knew and can't wait to try," she added. "I'll have to thank your brother when we see him."

"See Ian? Do you think we ever will?"

"You just find out where he is," she said, her eyes narrow with determination. "We can do anything. You saw that already. No one's gonna stop us."

She returned quickly to the book.

Maybe she was right. Maybe we could visit Ian. After all, Ian had gotten him and me in to see our mother all by ourselves. Alanis wasn't anywhere as smart as Ian, but she seemed to know how to get things done.

"Here's a word I heard but never knew what it meant: erogenous. We have erogenous zones." She looked up at me, her eyes wide as she smiled. "It says here there's nothing wrong with experimenting with your own body to learn about yourself. I didn't need a book to tell me that, but the school nurse never mentioned any of this in that health class I had to take. You know what?" she said.

"What?"

"We'll form our own health class, a secret club, and call it the Erogenous Club. Just us. After I read all this, I'll be like the teacher, too."

She thought a moment, looked at the page she was reading, which had an illustration on it I didn't understand, and then nodded at my bedroom door.

"Close the door," she said in a hoarse whisper. "We can't take the chance of even your great-aunt overhearing us. We don't tell anyone else about your book, okay?"

"Okay," I said and closed the door.

"This is the biggest secret we'll have, Jordan. You swear you won't tell anyone."

"About what?"

"The book, the club!"

"Okay," I said, although in my heart of hearts, I wasn't sure Ian would approve. Then I had an idea why Ian would approve. "I won't tell if we call it the Erogenous Project instead of the Erogenous Club."

"Good idea," she said. "Makes it sound scientific and makes me sound more like a teacher, too. Good." She waved me off. "Don't bother me for a while," she added. "I've got a lot to read, and usually I hate to read."

Like someone starving, she attacked the words and the pages while I sat looking at my pictures of my mother, father and Ian and wondering where and when we would find ourselves doing the simplest things together again, like sharing a dinner or riding in a car. At the moment, as I watched Alanis reading excitedly, I thought going back to the way things once were was as hard as being reborn.

11

Tadpoles

"I just got another great idea," Alanis said, sitting there on the floor by my bed and looking around my room. She nodded. "A really great one."

"What?"

"I should move in here with you."

"Move in here?"

"Yes. I sleep on a sofa now, and I have about as much privacy as a goldfish. Granddad is always complaining about how much time I take in the bathroom. We've only got one. Besides, I can see where you need me around more. Your great-aunt is more than a handful. I know I can convince my mother. I'll promise to do all the housework here. We both will. She'll be happy about that and take my side against my granddad in case he puts up opposition."

She paused and looked up at me.

"Why don't you say something? Don't you want me to move in with you?"

"Yes," I said, even though I wasn't really sure I did. I'd never even had anyone sleep over for a night when I was at Grandmother Emma's, and sometimes Ian had been so involved in his projects, I hadn't seen him much at all.

"We have a lot to do. It's best that I'm here," Alanis said, nodding like someone convincing herself.

She rose quickly and went to the closet.

"What is all this?"

"My great-aunt's things."

"Well, why are they in your room?"

"This was once her room and she hasn't gotten around to getting her things out. She said some of it could fit me or you. She told me she would give away whatever didn't fit us."

"I wouldn't be caught dead wearing any of this," Alanis said, sifting through the clothes. "And neither should you. C'mon. Let's get it all out of here so there's room for my things, too."

She started to pull clothing off hangers and toss garments onto my bed. When she started on the shoes and boxes on the closet floor, I lunged forward, realizing she would discover the bag of Ian's letters.

"What's that?" she asked when I took it out quickly.

"Nothing," I said.

"It can't be nothing."

"Just some old letters I kept."

"From who? Your brother?" she followed quickly.

"Yes, but I'm not supposed to let anyone else read them. I'm not!" I said firmly, tears coming to my eyes.

"Okay, don't bust a blood vessel. I won't read them. I'm sure they would be boring anyway." She paused, then turned back to me. "Isn't there a return address on the letters? That'll tell you where he is."

I shook my head.

"Someone ripped it off all the envelopes."

"Who would have done that? The Grandmother from Hell?"

"I don't know," I said.

"Whatever," she said and shrugged as she went to the dresser drawers. "I can't believe she left all this in here." She started flinging things out of the drawers. "I'll need at least three of these drawers. Put some of this in that carton now," she told me. "I'll get some big garbage bags for the rest and we'll take it all down to the basement. Aren't you excited about us being together all the time?" she asked when I just stood there clinging to the bag of letters and looking at the clothing on the floor.

I nodded.

"You don't look very excited. But don't worry," she said, smiling and tapping the book Ian had given me. "I'll show you how to get excited. Okay, I'm heading over to Granddad's to break the news to them. I'm telling them you asked me to stay here, so go down and tell your great-aunt you did and ask her if it's okay."

"What if she says no?"

"She won't. Tell her I'm helping with the housework, the cooking, everything, and with your homework, too! Don't forget that. She likes the idea of my being your big sister. This is perfect," she said, looking around the room. "The bed's certainly big enough for both of us."

"The bathroom's very small," I said. "There's hardly room for my things."

"Don't worry about it." She looked at the book. "For now, let's keep this under the bed." She slipped it under. "I'll be back with the garbage bags. Don't just stand there. Get everything in a pile and go down to tell your great-aunt."

She rushed out. I felt swept along in a wind swirling about the room. My first thought was, *Where do I hide Ian's letters?* I didn't trust that she wouldn't sneak into the bag to read them, and I still had many more to read myself. I decided the best place to hide anything was in the untouched room, the room reserved for Grandmother Emma. I hurried down to it and put the bag of Ian's letters in the closet. Then I returned to my room, piled up the clothing Alanis had tossed around, and went downstairs to ask Great-aunt Frances if Alanis could move in. A part of me was hoping she would say no. I couldn't help being afraid of having Alanis actually live with me.

"She wants to move in?" Great-aunt Frances said, sitting up on her sofa. Her show had just ended. "What a wonderful idea. She'll really be like your sister then, won't she? And you say she'll help us with the cooking and cleaning?"

I nodded. "She already took all your old things out of the closet and drawers to make room for hers."

"That's okay. That's fine. Remember I told you to put whatever you don't want in bags and we'll give it away?"

"Yes."

She clapped her hands together. "Oh, this will be fun. The three of us will dress for dinner tonight. We're going to have steaks and potatoes and peas. We'll make the steaks on the grill in the back. It's going to be a Western dinner, so I'll go look for the cowboy hats I have and some great skirts and blouses. We used to wear them to a barbeque."

"Alanis might not want to," I said.

"Of course she'll want to. You tell her. Oh, I don't remember if I defrosted the steaks."

She rose and went to the kitchen. I followed her.

"Oh, dear," she said. "I did forget. Well, it will just take a little longer to cook them, that's all."

She took the packages of meat out of the freezer and put them on the counter. They were like rocks.

"I'd better go look for the clothing," she said. "This will be great fun."

I decided to wait for Alanis upstairs. I wished I could be as excited about it all as Great-aunt Frances seemed to be, but it still made me nervous to think of someone sleeping in my bed and sharing my room. I didn't want to say anything that would make Alanis angry, though. What if she could help me find out where Ian was and we did visit him? Maybe she could help me get to visit my mother.

I went into the bathroom to see how I could re-arrange some things to make room for hers. Once she discovered the untouched room reserved only for Grandmother Emma and she saw that bathroom, she would want us to use it for sure. I knew that would upset Great-aunt Frances. I wondered what Grandmother Emma would say when she found out Alanis had moved into my room. Felix would surely tell her. *Maybe her granddad won't let her do it,* I thought.

I heard the front door open and close. Alanis, car-rying full garbage bags, started to charge up the stairs, then stopped when she saw me in the hallway at the top of the stairway.

"Well? What did she say?"

I told her everything, adding, "She went into the basement to look for things for us to wear to a barbeque."

"That's great. I'll put on the costumes, wigs, masks, anything to move in," she said and continued up.

"But you laughed at us when we did it before," I reminded her.

"We have to make your great-aunt happy. My mother couldn't care any less about my moving in, especially when I said I'd do all the work. Granddad wasn't there so he doesn't know yet, but he'll have to accept it because I'm doing it," she said with determination. "These bags are full of my things. We'll empty them, put my things in the closet and dresser and fill the bags up with those old clothes. C'mon, let's finish setting up our room."

Our room?

I followed her into the bedroom. Sometimes, I thought, everything just happens so quickly that you hardly have a chance to think. That seemed to be the rule for my life. I felt like someone caught in an ocean current and carried along. I remembered when that had once happened to me and my mother had pulled me out of the water. It hadn't mattered one bit if I had been able to swim or not. The ocean had just been too powerful, and so were all the things happening to me now.

Alanis took her things out of the bags as if she thought someone would stop her if she didn't empty them quickly enough. I saw she didn't have all that much more clothing than I had. At the bottom of one bag was all her makeup, hair sprays and brushes. She showed me the CD player and discs, too.

"I still have Chad's CD player. We'll listen to music every night while we do homework, whenever I do it, that is." She looked around as if my room had been a palace. "This is going to be so great. Even when my father was with us, I didn't have a room this big. C'mon, let's get rid of her things and make more room for ourselves."

She began to fill up the emptied bags, and I started to do the same. When we had stuffed most of Great-aunt Frances's clothes into the bags, Alanis hung up her things and put other things in the drawers she had emptied.

"I have to tell you something," I said as I watched her organizing her things so happily.

"What?"

"There might be a ghost in this house."

She stopped and looked at me.

"What did you say?"

"There might be a ghost. Sometimes at night, I hear crying, and it sounds like someone moving through the walls."

She stared at me. "If you don't want me moving in, just come out and say it directly."

"No, I want you to move in."

"Then don't talk stupid," she said and returned to her clothing.

"My great-aunt forgot to defrost the steaks for the barbeque," I said. "My brother would say she was absentminded."

Alantis paused and shook her head. "She sure

is. Who knows what's in her head? That's why it's good I'm here. We need to take complete charge of everything as soon as possible. It's best for your great-aunt."

"Here she comes," I whispered, hearing her footsteps in the hallway.

She appeared in the doorway with armfuls of clothes, hats and even cowboy boots.

"Okay, wranglers, here we are," she announced and dropped everything on the bed. "Pick out your outfit. I have mine in my closet."

She looked around the room as if we had already done loads of things to change it. Her eyes fell on my pictures, and she went to them quickly.

"This is your mother and father?"

"Yes."

She stood there studying the picture.

"What a good-looking pair they are. Your father looks a lot like Blake," she said softly. She touched the picture as if she'd been touching both their faces. Then she put it down and looked at Ian's picture. "Your brother reminds me of my cousin Harris. He was very nice. I felt sorry for him because he had a lung disease and died in his teens. Emma was never very nice to him. She treated him like a leper. You know what a leper is?" she asked us. Alanis was already sifting through the Western clothing and not really listening.

I shook my head.

"People who had leprosy were called lepers and made to live in leper colonies. Sometimes," she added, her voice starting to drift and her eyes turning vacant, "I felt like I was a leper, especially after my father died.

"Oh," she cried, recuperating from her sadness instantly, "no time for unhappiness, ever. Let's get started. Welcome to our ranch, Alanis. Partner, I mean." She clapped her hands to drive away the heavy moment and hurried out of the room.

"She's bonkers," Alanis said, nodding after her, "but that's good for us. I'm wearing this one," she said, holding up a Western-style blouse. "This skirt isn't really all that bad either," she added. "It goes well with my hat, and these boots actually fit me. Maybe there are some things I can use here. We'll take our time searching this house. I'll bet it's full of all sorts of treasures. Here," she said, tossing some garments at me. "Try these on. Let's get moving. We need to start the barbeque before Granddad comes over to raise hell."

After we both dressed in the Western clothes, we went down and found Great-aunt Frances in her embroidered red-and-brown shirt, a pair of very baggy jeans and a red cowboy hat. She had put on a pair of brown boots that were obviously men's boots a few sizes too big.

"Oh, Alanis, darlin', can you light up the fire for us?" she asked in a Western accent. "Ma hands are busy lassoing our fixin's."

Alanis widened her eyes, looked at me, and hurried out the back.

"Why don't you see about settin' the table, Jordan, honey. The men will be comin' in from the roundup any minute. There's a tablecloth in the top drawer there," she added, nodding at a cabinet.

I took out the tablecloth and some dishes. Alanis came back in; she had already started the barbeque.

"I watched Granddad do this for her sometimes," she explained. "We got steak dinners that way. That meat's going to be tough because it wasn't defrosted, but that's okay. She's happy. Granddad won't be able to say she doesn't want me here."

I set the table and hurried back and forth with silverware, napkins and glasses. Minutes later, Alanis had the steaks cooking. She was right about her granddad. Mr. Marshall came charging around the corner of the building, looking like he was bound to beat her. Fortunately, Great-aunt Frances came out just as he arrived.

"What's going on here, Alanis?" he asked, stopping and putting his hands on his hips. "What do you think you're doing, girl?"

"Why, Tex," Alanis said. "You're just in time for the roundup dinner."

"You are certainly invited, Lester," Great-aunt Frances said.

He looked at her but turned back to Alanis quickly. "Your mother said you took your clothes to sleep over here," he continued.

"Not just sleeping over, Granddad. I'm settling in here." Before he could respond, she added, "Miss Wilkens has invited me, and I'm going to help out with all the chores."

"Now see here, girl—"

"Oh, she can stay, Lester. She's welcome."

Alanis smiled victoriously and her granddad stood speechless, fuming. Then he pointed at her.

"I know you're up to something, Alanis King. You don't volunteer for work. You do one wrong thing and make trouble for Miss Wilkens and I'll have you in the woodshed," he told her.

"Oh, she'll be no trouble, I'm sure, Lester."

He looked at us all again, shook his head and walked off.

"Thank you kindly, Miss Wilkens," Alanis said. "I sure do appreciate your hospitality."

Great-aunt Frances smiled at Alanis's Western accent.

"Why, you're as welcome as warm sunshine, darlin'."

Alanis beamed a smile at me, then leaned over to whisper. "See?" she said. "This will be easy as long as we play in her little shows. We're in control."

It sounded good and she looked very happy, but it made my heart flutter.

Alanis and I heard the phone ringing, but Great-aunt Frances acted as if she didn't hear it.

"Your phone's ringing, Miss Wilkens," Alanis told her.

"Phone? I don't know what that is, darlin'. Phones haven't been invented yet," she said and ignored it.

Alanis raised her eyes toward the sky and handed me the barbeque fork. "Turn over the steaks," she told me and started toward the house.

I had never helped make a barbeque. Everything that had been prepared for us outside had always been done by a caterer Grandmother Emma had hired. A staff of at least a half dozen people had done everything, and we'd just gone out to sit at the tables and eat.

"We're having a guest," Alanis cried from the back door. "He just rode into town, so I thought it would be decent of us to invite him. I hope you don't mind, Miss Wilkens."

"Oh, my," Great-aunt Frances said with her hand over her heart, "a guest. Who is it?"

"Captain Stuart Gavin of the U.S. Cavalry. He'll be here in a little while."

"Oh, then, Jordan, why don't you bring out another setting and another steak," Great-aunt Frances said. "I'll put up another potato."

She hurried into the house.

"How can he come here?" I asked. "Didn't he tell us his father told him he had to stay at home?"

"Stuart's father and mother got called away. His father's brother had a heart attack," Alanis told me. "I told him to put on his cowboy hat. See? If I had asked my granddad if we could invite someone over, he'd say no for sure. Like I told you, we're in charge," she emphasized. "Hey, the steak has to be turned. You're not minding your chores."

She pulled the fork from me and attended to the meat while I went in to get another setting and another steak. Great-aunt Frances was preparing another potato. She couldn't have forgotten what had happened to Stuart Gavin, I thought, or the phone call she had received from Mrs. Browne, yet she hadn't mentioned any of it when she'd heard he was coming.

I truly felt as if I had left the real world, as if I had been placed in a great dollhouse. Alanis was right. We would have no one telling us what we could and couldn't do. If we didn't feel like bathing, we wouldn't. If we didn't brush our teeth, no one would yell. We could eat whatever we wanted, go wherever we wanted, stay up late, maybe even stay home from school. None of it would make any difference. No one would punish us. The very thought of having a party like this on a school night wouldn't have risked coming into my mind back at the March mansion. It made me feel as if I was in charge of myself. And yet, I felt bad about doing these things. We were taking advantage of Great-aunt Frances.

"Isn't this fun?" she asked me. "Nothing chases the darkness out of the corners as quickly as smiles and laughter," she added and hurried out with bottles of soda.

Once again, I felt swept along, and followed her with Stuart's place setting and steak.

When he arrived, he stood there smiling at the scene before him.

"Wow," he declared. "This is a picnic."

To explain his arm in a cast, Alanis told Great-aunt Frances he had been wounded in a battle with Indians. I could see Great-aunt Frances thought that was perfect. Stuart had no idea what was going on, but he was happy to play along. The potatoes, peas and bread were all right, but the steak turned out so tough that it took forever to chew a piece.

"I was just going to make myself a cheese sandwich for dinner," he said.

We saw Bones hanging back, watching us. The aroma of the meat had made him braver, and he came closer and closer until Miss Puss appeared and raised her back.

"Oh, leave him be," Great-aunt Frances told her cat. She scraped up some meat and brought it to Mr. Marshall's dog.

"What's going on here?" Stuart finally asked when

Great-aunt Frances stepped away from the table. "Why are you all wearing the funny clothes and talking like you're in a movie or something?"

"Jordan's great-aunt likes to pretend when she has dinner. It's like being in a play or in a movie. And don't you make fun of it either," Alanis warned him.

Stuart grimaced. "It's weird," he said.

"So, it's weird. You don't think you're weird."

"Don't get so mad. I don't care."

"Besides," Alanis continued, "I've been invited to move in with Jordan. We're going to do lots of things together from now on."

"Move in? You mean, you're going to live here, too?"

"Yes, Stuart, hello. That's what moving in usually means." Alanis sat back smiling. "It's our house now. You can come by when we invite you, if you're good, that is. When are your parents returning?"

"Tomorrow, I guess," he said.

"We might let you stay overnight."

"What? Really?"

"We'll see," Alanis said. "You have to go through a test first," she added.

"What test?"

"You'll see," she said. He looked at me, but I had no idea what she meant.

She leaned over to whisper. "Boys have erogenous zones, too," she said to me and turned back to Stuart. "Jordan and I have a serious science project we've begun. It involves sex. Do you want to be part of it?"

"Sex?"

"Yeah, you ever hear of it?"

"Sure I heard of it. What is the project?"

"You'll see. Maybe. It's a very secret project. We have to be sure you won't go blabbing."

Stuart shrugged. "I can keep a secret as good as anyone else."

"Maybe," Alanis said. "Don't say anything else about it just now," she warned as Great-aunt Frances returned.

"That poor dog. Do you feed him?"

"He eats scraps every day," Alanis said. "Besides, it's Granddad's dog. He should be worrying about it, not me and my mother."

"Oh, we should all look after each other," Great-aunt Frances said. She sat and looked about with a wide smile across her face. "Isn't it just beautiful here? You can feel like a pioneer living here."

Stuart looked around as if he had never been here. "My dad always said this was a nice property, especially because of the big pond."

"Yes," Great-aunt Frances said. "The pond is special. I used to spend a lot of time just lying in the rowboat and letting the breeze blow me here and there while I looked up at the clouds. You can almost feel yourself falling into them."

She looked lost in her memories for a moment. We were having a warm September. The leaves of the trees didn't even have a hint of changing colors. The air was perfumed by the rich aroma of the newly cut grass, and it reminded me of the times I'd followed Ian around Grandmother Emma's mansion while he'd searched for interesting insect specimens. Most of the time it had been as if I'd been alone, but sometimes he had gotten so excited about a find, he'd called out to me and I'd come running. Of course, none of it had been interesting to me, but I'd pretended as best I'd been able. I'd been happy for him. *He'd have so much to explore here,* I thought. *Why couldn't they let him come to live with Great-aunt Frances, too?*

She reached out to touch me, as if to be sure I was really sitting there.

"What a sweet child. Look at all the happiness you've already brought. I'm so happy they sent you to be with me. I've got a family again."

I didn't know what to say. Both Alanis and Stuart just stared.

"I guess we should clean up," Alanis said.

"Oh, no," Great-aunt Frances said, rising and waving her hands frantically. "Not yet. I have a surprise for dessert. I forgot all about it because it was so deep in the back of my freezer."

"What is it?" Stuart asked quickly.

"An ice cream pie in a graham cracker crust."

"Chocolate?"

"And vanilla, too, with whipped cream on top," she declared. "You kids just sit tight. I'll go get it."

"Hey, I might wanna move in here too," Stuart quipped when she walked into the house. "Maybe you can get your great-aunt to adopt me."

He sat there smiling like a contented cat. Alanis stared so hard at him that he looked at me and then back at her.

"What?" he asked.

She looked at me and then leaned toward him.

"You know what a tadpole is, Stuart?"

"Sure, why?"

"You know you have them living in you, don't you?"

"Get outta here."

She smiled at me. "Stuart's got a lot to learn," she said. "And we'll teach him. You want to learn about sex, don't you, Stuart?"

"What's there to learn?"

Alanis laughed so hard I had to smile. He looked at both of us, and then, not knowing what else to do, he laughed himself.

"Here we go, partners!" Great-aunt Frances cried from the rear house entrance. She carried the ice cream pie out to the table. "Let's eat it before it melts."

Despite the tough steak, we did enjoy our Western picnic. When it was over, Alanis and I, with Stuart helping as much as he could, cleaned up. We told Great-aunt Frances to go watch her television show while we washed the dishes and put everything away.

"This is like having servants again," she declared. "Wouldn't Emma be jealous?"

"Who's Emma?" Stuart asked.

"Jordan's grandmother. Don't ask questions. You have one good arm. Take out the garbage," Alanis told him.

When we were finished, she decided we should go up to what was now our room. Stuart followed, looking frightened and confused.

"Close the door," Alanis ordered, and he did so.

He stood there looking around. "I never was in this house. It's pretty big."

Alanis knelt down and reached under the bed.

"Why do you have a book under the bed?" he asked.

"It's our project workbook," she replied. "We're up to erogenous zones."

"What's that?" he asked.

"Places on your body that when touched get you excited."

He opened and closed his mouth, then smirked skeptically. "What is this, another joke? I know you're up to stuff, Alanis."

"What you know couldn't fill a button hole, Stuart. You're either going to participate or go home."

"Participate? What do I have to do?"

"Just shut up for a moment while I read and think about it," she said. "We'll all sit on the floor. Go on. You know, I'm really doing this for you and Jordan. I know all about it. I don't need any sex science projects."

Slowly, he sat across from Alanis and me.

She shook her head. "It's not going to work with clothes on."

"What?"

"You have to take off your pants and underpants at least, Stuart."

"Get outta here. I'm not taking off my clothes in front of you."

She put the book down slowly and turned to me. "Are we doing an important scientific experiment or not?"

I looked at Stuart.

"Jordan?"

I nodded.

"Jordan is not afraid to take off her clothes, Stuart. She knows it's important. Jordan." She nodded at me. "Do it or he won't," she whispered.

I looked at him. Do it?

"Just slip off your skirt for starters," she added. I still hesitated. No boy except for Ian had ever seen me without clothes. "It's important or I wouldn't tell you to do it," she insisted. "You'll ruin things if you don't," she whispered. "He's scared. Go on. Do it."

Reluctantly, I stood up and unbuckled the Western style skirt. Stuart's eyes widened with surprise when I let it fall.

"See? Jordan's not afraid. Pants, Stuart," Alanis said.

He looked at me, and then at her, and shook his head.

"Do you want help? Is that it?" Alanis asked. She put the book down and started toward him.

"No," he said, pushing himself backward with his feet. "I don't need help."

"It's no big deal, Stuart. I've seen it many times," Alanis told him. "You like Jordan, don't you?"

"Yeah, but . . . I don't like you being here, too," he said.

"But I'm the teacher, Stuart. I'm the one who's reading the book. You're not ashamed of what you look like, are you?"

"No. That's not it. Look, I'd better go," he said, standing. "My father might call the house and find out I'm gone. It's late, and it'll be dark soon, and the motor scooter's light isn't too strong."

"I can't believe you're running away, Stuart," Alanis said. "What would your friends say, if you had any friends?"

"I have friends."

"Running away, like some frightened little mouse," she taunted.

"I'm not running away. I'll be back when I can."

"We might not want you back, Stuart. We might

find someone more grown up to participate in our project, someone else who might like to be with us, with Jordan," she emphasized.

He hesitated at the doorway.

"Someone who isn't afraid of sex," she added.

His cheeks reddened.

"I told you. I'm not afraid."

She smiled at me, then shook her head at him.

"I'm not."

"All right," Alanis said. "You don't have to be totally naked. Just take off your pants and come sit across from us again."

He considered, looked at me, and then unbuckled his pants, lowered them, kicked off his shoes, and stepped out of his pants.

Alanis smiled. "Now," she said, "we'll tell you about tadpoles."

12

Erroneous Zones

"**Y**ou see this?" Alanis asked Stuart, pointing to the picture of sperm. "Tadpoles."

He squinted, looked at me, and then at the picture again.

"They actually swim inside a girl," Alanis continued. "Don't laugh at me, Stuart," she said when he started to smile. "I'm reading right from the book."

He looked at it again. She glanced at me, smiled and pulled the book out of his hands.

"They come jumping out when a boy gets excited," she continued. "That's his erogenous zone. Now you get it? How many times you get excited, Stuart? Any boy I let be with me always gets excited. I bet you've gotten yourself excited plenty of times, haven't you, Stuart? You could show us how. It would be like a laboratory demonstration Mr. Beamer does in science class. How about it?"

Stuart's face reddened so brightly that I thought he might go up in flames. He pressed his lips together, then suddenly stood up and reached for his pants.

"What's the matter now, Stuart?"

"I gotta go home," he muttered and struggled with his one good arm to put on his pants.

"What are you going to do when you get home, Stuart? Won't it be more fun to do it here with us?" Alanis asked him, smiling at me.

He ignored her and struggled to dress quickly.

"You want us to help? Jordan, go help Stuart put on his pants."

"No," he said. "I can do it."

He twisted and turned and struggled until he got his pants on.

"Don't you want at least to tell us anything about your erogenous zone? We need information for our project, Stuart," Alanis said as he turned to the door. "We don't know about boys, only girls. That's why we asked you to be part of the experiment. We also thought you were mature."

"I am mature."

"Then come back. It's not going to hurt."

"I know," he said. "I gotta go. Thanks for inviting me to dinner," he said. His eyes averted, he rushed out.

"C'mon, Stuart, don't go. Everything you tell us will be kept secret," she called after him.

We heard his footsteps as he pounded down the stairs.

Alanis laughed. "See how easy it is to tease boys. We're going to have lots of fun together now, Jordan. Lots. For now, we don't need him. We've got a lot to talk about ourselves."

She started to look at my book again, then stopped when we heard Great-aunt Frances calling to us as she came up the stairway and down the hallway. Alanis quickly shoved my book under the bed again.

"Put on your skirt. Quick," she urged, and I went off to the side and did it just in time.

"Hi, girls. I saw Stuart leave quickly. Is everything all right?" Great-aunt Frances asked from the doorway. Miss Puss was at her feet, rubbing herself against her ankles.

"He promised his father he would be home early and he just realized how late it was," Alanis told her. She could spin lies as easily as a spider spun a web, I thought, and make them sound perfectly true. Was that a good thing or bad?

"Well, that's a good boy then," Great-aunt Frances said. "I'm going to change and go to bed early tonight myself. I like being around you young girls and boys, but I'm not used to all the excitement. You both did a wonderful job helping with dinner and cleaning up for me. The kitchen looks like no one's been in it. Thank you," she said. "Can I get you anything, Alanis?"

"No, I'm fine, Miss Wilkens. Thank you."

"Well, you two go on with your schoolwork. Just remember to go to bed early. Early to bed and early to rise makes a man healthy, wealthy, and wise. Women, too, of course. Emma can attest to that. Nothing displeased her as much as my sleeping late or being late for an appointment. She said it was a sign of poor breeding. She made it sound like we were raised to be racehorses or show dogs. She would get so angry at me if I told her that, but I'll tell you a secret," she said, leaning in and whispering. "I knew she was right.

I just didn't want her to know I knew." She smiled and stepped back. "Enjoy your first night together, girls. I so wish I had a girlfriend to stay with me when I was your age, Jordan. I so wish I had a sister who cared," she added and then quickly snapped out of her sad moment. "Sweet dreams."

She shuffled off.

But a moment later, she was back, poking her head in the door. "Oh, Jordan, did I tell you Mr. Pond called for my sister to see how you were getting along. She wanted to be sure you didn't need any medical attention."

"Why would she?" Alanis asked before I could respond.

"That's my sister. Always thinking and worrying. I told him everything is fine."

She turned and started away again.

"Medical attention? Why would your grandmother think of that?"

"She's that way," I said. I didn't want to get into how she had reacted to discovering how physically mature I was already. "She has to have everything perfect."

"Oh, one more thing," Great-aunt Frances said, returning to the door again, "I asked Lester to bring us more eggs. They should be there before you go down to breakfast."

She shuffled off once more.

"This is no good," Alanis said. "She'll keep poking her head in all night. C'mon," she decided, reaching under the bed for the book and then standing.

"Where?"

"To the basement, our private and special club-house. Where else?"

She started out.

"Shouldn't we start on our homework?" I asked, looking back at the books on my desk.

"We have plenty of time. Stop worrying," she said. "C'mon."

She started down the hall toward the stairway. I looked at my books again. It was as if I could hear them calling to me in Mrs. Morgan's voice.

"Jordan?" I heard Alanis say in a loud whisper, and then I followed her quickly.

"Why do we have to go to the basement to read my book?"

"We have to be careful about your great-aunt. She would never understand what we're doing if she saw us," Alanis said. "She probably forgot what sex is or never knew. The way she is, it might make her hysterical or something and then my granddad might find out and there would be hell to pay."

She opened the basement door and flipped the light switch.

"Quiet," she warned as we started down the stairs. When we reached the second door, she paused. I was surprised, because she stood there with her hand on the knob, not moving. Was she changing her mind?

"What's wrong?" I asked.

"Be quiet," she said and listened.

Then I heard it, a soft laugh and the muffled voice of a man.

"Who's in there?" I whispered.

Alanis didn't answer. She stood there holding the

knob and looking frozen. We heard another laugh and then a man's laugh.

"Go back up quietly and turn off the light," she said. "I want it dark before I open this door. Go on," she urged when I didn't move fast enough.

I went up, switched it off, then stood there for a moment. It was so dark. I opened the basement door a little, and that gave me enough light to go down the stairs again. Alanis looked back, thought a moment, then opened the second door very slowly and very slightly. We could just see the sofa. We heard the laughter, and a moment later, we saw Mae Betty dressed only in her panties. She pulled on a man's hand and he came into view. They kissed. It was a long, hard kiss. He ran his lips down over her cheek to her neck and over her naked breasts. She threw her head back, moaned and seemed to sink in his arms.

He scooped her up and placed her on the sofa. Then he stood back and began to unbuckle his belt, laughing as he did so. We could hear her squealing in anticipation.

Alanis closed the door softly and turned away. She didn't say anything. She just started up the basement stairs with her head down. I followed. We stepped out in the hallway and I closed the door behind us. She looked at me, and I saw that the hardness and confidence were all gone. Her eyes were glassy with tears. She sniffed and pressed her lips together. I didn't know what to say. I followed her in silence as we returned to the stairway and back to my room. Once there, she shoved my book under the bed. When she stood up, she slumped and stared at the floor for a moment.

"Who's that down there with your mother?" I asked.

"I'm going to go put some of my things in the bathroom," she said instead of answering me. "You better get started on your homework."

She took her things and left. I went to my desk and opened my books. I started to read the assignments, but I kept one eye and ear tuned to the doorway, waiting for her return. When she finally did, she looked like she had been crying.

"I hope you don't need help with any of that," she said. "I was never a good student."

She went to the bed.

"Which side of the bed you want?" she asked me.

"I don't care."

"I'll sleep on the right," she said and began to undress. She put on a dark gray nightshirt, then crawled under the blanket, turning her back to me. "Don't worry about keeping me up," she said. "Just finish what you have to finish. The light don't bother me. Sometimes, I got to go to sleep while my granddad's still watching television."

Even though she said that, I was uncomfortable working with her in bed trying to sleep. I knew I wasn't doing as well on my homework as I had the night before, because I rushed through it. Afterward, I prepared for bed and put on my pajamas. I thought Alanis was already asleep by the time I crawled under the blanket and turned off the light, but she started to talk as if she and I had been talking all the time.

"I knew that was my mother even before I opened the door. It didn't surprise me seeing her down there. I told her about the basement. I shoulda known she'd go and use it herself. She can't bring a man to my grand-dad's house. She'd bring one into the barn sooner than that."

"Who was he?" I asked again.

"Anybody," she said. "She thinks she's getting back at my father by being a tramp herself, but she ain't. He's long gone and she's outta his mind for sure. I don't know who started it first. Maybe she did. Maybe that got him started. I don't know."

"Started what?"

"Doing it with other men and women even though they was married."

"Your father womanized," I said. The word came back to me as if Ian had been there whispering in my ear.

"Yeah, he womanized. You know about that, do you?"

"My mother found out my father did it," I said. "That's why they had the fight and my mother wanted to get a divorce."

She turned. "Oh, yeah? What happened then?"

"My grandmother came to see us. We were up in the cabin in the Poconos and she talked my mother into giving my father another chance. We went home with her, and my father went up there to talk."

"To lie to each other some more is all," Alanis said bitterly. "So, they got back together, did they?"

"They were supposed to," I said. "But that's when they got into the automobile accident. Ian said it was Grandmother Emma's fault, because she called and told them about Ian and the Sister Project. They came rushing home in a storm and crashed."

Alanis was silent so long that I thought she might have fallen asleep.

"No matter who you are or how much money you have, bad things still happen," she said. "If all this bad stuff happened to a girl like you, what chance do I got?"

"Maybe your father will come back for you some-day," I said. I wanted her to have hope. She sounded so terribly sad.

"It's no different than your mother being in a coma. He might as well be in one, too. I ain't holding my breath, and I don't know if I would go off with him anyway. He don't want a girl my age on his tail.

"I'll tell you this," she said after a moment, "as weird as it sounds, your great-aunt even though she's bonkers is nicer than my family. I hope she lets me stay here all year."

"She will," I said.

"Yeah, but that chauffeur might not like it and he might tell your grandmother and they'll make me leave."

"I'll tell them you have to stay," I said.

"You would?"

"No lies, no secrets," I said, and even in the dark, I could see her smile.

"Okay," she said. "I'll tell you a big secret, and it will be just between us. My best friends don't know it, but you're my best, best friend."

I held my breath in anticipation. What possible secret could she have? Had she done something ter-rible? Did I want to know? My ears cringed in antici-pation. If it was something horrible, I wouldn't be able to sleep next to her.

"You ready?"

"Yes," I said weakly.

"I never did it with any boy," she said. "I come close, but never did yet."

"Did what?"

"Did what? You kidding? What have we been talking about? Took some tadpoles into me," she added and laughed. "I swear, you are just a sweet child after all."

She got serious quickly.

"Don't tell anyone what we saw in the basement."

"I wouldn't."

"It's 'cause of her my granddad is so hard on me. He thinks that's the way to keep me from being her. I'll never be her," she vowed.

We were both quiet. I didn't know whom I should feel sorry for more, myself or her. Finally, I decided that as bad as everything was for me, I should feel sorrier for her. My mother was in a coma, but I would never say I didn't want to be just like her. I always wanted to be just like her.

Without anyone to love and want to be like, you were really alone, I thought.

Sleep started to seep into my body from every direction. I welcomed it as I would a warm bath on a cold day. I sank quickly into my own safe darkness, just barely hearing Alanis whisper, "Good night."

Both of us forgot to set my alarm clock for the morning, but Great-aunt Frances didn't forget.

"Girls, girls, girls," she cried at the foot of the bed. "Rise and shine."

Alanis groaned and sat up slowly. "I guess I need Granddad every school morning after all," she said and slipped out of bed. She stood there for a moment looking at me. "Listen," she said, "in the middle of the night, I thought I heard what you said you heard."

"What?"

"Sobbing. It sounded like it was coming from above us. I tried to listen, but I fell asleep. Don't go telling me it's a ghost," she added quickly.

"Well, what is it?"

"I don't know. Maybe you just put the idea in my head. Go on to the bathroom first. I can wait," she said.

I did, but when I came out, she was returning from down the hall.

"My mother never told me what was up here," she said. "There's a whole other bedroom and bath just down the hall."

"That's Grandmother Emma's room."

"So? She ain't here. She's never here, and you said she was in a hospital anyway."

"Great-aunt Frances doesn't want anyone to use it."

"That's stupid. I already did anyway," she said and marched into the bedroom to finish dressing. "We just won't tell her. Don't worry. I'll keep it clean," she said as she dressed. "Here, put this on," she told me and tossed me her hat.

"But this is yours."

"Just take it. Don't worry about it. I think you'll look cute in it," she said.

I put it on slowly and looked at myself in the mirror.

"See?" she said. "I was right."

I did like how it looked on me.

"I'm not wearing it in school," I warned.

She laughed. "That's okay. Just don't lose it.

C'mon. Let's get some breakfast. I'm hungry this morning."

Afterward, when we stepped onto the bus, we found Stuart sitting in front next to another boy. He glanced quickly at us and looked away.

"Hi, Stuart," Alanis said anyway. "Did you get excited this morning? Rile up your tadpoles?"

He wouldn't answer or look at us. Alanis laughed, and the bus driver told us to get seated. As we continued, Stuart stole a glance at me, and I felt sorry for him. When we arrived at school, he got off the bus quickly and disappeared in the crowd of other students getting off other buses.

"Chances are Stuart will not join us for lunch today," Alanis said.

I took off her hat as we entered the building. She didn't want it back. She told me to hold on to it until lunch.

"They don't mind you wearing a hat in the cafeteria," she said. "I'd like other boys to think about you, and you look cute in it, cuter than I do," she said.

Mrs. Morgan collected our homework this time as soon as we started the school day. We were given another assignment to read in history and made to write out answers to questions while she reviewed our work. When she passed our papers back, I saw she had given me a very low mark.

"Did someone help you with your homework the first night?" she asked. "Is that why it was so much better than this?"

"No, Mrs. Morgan. I did it all myself both times."

"Humph," she said and moved on. I could see from the smiles on the faces of some of the other girls in the class that they were happy I hadn't done well. None of them had said anything nice to me yet even after they had read my autobiography. Meanness seemed to be in the air we all breathed.

Alanis was right about Stuart. He sat with some of his friends across the cafeteria. When Nikki and Raspberry asked about him, Alanis told them he had snuck over to my great-aunt's house for dinner. She then told them she had moved in to live with me. They didn't believe her until I told them it was true.

"I was wondering why you gave her your hat," Nikki said. "I thought you were born with it on and it was attached to your skull."

"I didn't have to pay her to move in," Alanis snapped at her. "I don't have to buy friends. She asked me to, and so did her great-aunt, but she looks pretty good in it, doesn't she?"

Nikki nodded reluctantly.

"So why isn't Stuart sitting with us?" Raspberry pursued.

Alanis looked at me, smiled, then told them about my book and what she had tried to do. They sat glued to her every word, only she made it sound as if Stuart wanted to be with her and not with me.

"As you know, I wouldn't waste my time with a boy that inexperienced," she told them.

"I'd like to see that book," Raspberry said.

"Soon."

"Why don't we all meet in the basement tonight?"

"We can't. We can't ever go back to the basement," Alanis told them.

"Why not?"

I looked at her, wondering what she would say.

"Her great-aunt got suspicious and found one of the alcopops we missed. She said she wouldn't tell anybody if we promised never to have a secret party down there again."

"Oh. That's too bad," Nikki said.

"Sucks," Raspberry added.

"We'll figure out another place soon. Don't worry," Alanis told them.

I didn't say anything, but all the while I kept my gaze on the table and my food. *Alanis swims in a pool of lies,* I thought. *She even has to lie to her friends.* I didn't know how to express it then, but in my heart of hearts, I knew she lied even to herself.

When we arrived home that afternoon, Great-aunt Frances invited us to watch the soap opera she had described to me my first day. I wanted to get to another letter from Ian and then right to my homework so I could do better than I had. Alanis decided to watch television. We both saw that Great-aunt Frances hadn't cleaned up after lunch. Jars were still open, and dishes were still on the table. Alanis said she would take care of it.

Taking advantage of the opportunity for privacy, I hurried up to Grandmother Emma's room and took out Ian's bag of letters. Then I sat on the floor with my back to the bed and opened the next one.

Dear Jordan,

As you know, I don't form friendships easily. I find friends to be a distraction and most of the time, a waste of my time, but I have formed a friendship with another boy here because he needs me. They have been telling him that he is eating away at himself, harming himself, cutting himself, even burning himself. He has marks all over his legs and his arms.

I studied them carefully and I had to inform him that he is being attacked daily by Cimex lectularius, *more well known as bedbugs. I explained how they don't fly but they can move over floors, walls and ceilings rapidly. They lay whitish eggs about the size of a dust particle so they can't be seen without a microscope. He didn't realize who they were because as they grow, they shed their skin five times. He was shocked to learn that they are disguised as the janitors and cleaning ladies here. While he is asleep, they feed on him. I explained how their bites are impossible to feel.*

Yesterday, he refused to come out of his room and he wouldn't let any of the cleaning personnel into it. They forced him out and then they took him upstairs and gave him some medication, I'm sure. I haven't seen him for two days, but I realized if they didn't have him to feed upon, they might start on me, so I stuffed my blanket and some paper under the door and blocked every possible opening. It might not work.

I told Dr. Walker about it and he promised he would keep them away from me. But this morning I found a bite on my arm. I'll try to write to you faster. I don't know how much longer I'll be able to before they take me upstairs, too. If my letters stop coming, you will know it's happened.

*And you will know it's our Grandmother's
fault.*

                                                                    Ian

I quickly opened the next letter.

Dear Jordan,
   I have made an incredible breakthrough.
   *I have found a way to speak to our mother. I
have been working on developing this skill for
a long time, even before I was brought here,
but ironically it is because I was brought here
and left alone so much that I have been able
to complete my effort to achieve what is called
telepathy. I know it's a big word for you and you
will be scared that you won't understand, but I'll
make it simple. It means talking with only your
brain. You think and the other person hears it.
It's like sending a radio signal. You know you
can hear the radio but you can't see the signal.*
   *To do this you have to be able to concen-
trate so hard your brain is sending out the
words through the air. Because Mother is in a
coma, she can't talk and this is the only way
she can be heard and only someone like me
who has developed the ability to do telepathy
can hear her.*
   *Don't worry. I'll tell you what she says and
what she wants you to know and to do, okay?*
   *After I speak with her and tell her everything,
I'll listen to what she has to say and I'll write it
down and send it to you.*

                                                                    Ian

I sat there trembling all over. It was possible that in some or all of the letters that remained, my mother would be speaking to me. I hoped she would tell me what I should do and when we would all be together again. Perhaps everything I dreamed of happening would soon happen and all because Ian had learned how to speak with her. My brother was wonderful.

"Hey," I heard Alanis call. I moved quickly to hide my letters and just scurried to the door when she appeared. "What are you doing in here? I thought this room was out of bounds for us."

I didn't know what to say. Lying didn't come as easily to me as it did to her.

"You hid those letters from your brother in here, didn't you?" she asked, smiling. "It's okay," she said quickly. "I don't mind, but you have to promise you'll tell me about them or show them to me one day, okay?"

I nodded.

She looked about the room and shook her head. "What a waste. A good part of this house is a waste." She smiled. "I couldn't watch that show with your grandmother too much longer. She talks to the characters as if she expects them to hear her, as if she's right in the same room. 'No, don't tell him that. No, don't go in there,' she cries and then she moans and gasps. I never saw anyone watch television like that. I guess she likes all the make-believe and that's why she wants to wear those funny costumes for dinner and pretend this and that." Her face turned hard, mean. "It's all just a bunch of lies, you know, the soap operas, the pretend dinners, lies. See? Everyone lies."

"No, it's not the same for her. It's different," I said.

"Why? How's it any different? It's not the truth, not real."

I struggled for an answer. The effort brought tears to my eyes.

"Forget about it," she said. "I don't care."

"It's not the same as lying," I insisted.

"Okay, okay."

"It's not the same because . . . because she isn't hurting anyone. It's not mean."

Alanis shrugged. "Maybe, but this house is full of lies," she said. "Just like mine."

"Why do you say that?"

She looked around Grandmother Emma's room. "This room, for example. It's being kept the best of any room for your grandmother, but she doesn't come here. She probably forgot what it looks like. Telling you it's reserved for her is a lie. It's pretending again, and that does hurt because we could really use this room!" she added. "So remember, don't tell her I'm using the bathroom. Besides, Jordan, something isn't a lie if you don't mention it, right? You're not lying to her unless she asks you if I'm using it. She doesn't do much, if any, cleaning, so she won't find out anyway.

"C'mon. Let's go read our book," she said and started out.

I looked back at the closet where I had hidden Ian's letters and followed, regretting that I hadn't been able to get to the next one.

"What's this door?" she asked and tried to open it. "It's locked."

"I know."

"Well, what is it?" She tugged on the handle, then knelt down to peek through the keyhole. "I can't see anything."

"Great-aunt Frances doesn't want anyone going in there, I guess," I replied, stating the obvious.

"Why not?" She stepped back and thought as she looked over the hallway and the ceiling. "You know what I think this is?"

I shook my head.

"I think it's the way to get to the attic."

"Then maybe it's just not safe to go up there and that's why it's locked," I said.

"Maybe." She pondered a moment, then shrugged. "Let's go read. We're going to China tonight."

"China? What do you mean?"

"Your great-aunt told me she's sending my grand-dad for Chinese food. We're going to Hong Kong or something. She has the costumes already laid out for us on her bed. I don't know if we're watching television or the television is watching us," she added and laughed.

While I started on my homework, this time determined to do well, Alanis returned to the book and sprawled on our bed to read.

"Don't you have any homework?" I asked her.

She didn't answer. She was so absorbed in what she was reading that I might as well not have been there. She didn't even hear Great-aunt Frances come to our room with the dresses in her arms. She was already wearing hers, a Chinese silk dress with an embroidered bird across the bodice. As with other costumes she wore, she was unable to pull up the zipper to the top, and the dress hung on her shoulders.

The moment Alanis saw her, she closed the book.

She didn't have to worry, because Great-aunt Frances obviously thought it was some schoolbook.

"I don't mean to interrupt you kids doing your schoolwork, but I thought you'd like to choose from these three," she said and put the dresses on the foot of the bed. Then she pressed her hands together, bowed, and shuffled in her slippers out of our bedroom.

Alanis turned to me and broke into laughter.

We looked at the dresses. Alanis decided to wear the long dress with a red cherry blossom pattern and thought I'd look better in the green, sleeveless minidress with the dragon and phoenix pattern. On me, it was well below the knees, and I needed only a few safety pins to keep it on.

We laughed at each other in the mirror.

"I don't look so bad, you know. I can tell you this," she said. "This is a lot more fun than eating at my house."

When her granddad arrived with the take-out Chinese food, however, he looked very angry.

"You don't belong here, Alanis," he told her. "I want you to come home."

"I don't have a home," she replied. "Besides, I'm in China now. It takes a long time to get home."

She hurried away to set the table and pretend with Great-aunt Frances.

Her granddad looked at me with heavy eyes. "Watch yourself," he warned and left.

I wished I could tell him it would all be fine, that Alanis was happier here and we were becoming good friends. We wouldn't get into any more trouble, and maybe she would even do better at school. Great-aunt

Frances certainly enjoyed her company. Now that Alanis had decided pretending was really fun, she was into it almost as much as Great-aunt Frances. She even struggled with chopsticks and refused to use the fork.

Afterward, we both pitched in and cleaned up the dishes, silverware and the kitchen itself even better than we had previously.

"You are two very nice young ladies," Great-aunt Frances told us. "You've already brought me more happiness than I had before you came."

"Maybe you can tell my granddad so he doesn't nag me to come home so much."

"Oh, I will," Great-aunt Frances promised.

Alanis gave me one of her satisfied expressions.

"I'm going to watch some television with your aunt," she said.

"Don't you want to do your homework?"

"I can do it all in a study hall tomorrow. Don't worry about it," she told me.

I was nervous about her watching television with Great-aunt Frances, however. Earlier, she had complained about how Great-aunt Frances talked to the television set and made it hard for her to watch television with her. Why did she want to do it again? Why wouldn't she want to come up to read the book, anyway? She saw my concern.

"Stop being a worry wart," she emphasized.

Not wanting to waste any more of my own time, I hurried upstairs and got into my homework again. I didn't want to do another poor job and have Mrs. Morgan scowl at me and give me a poor grade. If I worked hard, I thought, maybe I would have time to read another of Ian's letters before I went to sleep. As long as Alanis remained with Great-aunt Frances watching television, I could return to Grandmother Emma's bedroom and take them out of the closet.

However, the schoolwork took longer than I expected again, and I was so tired that I lowered my chin to my hands, propped up on my elbows. I nearly fell asleep at my desk. I opened my eyes when I heard Alanis enter the bedroom. She stood there smiling at me.

"Guess what?"

"What?" I asked, rubbing my eyes and sitting up.

She held up a key.

"What's that?"

"I asked your great-aunt a lot of questions about the house and she gave away where the old keys to things were kept. They were in a bottom drawer in the food pantry."

"So what's that key for?"

"I was right about that locked door. It does open to the stairway that goes up to the attic, and this is the key to that door," she said, adding, "which may lead us to our new clubhouse."

"How do you know that's the key?"

"I tried it and the door unlocked. I came to get you before I went up. C'mon."

I started to shake my head.

"What?" she demanded. She frowned and put her hands on her hips. "You're not going to start on that ghost thing again, are you? Well?"

"No, but—"

"But nothing. I'm going up there to check it out. You coming or not?"

It was just like that telepathy thing Ian had written about in his letter.

I could hear his voice.

"No," he was saying. "Don't open that door."

13

A Real Mystery Story

Alanis couldn't understand my reluctance.

"C'mon," she pleaded. "Your great-aunt will be downstairs for a long time yet. Who knows what we'll find? Maybe all that money that's hidden here is hidden up there. Whatever it looks like up there, we might be able to fix it up for ourselves to use instead of the basement. And we won't tell anyone else about it, even Nikki or Raspberry, until we both decide to tell, okay? It will just be our secret place, a place for just you and me."

I didn't move, and she grimaced, her hands on her hips.

"Don't you want to have fun? I'm living here with you to have more fun and I thought you'd like that. Well?" she asked, the ire in her eyes reminding me of her mother's eyes.

"Okay," I said, closing my books. "But we better not stay up there long. And what if it's dark? And—"

"And, and, and . . . you sound like some old lady. Darkness, ghosts," she said, laughing at me. "I checked. The switch worked and the lights go on up there. The ghosts will hide. C'mon," she urged and started down the hallway, still laughing to herself.

I thought if anything was funny, it was that we were still wearing the Chinese dresses. As we passed Grandmother Emma's room, I looked longingly through the doorway at the closet. In my mind Ian was standing inside it, calling to me, waiting for me to open the closet door.

She opened the attic door and turned to me.

"See? This is the key."

She flipped the light switch. I was surprised at how brightly the light lit the stairway and everything above. The stairway wasn't just an ordinary wooden step stairway for an attic either. It had dark gray carpeting, and the carpeting looked better than the carpeting on the main stairway in the house. There were ten steps to the top with no banister. Alanis glanced at me, excitement lighting her eyes, then started up. I followed slowly, half-listening for Great-aunt Frances below. Our stealing the key and sneaking up here would be sure to upset her. I was set to turn around and rush out the moment I heard anything resembling her footsteps on the stairs. Alanis paused at the top.

"Wow," she said. "You're not going to believe this. What you dragging your feet for? Get your booty up here."

She turned and walked into the attic. I hurriedly followed now that she had whetted my curiosity. She was right. It was surprising. The attic was a like a separate apartment within the house. There was a bedroom and an area with a small kitchen and another area with a sofa, table and chair, with a small television set on a table across from the sofa. To the right there was another door. She opened it and turned to me.

"It's a bathroom with a tub," she said. "Just about as big as the closet we're sharing now."

I stepped up beside her and looked in at the sink, tub and toilet. It was all clean, with no rust, but there were no mirrors. The floor was a dull cream linoleum.

The walls of the attic were papered in a light blue, but there were no pictures or shelves. Alanis moved slowly, looking at the furnishings until she reached the queen-size bed, which had a dark cherry headboard. It looked freshly made with a dark blue comforter and fluffy big pillows. It was made even more carefully than the bed in what was supposedly Grandmother Emma's room. She paused, then held up her hand, as if she wanted me to remain still and quiet.

Then she turned slowly.

"Come here. Look at this," she said.

I stepped up beside her and looked.

"What is it?"

"What is it? Don't you know nothing? That's a baby's bassinet. It's what they call a Baby Moses basket. My granddad still has the one my mother slept in right after she was born. She was born in a house, not a hospital. Maybe that's why my grandma died. If she was in a hospital . . ."

"Your grandmother died when your mother was born?"

"Never mind," she said, waving her hand as if she'd been talking to herself aloud. "Who lived up here? Whose baby slept in that? Why is all this locked away?

Huh?" she asked me as she looked around. Then she paused and looked at me, waiting for an answer, suspicious of my silence.

"I don't know. How would I know?"

"I just thought she might have said something to you about it."

"No, she didn't."

She went to the small television set on a table across from the sofa and turned it on. The screen lit up with a picture, and a smile exploded across her face. "This is better than the basement, way better. It has a kitchen and a bathroom, too. This really is a private apartment!"

She shut off the television set and went over to the sink to turn on the faucet. Dirty brown water came out but started to clear as she ran it. We heard the sound of what seemed like a bang in a pipe, so she turned it off quickly. We were both quiet, listening.

"Don't worry. I doubt she heard anything. She plays that television too loud," Alanis said and continued to explore the attic, looking in the dresser drawers. She held up baby clothes. "No question that there was a baby up here once. It's all blue and green and yellow. Bet it was a boy. Why keep it up here?"

"Maybe it was the maid's quarters," I suggested. "And she had a baby."

"How can you be a maid and have a baby in the house? Who would watch it while you worked, and where was the daddy?"

"I don't know. Maybe someone lived up here before my grandparents bought the farm."

That gave her pause.

"Yeah, maybe. I'd ask my granddad. He's been here

forever and would surely know, only then he would know we got the key, unlocked the door and snuck up here. I better not say anything to him."

"I don't know why it's important we find out anyway."

"Hmm," she said. "You know what we'll do?" she said, smiling. "We'll pretend this is our own private home. Yeah, that's what we'll do. We'll even bring food up here and have our own parties again."

"But Great-aunt Frances might not like it," I said. "The door was locked and she never told me about it."

"Well, we just gotta be careful so she don't find out, right? Right?" she punched at me.

"Right," I said.

"We'll just use it on weekend nights. We'll come up after she goes to sleep. For now, I don't want to even tell Nikki or Raspberry about this, so don't mention it in school. They can be big gossips."

She continued to search the dresser drawers. When she opened and sifted through the clothing in the bottom one, she paused and took out a piece of small notebook paper. She read what was on it.

"What is that?" I asked.

"Woman's name and telephone number. Toby DeMarco, 555-4343. I wonder if this was the woman who lived up here."

"Why would she have her own number in a drawer?"

"Maybe she left it after she left the house. Just in case she forgot something or something. I don't know all the answers. You know what we'll do? We'll just mention her name to your great-aunt and see if she says anything. If she wonders how we know the name, we'll say we heard someone say she lived here once."

Once again, I shook my head at how quickly Alanis could come up with stories and lies. It was as if they were all lying just under the surface, waiting anxiously for a chance to pop up.

She continued to explore the attic. I looked closer at the bassinet. It seemed very new, maybe even never used.

"Maybe this was all fixed up for someone and she never lived in it," I suggested.

"Yeah. That could be. You know what I noticed about this attic?" Alanis said, settling on the small settee.

"What?"

"It's clean. Look at the coffee table," she said and ran her hand over it. "Not much dust. Nothing like some of the furniture in the house."

"Maybe your mother cleaned it."

"My mother? No way. She don't do one thing more than she has to," Alanis said. Then she smiled. "Neither do I."

We heard what sounded like a door open and close below.

"Let's get down," she said, rising quickly. "But remember. This is our new secret."

She hurried ahead. We descended the stairs as quietly as we could. At the bottom, she checked the hallway first, and then we slipped out. She locked the door again.

"I'm going to put this key back, too. Just in case," she said. "I'll go down and spend some more time with her so she don't get suspicious."

"Why should she?"

"I don't know. I wanna watch some more television anyway. If she's asleep, I'll turn on something I like." She patted the door with her palm. "Our place," she said. "What should we call it?"

I shrugged. "I don't know."

"How about Hideaway Hotel? Every time we go there, it will be like checking into a hotel someplace."

"Okay," I said. Why did we have to call it anything or pretend anything? She was getting to be like Great-aunt Frances, pretending and creating her own little world, I thought.

"Damn, girl. Stop scowling. We're gonna have fun whether you like it or not," she said as she turned and headed for the stairway. I watched her go, and then, instead of returning to my room, I returned to Grand-mother Emma's and Ian's letters. I really felt I needed to be close to him at this moment, even if he was writing things that made little or no sense to me.

I took out the bag and plucked the next one, slipping it out of the envelope.

Dear Jordan,

Today I spoke to Mother using telepathy. I could hear the joy in her voice when she realized it was I. She thought we had deserted her. I explained what I could, but I don't know where you are or what you're doing since I have had no letters back from you and Grandmother Emma's attorney won't tell me anything. Mother immediately said your not writing back to me was probably Grandmother Emma's doing and then I told her about Grandmother Emma being in the hospital. I told her everything Grandmother Emma's lawyer would tell me.

She felt sorry for you because you were alone in that big house. She told me to tell you not to worry, that she would get better someday soon and she would come for you. She asked that you just be patient.

Of course, I told her where I was and what was happening around me. Guess what? She said she already knew. She said Father had come to see her and told her everything. She said he sat there for an hour in his wheelchair and he cried and apologized.

I told her to be careful about believing anything he says.

She was sorry that I was so skeptical. That means doubting.

She asked me to be patient, too, but I don't think I have much more time. I'll explain why in my next letter.

Ian

I wondered when our father had been there with our mother. Why hadn't he ever told me or taken me? Unless he'd gone there after I'd left the house, but then why hadn't he told Mother where I was? I'd have to get Great-aunt Frances to send out my letter as soon as I finished reading all of Ian's. He would know the answers.

I immediately took out the next letter. My fingers fumbled with the paper because I was so nervous, not only because of what I was reading but because of Alanis discovering me.

Dear Jordan,

 It began today.

 I am slowly being drawn into a cocoon. I am not sure yet what sort of an insect is doing this to me, but it's happening ever so gradually.

 Whatever it is, it is weaving itself around me from my feet up and doing a good, tight job of it. Today, I was unable to get out of my room. When I stood up, I fell over. I was lying on the floor for some time before I was discovered.

 Dr. Walker came immediately. I told him what was happening and he tried to convince me it wasn't true. I listened and listened and smiled and nodded and then he left. They had to bring my food to me.

 I can still sit up well enough to write to you.

 But don't worry. I will think of some way to get out.

 I didn't tell Mother about it. Why worry her any more than she is worried about both of us? If you get to see her, don't say a word about me.

Ian

How horrible for him, I thought. Father should help him. I tore open the next envelope. The next letter was very short.

Dear Jordan,

 It's around my knees.

Ian

I heard footsteps on the stairway, stuffed the bag of letters back into the closet, and hurried out just as

Alanis turned toward our room. She didn't hear me hurrying behind her, but when she saw I wasn't in the room, she turned.

"Hey. Reading those letters again?"

"Yes," I said. I didn't want to lie about it. It might only make her more curious. She wasn't that interested anyway. I was sure she thought it would be boring.

"I have some interesting news for you."

"What?"

"I did just what I said. I mentioned Toby DeMarco and your great-aunt became very disturbed. She wanted to know exactly where I had heard about her and I said I couldn't remember. I asked her who she was and she shook her head and said she forgot. Isn't that silly? First, she gets agitated at the mention of her name and then she says she doesn't know who I'm talking about. We got to find out ourselves somehow."

"How?"

"I don't know. We'll call," she said and showed me she still had the slip of paper with Toby DeMarco's name and number.

"What will we say?"

"I don't know. Jeez. Give me time to think, will you?"

"Why do we have to know anyway?"

"Ain't you curious?"

"No."

"Yes, you are." She stared at me a moment. "You look upset, flushed. What did your brother tell you in his letters? Did he tell you something bad or something sexy?"

"No," I said quickly.

She pressed her lips together and shook her head.

"Your face might as well be made of glass," she said. "You can't hide much." An idea occurred to her. "He didn't mention that attic by any chance?"

"No. He didn't say anything about this house or anyone in it. I swear," I said. "He never knew much about Great-aunt Frances either and he was never here, and he doesn't know I'm here. No one has told him about me, and my letters were never sent to him."

"Maybe." She smiled. "Anyway, we sure got ourselves one sweet hangout, Hideaway Hotel. I feel so good about it all, I think I'll do some homework to make my teachers happy. You finish all yours?"

"I have a little more to do," I said.

"Well, let's get to work," she said. "If we both do poorly, my granddad will have an excuse to make me leave," she added and went for her books.

She sprawled over the bed to read and do problems, and I continued at my small desk. That was the way Great-aunt Frances found the two of us a little while later.

"How wonderful," she said. "The two of you working so hard on your schoolwork and helping each other. If Emma had helped me, I might not have had so much trouble graduating."

"Did you?" Alanis asked her.

"Graduate? Yes, but my daddy had something to do with it," she said with a short laugh. "That's all right. No one expected me to go to college anyway."

"What you do after you left high school?"

"I worked for my father for a while."

"You never met anyone you wanted to marry or who wanted to marry you?" Alanis pursued.

I held my breath, waiting. These were questions I always wanted to ask.

Great-aunt Frances tilted her head and smiled.

"There was someone once. His name was Alex Foster and he worked for his father, too. His father had an export-import business. They were very wealthy people. Very snobby people, too. Alex was very handsome and he was head over heels in love with me, but his mother and father wanted him to marry someone else, someone wealthier. He was very upset about it. They wouldn't stop hounding him until . . . until one day he took his own life. Ever since then . . . oh, why did you ask me?" she cried, pressing her hand over her heart. "I don't like remembering sadness, remember? Besides, don't think about me. Think about yourselves and your wonderful futures. I'm an old lady now. Sweet dreams, girls," she said, smiling, changing expression as fast as she could change the channel on a television set.

She walked away.

"Jeez," Alanis said. "I don't believe it."

"Maybe it's true. She never married anyone," I said.

"No, it's not true."

"How do you know?" I asked angrily. She was too positive about everything she thought, and it was beginning to upset me.

"I know because that was the movie we were just watching," she said.

"It was?"

"Yes, it was. You would think she would remember I was sitting there with her watching it. She is bonkers. I wonder if she was always this way."

She thought a moment and then looked at me hard. "Your family's rich and stuff, but you sure have nutcases in it . . . your great-aunt, your brother, and from what you've told me, your grandmother ain't all there either. Your father sounds weird, too. You can inherit being nuts, you know."

I felt the tears coming to my eyes.

"No, you can't. Ian would have told me."

"Yeah, right, Ian. Don't worry about it," she said quickly. "I'll let you know if you do anything crazy or you're about to. I'm here to be your best friend, remember?"

I nodded, but I still didn't like what she had said. I tried to finish my school assignments, but the words became hazy on the page. I rushed to end it and then I got myself ready for bed. Alanis went downstairs when I was in the bathroom. I was already in my pajamas and in bed when she returned.

"Well, I got some news," she said. "That telephone number? I called it and a man answered. He told me Toby DeMarco was his mother and she was in the Sisters of Mercy nursing home in Johnsville. It's not that far from here. I thought he might have been the baby in the Moses basket, so I asked him where he was born and he got very uptight, demanding who I was and what I wanted, so I just hung up. What do you think of that?"

"I don't know."

"Why did we find his mother's name and telephone number up there? Why is that attic locked away? Why did your aunt keep it the way it was all this time? Why did this man get so upset when I asked him stuff?" she rattled off at me.

"I don't know."

"I don't know. I don't know. Is that all you can say? Don't you want to know?"

Should I tell her about Ian? I wondered. *Tell her about that thing he called telepathy and how I hear him warning me all the time? Would she think I am crazy already, too?*

"This is like a real mystery story," she continued as she undressed for bed. "I think we'll be like two detectives. I know what," she said as she was crawling in under the covers, "I'll make it up with Chad and we'll get him to drive us to that nursing home. Maybe we'll go there this weekend. I can make him do whatever I want. Okay?"

When I didn't answer right away, she added, "Don't say I don't know or I'll throw you out the window."

I didn't say anything. She turned over to go to sleep, but a moment later, she turned back.

"Maybe we'll learn something that will help you help your brother. You'd like that, wouldn't you?"

"Yes," I said.

"So there. This could be more than just some fun. Good night," she added.

Was she right? Did this house hold the answers to questions that would help Ian and me? Even Great-aunt Frances? I was so tired, but I was afraid that the moment I closed my eyes, Ian's letters would give me nightmares. I tried thinking of happy things, but in the end, I cried silently to myself until I was too tired to even dream.

Alanis was up ahead of me in the morning and shook me awake. When I opened my eyes, she was kneeling beside my bed to look into my face.

"What is it?" I asked.

"The ghost," she said.

I ground the sleep out of my eyes and propped myself up on my elbow.

"What?"

"It's not a ghost. It's your great-aunt. She goes up there and cries and then comes down. I heard her and watched for her. Don't worry. She didn't see me. Now I really want to know who Toby DeMarco was," she added. "And so do you, so don't even think of saying you don't. Get up. We have lots to do and talk about. Your great-aunt's trapped more in her lies and secrets than a fly in a spider's web. If we're smart, we'll unlock more than just an attic door in this house."

Why did she mention spiders and flies? Had she snuck into Grandmother Emma's room and read Ian's letters?

I didn't like spying on Great-aunt Frances, but I couldn't deny I was very curious about it all now. She was as chipper as ever in the morning, making sure we both ate a good breakfast even though she didn't herself.

"Tomorrow, Jordan and I might have a chance to go visit a friend of mine who has a nice house with lots to do in it. There's a game room with a pool table and all sorts of stuff. I have a friend who can take us," Alanis said. "Will that be all right with you, Miss Wilkens?"

"Oh. Well, what does your grandfather say?"

"He says if it's all right with you, it's all right with him," she lied.

"As long as you're both back in time for dinner. I

have some plans for our Saturday night dinner. Something special," she added.

"Oh, how can anything be more special than what we've had already?" Alanis cried. "It's so much fun living here, especially with someone as kind and as generous as you, Miss Wilkens."

Great-aunt Frances smiled. I looked down. Surely if I didn't, she easily could tell how much I hated seeing her fooled, I thought.

"Well, nothing makes me happier than seeing the two of you happy," Great-aunt Frances said.

I looked up at her and struggled not to shout out the truth: We snuck up into the attic, we found things and we're about to spy on people. The words got stuck in my throat and made my eyes tear. Great-aunt Frances thought I was just being grateful. She smiled at me and stroked my hair.

"Sweet child," she said.

"C'mon, Jordan," Alanis urged, poking me. "We don't want to miss our bus."

"Oh, I just remembered," Great-aunt Frances said, dipping into her housecoat pocket. "Here's your lunch money again. I hope this is enough for the both of you." She handed me a twenty-dollar bill.

"Oh, it's perfect," Alanis said.

I hesitated to take it but saw if I didn't, Alanis would. Once I had, she practically tugged me to the door.

"Bye. See you later, Miss Wilkens."

"Have a nice day, girls," Great-aunt Frances called back.

"You almost gave us away in there," Alanis complained. "Stop looking so guilty all the time. We're not doing anything so terrible. This money and what we have is important. We'll have to give Chad some for gas."

"What if she asks your grandfather if he said yes to your going tomorrow?"

"She won't, and even if she does, I'll tell him she got confused over something else we're doing. You're just a bundle of worry," she said.

You're just a bundle of lies, I thought.

When the bus pulled up and we stepped on, I saw immediately that Stuart Gavin was nowhere in sight. Alanis was curious about it as well and found out from another student, one who lived next to him, that his uncle had died and Stuart and his family had gone to be with the uncle's family for the funeral.

"And I was so prepared to pick on him again," Alanis said.

We parted as soon as we entered the school building because she saw Chad down the hall and went after him.

"Worry not," she threw back at me as she walked off. "He's wrapped around my finger."

She stepped right beside him and put her arm through his. He paused, smiled and walked on. She glanced back once with an "I told you so" expression.

Alanis sure does know a lot about boys, I thought. In her way she was as smart as Ian when it came to sex. I hurried on to my classroom. Maybe it was because I had begun hanging around in school with Alanis and her girlfriends, or maybe it was just because of what I looked like, but still none of the other girls in my class showed any interest in becoming my friend. Would I always feel like so much of an outsider?

Mrs. Morgan didn't collect the homework this time, but she called on us to read our answers aloud, and it seemed to me that she called on me more than anyone else in the class. Some of my answers were very good, but she poked holes in others. Then she announced grades on yesterday's work. She didn't care about everyone knowing everyone else's marks. I wasn't the lowest she gave, but I was barely acceptable. Although I knew she knew I had not been left back or was too old for my class, she treated me as if I had been. I could see it in the satisfied faces of the other students who looked at me.

Later, at lunch, Alanis sat with Chad. Nikki and Raspberry were annoyed.

"I thought she was giving him his walking papers," Nikki told me. "Why is she back with him?"

I closed my eyes for a moment and tried to do what Alanis taught me, pretend I believed what I was about to say.

"I don't know," I said.

I still wasn't good at it. They both looked at me suspiciously.

"I called her house last night and her grandfather said she was still staying over at your great-aunt's house with you. You two have a party in the basement with Chad and someone else?" Raspberry asked me. "I bet you kept all the alcopops and didn't throw any of it out, huh?"

"No."

"Don't go lying to us, girl," Nikki said.

"I'm not. We didn't have a party. Didn't you ask her?"

"Yeah, we asked her," Raspberry said, glaring at Alanis. "We know enough to know you can't believe

Alanis or trust her. She's acting pretty secretive, too. She got something planned and we bet you know what it is."

"I thought she was your best friend," I said.

"She was, but we think she's getting stuck up because of you," Nikki said.

"Me?"

"Yeah. You're a rich kid, right? She has more money on her than I ever seen her have," Nikki said. "All of a sudden we ain't gonna be good enough for her."

I didn't know what to say. I looked to Alanis, who was flirting so much with Chad that the teacher monitor was looking at them angrily.

"Don't you two go having a party without us," Raspberry warned.

"We're not," I said. I couldn't eat fast enough and be happier when the bell rang to return to class.

Afterward, Alanis met me in the hallway.

"It's all set," she said. "He's coming by to pick us up at ten tomorrow. I didn't tell him where we're going exactly or why, so don't say anything. I'll do all the talking."

"Nikki and Raspberry think we're planning to have a party without them," I said. "They're mad at you. They think you're getting stuck up and they're blaming me."

"Forget about them for now. I don't have time for fools," she said and hurried off.

When I turned, I saw Mrs. Browne standing in a doorway with one of the teachers, looking at me. Her face was full of disapproval and suspicion. The two of them began speaking very low as they stared at me. I walked faster, but I could feel her eyes following me down the hallway to my classroom. It actually felt as if they'd been inches from the back of my neck.

In the world I had come from, I couldn't recall any teacher ever having looked at me with anything but a smile on his or her face. What dark boundary had I crossed? Who had I become?

Once again I felt as if events were carrying me off like an ocean current. Would I drown or end up someplace better?

14

Sisters of Mercy

As soon as we stepped off the bus, we saw Alanis's grandfather coming down the driveway. He was walking so quickly and looked so upset that I thought Great-aunt Frances had told him about our trip tomorrow after all and, despite what Alanis planned to say, he knew she was up to something. Her lies wouldn't work as easily with him as they did with other people.

"I want you over to our house right off, Alanis," he said as we walked up. He pointed to it. "You just get yourself over there right now."

"Why?" she cried. "I'm living in Miss Wilkens's house."

"Why? I don't care if you've moved into Miss Wilkens's house to be with Jordan, but you still have chores to do at our house."

"Why can't Mama do it?"

He looked away.

"It's not fair," she shouted. "I'm doing all her work at Miss Wilkens's house, ain't I? There's not half as much to do in your house, Granddad."

He glanced at me and then in a softer voice said, "She's not here." It was almost a whisper.

"Well, where is she? She don't hafta be at work this early. I—"

"Your mother's gone off with that bum Olsen, the bartender. It's just you and me," he added quickly, turned, and walked toward the barn.

His words lingered in the air like heavy, smelly smoke. Alanis stood there looking after him. For a moment she looked as if she would begin to cry. Her cheeks twitched, her lips turned in and out on each other, and her eyes grew gray as a film of tears came rushing in and over them, but if Alanis ever did cry, she didn't cry in front of anyone, I thought.

"You see? I'm right. Be no different if my mother was in a coma, too," she muttered.

She glanced at me and then stomped up the drive-way, veering off to the right toward her grandfather's house, her head down, her hands clenched into fists pounding at her own thighs as she walked.

"See you later," she called back without even turn-ing toward me.

I continued to the house, and as soon as I stepped in, I heard Great-aunt Frances call for me. She was in the living room watching her afternoon soap opera, and she wasn't waiting for the commercial.

"Guess who called about you today," she said when I appeared in the doorway.

"Grandmother Emma?"

"No. Your father. I can't remember when I spoke to him last. It seems to me he was just a little boy."

"My father? I thought he went on a vacation."

"I don't know where he was when he called."

"What did he say? Did he say anything about my mother?"

"He asked how you were doing. I thought he sounded sad," she said. "Very sad. I can tell when someone is sad. It's like hearing a familiar song. I asked him if he wanted you to call him and he said no. He said he would call again."

"And he didn't say anything about my mother? You didn't ask?"

"I was so surprised at hearing his voice that I didn't think to ask. I'm sorry, dear. I didn't even ask about Emma. He promised he would call again soon. Oh," she said as I started to turn away. "He said to tell you he sent your letter to Ian."

"He did?"

"That's what he said."

"Then maybe Ian will write me here. We'll have to look at the mail every day."

"I don't get any mail," she said. "Lester gets anything important and takes it to the bank or sends it to Emma's lawyer. The rest, he says, is just junk mail."

"I'd better tell him not to make a mistake and throw away a letter from Ian."

"He won't if your name's on the envelope."

"I'll tell him anyway," I said, excited and not wanting to take any chances. I turned and ran back out of the house. Daddy had called about me and he had fulfilled his promise about my letter. It was as if an overcast sky had started to part and let in some blue hope.

Alanis's granddad was feeding the chickens. He was mumbling under his breath, either to himself or to the chickens, and didn't hear me when I called to him.

"Mr. Marshall," I called again.

"Yes?" When he turned to me, I thought he looked so much older, aging almost in minutes.

"My father called. I might get a letter from my brother any day now. His name is Ian March, so any envelope with that name on it is for me."

"Well, well now, that's nice. I'll be sure to get it to you," he said.

He didn't smile like he almost always did when he spoke to me.

"I'm sorry Mae Betty left," I told him, and his eyes widened a bit.

"Yeah," he said, and then he added something very strange. "Maybe we'll be better off."

I didn't know what to say. How could Alanis be better off without her mother? I certainly wasn't. And why was he better off without his own daughter? I turned and ran back to the house, practically charging up the stairway to Grandmother Emma's room. There were two more of Ian's letters to read. I seized the bag and sat on the floor.

Dear Jordan,

I am now wrapped around my waist so tightly I can't sit up. I am writing to you lying on my back so my writing might look funny.

It all happens to me at night. It happens very slowly, so slowly that I can't feel it happening and can't stop it.

The nurse and Dr. Walker pretend they don't

see it. They spend most of their time trying to convince me I am imagining it. They plead with me to move my legs and now to sit up. I just smile at them. I know this is a charade they must go through in case some health inspector arrives or in case the highly doubtful thing occurs and Father comes to visit or inquires about me. Of course, they have to be sure Grandmother Emma hears only good things, too. She will. My lawyer, Jack Cassidy, pretends to be very concerned and stands in the doorway looking in at me and nodding his head and shaking his head as Dr. Walker fills his ears with one lie after another.

I don't want you to worry because no matter what they do to me, I will still be able to speak with Mother. I don't have to move my mouth to speak with her, remember. It's all done with my brain and with hers, so even if they put me into a coma finally, it won't matter.

What's ironic, and that means funny in a serious sort of way this time, is that I am talking more with her now than I did when we were both at the mansion and free. Maybe it's because neither of us has much else to do.

However, I am afraid that some medication they will give me might cloud my brain and make it impossible for me to continue to talk with Mother, so I want you to start practicing telepathy.

Here's what I want you to do, Jordan. I want you to sit quietly someplace where no one can disturb you and where you won't be disturbed

*by anyone talking to you or any noise and I want
you to try to picture Mother in your mind and
just keep sending out a call to her. Work hard on
it and one day, you will hear her voice. It's that
simple, but it won't work unless you have a place
to go where you can be undisturbed.*

*I have to stop. My arm is aching and so are
my shoulders.*

Ian

Where could I go to do what Ian suggested? I wondered. And then I quickly realized, the attic. I would
go up there when I could go up alone, go up whenever
Alanis had to be at her granddad's house cleaning. I
just had to know where the key was. Excited about it, I
was now happy Alanis had made the discovery.

I opened Ian's last letter in the bag. It was in scribbling so awkward and clumsy that I had to study it
hard to understand. It was all over the page, too, some
words even sideways.

Dear Jordan,

*My arms are wrapped. I can just move my
wrist. Tomorrow, I won't be able to do that.*

Good-bye.

Ian

For a long time, I sat there staring at the scribbling.
I was surprised at the tear that fell on the paper and
realized it was mine. It had come from my eye and
was being followed by eager brother and sister tears
charging down my cheeks and leaping off to join the
first. What did this mean? Would he never write to me

again? What good was Daddy sending him my letter finally?

My shoulders shook and my chest began to ache. I rolled over on the carpet and brought my knees up against my stomach to make it feel better. I closed my eyes and rocked and rocked until I was too tired to continue.

And after a while, I fell asleep.

I woke when I heard Alanis's laugh. She was sitting on Grandmother Emma's bed reading Ian's letters.

"Stop!" I cried, grinding the sleep out of my eyes and sitting up. I reached for Ian's letters. "Give them back to me now."

"Talk about being bonkers," she said. "Your brother is really nuts. No wonder why you didn't want me to read these letters."

"He's not nuts. He's very, very smart," I said.

She smirked. "Yeah, right. The rest of the world is nuts."

She put the letters down, and I started folding them back into their envelopes.

"I told you not to read them. Ian wanted only me to read them."

"Don't worry about it. I'm not going to tell anyone. Remember? Real friends keep secrets for each other. Besides, this isn't important. Our discovery is what's important."

I thought about Ian's instructions about telepathy.

"Where did you say the key to the attic is?"

"The bottom drawer in the food pantry. It's the only one with a little blue stain on it. I don't know if there is more than one, so we have to be sure to put it back after we use it each time," she instructed. "I just told your aunt that you and I are going to make her a surprise for dinner so she doesn't have to think up any silly costumes or anything tonight. She looked tired anyway and was happy to hear it."

"What are we going to make?"

"I can make macaroni and cheese. You make the salad. Granddad bought a nice bread and a pecan pie, which is one of her favorites. It's Friday night so we'll watch television with her and keep her mind off asking about our trip tomorrow. We'll wake up, have breakfast and go before she realizes she had said it was okay. Granddad does most of his other shopping on Saturday so he won't see us leave. It's perfect as long as you don't say anything stupid."

"I won't say anything stupid."

"Just remember what I told you about speaking to adults. Take your time before you say anything. Count to five after they ask you questions so you don't accidentally blurt out the truth."

"I told you," I said. "I don't like lying."

"Then don't talk much," she advised. She looked very angry suddenly. "Don't you see how the truth just hurts most of the time? My granddad has to face the truth about my mother. She's a tramp. He can't pretend things like your great-aunt. All he can do is suffer. Anybody asks me where my mother is I'll tell them she's visiting relatives. Or would you rather I tell them the truth and say my mother ran off with a no-good man and didn't care she left me behind? Huh? Which would you say? Huh?" she pursued.

"I don't know. My mother never ran off."

She shook her head and sighed. "Sometimes, talking to you is really like talking to someone from another world," she said, glancing at Ian's letters. "What did you tell the other kids in your class about your brother when you wrote that autobiography the first day? Huh?"

I bit down on my lower lip.

"Well?"

"I said he was very smart."

"And?"

"That he wants to be a medical research scientist."

"And?"

"That's all I said."

"See? You didn't tell them about the minder or where he is. The truth hurts, so you didn't tell it."

I looked away, the tears threatening to return.

"I'm just trying to tell you how to get along, Jordan. I'm not trying to hurt you. C'mon. Let's get started on the dinner. We'll pretend we're the cooks on a cruise ship or something. We can have some fun and forget anything sad."

I turned to her sharply. "I thought you said we wouldn't pretend."

"I'm feeling sad all of a sudden. I'd rather pretend."

"You sound more and more like my great-aunt Frances," I said.

She smiled. "So? Maybe she ain't so bonkers after all. C'mon," she urged and got up.

I put Ian's letters back in the bag and the bag back in the closet. Then I followed her out and down the stairs. She thought it would be a good idea to make the dinner seem special by dressing the dining room table instead of eating in the kitchen. Great-aunt Frances poked her head in to watch us work. She laughed and clapped her hands, then told us that since we were eat-

ing in the formal dining room, she had decided she had
to go upstairs and dress in something nice, fix her hair
and put on some makeup. Alanis thought it was a good
idea, and she and I went up and put on prettier clothes.
When we came down, we set up candles and Alanis
found some old tapes to play on the stereo system. It
wasn't music she liked, but she said we should play it
for Great-aunt Frances, who, when she heard it, wore
a brighter, happier smile. She did look the nicest I had
seen her look since I had come to live here.

Although I had made a simple salad and Alanis had
only opened a box that had everything in it, Great-aunt
Frances thought we had made the most wonderful
dinner, especially with the candlelight and the nice
dinnerware. It stirred more memories about her youth,
and she began telling us about some of the wonderful
dinners her mother had made and some of the family
events, especially when relatives had visited.

"Emma was particularly fond of our uncle Bronson.
He was our father's younger brother, a dashingly handsome man who was a private plane pilot. He worked for
a corporation and flew all over Europe as well as America. He had wonderful stories for us and was always
urging us to think about traveling. Emma did a lot of
traveling after she was married, but I didn't do any.

"Once, Uncle Bronson took us both for a plane ride.
He rented a small plane. My mother was very nervous
and so was Emma, but she wouldn't admit it. She
didn't care that I was the one Uncle Bronson wanted to
sit up front. When I looked back at her, she always had
her eyes closed. Once," she said, hesitating, "I told her
she had her eyes closed most of her life and she got
very angry. You know why she got angry?" Great-aunt

Frances asked us. Neither of us had moved an inch or uttered a word the whole time she'd spoken. I could see that Alanis never expected Great-aunt Frances would talk like this. She was surprised and fascinated. "You know why?" Great-aunt Frances repeated, now really looking at us and not at her memories.

I shook my head. Alanis didn't move or speak.

"She got angry because she knew it was the truth," she said. "And she didn't want to hear the truth."

I looked at Alanis.

She was smiling.

Her whole face was saying, "See?"

The pecan pie cheered Great-aunt Frances up and turned her back to the childlike adult I knew. Afterward, we sent her to watch television while we cleaned up. As we promised, we joined her to watch one of her romantic movies. Alanis even joined her when she spoke to the set and told actors what to do and not to do. Finally, Great-aunt Frances got so tired that her eyes began to close. Alanis said she was tired herself and told me she wanted to go up to finish reading the book Ian had given me. She said she was nearly done and it would be the first book she had really read cover to cover.

"Most of the time, I skip stuff," she admitted. "Or I get someone else to tell me the story."

"I'll stay a little longer with Great-aunt Frances," I told her. It was a lie. I was getting better at it because she nodded, believed me, and left.

Great-aunt Frances was sleeping soundly now, so I tiptoed out and went to the food pantry. I found the attic key and then, as quietly as I could, I went up the stairs and opened the attic door. I slipped in without putting on the light. There was enough moonlight coming through the attic windows for me to clearly make out the stairway. I went up and sat on the sofa in the dark with the silvery moonlight draped around me like some magical blanket, and then I tried to do what Ian had instructed.

Only, when I pictured Mommy, I called out to her instead of using only my brain. I realized it and stopped myself, but it was hard. I sat there as long as I could and waited to hear her voice. There was just silence, a silence so deep that I could hear my own heartbeat.

Finally, I gave up. I imagined it would take a lot more practice. How could I expect to be as perfect as Ian right away? I told myself and tiptoed back down the stairway, taking great care with the door and lock. I returned the key to the drawer. By the time I went up to the bedroom, Alanis was asleep on the bed, still fully dressed, the book in her hands. I tried making as little noise as possible, but she woke.

"Oh," she said. "I must have fallen asleep. Your great-aunt still downstairs?"

"Uh-huh," I said, and then we both heard her come out of the bathroom.

"How could she get upstairs that fast?" Alanis asked.

I didn't know what to say. She would question me now and discover I had gone up to the attic alone. She would want to know why. Her eyes narrowed suspiciously.

"You fell asleep down there yourself, didn't you?" she asked and smiled. "Didn't you?"

"Yes," I said. She laughed.

"It's all right," she said. "Don't be embarrassed. I did, too. I'm getting ready for bed," she told me. She left to sneak into Grandmother Emma's bathroom.

That lie was even easier than before, I thought.

Lying to the expert liar wasn't as hard to do as I had thought. I must be getting better.

We talked for a while after we were both in bed and the lights were out. Alanis admitted being more than just annoyed at her mother.

"She would go off on a drunken bender for days when my father was still with us. Sometimes, I can still hear the shouting and yelling in my head. It rumbles about in there like tin cans. I can't tell you how many times she told me she wished she had never been married and never given birth to me."

"She said that?"

"Many times."

She was quiet and I was quiet, and then she turned on her side and, minutes later, was asleep. I thought I heard her sob in her sleep. As I lay there, I wondered how Ian actually felt with his body being wrapped. I tried to imagine it and pretend it was happening to me. It frightened me and I turned over, too, and tried to sleep.

Alanis was up ahead of me in the morning, excited about our trip. She wanted us to get downstairs and start breakfast before Great-aunt Frances had awakened. She said we'd both bring her breakfast up to her.

"We'll keep stroking her like this so she's in a good mood and doesn't ask too many questions about the trip," Alanis said.

I made the hot chocolate and Alanis prepared the

eggs and bacon, toast and jam. She was a better cook than she had said she was. While she worked, I learned she had been cooking and fixing breakfasts, lunches and dinners ever since she was five.

"Even though I was young, I couldn't wait for my mother to get over a hangover or something," she said.

"What about your granddad? Who's helping him with his meals now?"

"He's good at taking care of himself. Granddad was always on his own. My mother didn't bring him much more than trouble when we moved in with him. C'mon," she said. "Let's bring this up to your great-aunt. Wait," she added just as she picked up the tray. She hurried out the back door and moments later returned with a handful of wildflowers. She put them in a tall glass. "Just like in a hotel," she declared, smiling.

We marched upstairs. Great-aunt Frances was just stretching. Miss Puss was curled up and asleep at her feet and didn't waken until we brought the tray to Great-aunt Frances.

"Oh, my, my, dear me!" Great-aunt Frances cried. "How beautiful. You two will spoil me rotten," she said and sat up. Alanis moved quickly to set up her pillows and make her comfortable.

"Take your time, Great-aunt Frances," Alanis told her. "We'll come up to get your tray before we leave."

"Leave?" she asked. She had forgotten. Alanis threw me a quick glance.

"We're just going to visit a friend, remember? We'll be back before dinner," she told her.

"Oh. Yes."

"I hope the eggs are okay," Alanis said, immediately getting her mind off in another direction.

Great-aunt Frances tasted them and smiled.

"They're perfect, dear. Thank you," she said.

"We'll just have our breakfast and come up to see you before we leave," Alanis told her quickly and hustled me out of the bedroom. "Chad better not be late," she said when we reentered the kitchen. She made us some toast and jam and put up some coffee for herself.

I told her I never drank coffee. "My grandmother said young people shouldn't drink it."

"You drank booze and alcopops, Jordan. You can drink coffee, believe me," she said and poured me some. I tried it but I didn't care for it. Like Great-aunt Frances, I preferred the hot chocolate.

"You better stay down here," she told me afterward. "I'll see to Great-aunt Frances. She's liable to start asking too many questions and you won't know what to say or she'll see right through that glass face of yours."

Soon after, she returned with the tray and told me Great-aunt Frances hadn't even gotten out of bed yet.

"Let's get going," she said. "We'll wait for Chad out on the driveway. I don't want to take any chances."

I followed her out. She was worried that her grand-dad hadn't left for the store yet, but his car was gone.

"All systems are go," she told me. "As long as Chad shows," she added.

We went down to the end of the driveway.

"Why are we going to see Toby DeMarco again?"

"It's a mystery, Jordan. Don't you want to solve it? It's more fun than sitting around watching your great-aunt fall asleep in the living room or reading your brother's nutty letters."

"They're not nutty."

"Whatever," she said. "I'd rather do this than think about my mother anyway," she added and kicked a stone down the road. Of all the reasons she gave, I thought that was the most important for her. We both looked at the oncoming traffic.

Above us, a hazy morning sky sprinkled sunlight like light rain on the surrounding fields and forest. There was a nice breeze, but I could feel the underbelly of the oncoming cool fall. A few leaves from older trees let go of branches and drifted lazily toward the ground.

Alanis paced impatiently, her arms embracing herself. She glared at the traffic, angry at every car that wasn't Chad's. She was still in a very bad mood because of what her mother had done. I wanted to suggest that if her mother had done this before and returned, maybe she would again, but I was afraid to say anything. I looked back at the house. Maybe a new letter would come from Ian today, I thought. Maybe my father would call again. Maybe I shouldn't leave.

"Here he comes," Alanis announced before I could change my mind.

A dark blue Mustang sped around the far turn. We could hear the thump, thump of the rap music. Chad deliberately sped up, then hit the brakes in front of us.

"Hey, girls," he said, leaning out his window. "Going my way?"

"Get in," Alanis told me and hurried around to open the passenger side door. I hesitated for a moment, then slipped into the backseat. "Go, before my granddad returns," Alanis ordered him.

"Yes, ma'am," he said and accelerated so fast that the wheels squealed. "Where we going in Johnsville anyway?" he asked after a few moments.

"Just drive. I'll tell you when we get there."

"It better be worth it," he said.

She dug out a twenty-dollar bill from her pocket and tossed it into his lap.

"Gas money," she said.

"Okay, but I'm not talking about money, Alanis," he said, smiling. "I deserve more than money."

"Don't worry. You'll get what you deserve," she told him.

"Well, why can't you tell me where we're going in Johnsville?"

"We're going to visit one of Jordan's relatives," she replied.

"Relatives?" He grimaced with disappointment. "What's so important about seeing relatives?"

"It's important to Jordan and to me. What do you care?" she snapped back at him. "You doing something better today?"

"I can think of something."

"Think later," she said. She turned up the music, more to drown him out than listen, I thought.

I sat back and stared out the window while they talked and mostly teased each other. I still couldn't throw off this feeling that I was being carried along in currents so powerful there was no way to turn back or to stop. There were no hands to reach for, no arms to embrace me and lift me into safety. Ian was so positive that everything had a cause and effect. One thing he'd always spent time explaining to me was why—why this happened or that or why this or that would happen no matter what.

What was the why about me? I wondered. Why was I here? Was it simply because my parents had gotten into a bad car accident? If I thought about that and how Ian had explained it, I could keep asking why forever. Why had Grandmother Emma and Grandfather Blake brought up my father to be the way he was? Why had they married? Why was Grandmother Emma so different from Great-aunt Frances? The why questions would go back so far until—and this made me smile when I thought of it—I would ask why this tadpole met this egg and turned it into me.

As Alanis and Chad continued to tease each other, laugh and listen to their music, I wondered if any of these sorts of why questions ever occurred to either of them. Did Alanis ever wonder why she had the mother she had? Should I ask her?

I thought not. I closed my eyes and thought about my mother. I listened hard for the sound of her voice and tried to not hear any other, but it was too hard to do in a car with music playing loudly. Ian had known what I had to do when he'd told me to find a very quiet place.

After what seemed at least an hour, Alanis turned to tell me we were almost there.

"When we get there, we might have to tell them you're her grandniece," she said.

"What do you mean, she might have to tell them? I thought she was visiting a relative," Chad said.

"She is, but the relative is old and has a bad memory," Alanis replied without skipping a beat.

I'd never met anyone who was as good or as fast at coming up with a lie as she was. When I'd first arrived, I would have said I wasn't interested in that, but now I thought it would be better to be able to make up stories sometimes. I couldn't help thinking I'd be better off being more like she was.

"Pull into that garage," Alanis ordered after we saw the sign announcing we had entered Johnsville. "I need to get us directions."

As soon as he stopped, she jumped out and went into the office.

"She's one crazy girl," Chad said, "but that's why I like her. You never know what Alanis is going to do or say next. She's an original. Know what that means?"

I shook my head.

"She's different from the other girls, who are boring and predictable. She's full of surprises. Say, I like her hat on you, by the way. That was another surprise. I never thought she'd give that to anyone. I thought it was attached to her head. She must like you a lot."

I didn't say anything. I wasn't sure Alanis wanted him to know we were being like sisters.

"Who is this relative?" he asked.

I felt myself panic, and then I remembered what Alanis had told him and said, "Another great-aunt."

He nodded and moved with the music until Alanis returned.

"Keep going until we reach the third traffic light and then turn left," she told him when she got into the car.

"Yes, boss," he said, saluted and drove on.

Johnsville was a prettier community than ours. The houses looked clean and newer or well kept, and their lawns and bushes were trimmed to look like they were in a painting. The streets had no potholes, and the stores we saw looked busy. What struck me about our town was the empty feeling in the streets.

After another turn, we saw a sign indicating we were closing on the Sisters of Mercy adult residence.

"That's it," Alanis told him.

"She's in one of these places?" Chad asked.

"Yes, so now you see why she couldn't visit Jordan."

The residence came into view just to the right up a long drive. It was a very large three-story building with a wide portico and stucco made to look like stone. The grounds were pretty and well manicured with concrete pathways, upon which we saw two people in wheelchairs, each wrapped in blankets, as if it had been very cold outside. Two nuns talked to each other while the residents sat staring at us as we drove up to the parking area. The nuns stopped talking and turned our way, too.

"Now what?" Chad asked after he parked.

"Wait here," Alanis told him.

"Wait here? And do what?"

"Twiddle your thumbs," she said. "C'mon, Jordan," she told me and opened the door. She pulled the seat forward for me to get out.

"You better not be long," Chad threatened.

"Tell you what," Alanis told him. "I'll stay with you as long as I'm in there."

He smiled.

"Okay, deal," he said.

"Why did you say that?" I asked her as we walked toward the entrance.

"It's what he wanted to hear," she said. "Always tell boys what they want to hear."

She opened the big door, and we stepped into the residence lobby. A half dozen or so elderly people were sitting in the lounge watching television. Two were playing cards off to the right. We could hear some soft music piped in over speakers in the walls.

As soon as we entered, a nun started toward us. She didn't look much younger than the residents at the home.

"Can I help you?" she asked us. She smiled. "I'm Sister Andrea," she added.

"Oh, thank you, Sister," Alanis said in the sweetest voice I'd heard her use. "My friend and I took a ride with my boyfriend, who just got his driving license. It's exciting when you first get your license."

"Oh, I'm sure it is," Sister Andrea said, looking more at me now. I thought I would just keep quiet.

"Anyway, there we were trying to figure out where we would go on our first big ride and Jordan here remembered her great-aunt Toby DeMarco was in this residence so we thought we'd stop by and say hello if we could."

"Really? Why, that's very nice of you, a very kind and loving thing to do. Unfortunately, our residents don't get that many visitors."

"Yes, ma'am. She, Jordan, hasn't seen her for a very long time. She was afraid her aunt might not remember her."

"Oh, Mrs. DeMarco has a very good memory."

"That's good. Our prayers worked," Alanis said.

What prayers? I wondered.

Sister Andrea smiled. "Come this way. She's in her room at the moment, but she's doing fine," she said.

We followed her through a door to a stairway and walked up one flight. As we walked, she asked us where we were from. Alanis mixed the truth with some fabrication, but she did it so smoothly that I almost believed her myself. At the second door on the right, she paused and nodded at it. The door was open. A slim woman with black strains still prominent in her mostly gray, short hair sat with her back to us, looking out her window. There was a large cross over the headboard of the bed and some pictures of family on the dresser and on the small round table to the right. A settee that could sit only two or three at most was just to the right of the table.

"Mrs. DeMarco," Sister Andrea called.

Slowly, Toby DeMarco turned around. Her face was narrow, her nose pointed and her lips thin. Her skin looked pasty and spotted here and there with brown age spots. She wore a dark green housecoat and a pair of fluffy white slippers.

"You have some visitors," Sister Andrea told her.

I held my breath. Would she come right out and demand to know who we were? She didn't move. Sister Andrea reached back to put her arm around my shoulder and bring me forward.

"Your great-niece, Jordan," she said.

Toby DeMarco said nothing. She didn't change expression. There was only a slight movement in her gray eyebrows.

"Tell her your full name, sweetheart," Sister Andrea urged me.

I glanced at Alanis, who waited with excitement and anticipation. She nodded for me to go ahead.

"I'm Jordan," I said. "Jordan March."

Mrs. DeMarco's eyes widened.

Then she smiled.

"I've been waiting for you," she said. "For a very long time."

15

The Secret of the Attic

"**H**ave a nice visit, girls," Sister Andrea told us and walked away.

"Come in," Mrs. DeMarco urged, beckoning and nodding toward the settee.

Alanis looked at me and saw I was hesitant. She wasn't afraid so much as she was amazed. She shrugged and smiled. "Go ahead," she urged, giving me a little push through the doorway.

I walked in slowly and sat on the small settee. Alanis followed and quickly sat beside me.

"Why did you tell the sister you were my grandniece?" Mrs. DeMarco asked immediately.

"We thought it would be easier to get in to see you," Alanis replied.

"Why do you want to see me?" she asked.

"We live with Miss Frances Wilkens," Alanis began.

She'd started to smile but stopped instantly when Alanis said that.

"Did Frances Wilkens send you here?" she asked quickly.

"No, ma'am. She doesn't know we've come to see you."

"Then how did you know to come here?"

"We found your name and phone number and called and your son told us where you were when I asked for you," Alanis replied.

She nodded as though she had expected to hear that as well.

"We found your name and number in the attic," Alanis added pointedly. "Miss Wilkens's attic."

"I see." Her eyes became deeper pools of suspicion, moving quickly from Alanis to me and then back to Alanis. "How is Frances?"

"She's all right. I mean, she's not sick or anything like that," Alanis replied and looked at me. I nodded.

Mrs. DeMarco concentrated her gaze on me.

"So you are a March?"

"Yes, ma'am," I said. She smiled warmly this time. Then she turned away quickly to look through the window, as if something had demanded her attention. Her smile evaporated. Alanis nudged me and nodded at Mrs. DeMarco. She wanted me to ask questions, but I felt as if I had just swallowed a rock and was afraid to utter a sound. She turned back to me.

"Why did you say you were waiting for her for a long time?" Alanis asked, which brought her around to us again. She stared at me again for a moment.

"Your father's name is Christopher?"

"Yes, ma'am."

"What about Emma?" she asked quickly.

"Grandmother Emma?"

"Yes," she said, drawing the corners of her mouth in and down, which shot a line through each side of her jaw. "Grandmother Emma. Did she send you?"

"Oh, no, ma'am. She's very sick," I said. "She's in the hospital."

"She had a stroke," Alanis added quickly.

"And who are you?" Mrs. DeMarco asked her with surprising sharpness.

"I'm Lester Marshall's granddaughter. Do you know Lester Marshall? He works for Miss Wilkens."

"No," she said. Then she thought a moment. "Maybe," she added. "He came later."

"Later? When later?"

"After I was gone," she replied.

Alanis glanced at me, a look of satisfaction spread on her face. We had come to the right person, the right place.

"Who was in the attic? Why was there a Moses basket? Did you live up there? Was the basket for your baby?" Alanis asked, firing her questions as if she was afraid that if she stopped, it would be too late.

Mrs. DeMarco looked from Alanis to me again, her forehead scrunching with thought, her eyebrows dipping toward each other as a crown of confusion settled on her.

"So you don't know who was in the attic?"

"No," Alanis said. "That's why we came to see you."

"Um," she said, nodding. She smiled as it all began to clear, like something foggy coming into sharp focus. "So you two don't know anything?"

"No," Alanis said.

She looked at me to confirm.

"No, ma'am," I said.

"And you're a March?" she asked again, this time sounding a little skeptical.

"Tell her about yourself," Alanis urged.

"Yes, tell me," Mrs. DeMarco said. "Your parents let you come here yourself?"

"Her parents were in a car accident."

"Oh?"

"They were in a bad car accident," I said. "My mother is in a coma and my father has to be in a wheelchair now."

"How terrible."

"She has a brother, too."

"You do?"

"Ian," I said.

"He's not with her. He's in an institution. He has some mental problems."

She nodded as if she had expected to hear no less.

"So with her father in a wheelchair and her mother in a coma, her grandmother made her come live with her great-aunt, Miss Wilkens."

"I see. Yes, Emma is good at deciding other people's lives," she added. "But I thought you said she had a stroke."

"She's in the hospital," I said. "She can't talk very much, but she gives orders through her attorney."

She stared at me hard. It made me feel uncomfortable. She looked like she was searching my face for some sort of clue.

"But her attorney didn't tell you to come see me?"

"No, ma'am. No one told us," I said.

That seemed to make her uneasy. She fidgeted, as if she was going to stop talking to us. Alanis sensed it, too.

"So why was your name in the attic dresser drawer?" Alanis pursued. She was probably thinking also about Chad waiting impatiently in the parking lot.

"I didn't put it there. I thought everything that had to do with me had been taken out of that attic. I thought it had been completely emptied, in fact."

"No, it's full of stuff, furniture," Alanis said. "And that Moses basket."

"So? How did you know to come here?" she asked again.

Alanis rolled her eyes at me. "I called the number we found in the attic and your son answered and he told me where you were. I asked him if he was the baby in the attic," Alanis said.

Mrs. DeMarco smiled.

"Hardly," she said. "You're sure Frances doesn't know you've come?" she asked, looking at me now.

"No, ma'am. She doesn't even know we were up in the attic. It's always locked," I said.

"I found the key and we went up there," Alanis said. "I'm living with Jordan now in Miss Wilkens's house. We're best friends," she told her.

She stared again, and then she looked away.

"You shouldn't have come here," she said without looking at us. "I'm not the one you should be asking these questions."

"We didn't know who else to ask."

"You should have asked Emma March."

"No, we can't. She's in a hospital and she can't talk," Alanis pursued. "I guess maybe we could have asked your father," she told me.

Mrs. DeMarco turned back to us.

"No, I doubt he could tell you anything. His father could have, but it's been some time since Blake passed on, hasn't it?" she asked me.

"My grandfather?" I asked, and she nodded. "I don't remember exactly. He was dead before I was born. My brother remembers him, but not all that much."

"He was a very handsome man." She smiled. "He reminded me of Clark Gable in *Gone With the Wind.*"

"Gone With the Wind?" I asked. I looked at Alanis. She nodded, understanding.

"That first dinner when you and Great-aunt Frances dressed like Southern belles."

I nodded.

"Frances is still putting on those dresses and pretending she's this one and that one?" Mrs. DeMarco asked us.

"Yes, ma'am. She likes to dress up in something for dinner. At least she has since I've come," I said.

"Poor Frances. She was caught somewhere between childhood and adulthood, afraid to step too far back and terrified of stepping ahead," she said. "Can't blame her. Look where it takes you," she added, nodding at her room. "Four walls and a window, cafeteria food, people having the same conversations day in and day out, forgetting they've told you about themselves and their families a dozen times, if they've told you once. I've got diabetes, a heart that's sick of hearing itself beat, and a closet full of old clothes I'm ashamed to give away. I get tired of the echo of my own thoughts, but when you're alone, it's all you hear."

"Doesn't your son come to visit you?" Alanis asked.

"Yes, when that wife of his loosens the leash a little. I've got a daughter living in Canada. Did I tell you?"

"No, ma'am," I said.

"If I repeat myself, you just let me know. I hate repeating myself."

"Why were you in the attic?" Alanis asked as if she hadn't asked before.

"Do you know what I did when I was younger?" Mrs. DeMarco asked instead of answering. She looked to me for a reply.

"No, ma'am," I said.

"All we know about you is your name, the telephone number and your son and this," Alanis said, holding out her hands.

"I was a pretty good nurse. You know, more often than not, a good nurse does as much as if not more than the doctor, especially when it involves women. I can't tell you how many times I've had to remind a doctor what was wrong with his patient, why he was treating this patient or that and what he had prescribed. Take my advice, don't get sick and if you do, stay out of hospitals. If you're not dying when you're admitted, you will be soon after," she said.

"But where else are you supposed to go if you're very sick?" I asked.

"Don't get very sick," she said and then smiled. "I'd know you were from the Wilkens line of women anywhere," she said. Then she straightened up. "I was a CNM, a certified nurse midwife. Do you know what that is?"

I shook my head.

"I'm not sure," Alanis said.

"Midwives are nurses who can assist in childbirth. We are trained in prenatal care, making sure the pregnant woman eats right, takes the right vitamins and supplements, exercises, avoids bad things. In short, my little Nancy Drews, there wasn't simply a baby living in the attic. There was a baby born in the attic, and I attended and oversaw the birth. If I didn't have this terrible arthritis," she continued and showed us how twisted her fingers were, "and I wasn't a severe and brittle diabetic, and I didn't have a traitorous heart, I might still be working and on my own out there," she said, nodding at the window. "Instead, I've been put out to pasture and this is the pasture.

"Some days," she continued, "I feel like getting up and going out and walking and walking to my grave plot next to my husband's and hopefully expiring right on it. But," she said, waving her hand and arm as best she could, "this isn't proper talk for you two young girls to hear. Old age is still a dream or a nightmare, some sort of fantasy to you. I'm sure you can't imagine being in this chair and in this place. I'm sure you never see yourself as old and crippled."

"No," Alanis said. I think she was thinking it so hard it just came out.

Mrs. DeMarco smiled.

"Nor should you. Now where was I?"

"You told us a baby was born in the attic," Alanis reminded her.

"And lived there for a short period, or at least until Emma was ready to take him away."

"So, her father was born in the attic?" Alanis quickly followed.

I looked at her and then back at Mrs. DeMarco. That wasn't what I had been told. Why would my father have been born in the farmhouse anyway? And why up in an attic? We were always a rich family. That made no sense. Maybe she was already losing her memory and getting things confused.

"Yes, that's correct," she said without hesitation. "I guess with Emma in a hospital and Frances dancing in another world, and especially with Blake March gone, I'm not bound by any promises and oaths. I didn't get enough for it all anyway," she added. She leaned toward me. "Sold my soul too cheaply."

Alanis smiled. "I bet I know what happened," she said. "Her grandmother had an affair and got pregnant, right? They kept it a big secret and she gave birth in the attic, right?"

"An affair?" I asked Alanis. "My grandmother?"

"Like my mother," she replied. I turned with surprise and shock to Mrs. DeMarco. Surely, not my grandmother Emma. She couldn't be like Mae Betty.

Mrs. DeMarco shook her head. "No. Emma March never gave birth as far as I knew."

Alanis sat back, her mouth slightly open. "She never gave birth?"

"But she's my grandmother," I said.

"No, dear. Your grandmother is Frances Wilkens. Emma March is your great-aunt."

Neither I nor Alanis spoke. Then Alanis smiled again. She thought this was even a juicier story. Her excitement annoyed me more than just a little, but I didn't speak.

"I shouldn't have to be the one to tell you all this, but I can see where you'd grow up never knowing the truth," Mrs. DeMarco said. "Maybe that's okay to some people, but to me, especially now, it seems like a sin, and I feel like I was part of it."

She did look happier to be telling us all this. She looked like she was taking a heavy weight off her shoulders.

"Okay," Alanis said. "If that's true, who was the father of Miss Wilkens's baby?"

"Why, Blake March was the father," she said.

"No wonder her grandmother, her great-aunt or whoever she is doesn't like her own sister," Alanis said quickly. "This is better than the soap operas she watches every day," she told me. "It makes sense to me. Miss Wilkens was very pretty once, prettier than her sister, Emma. She seduced Blake March, Jordan's grandfather, right?" she asked Mrs. DeMarco.

"No," she said. "There's much more to this than a sister seducing another sister's husband. In fact," she said, struggling to get up, "it was Emma who seduced Frances."

She went to her window and tried to open it wider. I jumped up to help.

"Thank you, dear. You're certainly a pretty little thing. Where did you get that cute hat?"

"It was Alanis's hat. She gave it to me," I said.

She nodded.

Alanis was staring up at her with her head tilted, as if she thought Mrs. DeMarco was either lying or, as she said about Great-aunt Frances, bonkers.

"How could Emma March seduce her sister and her sister have a baby, Mrs. DeMarco? That doesn't make sense."

"No, on first blush it doesn't," Mrs. DeMarco replied. "Looks like a nice day."

"Do you want us to take you out?" I asked her.

"No, no, thank you, dear. I'm actually a little tired. By this time of day, I usually take a nap, sometimes sleeping until dinner. As you get closer and closer to the end, you sleep longer and longer. Your body is getting used to it."

"Can you tell us what you meant about Emma seducing Frances?" Alanis pursued. "We have someone out there waiting for us, and he is not a very patient person."

"Yes, well, someday he'll realize rushing your life along just gets you to the end faster."

She returned to her chair and closed her eyes. We didn't think she was going to continue. Alanis fidgeted and smirked and then cleared her throat loudly.

"I didn't know what had gone on when I first started caring for Frances," Mrs. DeMarco began again, keeping her eyes closed, as if she was trying to picture things. Then she opened them. "Like you, I assumed Frances had an affair with Blake March. In those days everyone knew everyone else's business. If you sneezed too many times, your neighbors heard. I had heard that Blake had been to the farm often without Emma. I must confess I rode by and strolled by a few times to catch a glimpse of him there. He drove into the village to buy things and was usually alone. If anyone asked after Emma, he had one excuse or another to explain why she wasn't with him. Rumors don't need much water and fertilizing to grow until they wrap themselves like vines around willing ears.

"Then, soon after . . . Frances seemed to disappear."

"Disappear?" I asked.

"No one saw her for some time, even delivery people. Emma and Blake were there and were seen, but Frances was just not seen. When they were asked about her, they said she had gone to spend time with some relatives. No one doubted it, but the theory was Emma found out Blake had been, shall we say, too attentive when it came to her sister and she had her sent off. That's the way it was for months and then, one day, Emma March called me to the farm.

"She met me at the door and took me into the living room, where Blake sat waiting. I must say he looked handsomer than ever," she added with a soft smile. "He was an elegant gentleman, your grandfather," she told me. "He was the kind of man who belonged in a previous age when etiquette and manners mattered. He rose when a woman entered the room and sat only after she sat. I tried to teach those things to my own son, but that was like pushing string uphill."

She sighed and again looked like she was going to fall asleep. Her gaze lowered, and her chin slowly sank toward her chest. She took a deep breath, though, and continued.

" 'We would like to employ you to help with a pregnancy,' " Emma began. She was always all business, Emma Wilkens, Emma March. There was never any time for chitchat. You could probably count on the fingers of one hand how many wasted words that woman spoke. I'm not saying that was a terrible thing, mind you. I'm sure Emma has been more productive than most women, and I'm sure she was in many, many ways a great assistant to Blake. I have no doubt that he wouldn't have reached the heights of success he reached without her at his side or, shall I say, right behind him.

"And I'll tell you something else," she said, nodding at me especially, "in his own way he loved Emma very much. He knew she was of the quality of woman he needed and wanted at his side. People here who had known them used to call them the king and the queen."

"Yes," I said, remembering. "Grandmother Emma's mansion was like a palace with palace guards. My mother said they were like old monarchs."

"Your great-aunt, not your grandmother," Alanis corrected.

I looked at her and at Mrs. DeMarco. I couldn't just drop the idea of Emma as my grandmother just because of what this woman was telling us.

"It's not important what she calls her now," Mrs. DeMarco told Alanis. "It's too late for it to matter, I'm sure. Anyway, Emma asked me what I charged and I told her and just like that, she waved her hand and said, 'We'll triple that.'

"Well, I can tell you, triple was a lot of money for me and my husband back then. I couldn't contain my excitement. 'Under certain conditions,' she added.

"Of course, all the while I was thinking she had found out she was pregnant and wanted private care.

" 'So,' I asked her, 'what are these certain conditions?'

" 'You are not to tell anyone now or ever what you do here and whom you do it for. Nothing that happens here shall ever be revealed. We will ask you to sign a paper to that effect, and if you violate it, not only will we expect all the money we've given you returned, but we'll sue you for breach of contract and cost you your home and all you have saved. Believe me, we have the lawyers and the funds to do it.'

"Well, I just sat there staring at her. I couldn't imagine what secret she wanted so guarded and I had no doubt she would do what she threatened. She could scare a spider out of its own web, that woman.

" 'I won't do anything illegal,' I said. 'I don't do abortions,' I added.

" 'Oh, we don't want an abortion. We want you for a birth, and hopefully a healthy, successful birth that results in a healthy child. We will not ask you to perform any medical duty other than what you are trained to do.'

"Well, that didn't sound bad. If she wanted to keep her pregnancy a secret and the birth a secret, what did I care really? It was her affair, not mine.

" 'We don't mean to sound threatening,' Blake said in a far softer, more pleasant-sounding voice. 'We just want our private business to remain private. It's very important to us. Doctors, lawyers and I suppose good private nurses like you have an ethical obligation to keep what goes on between them and their patients and clients privileged information. You've done that before, I'm sure. I'm sure there are plenty of good stories you've buried away.'

" 'Yes, sir, Mr. March, that's for sure,' I told him. There certainly were.

" 'Please, call me Blake,' he said. I could see Emma didn't like that much, but I smiled.

" 'Are you willing to follow and obey the conditions we set down then?' she asked.

" 'Yes, I can do that,' I told her. She looked at Blake and he nodded.

" 'Okay then,' she said. 'You can begin tomorrow. One more thing,' she added.

" 'Yes?' I said.

" 'We'd like you to move in and stay here for the duration. Of course, you can take off two days a week and holidays that fall in between.'

" 'Move in? Right from the start? I mean, I stay when birthing is close at hand, but—'

" 'We need you full time,' she interrupted. 'We want to restrict access only to you. Mr. March will be coming and going, but I will remain here once you begin.'

" 'Well, why would you need me here full time? I'm not a maid or a cook, Mrs. March.'

"She looked at Blake. 'We'll double what we've tripled,' he said, 'if you will take on as much of that as you can.'

"Well, my jaw nearly dropped in my lap. We were talking big money now. In seven, eight months, I could make what it took my husband three years to make. And then Blake added, 'And if all works out well, there will be a significant bonus, say equal to the total you've been paid.'

"I could have fallen out of the chair if I didn't grip the arm firmly. 'There won't be more than the three of us to care for,' he added. Of course, I thought he meant me and them.

" 'All right,' I said. 'I'll do it. My son's away at college now so that won't be a burden and my husband can care for his own needs while I'm here.'

" 'Your husband owns that small garage and body shop just outside of the village, doesn't he?' Blake asked me. 'Yes,' I told him. 'DeMarco Station.'

"He nodded and then he said, 'Tell him I have two

dozen trucks that make a run near here twice a week. They'll be directed to fill up at his station and go there for any minor repairs. We'll, in fact, draw up a contract for the service,' he added.

"Two dozen trucks twice a week and minor repairs! *What a carrot,* I thought. *My husband will be beaming from ear to ear.* 'I'll call him first thing in the morning,' Blake added.

" 'Thank you, Mr. March.'

" 'Blake,' he repeated.

" 'Well now,' I said, turning to Emma. 'How long have you known you were pregnant?'

"She didn't reply. She got up. 'Follow me,' she said and led me to the dining room table, where there was a paper for me to sign. I looked at it and saw it basically said what she had told me it would say. For a moment, only a moment, I hesitated. My heart was warning me, you see. Then I signed it and she said, 'Come along.'

"We went upstairs and then to the attic door. She took out a key and unlocked it. Really confused now, I followed her up the stairs, and there, lying in bed, looking as contented as a well-fed cat and reading a romance magazine, was her sister, Frances. The shades were drawn closed on the windows."

Mrs. DeMarco paused and closed her eyes.

"I'm afraid," she said, "I have to lie down. Just help me to my bed. I'll finish telling you everything lying down," she added.

Alanis sprang to her feet and took her right arm. I took her left and we helped her rise and guided her to the bed. She sat and I fixed her pillows. She smiled at me and lowered herself.

"Go to the sink, dear, and get me a glass of cold water, please," she told me.

I hurried to do it and returned. She drank some, then handed me the glass.

"Well," she began again, "you can just imagine. Like everyone else, I thought Frances was somewhere else. 'How long have you been up here?' I asked her. She looked at Emma, either because she forgot how long or she wanted permission to tell me.

" 'She's been here a little more than a month now,' Emma said, 'and she's more than a handful. Don't worry,' she continued, 'you'll earn every penny of what we're paying you. Frances,' she told her, 'Mrs. DeMarco will be taking care of you now. She'll be with you until it's over. You are to listen to her, obey her and not make her job any more difficult than it already is. Understand?'

" 'Yes, Emma,' Frances said.

" 'Please give us a list of what you will need in the way of medical paraphernalia, Mrs. DeMarco,' Emma told me, 'and medicine or whatever,' she said.

" 'Okay,' I said.

" 'In the meantime, are there any questions I could answer for you?' she asked.

"I looked at Frances. She looked sweet and young and so vulnerable that my heart went out to her.

" 'Hasn't she been out of this room, this attic, during this time?'

" 'No,' Emma said, 'and I'm afraid that is how it has to be until it's over.'

" 'But walking, fresh air—'

" 'Open the windows, but keep the shades down and her from standing in them if they are opened. We don't want anyone to see her. Walk her all over this house, if you like. I understand going up and down stairs is helpful.'

"She gave me one of her official smiles, and I thought what you thought, of course: Frances is having a baby out of wedlock and Emma wants it to be kept secret. At that moment I didn't think Blake was the father. Why would a wife want her husband's mistress and the resulting child well cared for like this? Frances Wilkens must have strayed and had some affair with a stranger or even someone in the community I knew, and Emma was embarrassed for the family.

"I could see Emma wasn't about to tell me anything more. 'I'll leave you to discuss the procedures, diet, exercise, whatever with my sister,' she said and left the attic.

"I was never a gossip. I asked Frances nothing about the father of her child. I went through the proper medical questions and the symptoms, performing the examination I always did with a woman who had realized she was probably pregnant or had been diagnosed as pregnant. I talked about food and the vitamins I'd be getting for her and then I left.

"Emma was waiting for me below. She locked the door as soon as I stepped out.

" 'Is that necessary?' I asked. 'Locking her in the attic?'

" 'Yes,' she said. 'At least for now. Never mind that,' she added, waving my question away like annoying cigarette smoke. 'How is she?' she asked after I followed her down the main stairway. I thought she was fine and told her so. Then I sat at the kitchen table and prepared a list of the things I would need and wanted for Frances. She said she would have it all by the time

I returned in the morning, and then she told me the most astounding thing of all."

"What?" Alanis asked, impatient.

"She told me to tell anyone who asks, especially my husband, that I was attending to her and not her sister, that she was the one who was pregnant and she had decided to spend her pregnancy here at their rural retreat where it was quieter and more pleasant. She said she would even appear pregnant and that I was not to contradict what people believed.

"I have to tell you I was speechless.

" 'Why are you doing this?' I asked.

" 'We're paying you enough not to ask,' she said and that was all she would ever say about it.

"It wasn't until nearly two weeks later that Frances confided in me and told me she was having Blake's child. Of course, I thought it was because they had a secret affair, but then she added that it was what Emma wanted."

Mrs. DeMarco closed her eyes.

"Excuse me," we heard Sister Andrea say from the doorway, "but there is a young man in the lobby asking after you. He says to tell you the meter's running, whatever that means. He's not a taxicab, is he?"

"Yes," Alanis replied. "Actually, that's all he is. Thank you. We'll be right there."

"Oh, well, Mrs. DeMarco is getting tired. You should let her rest anyway, girls."

"We will. We just want to say good-bye," Alanis told her.

She nodded and left. We looked at Mrs. DeMarco. She seemed to be asleep already.

"Mrs. DeMarco. Why would Emma want that?"

She opened her eyes slowly. She looked half asleep already, and then she closed them again.

"Mrs. DeMarco?"

She didn't open her eyes.

"We better go," I told Alanis.

"Good-bye, Mrs. DeMarco," Alanis told her. "Maybe we'll be back. Thanks."

"Good-bye," I said, but when I turned to follow Alanis out of the room, Mrs. DeMarco seized my wrist. Her eyes popped open. "Alanis," I called, and she turned back.

"I never had a full, head-on conversation with Emma March about it," she told us. "You don't question Emma March, but I picked up things, read between the lines. Emma convinced her sister to be her surrogate mother. She didn't want to go through a pregnancy, but Blake insisted on having a child, and if the child wasn't a boy, he would want another. She promised Frances all sorts of things, but mainly her everlasting love, which is all poor Frances ever wanted from her anyway. That's why I said Emma March seduced her sister."

She closed her eyes again. I looked at Alanis, whose face was bursting with excitement because of the revelations. We started out again, and again Mrs. DeMarco called to us. She pointed at us.

"I knew," she said. "I've always known that Emma March hated her sister for the loving gift she gave her, she demanded of her. But believe me, my little dears, in the end, probably right now, she hates herself for it even more.

"I shouldn't be telling you two all this," she said, suddenly full of regret. "You're both too young, and

I'm only stirring up sleeping hornets, and what for? What's done is done. I'm sorry. I'm sorry," she said.

She closed her eyes firmly this time, and we left. In the hallway Alanis paused and reached out to take my hand. I felt that if she hadn't, I would have risen like a hot air balloon and drifted away with my heart pounding like a funeral drum.

"Well?" she asked me. "Aren't you happy we came here? You found out all your family secrets. Thanks to me," she added. "Aren't you happy?"

"No," I said.

"Why not?"

"I don't know."

"You're just stunned a bit. You'll be happy about it someday. I'm sure."

I'm not, I thought. *I won't ever be happy about it.*

In fact, I was afraid that when we stepped outside, the wind would carry me off like a leaf discarded too soon and bewildered by the notion that it had to be something by itself, unattached and forever alone.

16

Locked in the Attic

"**W**hat the hell you two been doing?" Chad demanded. He was pacing in front of the entrance now and smoking a cigarette.

"Playing tiddlywinks with manhole covers," Alanis said and laughed. "That's what Granddad always says," she told me. She put her hands on her hips and leaned toward him. "We were talking with her great-aunt, like we said, Chad. The poor woman hasn't had a visitor for months and months and was starving for conversation. Ain't you got any compassion for old people?"

He smirked. "Since when do you?" he fired back at her and headed for his car. We followed.

"Since I decided to become a lady," she replied. "Now, a gentleman opens the car door for his female companions," she continued, folding her arms and stepping back from the automobile. "Just like Clark Gable in *Gone With the Wind* or something."

"Huh? My name ain't Clark Gable, whoever that is. Get in yourself," he replied.

"How uncouth," she told me.

I was still feeling too stunned and confused to fool around with Chad.

"I'm hungry," he said, flipping his cigarette behind him and getting into the car. He held up the money Alanis had given him. "This twenty is for gas. You got money for lunch?"

"As it happens, we do," Alanis told him. "Stop at that Fast Freddy's Grill Burger joint that was on the right just as we entered town," she directed.

I had no appetite, but the two of them were famished. I nibbled on a grilled chicken sandwich and sipped a Coke. We ate in the car. Chad wanted to know what we'd talked about with "the old lady," but Alanis didn't reveal anything.

"Well, when we getting together then?" he demanded. "Tonight?"

"We'll see," she said, twisting her shoulder and dangling hope in front of his eyes. "Maybe if you're good."

"Ahhh," he said, pushing her away. "Just say when."

"We have to work on my granddad," she added quickly. "I've been grounded because of failing my first math, science and English tests."

I didn't know if that was true or not, but the explanation was credible for Chad.

"Well, if you're living with her in the big house, we should be able to meet in the basement anyway. What time?"

"We can't meet in the basement anymore. Her

great-aunt found some alcopops down there and it's off bounds."

"What alcopops? You had a party down there without me? That was true what I heard about Stuart Gavin?"

"No, silly. We took some from him and the girls and I had our own little girl-talk get-together. No boys allowed. Right, Jordan?"

He considered her stories, glanced back at me, then started the car. I didn't say a word for fear he would know it was all a big lie.

"So where we gonna get together and have our own little party?" he asked.

"We might figure out a way to sneak you in after her great-aunt goes to sleep," she offered. "I'll call you. Stand by."

"Stand by? Where should I stand by? You playing me, Alanis?" he asked.

"Why would I do that, Chad? Don't you think I want to have fun, too?"

"I don't know," he said. "You better," he added. "I don't want to be made a fool."

She glanced back at me and winked, but I was only half-listening to their chatter now. My brain was still reeling with the information we had just gathered. How desperately I needed to speak with Ian, I thought. Or my mother, but neither could hear me. Who could I turn to? Who would help me understand? How could I tell my father any of this? What would he say? Would he believe it, believe his mother was really Great-aunt Frances? How do you tell someone his mother isn't really his mother?

Either out of fear or frustration or maybe because

of both, I started to cry silently. Chad and Alanis were into their own conversation, teasing each other again, listening to their music. Neither noticed me all the way home. As soon as we pulled into the driveway, her granddad, who was on the tractor cutting more of the overgrown grounds, stopped and turned off the engine. He sat there watching us for a moment, obviously poised to come at us as soon as we stepped out of the car.

"Let me do all the talking," Alanis told me quickly as we got out of the car. "Get outta here quick, Chad," she told him. "I'll call you."

"You'd better," he said, backed up, and drove fast down the driveway, kicking up stones and dust.

Alanis's granddad hopped off the tractor and started toward us. He was as angry-looking as he had been that day at school when he'd slapped her behind the head and pushed her into his car. He even frightened me.

"Where you been?" he asked halfway to us.

"We just went for a ride to visit one of my friends. It's the weekend, Granddad. We can have some fun," she whined.

"You're lying, Alanis, and you lied to Miss Wilkens. I'm disappointed in you going along with this, Miss Jordan," he told me. "That woman trusts you and you go and help make up stories and go someplace you ain't supposed to go."

I looked down quickly.

"We didn't lie," Alanis began, "we told her we—"

"Don't even start, Alanis. You might be pretty good at pulling the wool over other people's eyes, but you know you're not good at it with me. And besides, Miss Wilkens got a phone call from Tom DeMarco."

I looked up quickly.

"That's right. His mother felt bad about things she said to you and she was worried. She called him and he called here and told Miss Wilkens everything. I never seen her so upset. She couldn't even talk. Where'd you go? Why'd you go visit his mother in a nursing home? What things did she say? Why is Miss Wilkens so upset she was crying? She never cries. No more of your lying, Alanis. What sort of mischief are you up to now? Doing such a nasty thing to that poor old lady. Go on, spit it out before I take a strap to you," he said without taking a breath.

I turned to her to see what she would say. Great-aunt Frances was very upset and was crying? This was terrible.

"I'm not lying! I don't know what you're talking about. Some old lady imagined things, that's all. We didn't do anything to anybody. You're always accusing me of things!" she screamed back at him. "No wonder my mother ran off. No one wants to live with you. I'll run off, too!"

Her granddad practically flew across the few yards between us and seized her at the shoulders, shaking her so hard that I thought her eyes rolled in her head. I stepped back, terrified. She looked like she might crack in two in his hands.

"You ain't running off, child. The only place you're going from here is some juvenile detention center. You lie, steal, drink my alcohol, smoke in school and now who knows what else. You're not just walking in your mother's footsteps. You're making your own and you're going down the same dark path to hell. Now, you go back into that house and you get your things and bring them back to our house right now, hear me? I told Miss Wilkens you can't stay there anymore, and she knows it. I don't want you having any more to do with this little girl either, hear?"

"I won't move back in with you. I won't! You hate me just as much as you hate my mother!" Alanis screamed and tore herself out of his grip. She fumed, and then she turned and ran down the driveway.

"Alanis King, you come right back here. Now!" he cried. "I'm not fooling with you. I'll call the police and have them pick you up, girl. You'll go to a juvenile home," he shouted as she rounded the turn at the bottom of the driveway. She didn't stop. In a moment she was gone.

Frustrated, Lester Marshall shook his head, then turned to me.

"Best thing could happen to you is she keeps going," he said. "You better go let your great-aunt know you're back and okay. You better tell her where you were and what you and Alanis did to make all this trouble," he said. "You got her in a terrible state. She was trembling something awful. I'm mighty disappointed in you, too."

He turned and started back toward the tractor. I looked down the driveway, hoping Alanis would return. I needed her help with my great-aunt Frances. What was I going to say? I waited a little longer, but she didn't come back. After a few more moments, I headed for the house, so exhausted from my emotional ping-pong that I didn't know if I could even talk.

When I entered, I was immediately struck by the silence. The television wasn't on, and Great-aunt Frances wasn't in the living room. She wasn't in the kitchen or anywhere else downstairs. I called for her, but she didn't answer. What's more, I didn't see Miss Puss anywhere either. *She could be outside,* I thought and went to the rear door.

I stepped out and panned the yard, looking down to the lake, but I saw no one. There was just the dull whirr of the tractor Lester Marshall was driving out front. I called and waited, called and waited, and then went back inside.

Slowly, I started up the stairway. When I reached the top, I stopped and listened but heard nothing. Now more frightened than curious, I hurried down to her room and looked in, expecting to see her curled up in her bed with Miss Puss curled up beside her. She wasn't there. She wasn't in the bathroom or my room either. When I started down the hallway, I stopped and froze the moment I could make out Miss Puss curled up at the door to the attic. Why would she lock out Miss Puss? I wondered. There wasn't anyplace in the house she didn't permit the cat to go. Sometimes, Miss Puss even went into the bathroom with her.

"Where's Great-aunt Frances?" I asked Miss Puss, who lifted her head but didn't move. "Why did she leave you out here?"

Cautiously, I tried the handle on the attic door and found it was locked. *It must be locked from the inside,* I thought. Now more suspicious, I put my ear to the door and listened. I was sure I heard soft sobbing.

"Great-aunt Frances!" I called. I knocked on the door. "It's Jordan. Are you up there? Great-aunt Frances!"

I listened, but I heard nothing, no footsteps on the stairway, nothing. I put my ear to the door and did still hear her sobbing. Again I called for her. When I knocked again, Miss Puss rose and stepped behind me. She stood still, watching, as if she knew something. Her behavior made me even more nervous. I knocked and listened and called again and again, but Great-aunt Frances didn't respond. There was only the sobbing. I waited and listened, and then I went to my room. Miss Puss followed slowly, but she didn't come in.

I thought about going out to tell Lester Marshall about Great-aunt Frances crying in the attic with the door locked, but he was so angry at Alanis and me that I was afraid to ask him for help. *Maybe Great-aunt Frances will come down soon,* I told myself and sat on my bed with my back against the pillows staring up at the ceiling. When I still didn't hear her after almost another half hour, I returned to the attic door. Miss Puss was nowhere around this time. Again, there was only silence.

I called to her but heard nothing.

Why won't she answer? I asked myself. I thought a moment, wondering if I had fallen asleep and not heard her come down. Maybe she had gone to her bedroom. I hurried back and looked, but she wasn't there, and neither was Miss Puss.

So frustrated I could cry, I returned again to the attic door and pounded it with my small fist.

"Great-aunt Frances," I screamed, "don't you want to start thinking about dinner with me?"

I listened and heard nothing, and then this time when I put my ear to the door, I didn't even hear the soft sobbing. Maybe she had come down without my having heard her, but she'd have gone downstairs and not to her room, I imagined, so I went downstairs, but she wasn't there. I did find Miss Puss in the living room, curled up below the sofa, as if Great-aunt Frances had been lying on it and watching television. The cat glanced at me, closed her eyes, and lowered her head.

I returned to the kitchen, got myself some cold apple juice and sat on the stairs, listening attentively for any sign of her. I heard nothing and began to hate the silence.

I wondered about Alanis, too, and went out to see if she had returned. Her grandfather was working behind the house now. I ran quickly over to his house so he wouldn't see me, and I knocked on the door. I called to Alanis, but she didn't respond, and I didn't hear anyone moving about inside.

Where was she? Where could she go? I wondered and slowly returned to the main house. When I entered the living room, I saw that Miss Puss had gone somewhere else. I tried to keep myself from thinking about everything and even thought if I turned on the television set, Great-aunt Frances would hear it and come down from the attic, but she didn't appear. Bored and worried now, I turned off the set and went back upstairs, where I found Miss Puss again lying by the door.

"What is she doing, Miss Puss?" I asked. The cat stared up at me as if she, too, was thinking the same thing.

I knocked again on the attic door. The silence frightened me. Why wouldn't she respond? Was she so angry at me for going with Alanis to see Mrs. DeMarco? That had to be it. She probably thought we had been sneaky. *She's just mad and in a sulk*, I thought.

"Great-aunt Frances," I called. "Please come down.

I'm sorry if I upset you. Please," I begged. "We were just curious. We didn't mean to make any trouble. I'm sorry."

I waited and listened and knocked and called, but there was still no response.

"I'm going to stay here until you come down, Great-aunt Frances," I declared and curled up on the floor at the door beside Miss Puss. I, too, could sulk, I thought.

My head felt heavy. All that we had learned had left me dizzy and even a little nauseous. I was sorry I had eaten any lunch with Alanis and Chad. The sandwich had been too greasy. I closed my eyes and soon fell asleep. I had no idea how long I slept, but when I woke, the hallway was dark and Miss Puss was gone. For a few moments, I was very confused. I forgot where I was. Since I had fallen asleep right at the attic door, I realized that Great-aunt Frances hadn't come down or she would have discovered me. I rose, rubbed my eyes and listened. The house was deadly quiet. I put my ear to the attic door but heard nothing.

Not sure what I should do, I went downstairs. There wasn't a light on, of course, so I had to put some on. I went to the front and looked out. It was very dark because the sky was completely overcast. In fact, when I opened the door, I saw there was a light drizzle. It was cold, too, so cold it made me shiver quickly. I closed the door and went into the living room, where I sat and waited and wondered what I was supposed to do. *Surely it's time for dinner,* I thought and returned to the attic door to knock and call to Great-aunt Frances. She hadn't eaten lunch. *She must be hungry,* I thought.

"It's dinnertime, Great-aunt Frances. Are you coming down? What should I make? Do you want to put on any special clothes?"

As before, there was no answer. *She's fallen asleep,* I thought. *She'll come down when she wakes up, I'm sure.* I went down to the kitchen and looked for something to make myself for dinner. Miss Puss appeared again, this time looking more alert and curious. I imagined she was hungry, too, so I poured some of the cat food into her dish and she went right to it. Then I found another box of macaroni and cheese and followed the directions. There was some bread and butter and some grape juice to drink.

Even though it tasted good, I felt strange eating alone in the silent house. Halfway through, I lost my appetite and dumped the rest of it in Miss Puss's plate. She smelled it, ate some, then left the kitchen. I washed everything and cleaned up. After that, I went to the living room and looked out the window. The world looked even darker to me. I felt as if I was shrinking under the enclosing blackness.

Without the television going or Great-aunt Frances moving about, and no one else here, silence fell like a stone curtain around me. I wondered if Miss Puss had gone back upstairs to wait at the door. I kept expecting Alanis, anticipating her bursting in and complaining about her granddad. I actually missed her company and hoped she would return, but the hours went by and I heard or saw no one outside. Every time I peered through the window curtain in the living room, I saw no one. Without lights and this far from the road, there was barely a glimmer.

It started to rain harder, and soon I heard thunder

and saw a flash of lightning. It drove me back from
the window. Ian loved to see lightning. He was in awe
of the energy and loved to count the seconds until we
heard a rumble or a roll of thunder.

I wondered how Great-aunt Frances felt about
lightning and thunder. I half hoped that it would ter-
rify her and drive her out of the attic and down to me.
When was she going to come out? How could she stay
in there so long? I wondered, and then I remembered
what Mrs. DeMarco had told us about Great-aunt
Frances being confined to the attic for months and
months, even locked in it. Surely, if she had been able
to stand that, she could stay up there now for a day.
But why would she want to? And why wasn't she worrying about me? She couldn't be that angry.

The rain sounded like bugs hitting the windows.
I could hear the wind sweeping sheets of it onto the
porch and against the walls. The wind itself was whis-
tling around the house, seeping in every crack. It was
a real Indian summer storm. I cowered on the sofa,
then decided to just go upstairs to bed. Sure enough,
Miss Puss was sleeping at the attic door. I listened,
put my ear to the door, knocked and called once more
for Great-aunt Frances, but she didn't reply and I
heard nothing. *She must have gone to sleep herself,* I
thought. Miss Puss was still asleep. My noise hadn't
woken her.

I washed, brushed my teeth and headed for my
bedroom. I thought I heard something and stopped
to listen, but it was only a window shutter rattling.
Practically diving into bed, I pulled my cover around
me, said prayers for my parents and Ian, then tried to
drown out the sounds of the storm by pressing my ear

to the pillow and practically pulling the blanket over my head. I wondered again about Alanis. Had she come home? Had she gone to a friend's house? *She couldn't be wandering about the streets in this storm,* I thought, and then I imagined that was just what she was doing and felt sorry for her.

Sometime after I had fallen asleep, I woke to the sound of a telephone ringing. I listened, and it stopped. I had no idea how long it had been ringing or what time it was.

"Great-aunt Frances?" I called to the open bedroom doorway and the hall. I waited, but I didn't hear her call back or moving about. The storm had stopped and there was just a light wind circling about the house now. I could hear the water still running down the gutters. It sounded like marbles. After a few more moments of listening, I fell asleep again and didn't wake this time until sunlight crawled over the bed and nudged my eyelids with soft fingers of brightness.

Eager now to see Great-aunt Frances, I rose quickly and dressed. Then I looked first in her bedroom and was terribly disappointed to see she wasn't there and the bed hadn't been touched. I hurried out. Miss Puss wasn't at the door, which gave me hope. I practically leaped down the stairway, calling for Great-aunt Frances as I descended, but when I reached the kitchen, I saw she wasn't there. She wasn't anywhere. I discovered Miss Puss in the living room near the sofa, and for a moment, I just turned about, stunned and confused.

She can't still be up in the attic, I thought. *She can't.*

Nevertheless, I returned to the attic door, listened, and knocked, and called. There was no response, and it was still locked. I couldn't help but start crying a little, and then . . .

I looked down and saw the ants.

They were coming out from under the door.

Ian's ants!

Streaming out in a thin line right toward me.

I screamed and backed away, nearly falling over in my haste to retreat. Spinning around, I charged down the stairway and tripped, just catching myself on the wobbly banister. I heard it cracking and let go, balancing myself.

Crying harder now, I continued down and charged out the front door.

Lester Marshall, wearing paint-stained overalls and carrying a can of paint and a brush, was heading toward me. He stopped for a moment. I simply screamed "Ants!" and he dropped the can of paint and the brush and ran toward the house.

"What is it?" he asked.

I was sobbing so hard that I couldn't breathe or speak. The words just wouldn't form.

"Miss Jordan, what's wrong?" he asked.

I was choking now. I felt the porch floor start to wobble and the whole world begin to turn, as if I'd been in a huge bubble and it had started to roll.

I heard him call out to me, and I felt his hands reach out and catch me under my back just before I hit the porch floor.

That was all I remembered until I woke up in the living room on the sofa. I felt the cold washcloth on my forehead. Lester Marshall was standing there looking down at me, a glass of water in his hand.

"Drink some of this," he said. He knelt down to

help me lift my head, then guided the glass to my lips. I drank some and closed my eyes. "Where's Miss Frances?" he asked.

"She's . . . up in the . . . attic," I said.

"The attic?"

"She's been up there all the time. The door's locked. And now ants . . ."

"Ants?" he said, twisting his lips. He stood up, looking very concerned.

"Ian's ants," I muttered. "He said to watch out."

"You babbling, child. You just rest here a while until I see what is what," he said.

He turned and left the living room. I heard him going up the stairway. Then I saw Miss Puss appear. She walked toward me, stood looking up at me, then curled up beside the sofa. I closed my eyes. My stomach was churning and turning, and I was still very dizzy.

I know I called out for my mother. It seemed as if I was doing it in a dream.

And then, I was sure. I was positive. I heard her. Ian was right. The telepathy would work. Mommy would hear me. She called my name. She told me not to be afraid. She said she would watch over me. She said everything would be all right. I felt myself relax, and moments later, I was asleep.

When I woke again, there was a great deal of noise and activity around me. A kind-looking woman in a paramedic's uniform was at my side, smiling down at me. She knelt and told me I shouldn't be afraid.

"I know," I said. "My mother just told me that, too."

"Oh, did she?" She held her smile. I thought she

had very pretty dark brown eyes, more like the shade of pecan brown with tiny gold specks. "When did you see her?" she asked.

"I didn't. She's in the hospital in a coma, but she talks to me through telepathy. Ian taught her how to do it."

"Ian? Who's Ian?"

"He's my brother."

"Oh. Well, that's very nice. I'm happy for you. Would you like to sit up? Do you want to eat something?"

I remembered being nauseous and shook my head.

"I was nauseous," I told her.

"I'll give you something to help that. In the meantime, I want you to drink some water and then we'll make sure you're fine, okay?"

I nodded.

She was very nice. *Mother would like her,* I thought. Ian might even trust her.

"Where's Great-aunt Frances?" I asked.

"We're taking care of her," she said. "Don't you worry. Your name's Jordan, right?"

"Yes."

"I'm Alexandra, but everyone calls me Alex."

I heard more noise just outside the living room and sat up to see other paramedics carrying a stretcher on which Great-aunt Frances lay. They had one of those bags with what looked like a wire going into her arm, just the way my mother had. *Oh no,* I thought, *she's in a coma, too.* I felt the tears filling my eyes.

"Great-aunt Frances is in a coma."

"No, she's not. She needs medical help, but she's not in a coma. Don't worry."

Everything started to come back to me. I rattled it off, babbling. Alex seemed to be pleased, though. Another paramedic arrived and spoke with her, and then he left. I saw Lester Marshall for a moment talking to what looked like a policeman this time.

"Is Alanis back?" I asked.

"Alanis?" Alex asked.

"She's Mr. Marshall's granddaughter. She ran away."

"Oh. I don't know. I haven't seen anyone, any other girls about."

"Where's Miss Puss?" I asked.

"Miss Puss? The cat?"

I nodded.

"Oh, I saw a cat in the hallway. I think she's just hiding from all the noise and people. I'm sure she's fine," she said, smiling.

The other paramedic returned to the living room doorway, and Alex went to speak with him. Then she returned to me.

"Well now, someone is coming for you, so I don't want you worrying any, Jordan."

"Who's coming?" I asked.

"Your father's coming," she said. "He'll be here as soon as he can."

"My father?"

"Uh-huh. Everything's going to be fine," she said. "Drink some more water for me, okay?"

I started to drink when I remembered something important.

"What about the ants?" I asked.

"Ants?"

"In the attic. Ian's ants."

"Oh, there weren't many ants. No problem," she said.

I suddenly became a little suspicious. Would Ian trust her after all?

"They were coming out from under the door," I said. "I saw them."

"If there were any, there were just a few," she said.

Lester Marshall returned and stood in the doorway, looking in at me.

"How's she doing?" he asked.

"She's stable. I gave her something for her nausea. She'll be fine," Alex said, smiling at me. "Right?"

I looked at Lester.

"Did you see the ants?" I asked him. "Coming out of the attic?"

He pulled his head back and then looked at Alex, who held her smile but widened her eyes.

"Oh," he said. "Right. There were some ants, but I sprayed. They're gone now," he said. "No worries," he told me. "You just relax, Miss Jordan. Your daddy's on his way."

"Is Alanis home?"

"She's home," he said, losing his smile. "Don't concern yourself about her."

I looked from him to Alex, and then I closed my eyes and lay back again. I don't know how long I slept this time, but when I awoke, I heard my father's voice. I heard Felix and I heard Lester Marshall. Moments later, my father wheeled himself into the living room. Felix was right behind him.

"Hey, Jordan," Daddy said, wheeling as close to the sofa as he could. "How you doing?"

I blinked and stared. Was he really here? Was I really awake, or was this another dream?

"Great-aunt Frances wouldn't come down from the attic," I told him. "And there were ants."

"Yes, I know. We'll talk about all that later," he said. "Nancy is upstairs getting your things together. I'm taking you home," he told me.

"Nancy?" I looked at Felix. "I thought Nancy wasn't working for you anymore."

My father laughed. "She's changed her mind. There are a few other changes at the mansion, too," Daddy said. "Kimberly is gone. She decided I wasn't quite worth all the effort after all. Your grandmother will be pleased."

"My grandmother," I muttered. Should I just tell him everything now?

I glanced at Felix, and his face seemed to have the word *Wait!* written across it. Was it possible that he knew everything?

"Yes, your remarkable grandmother," he said. "She's sitting up, writing, getting speech therapy. There's the terrifying possibility she'll be coming home soon," he added and laughed.

"I spoke to Mommy," I told him.

He raised his eyebrows

"Ian told me how to do telepathy."

"Is that so?"

"I knew everything would be all right. She told me it would be."

My father looked up at Felix and then back at me.

"Well, maybe. Who knows what is and is not possible anymore? Certainly not me," he added.

We saw Nancy in the hallway. She had my suitcases. Felix moved quickly to take them from her. Then she came in to see how I was.

"I missed you," she told me. "Your room is all set for you at home."

"I'm not going to live here anymore?" I asked my father.

"No. Your father is going to try to be a responsible adult again. Not that I ever was, according to your grandmother," he added. "There's no one to look after you here anyway, Jordan. Great-aunt Frances needs care herself."

"What happened to her?" I asked.

"Something upset her and she took a few too many sleeping pills, but fortunately, thanks to you, she'll be all right. Later, you can tell me what upset her." He smiled. "You do know what upset her, don't you, Jordan?"

I wanted to shake my head. I bit down on my lower lip. Felix wasn't there. Nancy was standing and looking down at me. Lester Marshall was doing something else with someone outside. Alanis wasn't in the room to help me make up a story. There was too much noise and too many people around me to try Ian's telepathy and speak with my mother.

I struggled with my thoughts, turning this way and that in my brain, looking hard for one of Alanis's convenient exits. Everyone has to lie, she'd told me. You'll find out. You'll have to lie, too.

Can you swallow down the truth? I wondered.

And if you do, will it keep coming up like a burp?

Until you can't stand it anymore and you have to get it out, just as Mrs. DeMarco had.

Daddy sat there in his wheelchair, already having spent months and months feeling terrible about himself, wishing he'd been dead, maybe looking to hide, hating everyone and everything, willing to give me up and disappear.

He looked like he was coming back, going home, just like me.

Should I tell the truth?

Grandmother Emma once told me people who lie are afraid and weak. Was that what I was? Afraid and weak? Or was Alanis right? Sometimes, you do it not to hurt someone you love.

No matter what, I couldn't help but love my father.

I shook my head.

"No, Daddy," I said. "I don't know why she was upset."

17

No Secrets, No Lies

Before we left, I did eat some hot oatmeal Nancy prepared. With the way she was flitting about the kitchen, I felt as if I'd already been back at the mansion. Afterward, I went upstairs to see if there was anything being left in my room that I wanted. I found the doll Great-aunt Frances had given me the first night and decided I would take it with me. I wondered if Grandmother Emma would remember it if I showed it to her.

"Won't I see Great-aunt Frances anymore?" I asked my father when I was ready to go.

"Oh, sure," he said. "We'll either come here or she'll be brought to see us."

"She should be," I said. "She says she has never been at the mansion."

"Yes," Daddy said. "As far as I know, that's true."

Felix wheeled him out and Lester Marshall helped

get him off the porch, because there was no ramp like we had at the mansion. I waited and watched while they transferred him into the backseat of the limousine and then folded and put his wheelchair into the trunk. Then I went around to get in when Felix opened the door for me. Before I did, I looked toward Lester Marshall's house.

"Who's going to feed Miss Puss?" I asked.

"I'll take care of her. Don't worry," Lester Marshall said.

"Can't I say good-bye to my friend?" I asked my father.

"Sure," he said. "Why not?"

I looked at Lester Marshall. He was not pleased about it.

"She's not coming out," he said. "And your daddy's got to get started."

"It's all right," my father told him. "I'm fine. Let her go say good-bye, Lester. I have a few things to discuss about the property with you while we wait."

Lester shook his head and then approached the limousine. I ran toward his house. Bones, as usual, had planted himself safely between the main house and Lester Marshall's. I saw that Miss Puss was lying near a basement window watching him. She was more of a guard dog than he was. Bones lifted his head and watched me hurry to the front steps. I knocked on the door.

"Alanis, it's me. I have to leave."

She must have been standing right there, because almost before I finished my sentence, she pulled the door open.

"What do you want?"

"I came to say good-bye."

"Good-bye," she said and started to close the door.

"Why are you mad at me?" I asked.

She held the door and looked down.

"I ain't mad at you. I'm just mad I got to come back here."

"Where else could you go?"

She looked up sharply.

"That's what I mean, stupid. I got no place to go. I got no rich family looking after me."

I winced and her face softened.

"It's not my fault," I said. It seemed silly to say it. How could it possibly be my fault? But I didn't know what else to tell her.

"I'm not saying it is. I said I'm not mad at you." She looked toward the limousine. "Where you going?"

"I'm going back to live with my father. I'm sure you could come visit. Maybe you could come with Great-aunt Frances when she's well enough."

"She's not your great-aunt."

"I know," I said. Now I was looking down.

"You didn't tell, did you? Well?"

"No."

"Why not?"

"I don't know. I didn't know what to say."

"It's not hard. You say that woman back at the mansion is not your mother, Daddy. She's your aunt and the woman you think is your aunt is your mother."

"I know," I said.

"You look like a big girl, but you're still a baby."

"No, I'm not. I just don't want to hurt anyone," I said. I saw her expression soften again.

"Well, my granddad got no right to be so mad at me

for taking you to see Mrs. DeMarco. You had a right to know the truth. What you do with it is your own business, I suppose, but he's got no right to be punishing me. Am I right? Well? Am I?"

"Yes," I said. She softened some more and stepped out on the porch.

"You're going back to that big mansion, huh? You going to attend a private school again, too?"

"Probably."

"We both got screwed-up families," she said, "but it don't hurt none to be the rich one."

"I didn't mind living here. We were having lots of fun."

She studied me to be sure I wasn't just saying it, and then she let go of her grip on a smile, let it out and nodded.

"I usually have a lot of fun no matter what."

"I'm glad you're my friend."

"Yeah, yeah." She waved her hand to shoo off a fly.

"I am. I didn't have any friends like you back at the mansion and probably still won't."

"Yeah, maybe," she relented. "Well, maybe I'll do you a favor and visit."

"Will you? Please."

"If Granddad takes off the ball and chain."

"What do you mean?"

"Lets me go, stupid." She smiled. "What are you going to be like when your brain catches up with your body, huh?"

"I don't know."

"I do. You going to have lots of boys' names to write on your shoes. You just make sure they don't write your name on theirs, hear?"

"Okay."

"Okay," she mimicked, then took me by surprise and hugged me quickly.

She turned and went back into the house. "You know why I'm coming to see you, don't you?" she asked, holding the door open. I shook my head. "I want to meet that weird brother of yours. I think I'd like him. You tell him I'm coming and you tell him I read his letters and I'm still coming, understand?"

I nodded.

"I'll look after your . . . great-aunt," she said and closed the door.

"And make sure your granddad feeds Miss Puss," I shouted.

Lester Marshall stepped back from the limousine and looked my way. I stepped off the porch, patted Bones on his head, and hurried to the limousine. Felix was still standing by the door, waiting. He smiled at me, and I got in. Nancy was sitting up front.

"You okay?" my father asked when I slid in and Felix closed the door.

"Yes, Daddy."

"Your friend can come visit, you know."

"I told her."

"Good."

Felix got in and started the engine. Lester stood there looking at us with his arms folded as the limousine started down the driveway. I turned and looked back at his house. Alanis had come out again and was standing on the small porch, watching us. She couldn't see I was looking back because of the tinted windows, but I saw her slowly lift her right hand to wave. Then she realized what she was doing, dropped her arm to her side and rushed back into the house.

The car turned at the base of the driveway and we were off.

"When is Great-aunt Frances coming home?" I asked my father.

"Very soon. I've arranged for someone to stay with her for a while," he said. "She needs a full-time housekeeper and companion. I'm informing your grandmother."

"What about Mommy?" I asked.

"We'll go see her."

"And Ian?"

"Ian hasn't been well, Jordan, so he's been moved to a different facility." He smiled quickly. "I understand he's doing better already, complaining and offering suggestions for improvements."

"He is?"

"Yes."

"Can I visit him, too?"

"We'll see. I have to get you organized first, get you enrolled in your school again," he said. "I'm making all the calls today after we're home."

"You are?"

He started to speak, then stopped and glanced out the window for a moment. "Yes," he said, still looking out the window. "It's time I accepted who I am."

The blood rushed to my face. Did he know? Had he always known or was the secret out?

He turned back to me.

"I'm Emma March's son," he said. "I have to start acting like a mature, responsible person. I resented my mother. I know there were lots of times I thought

I hated her and there were lots of times she wasn't really a grandmother to you and to Ian, and certainly not a mother-in-law to Caroline, but life's too short to fill your time with resentment and," he said, smiling, "self-pity. If she says that to me one more time . . ." He shook his head. "It's too easy, too convenient to blame other people for your own mistakes, Jordan. Yes, it makes you feel better on the surface, but deep down inside you know you're lying to the most important person in your life."

"Who?"

"Yourself," he said. "Lies are the worst kind of ghosts . . . they constantly haunt you. They wait behind the mirror and emerge every time you look at yourself."

No lies, no secrets, I thought. If that was the pledge between two best friends, why shouldn't it be the pledge between a father and a daughter? *I have to tell him.*

But he wants to be Emma March's son now, another voice inside me said. *He's finally become comfortable with it. How can you send him reeling back into what Ian would surely call a web of deceit? How can it be right to hurt him so much?*

Besides, you're not the keeper of this truth. It belongs to Grandmother Emma. She is the only one who can unlock it, if it is to be unlocked.

Oh, how I miss my mother, I thought. *She would surely know what I should and shouldn't say.*

"Isn't Mommy getting any better, Daddy?" I asked. My eyes started to fill with tears just asking.

"Yes, there's improvement. I don't want to build up your hopes too much. I don't know how long it will take or if it will ever happen that your mother returns to us the way she was. We can only hope and pray."

Will we pray?

When did we pray together last?

Isn't it stronger when we're all together or there is more than one of us saying the same prayer? Won't our voices be louder?

"You and I should go to church and pray then, Daddy," I said.

He looked at me, smiled and nodded.

"Yeah, maybe," he said. "Hey, Felix, does our church provide for the disabled?"

Felix looked in the rearview mirror.

Daddy was smiling.

"Mr. March, everyone who goes to church comes with some disability or another."

Daddy laughed.

Laughter, I thought as we rode on. What a sweet sound when it comes from the people whom you love and who love you. It's as comforting as warm milk. Maybe that was why Great-aunt Frances wanted it so much in her life and turned everything she could, even a simple dinner, into a party.

As soon as we arrived at the mansion, Daddy was surprised to hear immediately from Mr. Pond, Grandmother Emma's attorney. He told him that she wanted me brought to see her as soon as possible. She was now at a special clinic for stroke victim's therapy. After my father spoke with Mr. Pond, he asked Nancy to tell me to come down from my room.

Although I had spent so much time in this room before I'd been taken to live with Great-aunt Frances, it seemed so strange for me to be returned to it. All of the things I had left in it were still there, of course, and there was nothing different about the room, nothing added or changed. Yet without Ian nearby or my parents down the hall, and without even Grandmother Emma close, I felt what everyone had feared I would feel—terribly lonely. I immediately fantasized bringing Alanis here to live with me and go to my school. It was an impossible dream, I knew, but I sat there imagining it, imagining how we would enjoy the mansion, the grounds, the pool, all of it. With a sister it would all make so much more sense, I thought.

"Apparently," Daddy told me after I came downstairs, "your grandmother thinks it's more important for you to see her before I even get you enrolled in your school. And," he said, smiling, "you're to visit her alone. She knows about Great-aunt Frances, of course. She knew almost as quickly as I did. She'll probably ask you a lot about it, and I'm sure, now that she knows you're here, she probably wants to find out the nitty-gritty about me as well. She wants to make you her little spy. That's all right," he added. "If I have to have anyone spy on me, I'd rather it be you."

"I won't be a spy, Daddy," I said.

"Whatever. Go make her happy. Tell her whatever she wants to know. She's still the queen. Felix will bring you there in the morning. I'll start the process to get you back into school. I've ordered that specially equipped car I told you about, by the way. Soon, I'll be the one who brings you to school and picks you up, when I'm not tending to business, but I promise, that'll be the only reason I'm not."

"I'd like that, Daddy," I said.

"Me, too. Nancy's preparing one of your favorite meals, Southern fried chicken."

I smiled. "I should get dressed up for it," I said.

"Pardon?"

"Get a *Gone With the Wind* dress."

"Huh?"

"Nothing, Daddy. Just kidding."

"Yes, well, that's something we haven't had around here for a long time, kidding. Go settle yourself in your old nest, little bird."

He smiled at me, and I stood there for a moment remembering an earlier time. I didn't know exactly when, but I remembered running up to him when he was sitting at the dinner table and him holding out his arms. He lifted me and put me in his lap and hugged and kissed me. Was it a dream?

He held up his arms, and I went to him now. He embraced me.

"I'm so sorry for everything, Jordan."

For a long moment, we just held on to each other. Then he kissed my cheek and I turned and ran to the stairway. The tears flew off my chin as I hurried up to my room.

I sat on my bed right where I'd sat the day Felix had come to take me away, only now I closed my eyes and worked hard on Ian's telepathy. I concentrated on reaching my mother, and I tried and tried until I was sure I heard her voice, heard how happy she was that I was home again. She promised me she would return soon, too.

It had been a long time since I'd sat and had dinner with my father. Of course, I missed Ian and my mother at the table, but Daddy talked about all his new plans.

He spoke to me as if I'd already been a grown-up and he wanted my opinions. After dinner, he went to the office and made some phone calls to see how Great-aunt Frances was doing. Later, he told me she would be heading home even sooner than expected.

"Won't she wonder where I am?" I asked.

"She's been told and she's also been told that as soon as she's strong enough, she's being brought here to visit you and me and, who knows, maybe even your grandmother."

"Good," I said.

I asked again about Ian, and he promised he would work on our visiting him as soon as possible.

"I've been speaking with your mother's doctor, Jordan. We'll be going to see her this weekend. I want to stress that you shouldn't get your hopes up too high, but they're leaning toward a more positive prognosis, which means more hopeful. It might take a long time yet, if at all. Okay?"

I nodded, too terrified that I might think or say something that would change his mind. He smiled.

"You are growing up so fast, I feel like I'm in a rocket ship watching."

Comforted with all this new promise and hope, I was able to curl up in my own bed and fall asleep quickly. I had once again been riding on an emotional roller coaster and was far more tired than I had imagined.

After breakfast the following morning, Felix took me to visit Grandmother Emma. For the visit, I put on the dress she had bought me on my birthday. *She'll be surprised to see me wearing a bra now,* I thought. I fixed my hair and put on a string of pearls my mother had given me some time ago. When I thought I looked good enough to make a proper presentation to my grandmother, I left the house and walked toward the limousine. Daddy wheeled out to wish me luck.

"Well, look at you, a young woman, a beautiful young woman."

"Daddy," I said, even though I soaked in the compliment. He laughed.

"I guess it all comes natural to you girls."

"What?"

"Never mind. You'll know. Now remember, you don't look the queen directly in the eyes," he joked. I started toward the limousine. "Tell her I made you sleep on a bed of nails in a closet," he shouted after me. "Tell her I installed the chair lift on her stairway."

"I will not, Daddy," I said, and he laughed.

Moments later, we were on our way, and my heart was beating as quickly as the wheels were turning on the road. The ride wasn't as long as I'd anticipated. Grandmother Emma was in a building that Felix said had been recently bought by a group of very wealthy people and was supported through charity balls and events and heavy donations. The building and the grounds had been constructed to make it look like anything but a place to house and treat stroke victims. In many ways it looked like the March mansion.

It was a large, light-gray stucco structure with beautiful stonework around its entrance and first-floor windows. With its round tower, it did look like the castle my grandmother thought she owned. I wondered if she now imagined she was really the queen she pretended to be.

The parking lot was in the rear so that anyone who

approached it and didn't know what it was would not
assume it was in any way a medical facility or any sort
of institution. There were no big signs announcing it
either. I asked Felix about that and he said, "If you
have the money to be brought here, you don't need
signs telling you you're here."

I guess he was right. Exceptionally detailed care
was taken with its grounds. The perfectly trimmed
hedges looked like they had been pruned with scis-
sors from a beauty salon. The small ponds had water
percolating over colored rocks, and there was statuary
placed everywhere I looked. Some of it was of people,
some of angels and some of birds. I saw some benches
and smiled in amazement at the beds of beautiful flowers full of rainbow colors. Were they real?

I saw the curtains on the windows as we drove
closer and then around the building. They looked like
velvet drapes. In the rear there were a few dozen auto-
mobiles and a large van. The rear lawn flowed on and
on in wavelike ripples until it reached a wooded area.
Two men on large grass cutters were busy leveling out
the autumn grass, and when I stepped out of the limousine, the sweet aroma perfumed the air around me.

There were still flocks of birds fluttering about
in the clear sunshine to make for a pleasant, happy,
melodic morning. If someone couldn't recuperate
here, I thought, they couldn't get better anywhere.
Looking out your window at this world certainly had
to raise your spirits.

Felix led me to the entrance off the parking lot.
Whoever had designed this place had basically put a
false front on it, because the real entrance opening to
the lobby and receptionist was here, and not up front.

Even inside it didn't look at all like a medical facility. The lobby was plush, with big, soft leather sofas and chairs, beautiful standing lamps and table lamps. There were flowers in vases everywhere and, spread evenly over the panel walls, large oil paintings of scenery, ocean views and lakes. The floor was an immaculate-looking black marble, so shiny it worked like a mirror reflecting all that was on it. Soft classical music was being piped in through invisible speakers.

A tall man in a dark blue suit, with curly light brown hair, and carrying what looked like a briefcase spoke quietly with a nurse in front of a counter that looked more like the kind seen in hotel lobbies. I saw another two women behind them working on files and papers, one at a computer. As we continued to cross the lobby toward them, the nurse and the man she was speaking to turned our way.

"Can I help you?" she asked Felix.

"Yes, I've brought Jordan March to see her grand-mother."

"Oh," she said and smiled at me. "I'm Mrs. Sand-ers," she said. "Chief administrator and head nurse." She smiled at me. "I know your grandmother is wait-ing anxiously to see you. She asked after you four times already this morning."

No one keeps my grandmother waiting, I thought. I remembered my mother once saying how she pitied a dentist who ran late and kept her in the lobby for nearly forty minutes. "He'll be wishing he were having his teeth cleaned instead of cleaning hers," she told me.

"Right this way," Mrs. Sanders said. "I'll have that report for you in the morning, Dr. Stevens," she told the man with whom she had been speaking. Doctors didn't look like doctors here either, I thought. He didn't wear a doctor's coat or carry anything that doctors carried. He looked more like a lawyer or a banker.

"Fine. I'll call first, Marion," he told her.

"This way, Jordan," Mrs. Sanders said, nodding at a door. I trailed just a little behind her.

"I'll be waiting here for you, Jordan," Felix said, moving toward one of the sofas and lifting a magazine off the side table.

I continued to follow Mrs. Sanders through the doorway and down a long, wide corridor.

"Your grandmother has made very good progress." She stopped and turned to me. "You know how we know?"

I shook my head.

"She doesn't stop complaining," she said and laughed.

That's what Daddy told me about Ian in his new place, I thought.

We walked on, then stopped at a doorway. She glanced at me, then knocked and opened the door. There was a small entryway with a closet on the right and a bathroom on the left. Instead of a rug or tile, the floor was a rich-looking dark wood. There was a king-size bed with a large headboard. The bed had matching end tables and lamps. The large television set was mounted on the wall across from the bed, and I saw there was a stereo unit of some sort beneath it. The wall to my left had shelves of books, interrupted by vases that looked like they contained fresh flowers.

This room is almost as big as Grandmother Emma's room back at the mansion, I thought. Directly ahead of us, there was a sliding glass door opening to a tiled patio with a table and chairs, potted plants and a view of one of the bigger ponds.

Grandmother Emma was sitting outside, wearing a fur-collared ruby robe. Her hair was spun and tied with a light green ribbon, and she looked a lot better than she had when I had seen her in the hospital.

"Your granddaughter has finally arrived, Mrs. March," Mrs. Sanders said.

Grandmother Emma didn't respond. She nodded at the chair across from her, which was her way of telling me to get to it and sit.

"Is there anything you want or need? Should I bring the young lady something to drink?"

"No," Grandmother Emma said with perfect clarity and sharpness.

Mrs. Sanders smiled at me.

"Enjoy your visit, dear," she said and walked out.

I took the chair and sat back with my hands folded in my lap.

When Grandmother Emma spoke, her lips seemed to writhe because some of the muscles in her face weren't working well. Her tongue looked swollen, which I imagined made it difficult for her to speak. The words streamed together, parts of one tacking onto another before it had been pronounced, but I could understand.

"I know about Frances," she muttered. "Tha . . . woman," she added, and I wasn't sure if she was complaining about Great-aunt Frances or Mrs. DeMarco.

For a long moment we just stared at each other. What was I supposed to tell her? Was she waiting for the story? Was she unsure about what I knew and didn't know?

She made it clear.

"What did she tell you?" she asked, this time almost perfectly.

"That Great-aunt Frances is really my grandmother," I replied. She was blinking fast, and her mouth opened and closed, opened and closed. She struggled to keep herself erect in the chair, and she pounded the arm in frustration. This time the words she wanted to come out were stuck in the mud. She took a deep breath. Then she just nodded.

"Does . . ." She had to wait, as if the air to make the words had been coming up out of her lungs like a bubble rising to the surface of the ocean. "Father know?"

I shook my head. She pointed at me.

"I didn't tell him," I said, understanding.

She nodded slowly, but I saw how her eyes focused on me, a slight relaxing in the corners. It was hard to tell whether she was smiling, trying to smile, or it was nothing.

"Why?" she managed to ask.

"Because he wants to be your son now," I said. Her eyebrows rose so fast that I thought they would lift off her head.

She pointed at me again.

I understood.

"It doesn't matter now whether she's my great-aunt or my grandmother. It's too late, but I love her." I wanted to add, "I love her more than I love you," but I didn't.

She sat back, nodding slowly.

"Do you want me to tell Daddy?" I asked.

She shook her head and pointed to herself.

"Okay," I said.

"Your mother?" she asked.

"She might be getting better," I said. "We're going to visit her. Ian's getting better, too. They moved him to a nicer place, Daddy says."

She nodded. She knew that.

"How long are you going to stay here?" I asked.

She looked at me and then shook her head.

"It's a nice place."

She grunted.

"As niiiice as a cema . . . cema . . ."

"Cemetery?" Figuring out her words was almost like playing a game.

She nodded.

"You're not dead," I told her. I said it so matter-of-factly that her eyebrows rose again, and this time I was positive she was smiling.

"Why did you send me to live with Great-aunt Frances?" I asked. "Did you want me to find out the truth?"

She just looked at me, her eyes saying nothing, her lips crooked, turning in and out.

"Why didn't you want to have your own baby?"

She shook her head.

"It was mean to leave her alone there."

She looked away.

"She wants to come to see you."

She looked at me with skeptical eyes.

"She does. Daddy said he would bring her to the mansion. He's taking me to see Mommy and Ian. He's getting a special car so he can drive me." Suddenly I felt a burst of verbal energy, a need to say everything. "He wants to be a better father. He isn't full of self-pity anymore. He's getting someone to be with

Great-aunt Frances. I made a friend named Alanis and she's . . . coming to see me, too. I learned how to talk to Mommy with telepathy and she's coming home. She is. We're all going to come home, and you should try to come home, too."

I thought that made her laugh, but she could have just been choking on her effort to speak. *Why did she have me brought here?* I wondered. *She is trying to find out things behind my father's back. She does want me to be like a little spy. Well, I won't be.*

I stood up. The anger in me felt like boiling oil.

"My daddy shouldn't have been born in the attic," I said. "You better come home and tell him the truth. No secrets, no lies," I declared.

Then I turned away and ran out of the room, not even looking back.

Epilogue

Daddy's car came, but he had to spend time learning how to drive it before he would take me anywhere in it. Felix drove us to my old school and wheeled Daddy in to meet with the principal and take care of the reenrollment. My teachers were happy to see me. I thought some of the students I had been with now looked at me in a very different way. It was almost as if I had been in some war or involved in some major event and had returned. I could see their curiosity, and afterward, many of them did attack me with questions about where I had been, what it had been like, why I had been brought home.

I found myself becoming Alanis, enjoying the elaborations and exaggerations I could create. They believed everything and were envious when I described the wild parties and being on my own. I could almost see the way their pity for me turned into respect.

Everyone seemed to want to be my new best friend. It was as if they expected I could guide them into maturity, teach them how to handle boys and be sexually sophisticated, especially when they saw the name *Stuart* written on my white shoes. They competed for my attention, each trying to impress me with what she already knew. Some even revealed things about their own sexual experimentation and experiences, begging me to keep their secrets locked away. When I looked at them all now, I thought my lenses had been washed clean and I could see each for who she really was. I felt I instinctively knew whom I should trust and whom I shouldn't.

Thank you, Alanis, I thought as I sauntered down the hallways, my head never held as high. Even my teachers looked at me differently. I could feel it in the way they spoke to me. They all saw me as older, wiser.

Was I really?

If only Ian could see this, I thought.

By the weekend, Daddy was confident enough in his driving to take me to visit Mommy. He'd even mastered getting his wheelchair out and unfolded, although I leaped to do that for him. The hospital had ramps, of course, and we took the elevator up to the floor Mommy was on.

When the elevator door opened, Daddy wheeled himself out, but then stopped. I stood there, waiting.

"Okay, Jordan," he said. "I haven't told you everything because I didn't want to get you frightened or disturbed when you were readjusting to returning home and your old school."

"Mommy's not better?" I asked quickly.

"No, she's better, a lot better. She's conscious, but—"

"But what?"

"She doesn't remember very much. It's like being in a haze or a daze."

"You mean she doesn't remember the accident?"

"No, honey. She doesn't remember anything. She didn't remember me, for example. She probably won't remember you, so don't be upset. In time—"

"She'll remember me," I said, smiling. "She's been talking to me, Daddy. Remember? I told you about the telepathy?"

He sighed deeply. "Okay, Jordan. Let's go," he said and continued wheeling himself down the hallway. I followed alongside.

The nurses at the station midfloor saw us coming, and I saw the nurse I remembered Ian calling the case manager. Her name was Mrs. Feinberg, and she had been very angry at us when she'd found out Ian had brought me here without permission. It seemed like just yesterday.

"Mr. March," she said, smiling as she drew closer.

"Hello, Mrs. Feinberg. I believe you know my daughter, Jordan," he said.

"Yes," she said, looking at me with her head tilted a little and a wry smile on her face. "How are you doing?"

"Fine," I said quickly.

"She's doing a little better every day, Mr. March," Mrs. Feinberg told my father. "It's going to take time."

"Yes," Daddy said. He started to wheel himself toward the room.

I felt as if my heart had become something so light and airy that it floated about in my chest. I know I was holding my breath. We entered the room. Mommy was propped up and looking vacantly at the television set as if she had been hypnotized by the light and had no idea what was playing or what people were saying. She looked at us, but I saw no recognition, no change in her expression. Daddy reached for my hand and looked up at me. I know he was expecting me to cry.

I didn't.

He wheeled close to her bed, and I followed.

"You can give her a kiss," he whispered.

I did. I kissed her cheek. She brought her hand to it and stared at me.

"Hi, Caroline. I brought Jordan because she's come home. Remember I was telling you how she had gone off to stay with Aunt Frances for a while? Well, she's back now. I enrolled her in school this week. She's doing fine," he added.

Mommy listened and then looked at me, but her expression didn't change.

"Talk to her," Daddy said.

"I have been talking to her," I told him.

"Talk to her some more, Jordan," he said, closing and opening his eyes.

He doesn't believe me, I thought. *That's all right. It's not important.*

I started to talk to her as if she knew everything already. I began with my return to the mansion and the school. I told her about my classes and all the things I hadn't told her telepathically. She listened, her eyes on me, her expression never changing.

Daddy sighed and shook his head.

"Patience," Mrs. Feinberg whispered. I hadn't realized she was standing behind us the whole time.

Daddy nodded.

"Keep talking to her," he said but without enthusiasm.

"Oh, I see the doctor is here, Mr. March," Mrs. Feinberg said. "Would you like to speak with him?"

"Yes," he said. "I'll be right back, Jordan. Just keep talking to her," he told me, turned his chair and wheeled out of the room.

Mommy followed him with her gaze, then looked at me.

Now that Daddy was gone, I began to tell her everything about my discovery, about Mrs. DeMarco and about visiting Grandmother Emma. She listened, and I could see her eyes darken and feel her fingers tighten a little in my hand.

"What should I do, Mommy? What should I do?"

Her fingers moved in my hand, but she didn't speak.

Daddy wheeled back into the room.

"How's it going?"

"Good," I said, and his eyes widened with surprise at my calmness.

"Okay. Now that you know how it is, we'll return regularly and hope for a quicker recuperation. We've got to leave now, honey. I have some other things to do."

"All right," I said.

He wheeled closer, took Mommy's hand, and told her we would return often and told her how much he wished for her to recover. She didn't say anything.

She's not ready to forgive him, I thought, but I knew in my heart she would someday.

He looked at me, turned and started to wheel himself out.

I leaned over and kissed her on the cheek.

I felt her breath on mine. *She's trying to speak,* I thought and leaned closer, bringing my ear to her lips.

I heard her.

No one would ever believe it, but I heard her.

"Don't tell him," she whispered.

I smiled at her and nodded. Then I kissed her again and hurried out after Daddy.

We did visit her frequently, and her return began first in small ways and then in bigger and bigger ones as the memories started to reemerge in her brain.

"She's returning from a dark place," Mrs. Feinberg told me one time. "It's like climbing out of a deep hole into the light. There's more and more as you get higher and higher."

"I know," I said with such confidence that she pulled her head back. "She told me."

Everyone thought it was cute or funny, but I didn't care. *I'm like Ian now,* I thought. *I know more than they do, and I'm comfortable about it. It doesn't matter what they think.*

On Thursday of the following week, I was called out of class to the principal's office. All I was told was that my father was coming for me. I was surprised to see Felix actually come to sign me out.

"Your father's in the limousine," he said.

"Why didn't he drive himself in his special car?"

"He wanted me to drive him this morning, Jordan," he told me.

I hurried to get into the limousine. Daddy was sitting in the corner, waiting. Felix closed the door.

"Why are you taking me out of school, Daddy?" I asked him.

"I'm afraid your grandmother has passed away, Jordan."

I'll never forget that for a moment I wondered whom he meant, Emma or Frances.

"Considering the limits to her recovery, it's probably for the best. My mother wasn't anyone who could accept anything less than perfection, especially for herself. I could almost guarantee you she decided her heart should stop, herself. She was always in charge. She would even tell Death what to do and when. Your great-aunt is being brought to the funeral," he added.

I didn't say anything.

We returned home, where we had a steady stream of visitors offering their condolences. Daddy wanted me at his side all the time. There were still many people alive who had been friends with my grandparents, even some former business associates from the steel company. Of course, there were all the people involved with all the charities Grandmother Emma had supported. It was, as Daddy would say, a true Who's Who. We even had a senator and two congressmen come to pay their respects.

I was impressed, but I waited eagerly for the arrival of Great-aunt Frances. No one was more important to me.

Felix brought her the day of the funeral. I was surprised at how good she looked. She had lost weight. Her hair was styled, and someone had helped her with her makeup, or else she'd finally realized how to do it conservatively so she wouldn't look silly. She wore a very stylish black skirt, blouse and jacket. I imagined that whomever Daddy had gotten to be with her had been a really good influence.

She was really happy to see me, even more than Daddy or the mansion. I was full of questions for her about Alanis, Miss Puss, and Lester Marshall. She was overwhelmed by all the attention and by the mansion. Daddy was very nice to her. She looked at me almost every time he spoke to her, and I thought, *She's wondering if I told him what Mrs. DeMarco told Alanis and me.* I didn't know how to speak about it. I was afraid I would stir up the same sadness in her that had driven her to lock herself in the attic and take sleeping pills.

How hard it must have been for her to give away her baby and be forgotten.

We were too busy all day anyway, with the church service and the burial with the aftermath, for us to have any private conversation about it, and I had the sense that it was something better left unspoken, sort of like her saying, "No unhappiness, no bad news in this house."

The church was filled to capacity, and more people came to the mansion afterward. To me it seemed to become a big party, almost a celebration. It was catered, and for a while I thought it looked like one of those extravagant golden age parties Grandmother Emma had been so proud to show us pictures of and describe. She would be pleased with my father, I thought, pleased with the man she'd kept her son, maybe dying to be sure she would never say otherwise.

So many people were introduced to Great-aunt Frances that I was sure she would remember no one. She obviously enjoyed the attention, however. *She should,* I thought. *It's way overdue.* Loneliness was a shadow that would never fall over her again.

Toward early evening, the crowd of mourners thinned out until there was no one left but Felix, Nancy, Daddy, Great-aunt Frances and myself. Daddy expected that Great-aunt Frances would be very tired, but the activity seemed instead to have energized her. I thought she looked upset it was all over, in fact.

As I watched him talk to her, I realized, of course, that Grandmother Emma's passing meant she wouldn't be telling him the truth. I wondered what I should do.

Before the sun went down, Daddy decided he needed some fresh air. Great-aunt Frances was eager to go out, too. I followed behind them, listening to Daddy's conversation. He had many questions about Grandmother Emma when she was a young girl, and Great-aunt Frances was happy to answer them. With Grandmother Emma gone, she was free now, I thought. She was unafraid.

But she was really not unkind. She said so many nice things about her sister that I wondered if she had made up the terrible ones, but then I thought about the truth and lies again. Great-aunt Frances was just too nice to say anything that might upset Daddy, I realized. Did that mean she was lying? Or did it mean she was more caring?

They got ahead of me on the walkway toward the pool area, passing gardens and fountains, weaving along through the hedges. Great-aunt Frances suddenly paused and began to wheel Daddy. I smiled to myself, wondering if she thought she was like a mother wheeling her child in a baby carriage. It was something she'd never gotten to do.

Would she bend down, lean toward his face and whisper in his ear, telling him she was really his mother?

Or was there something magical that would happen, if not now, someday when Daddy would look at her and realize the truth?

Maybe he would learn how to do Ian's telepathy and he would hear Great-aunt Frances's thoughts.

The simple word would unlock his heart.

The word every child knows in his or her very soul even before birth.

Mother.

A week later, a letter came for me.

It was from Ian.

Unopened, it was waiting for me on my bed in my room. My fingers trembled as I tore the envelope and pulled out the paper.

Dear Jordan,

I suppose you know I'm in a new place.

You know the reason why they wanted to move me.

I'm stronger now, so they're probably sorry.

And I've decided it's more important for me to get them to let me come home. I have spoken

*with Mother about it and it's what she wants as
well. Father was here to see me and told me he'll
be bringing you soon, too. He seemed different. I
think he has changed or as Grandmother Emma
might say, grown up.*

They told me about her passing away.

*I told them I knew and they just shook their
heads of course.*

*They continually ask me if I am sorry about
anything I've done.*

*I am sorry, but not for the reasons they would
like to hear. I am not going to lie about it.*

*I am sorry because I realize I have left you
alone out there.*

*So I have decided to do everything possible to
come home.*

*Mother has told me she will need me as well
and from what I can see of Father, he could use
my assistance.*

*You only have value in relation to how you
can help other people.*

*I told my new doctor that and he was very
impressed.*

*I wouldn't tell him and I wouldn't tell Daddy
and I won't even tell Mother, but I'll tell you
because you can keep a secret. We both know
that.*

I'm tired of being alone.

Ian

The day after they brought Mommy home, Ian
returned.

Great-aunt Frances was moved into Grandmother Emma's bedroom.

Alanis was coming to visit me.

And suddenly it seemed like we had all been reborn, metamorphosing like one of Ian's caterpillars.

When I looked out my window, I saw the world was filled with butterflies.

POCKET STAR BOOKS
PROUDLY PRESENTS

SECRETS IN THE ATTIC

V.C. Andrews®

Available in paperback
October 2007
from Pocket Star Books

Turn the page for a preview of
Secrets in the Attic. . . .

Prologue

As young girls living in a peaceful and relatively crime-free community, Karen Stoker and I should have had an adolescence full of hope, an adolescence of bright colors, sweet things and upbeat music. No one season should have looked drearier than another. Winter should have been dazzlingly white with icicles resembling strings of diamonds and the air jingling with our laughter at the crunch of snow beneath our boots. Spring, summer and fall would each have their own magic. In fact our lives should have been one long and forever special day protected by loving parents and family.

Ghosts and goblins, creatures from below or out of the darkness were to be nothing more than movie and comic book creations to make us scream with delight in the same way we might scream sitting in a roller coaster car plunging through an illusion of disaster. Afterward we would gasp and hug each other in utter joy that we were still alive. Our excited eyes would look as if tiny diamonds floated around our pupils. Our feet would look like we had springs in them when we walked, and all the adults in our families would cry for mercy and ask us to take our boundless energy outside so they could catch their breath.

That was the way it should have been, could have been, but there was something dark and evil incubating just under the surface of the world in which we lived, in which I, especially, lived. I was in a protective rose-colored bubble, oblivious and happy, pirouetting like a ballerina on ice, unaware of the rumbling below and never dreaming that I could fall through into the freezing cold waters of sorrow and horror, the parents of our worst nightmares.

It was Karen who showed me all this, Karen who pointed it out, lifted the shade and had me look through the window into the shadows that loitered ominously just beyond our imaginary safe havens. I thought Karen was like Superwoman with X-ray eyes that could see through false faces and through false promises.

I wanted to be Karen's best friend the first moment I set eyes on her after we had moved into the Doral House, a house made infamous by its original owners because the wife, Lucy Doral, was said to have murdered her husband, Brendon, and buried him somewhere on the property. His body was never found and she was never charged with any crime because she claimed he had run off, and back in the nineteenth century it was much more difficult to track people. No one could prove or disprove what she had said. However, the house had a stigma attached to it, and it remained abandoned for many years before it was bought and sold three times during the past eighty-five years. Each owner made some necessary upgrades in plumbing and electric, as well as expanding the building.

My brother Jesse saw the house briefly when my father took a second look at it and brought him along, but Jesse went off for his college orientation in Michigan a week before we moved in so he didn't spend any real time at our new home until his holiday break at Thanksgiving, and he was too excited about going to college to really think about where we were going to live. Later, when he did spend time in it, I found him surprisingly aloof and disinterested. It was as if he was already on his way toward his independent life and we were now merely a way station along that journey.

Karen claimed she understood his attitude.

She and I often sat upstairs in the attic in my house to carry on our little talks because it was such a private place, away from the newer, expanded kitchen and living room below that had been part of an add-on. There was a short stairway on the south end of the upstairs level that led up to the attic. It had no banister, and the old wooden steps moaned like babies with bellyaches when we walked up them. For me, and even more for Karen, the most interesting thing about our house was exploring it and the grounds around it.

"Maybe we'll discover the remains of Mr. Doral," she said, "or at least some important evidence. She could have sealed him in a wall as the character did in Edgar Allan Poe's 'The Cask of Amontillado,'" she whispered, and put her ear to the wall as if she could still hear the poor man moaning and begging to be freed.

As soon as Karen laid her eyes on the attic, she declared it was the most fascinating part of the house because it was large and contained so many old things, furnishings, boxes filled with old sepia pictures, dust-coated lamps, a few bed mattresses, and some pots and dishware that previous owners didn't care to take with them. There was even some costume jewelry. Karen thought they might have forgotten they had put it all there. She said everything looked as if it had been deserted. She almost made me cry with the way she embraced a pillow or caressed an old dresser claiming all were on the verge of disappearing and were so grateful we had come up to befriend and claim them. She said it was a nest of orphans and then she clapped her hands and declared that we would adopt them all and make them all feel wanted again.

"I know just what your brother is feeling about

this place, this town," she told me after he had returned to college at the end of his Christmas holiday recess, and I had complained to her about how indifferent he seemed to be the whole time he was home. He didn't care that we had to drive miles and miles to go to a movie, or that there were no fancy restaurants in our village. He didn't care that there were no streetlights on our road or that our nearest neighbor was a half mile away.

Karen and I were sitting on an old leather settee that had wrinkled and cracked cushions, reminding us of an aged face, dried close to parchment by Father Time. After only our second time up there, Karen christened the attic "Our nest." Neither the stale, hot-trapped air nor the cobwebs in the corners bothered her. We aired it out and dusted as best we could, but it never seemed that clean. She told me we shouldn't care because clubhouses, secret places, were supposed to look and be like this, and we were lucky to have it.

The day we talked about Jesse, we had both put on old-fashioned dresses with ankle-length skirts and lots of lace, wide-brim flowery hats and imitation diamond and emerald earrings we had found in an old black trunk that Karen said were like those that had gone down with the *Titanic*. I wore an ostentatious fake pearl necklace that had turned a shade of pale yellow. Karen wore a pair of black shoe-shined old-fashioned clodhoppers, too, and a pair of those thick nylon stockings we saw elderly women wear, the kind that fell in ripples down their calves and around their ankles.

"Oh really? What's my brother feeling?" I asked, a little annoyed that she thought she could interpret him better than I could.

"It's simple. Don't be thick. You think I'd be here if I didn't have to?" she asked. "If I were in college like your brother, I wouldn't come back even on holidays. Not me. I want to live in a big, exciting city that never sleeps, a city with grand lights and continuous parties, traffic and noise and people, a city with so much happening, you can't decide whether to go uptown or downtown. Don't you?"

Her eyes filled with such exhilaration it was as if she had the power to lift us up and carry us off on a flying carpet to her magical metropolis. She held out her arms and spun around so hard she nearly fell over from dizziness, making me laugh. I had lived in Yonkers, which was very close to New York City, and didn't think big-city life held all the enchantment she thought it did, but I agreed with everything she said because I wanted so to be her dearest friend, and I enjoyed listening to her fantasies and dreams.

I was ever so grateful that I had this house, this attic, this stage where we could act out our imaginings, or look at the faded sepia pictures of young men and women and make up romantic stories about them. This one died in childbirth, that one took her own life when her lover betrayed her or her father forbade she marry him. Karen never failed to come up with a plot or a name. All her stories were romantic but sad. She seemed capable of drawing these tales and the characters out of the very attic walls.

I did come to believe there was something magical about being in our nest, something that helped us mine our imaginations with ease. There were only two naked light fixtures dangling from the attic ceiling, casting uneven illumination, but Karen didn't complain about it. She said she rather liked the eerie and mysterious atmosphere it created, and I tried hard to feel the same way. Putting on the old clothes, sitting amongst the antiques, gave us the inspiration to fantasize and plan, she more than me, but I was learning fast to be more like her and let my imagination roam.

I told her so.

"Yes, why not?" she asked, lifting her eyes and looking as if she was standing on a stage. "After all, it's our imagination that frees us from the chains and weight of our dull reality. Come dreams and fantasies. Overwhelm me."

She could make statements and gesture with such dramatic flare, I could only stare and smile with amazement. I told her she should go out for the school plays. She grimaced.

"And be confined by someone else's vision, plot, characters? Never," she said. "We must always remain free spirits. Your house, our nest, is the only stage I want to be on."

Our new home was on Church Road in Sandburg, New York, a hamlet that Karen claimed gave credence to the theory that some form of sedative had seeped into the ground water. Karen said there was a picture of the hamlet next to the word *sleepy* in the dictionary.

"People here have to be woken up to be told they've woken up," she told me.

"Maybe that's why it's called Sandburg. They named it after the Sandman," I added, always trying to keep up with her wit.

"No, no one was that creative. It's named after the nearby creek. Speaking of names, I like yours," she told me.

"My name? Why?"

"I envy people with unusual names. Zipporah. It shows your parents weren't lazy when it came to naming you. My name is so common, my parents could have imitated Tarzan and Jane and called me Girl and it wouldn't have made all that much difference," she said, the corners of her mouth turning down and looking like they dripped disgust. I couldn't imagine how someone like her could be unhappy with herself in any way.

"It's not so common. I like your name. It takes too long to say mine."

"It does not. Don't let anyone call you Zip," she warned. "It sounds too much like the slang for zero, and you're no zero."

"What makes you so sure?" I asked. How had she come to that conclusion so quickly? I wasn't exactly Miss Popularity with either the girls or the boys at my last school. In fact, I had yet to receive a single letter or phone call from a single old friend.

"Don't worry. I have a built-in zero detector. I'll point out the zeros in our school and you'll clearly see that I know a zero from a nonzero."

It didn't take long for me to believe she could do that. Anyone she disliked, I disliked; anyone she thought was a phony, I did as well.

Both Karen and I were fifteen at the time, less than a year away from getting our junior driver's licenses. She was two months older. With passing grades in the high school's driver's education class, we could get our senior licenses a year earlier at seventeen, which meant we could drive after dark. We would also get a discount on auto insurance. This was all more important to me than to her because I was confident I could eventually have a car of my own. Jesse had his own car, a graduation present, so I assumed I would as well.

We talked about getting our licenses and a car all the time, dreaming of the places we would visit and the fun we would have. Sometimes up in the nest we pretended we were in my car driving along. We'd sit on the old sofa and as I simulated driving she pointed out the scenery in Boston or New Orleans and especially California, shouting out the names of famous buildings, bridges, and statues. We used travel brochures and pretended we were actually plotting out an impending vacation.

We considered a driver's license to be our passport to adulthood. As soon as the motor vehicles bureau issued it to you, your image among your peers and even adults changed. You had control of a metallic monster, the power to move over significant distances at will, and you could grant a seat on the journey with a nod and make someone, even someone older, beholden.

"Of course, it's obvious we don't need a car to get around Sandburg," Karen said. "It's so small the sign that says 'Leaving Sandburg, Come Visit Us Again,' is on the back of the sign that says 'Entering Sandburg, Welcome.'"

When I told Jesse what Karen had said, he laughed hysterically and said he was going to try to get a sign made up like that to put in his dorm room. He was so excited about the idea that I wished I had been the one to say it, especially after he remarked, "Your girlfriend is pretty clever and not just pretty."

The imaginary sign wasn't all that much of an exaggeration. There was only one traffic light in the whole hamlet. It was at the center where the two main streets joined to form a T, and because this was a summer resort community, during the fall, winter and spring, the traffic light was turned into a blinker, more often ignored than obeyed. If Sparky, the five-year-old dog, a cross between a German shepherd and a collie owned by Ron

Black, the owner of Black's Café, located near the light, could speak, he would bear witness against three-quarters of the so-called upstanding citizens who ignored it. Whenever he was sprawled on the sidewalk, both Karen and I noticed that Sparky always raised his head each time a car drove through the red light without stopping. He looked like he was making a mental note of the license plate.

We laughed about it. Oh, how we laughed at ourselves, our community, our neighbors back then. There seemed to be so much that provided for our amusement, like the way Al Peron, the village's biggest landlord, strutted atop the roof of one of his buildings with his arms folded across his chest, his chin up, as if he was the lord of the manor, looking over his possessions. We called him Our Own Mussolini because he resembled the Italian dictator as pictured in our history textbook. We giggled at the way Mrs. Krass, the wife of Mr. Krass who owned the fish market, swayed like a fish swimming when she walked. Stray cats followed cautiously behind her as if they expected some fresh tuna to fall out of her pockets.

We laughed about Mr. Buster, the postal clerk whose Adam's apple moved like a yo-yo when he repeated your order for stamps as he wrote it down on a small pad before giving them to you, and we shook our heads at the way the Langer Dairy building leaned to the left, a building Karen called The Leaning Tower of Sandburg.

"If too many customers stand on one side, it might just topple," she declared. Mrs. Langer wondered why Karen and I shrieked and then hurried from one side to the other when people came in behind us.

Karen and I observed so many little things about our community, things that no one else seemed to notice or care to notice. I began to wonder if we indeed had a bird's-eye view of everything and floated far above our world. Whenever I mentioned something Karen and I had noted, my mother or father would say, "Oh really? I never thought of that," or "I never realized it." Maybe adults see things too deeply, I thought, and miss what's on the surface. They were once like us and saw what we saw, but they forget.

Karen agreed.

"Time is like a big eraser," she said.

It was Karen's idea that we should write down all these insights and discoveries some day because it was a form of history, our personal history, and we would become like our parents, oblivious, distracted.

"Years and years from now, when we're both married and have clumps of children pulling on our skirts wailing and demanding, and we look like hags with a cigarette dripping from the corner of our mouths, we'll remember all this fondly, even though we make fun of it all now," she said. "That's why it's so important."

It did sound important enough to write down,

but we never created that book together. We often talked about doing it. Later when we had little else to do, we passed some of our time remembering this and that as if we were both already in our late seventies reminiscing about our youth, looking back with nostalgia and regret.

It was lost for both of us just that quickly.

Look for the film adaptation of

V.C. ANDREWS'S bestselling novel

RAIN

STARRING:

★ Faye Dunaway

★ Robert Loggia

★ Khandi Alexander

★ Giancarlo Esposito

And introducing
Brooklyn Sudano as Rain

Produced by Merv Griffin Entertainment in assocation
with Bigheadz Entertainment and Lexi Dog Media Group

POCKET
STAR BOOKS
A Division of Simon & Schuster
A CBS COMPANY

14730
www.simonsays.com